Better Without You

Ava Madden

“It is said, your emotions are the slaves to your thoughts, and you are the slave to your emotions.”

—Elizabeth Gilbert

Prologue

1966

It had haunted me all my life.

Maybe even formed who I was.

I'll never know, because I can never undo what happened and see the person I might have been.

My thoughts drifted back to that sound of the big, fancy door, always that door, which slammed behind me, as the memories rushed over me yet again.

Mommy dabbled her fingers in the holy water, on the wall near the door, and blessed herself. I stood on my tiptoes and dipped too. Even though it was a holy place, it seemed creepy and made me stop. I turned and stared up at Jesus on the cross, towering behind the altar. The sun was streaming through colorful, stained-glass windows: Jesus, Mother Mary, and the saints were trying to tell me something. A secret?

A long chord rang out.

The organ player had just sat down to practice. I ran down the aisle to catch up to Mom.

The pews were empty. Well, except for my classmates and me. Mom knelt and blessed herself again. I did the same. I sat with my classmates in the last rows nearest the two confessional booths, waiting to go in. I was only seven—what sins would I have? I didn't even talk back to anyone. *How can a seven-year-old have a mortal sin?* I wondered. I didn't even have a venial sin; I never lied, stole, or said the Lord's name in vain. I was afraid of the priest. Maybe because to me he was like a god. But it didn't matter what I thought; this was tradition. And besides, I could hardly wait to look like a bride—they were always so beautiful—with a white veil and dress on Sunday, to receive my first communion.

Did this mean I'd be married—to God?

Still, why did I have to talk to a stranger? I wanted to talk to God in private, the way I did at night in my prayers. Repent what? And what would I be saved from? My parents? My teachers? The bullies? The boogieman? And what the dickens was purgatory.

The closer it got to my turn, I thought my heart was coming out of my chest, it was beating so hard. My whole body was shivering. Then I was up! It felt like I couldn't move—my fear was so bad. My mother grabbed my bony arm, yanking me from the pew. I saw my classmates staring. I wanted to scream out, "I'm not going in there!" Or maybe I did scream out. With tears in my eyes, I silently rehearsed, "Bless me, Father, for I have sinned." But I had no sins. What should I say? Should I lie? I never had. Should I tell him about the time in the woods?

"Kneel. He will open his little window. God will punish you if you don't confess the truth," Mom said.

"But I don't remember—I just remember what you've told me. Do I have to tell the priest—if I don't remember?"

"Yes, you will go to hell if you don't."

"Oh, Mommy, I don't want to go to hell," I cried.

"No, Father," I said, my head shaking violently. "I didn't do anything with anybody." *What is he saying—accusing me of?* Mom said I was three and the older boy, named Damon, played doctor on my private part.

"Here's your penance: You say seven Hail Marys and seven Our Fathers."

But I have not sinned. I have done nothing wrong.

"Father...," I begged, but it came out low, a mere whisper.

He closed his window.

Chapter I

2008

The drive from Yarmouth Port to Sandwich was dark and the winding roads less traveled now, curling from town to town. Summer had faded into autumn. The days were still warm, but chill dominated the evenings. It didn't matter to me; I kept the window open to catch every scent. The truck's headlights illuminated the golden, copper, and scarlet flames of the oak and maple trees. Every season to me was a new opening. A new beginning. The transition of the four seasons not only changed the surroundings but altered me in a subtle way, each one giving me a sense of intimacy with their characteristics. Now, I wanted to rejoice in autumn's glory, dance and sing, kick up the leaves.

Instead, as Steve pulled up to a stop sign, my attention was drawn to parishioners exiting a church. An early evening Mass, I assumed. Smiling faces were standing in line to shake hands with the priest. Many of them were dressed casually, but some elderly gentlemen wore hats. My eyes fixed on a young girl, around seven, thin with long, blonde hair. She was wearing a long paisley dress. Her mother was holding her hand. The little girl never raised her head when the tall priest bent over to speak to her.

Cold fear filled me. Was she suffering as I had suffered?

My mind drifted back. 1966.

"I'm to watch you until your mother is finished working. "Come," he says, holding out his hand. I eagerly take the hand of the man who represents God.

From the window of the truck, I saw the little girl's mother tugging her arm, and she looked up. Even though it was warm in the truck, and I was comfortably dressed in jeans, pullover sweater, and a lightweight jacket, cold goosebumps ran through me. I rolled up the window and maneuvered my trembling fingers into my gloves, wrapping one hand around the other.

Two more blocks and we arrived. The driveway was narrow, with cars parked over the rough, barren landscape scattered with pitch pine trees. A lovely brick patio led us to the entrance of the saltbox house, with a potting shed flanked with 'mums to the left.

Inside, other than the hosts, Diane and her husband, Joe—I only recognized a few familiar faces. I think Diane had spent all day in the kitchen preparing this Oktoberfest gathering: sirloin and pork, a spinach pie, roasted beets on greens, meatballs, marinated steak tips, several casseroles, and even mussels that Joe must have harvested during the low tide that morning on the Sandwich flats.

I saw Diane taking more food from the refrigerator to the oven. She stopped and greeted us. I handed her the cake I made.

"So glad you could make it," she said with a smile, taking it from me.

I nodded. "Me too. Can I help?'

"No, no, you go enjoy," Diane said, waving us on.

Diane had insisted that I come tonight because she'd invited a couple of band members from the Beloved Townies. I was excited about it. The group had been popular here on the Cape in the late '60s and '70s, and I felt fortunate to have had them perform at my sixteenth birthday party, attended by a hundred kids from my high school. Soon after, the band cut a record that made number one on the charts back in the late '70s, their name becoming famous in the United States and the United Kingdom.

My father and mother, though divorced, planned the event so meticulously, at a local hall, complete with a wedding-size birthday cake and a professional photographer. There was even a guestbook. Mom worked countless hours on the dangling, colorful tissue decorations that resembled full-blossomed rhododendrons. My best friend, Eileen, and I shopped on Newbury Street; Boston was the best place to get the latest fashions. In a small boutique, Eileen found floral bellbottoms with wide slit flares from knee to ankle and a matching top with wide bell sleeves. I was captivated by a beautiful midi dress in a white Chantilly lace with overlay ruffled sleeves and found a pair of white leather platform sandals that were a perfect match. One might have thought I was getting married that day. How fast the years have passed.

Steve knew more people at Diane's party than I did; many of them were in the building trade like him. So while Steve mingled, I stared at the food I couldn't eat, since finding out I had an intolerance to gluten.

Steve was fine-looking in his L.L. Bean dress pants and shirt. Even though he was developing that middle-age stomach, it was barely noticeable with his tall, strong build. His hair, though mostly gray, had wisps of reddish blond, and his smooth skin was mottled with freckles. I heard one guy say to him, "Steve, you clean up well."

Steve was rarely seen without his work clothes on—but he looked good no matter what he wore.

Steve introduced me to a couple who had just been married the year before. After talking with them, I remembered babysitting the wife, Charity, when I was seventeen. She was a toddler at the time. She now had her own baby, whom she'd brought to the party. Charity was visibly exhausted—dark circles around her eyes and hunched shoulders—from the burdens of caring for a newborn. Yet she was gracious and friendly. As we talked, I reached over and touched the baby's tiny hand, skin like freshly spun silk. The old sting of not having a child of my own, buried for years, hit me again. When I glanced at Steve, he gave me a quick and neutral nod before turning away. I wondered if he ever sensed my longing; but that door seemed to be closed.

Like so many other doors in our marriage.

"I used to babysit you and your sisters when you were kids," I said.

"I don't remember much. I was so young. My sisters were older," Charity said.

"That's okay. I was only a teenager—I don't recall too much either except being afraid of your dog. He was so protective of you girls."

"Yeah, Denver was a great watchdog."

I nodded. "He was a Doberman, wasn't he? They get such a bad rap."

"That's right," Charity said. "He was so sweet. I still miss him." Her voice trailed off.

By nine, the musicians still hadn't arrived. So, I assumed they were a no-show. Just as Steve and I were talking about leaving, two scruffy, gray-haired guys carrying guitar cases and amplifiers walked through the door. God, they looked so old! Had it been that long? So many of the photographs I had saved from my big and unforgettable sweet sixteen party showed the band. Neither of these disheveled fellows looked like Sam or Rob Stone, the musical brothers in my pictures. Then again, over three decades had passed.

Of course, we stayed. It took forty-five minutes for the musicians to set up their gear in the center of the room, grab a bite from the buffet, and visit the bar before they finally began playing. Steve and I sat beside another couple on a sofa to the right of the musicians. The rest of the guests were either consumed in conversation, getting a drink, or refilling their plates. In any case, they seemed uninterested in the music. We listened as the two former Beloved Townies played and sang some oldies. Then I went over and asked Rob if he'd play "Love Won't Let Me Wait" by Major Harris. He had sung that song at my birthday party, and I'd never forgotten how special that was. The brothers sounded great, although Sam appeared to be having some difficulty. Even though he hit every note with accuracy, his voice had aged. I could see the pain in his face as he reached for the notes. The veins in his neck protruded as he harmonized with Rob. My eyes welled up. Was I moved by the music? Or was I concerned for Sam's well-being?

Watching Rob, I wanted to change his oversized flannel shirt and his natty-looking shoe boots. Yet I didn't know what I expected him to be in. Maybe a fitted Henley and new hiking boots or even a pair of sandals? Barefoot? Something more appealing. Sexy. I wanted to cut his long, curly gray hair too. But why? What did I care?

After the guys finished performing, everyone got up. Steve and I went for another drink at the bar. He had rum and Coke while I stuck with just Coke.

When Steve handed me the glass of soda, he bent over and whispered in my ear. "Why don't you have a real drink. You might loosen up, instead of looking like a fuckin' wallflower."

"Go to hell," I hissed under my breath.

Steve always did this. Just when I thought we might get through an evening without an insult, it came at me like a stab from a knife and the disappointment—yet again—sliced through me. Why I should care after all this time, I don't know. Steve seemed to have a devil in him. Whether it was just black moods or something more serious—maybe bipolar—I don't know. But every time, even though I knew it would probably happen, it hurt.

Diane and I agreed the music was great. While she went to get more hors d'oeuvres, Steve went to talk with some friends. I sat down at a table across the room, my insides stewing from Steve's remark. I was so stupid to think that one day we'd go out and have a good time, that he'd be nice and not say something unkind or hurtful, that left me feeling like crap.

My eyes met with Rob's. He raised an eyebrow and looked puzzled as he rubbed his chin. In a moment, he was coming towards me. "Do I know you from somewhere?"

"Well, yeah, but it was a long time ago. My name is Aimee, Aimee Parker. You played at my sixteenth birthday party."

"Umm...," he said, his eyes rolling upward, obviously trying to recall.

"It was like a hundred years ago—I'm sure you wouldn't remember."

Rob laughed. It was a pleasant sound after my husband's sarcasm. "We did so many parties in those days. But you do look familiar."

"I have a familiar face," I said with a smile.

At least that's what I've been told, more so when I was younger. By sixth grade, my straight sandy blonde hair was darkening and becoming wavy. I had towered over most of the kids which made me feel totally awkward, but thankfully I'd stopped growing after that. In high school, my lanky five feet seven-inch frame was shaping up nicely, and I was getting attention from boys. Once I was told I looked like Sandra Bullock. I think that guy was just hitting on me, although I guess Sandra and I did and still do have a similar figure and hair color. I was grateful I'd inherited my dad's long, thick eyelashes and bottle-green eyes to compensate for my ski-slope nose.

There was an awkward silence.

"Have you always lived on the Cape?" Rob asked.

"Yeah. My roots are here," I said, thinking about all the times I'd wanted to move away. "Diane said you live in Oregon."

"Yes, we've been living in Oregon for quite a few years now. We came looking at colleges with our oldest son and ended up staying."

"Oh. Nice."

"I do miss the Cape—old friends and the beaches."

I nodded.

Then Rob mentioned his new CD.

"Diane said it was fantastic. Where can I get it?" I asked.

"I'll send you a copy."

"Oh, no, that's kind but please let me buy it."

"We artists need to support one another," he said, his molten-brown eyes penetrating mine. "Look at it as a belated birthday present."

I froze, but my heart rate didn't, and I felt a thrill run through me. "Okay. And… thanks."

I blushed too. That comment about being an artist and supporting each other meant Diane must have told him about the silly romance novel I wrote when I was a teenager, but never published. Until recently.

Then out of the blue, in a hushed tone, he said, "A week after my mom died of cancer, my dad killed himself."

"Oh! That's horrible." The word felt inadequate.

"Yeah. He blew his head off. It was nearly three years ago now, but it still seems like yesterday."

"I'm sorry" was all that I could mutter. I wondered what my expression might have revealed. I wanted to ask if he was present or if he had found him. It had to be traumatizing. I'd be so screwed up if I'd witnessed something that horrific. I could only imagine the gory details and what a friend or a loved one or the police had discovered. I wanted to ask more, but I didn't think it was right.

Did his father love his wife that much that he wanted to be with her in the hereafter? Can one truly achieve real and abiding happiness by dying for another? Or maybe he just couldn't stand the idea of being alone. His father may have felt guilty for taking her for granted, cruelly abusing her, and cheating on her, like my dad did to my mom. But I wondered why he was telling me all this.

I really didn't know this man. I was surprised he'd talk about such a personal tragedy with a pure stranger, but I liked his openness. I wanted to hear more. Was he looking for sympathy? Was he lonely?

Or was I the lonely one and he could tell?

We exchanged email addresses. When there seemed to be little else to say, he stood up and walked away. I wanted him to stay. This was the only notable conversation of my night.

He turned around. "Hey, I'm going to look up your book."

I smiled. I wished Steve had that much interest.

Later, I saw him again in the kitchen. "I made this great cake. Even though it's gluten free, you can't tell. I mean, it tastes really good," I said.

"I'll have to try it. I've been having some stomach issues lately when I eat gluten."

"I hear more and more people say that."

"I have too," he said.

I didn't find Rob good-looking. He was shorter than average. His attire was bland. But there was this presence about him. I wasn't sure if it was his voice or his compassion. But, in this strange way, he moved me. He had this irresistible magnetism, and I could have listened to him all night.

Steve gave me the signal that he wanted to leave. Rob was leaving at the same time so he stepped outside and escorted me to the car, Steve trailing behind. We walked side by side talking, like there was no one else around. When his shoulder brushed against mine, something in me stirred.

Chapter 2

I parked my Toyota Camry in the closest visitor's spot. Then I grabbed my purse and the bag of groceries and headed toward the cement walkway. Maple and oak trees spread across the well-maintained grounds of the single-floor apartment complex. Purple and yellow mums were bursting in window boxes.

My mother's next-door neighbor, Jackie, was outside in an orange chaise lounge, festive for the season, knitting an Irish sweater, her dark-framed glasses perched on her nose.

I waved.

"Feels like we're having an Indian summer," Jackie said.

"Yeah, sure is warm today."

Jackie was one of the youngest in this senior housing complex. At one time my mom was the youngest. In a few months, she would be seventy. Where did the years go? Mom moved there after Steve made arrangements with his friend, Tom, the owner of the complex. He had to get Mom into one of these apartments. Either that or he was going to throw her out of our place on her ear. Tom obliged within a month. I was thankful since Mom and Steve were not fond of each other. Maybe because they were so much alike.

Jackie was pleasant but displayed mood swings when she'd forgotten to take her medication. Her long dark hair and dark, peering eyes reminded me of Morticia, the aloof matriarch of the Addams family. My mother and Jackie became friendly. And I was glad Jackie's door was only a few feet away in case Mom needed to call out in an emergency. Some of my mom's older neighbors used to come by regularly to visit, but as she became more confused, fewer showed up. Maybe they thought dementia was contagious.

Jackie signaled me with her index finger. I walked closer to her.

"Your mom was outside in her underwear, hanging her clothes," she whispered.

"In her underwear?"

"Yes—I was going to call you, but I couldn't find your number."

"Thanks. I'll talk to her."

"Don't say I said anything."

I shook my head. "I won't."

A pair of tan casual slacks and cotton underwear were hanging on a wooden clothes rack outside Mom's door. She must have wet her pants again and handwashed them. My mom, the most modest woman I knew—outdoors in her underwear? She never wore a bathing suit after her thirties and never exposed any skin after fifty.

I opened the screen door and walked in. Mom was fully dressed, drinking coffee in the electric recliner I had found at an estate sale. It lowered for sleep and rose when she needed to stand. Since she refused to sleep in her bed and needed her oxygen beside her, it was the perfect solution.

"Hi, Mom. How are you doing?"

"Good. What are you talking to *her* for?"

"She was just being friendly, saying hello.... Mom, were you outside in your underwear?"

"Yeah, so what?"

"What if somebody walked around the corner and saw you?"

"I don't care!"

"You should care. People get arrested for doing that." I thought if I told her she could get in trouble it would scare her, but she seemed oblivious. Which scared *me*. What else might she do?

"I peed my pants."

"That's okay—it can happen to anybody."

"I washed my clothes!"

"Yeah, I saw that. Please don't walk outside again without pants on."

"What are you suddenly—my mother? Miss Righteous!" All that barking and then she rolled her eyes. Like she did to me as a child.... I hated that—so dismissive.

Mom's small apartment gleamed—a real estate showpiece. I could eat off the floor of her galley kitchen. Not a pan or dish to be seen. The carpet throughout was spotless. Even the glass mirrors, kitchen table, and coffee table were clear of dust, fingerprints, or smudges. The apartment would surely pass the white-glove inspection.

The wooden TV cabinet had side shelves full of imitation Hummels I had found at yard sales. The opposite side held my high school photo and a few framed family photographs.

Mom hid the photo of her only living sibling, Sara, who was a year older than her. Mom had this vendetta against her. Aunt Sara must have done something Mom didn't approve of. And now that Mom's mind is waning, I'll probably never know.

In the bedroom, a navy and white Ralph Lauren comforter covered her queen size bed. One that was never slept in. I couldn't understand what kept her from getting under those sheets. Maybe sleeping alone was too painful.

"Mom, come sit on the sofa," I said, patting an area next to me. "Let me brush your hair."

She sat quietly as I gently moved the soft bristles through her fine gray hair. I patted down the fly-away strands. Her face relaxed, and her head tilted back in contentment.

"Does this feel good?"

She murmured, "Yes."

"Oh, Mother, everyone needs to be touched in some way. Even someone running their fingers over your arm feels wonderful." It must've been years since any man stroked her, caressed her, given her any kind of pleasure. *She couldn't have forgotten what it felt like to have a man in her life. Or could she…?*

My phone rang, interrupting my thoughts.

"Where are you?" Steve asked.

"With Mom."

"Supper is almost ready."

"Okay. I'll be along shortly."

Click.

Mom seemed quite content for the first time in a long while. It was amazing what human touch could do. "Mom, I have to go now. It's getting late."

"You can stay the night."

"I can't. Maybe another time."

"You're always rushing off!"
I kissed the top of her head and left.

Chapter 3

As I pulled into the driveway, Steve had just finished cutting the grass. I deeply inhaled the pleasant fragrance. After all these years of hard work, he'd finally broken down and gotten himself a well-deserved John Deere riding mower.

I remembered one glorious, late July afternoon when we first married. We couldn't afford much. Steve had come home from the dump, joyfully yelling from his pickup, "Aimee! Aimee, come see!" I was putting away laundry upstairs and heard him from an open window. He was always finding treasures; people would discard stuff that had broken, or things they just didn't want anymore. It was his joy to bring them back to life for us. I ran outside to see what he'd found this time. We laughed as we took turns pushing that mower around the yard. Afterward, we lay in the lush grass, kissing tenderly till moonlight filled our universe. Then we made newlywed love and traced the constellations.

Seeing the steaming pans on the stove, I walked over and lifted the covers to see what was in them. Steve appeared from the living room. "Hi," I said, turning. "How was your day?"

"I'll tell ya when we sit down."

"Okay."

I went to the cabinet and pulled out the Currier and Ives dinner plates that my grandmother had given us when we married, grabbed the silverware from the drawer, and set the table. Steve took the swordfish and baked potato from the oven while I dished out the collard greens.

After I tried the swordfish, I saw Steve looking for my approval. "It's good," I said, after swallowing.

"That's it?"

I said nothing.

"If you got your ass home on time, it would have been fine. I'm making dinner—I work all day."

You told me you'd go out of your mind if you had to sit home. And you love cooking.

"Mom went outside in her underwear—can you believe it?"

"How do you know that?"

"Her neighbor—you know, Jackie—told me."

"Do you believe that nut bag?"

"Why would she make it up? Mom didn't deny it when I asked her. I know it's not like Mom to do something like that, but she is changing."

"Yeah, we're all changing," Steve said and stormed out of the kitchen.

I cleared the table, rinsed the dishes, and stacked them in the dishwasher. I washed the pots and pans by hand, dried them, and put them away. Then I went downstairs to the basement, unloaded the dryer, and brought the clothes upstairs to the living room to fold them. Steve was on the sofa watching an antique car program on TV, something I wasn't interested in. So, after putting the clean clothes away, I picked up a novel I'd begun the week before.

"Quick, that's how it used to look," Steve said, pointing.

"Huh?"

"That old '62 Corvette. Now look at it—it's been totally restored."

I glanced at the TV. "That's nice," I said and went back to reading.

My phone rang. I slid my index finger across the screen; it was my friend Vicky.

"Hi, how are you?" I asked.

"Shut up, I'm trying to listen," Steve bellowed.

I walked into the kitchen with the phone and spoke more quietly. "At the cinema? What time?"

"Yeah. The movie starts at seven. If you want to come earlier—I'm going to make soup."

"Sounds good. See ya then."

I went back into the living room, picked up my book, and curled up on the sofa.

"Who was that?" Steve asked.

I looked at him. "Vicky."

"What does she want?"

"Nothing really. She just wanted to tell me about this romantic movie we both wanted to see that's playing at the cinema now."

"Oh." Romantic films never interested Steve.

Bringing flowers and giving a card that expressed how much he loved me on birthdays and Christmas was his concept of romance. Not mine.

"We're going to see it."

"When?"

"Tomorrow night. I'll probably eat with Mom or Vicky if that's okay with you."

He grunted. "I don't care."

Why did I bother telling him?

On the sofa, he was at one end, me at the other, for the rest of the night. I read a mesmerizing story of a woman who had suffered from PTSD because of family abuse. I thought you could only get PTSD from being in the military, witnessing and experiencing horrific events. I was so absorbed in the book that I never noticed he went to bed.

Chapter 4

I drove east down Rte. 6A till I reached a long, shell driveway. Braids of mist filtered through the yard of the old, miniature Victorian-style house. Vines coiled around oak and maple trees; yellow finch, blue jays, and bright, red-crested cardinals fluttered. I knocked and then turned the doorknob. The scent of sage wafted through the air. My dear, new friend and confidante, Victoria Steinbeck, had been cleansing her house of any negativity. I knew I should be doing the same. I took a deep breath, letting it seep in, exhaling the day's stress. I had met Vicky at a Reiki session one year ago and we connected immediately.

Vicky was sitting at a round, rattan table in her sunken living room. The knotty pine walls were adorned with several still-life paintings. She was dressed in a denim dress with floral embroidery on the back. She was coloring with gel pens; flowers sparkling in glitter jumped off the page.

"Oh my gosh—that's beautiful. The colors are amazing, and the flowers so detailed. What a great concept! Coloring books for us older people."

Vicky laughed. She let me skim through the pages.

"You should order one. You can get butterflies, birds, animals..."

"Amazon?"

"Yeah, I'll send you the link. I find coloring very healing."

"I'm sure—I'm going to order one tonight."

Vicky closed her coloring book and poured each of us a cup of herbal mint tea from an antique porcelain Japanese tea set she had inherited from her mother. Afterward, she handed me a bowl of pea soup, and we sat on rocking chairs in front of the hearth gazing into the flames.

"What do you think?" she asked, showing me a pic of a guy on her phone.

"He's cute," I said, thinking he looked half her age. Vicky was eight years my senior, although for fifty-seven she looked great. Her smooth skin and long, wavy white hair and azure blue eyes reminded me of some fairytale character I remembered seeing in a movie once when I was young.

"We've been writing back and forth since the middle of the night."

"What does he do for a living?" I couldn't help but wonder what job would allow him to be up all night messaging her.

Vicky had been trying out a variety of men for a while now. She had one long relationship with a guy from Colorado she went to visit and ended up staying. But in three months it was over. She had the freedom to do things and go where she wanted. I was envious of that. She seemed to be searching for love, but with all the wrong prospects. She said she didn't want a man her own age for fear he would get ill, and she'd have to take care of him—like she had done with her ex-husband. Then he ran off with another woman anyway.

"After the last fiasco, I'd rather not get into it until I learn more about him, if that's okay with you," she said.

"Of course."

"Did those two musicians show up at the party?"

I had told Vicky that the Stone brothers were going to be at the party—the reason I was excited about going. "Yes. Just as we were about to leave."

"Did either of them remember you?"

"Nah, too many years ago."

"Did you remember them?"

I shook my head.

I felt there was no purpose in mentioning the talks I'd had with Rob at the party. They were only casual exchanges really, yet I found him interesting. I wasn't sure if *interesting* was even the right word. I certainly wasn't going to tell her that his father committed suicide. That was private. Why he revealed something like that to a stranger still mystified me.

Since it was getting late, we brought the dishes into the outdated, windowless kitchen with its worn wide-pine floor and deposited them in the sink of dirty pans. We headed to the 7:00 p.m. movie at the cinema. We had both seen the previews a few months back and vowed we were going to see it. It was about a struggling writer, Jack, who had fallen in love with a librarian named Caroline, whom he'd met at a local café. But after learning she was married to a wealthy businessman, he decided it was pointless to carry on.

Both Vicky and I were old romantics. She was single though, and seeking a passionate relationship, while I was married to a man who was a world away from that. If someone had asked me how I'd rate the movie, I would have given it three stars. Even though it was done well, and the actors did a great job, I guess I was disappointed with the ending. But realism can be cruel.

"So, what'd ya think?" Vicky asked, on the way back to her house.

"I wanted those two back together."

"Me too."

"They loved each other so much. She didn't belong with that pompous ass," I said.

"I think Jack believed he couldn't give her the life she was used to."

"Maybe Caroline didn't care about that."

"Maybe she didn't at first. I'm sure he thought it over carefully."

"Yeah. People overthink too much—that's why things get ruined."

I dropped Vicky off at her cottage and went straight home, knowing Steve would be waiting up for me. He was lying on the sofa and sat straight up and glanced at the clock when I walked in the room. I knew he wouldn't ask me anything about the movie, so I volunteered.

"The movie was good, but it didn't have a happy ending."

"How come—aren't they supposed to?"

"No, but it's always nicer." *I guess it was more like reality.*

He didn't say anymore, so I went upstairs, donned my pajamas, and washed up. When I came back down and sat on the sofa, Steve got up and went to bed. I picked up the book I had been reading and bounced between paragraphs and *NCIS* for an hour or so before turning in. I slipped under the covers next to him; I knew he was still awake by his tosses and deep sighs.

"What's wrong?" I asked.

"I can't sleep."

"Is something on your mind?"

"No."

I said no more and lay quietly till my sleepless mind fell into a kind of dreaming. Steve never wanted to talk about what was really bothering him. He never wanted to talk about anything. Anything deep. Like feelings.

Chapter 5

Two weeks later, Joe and Steve had breakfast together at the Daily News. This was the first time Steve had seen Joe since his party in October. Diane had received a CD from Rob in the mail with a note asking her to get it to me. So, after changing hands from Rob to the mailman, to Diane, to Joe, to Steve, it was finally mine! I set the CD aside and played it that afternoon in the car on the way to Mom's. Rob's voice was much like Lionel Richie—soothing, and his tone ethereal. I remained in the car and played the CD repeatedly, listening to his romantic ballads. They moved me; I liked his style. I emailed Rob when I got home.

I got your CD. I love it!

He must have been on the computer because he emailed me back right away.

That's great. So glad you liked it.

I wrote back hoping he was still there. *I seriously did. I think you have a really nice voice.*

I waited to see and almost instantly got another email from him. *Thank you. My son and I perform together. He's got a nice voice too.*

Maybe you both could come and perform at one of my parties if you are here. Parties? What parties? We rarely had company these days.

Yes, when you are ready, let me know.

I will. Thanks.

I was about to walk away from the computer when another email came.

Hey, are you on FB? I am on there a lot. We could send messages back and forth if you were.

Sorry no. I don't know too much about it. I could try.

What prompted me to say that? I knew nothing about social media, and I had no real interest. I'd always been a private person. But I figured it wouldn't hurt to check it out.

Maybe I'll see you on there. Bye for now.

Yeah maybe. *Bye.*

Without hesitation, I called our neighbor's daughter, Carrie Greene, who was fifteen. I assumed all teenagers would be familiar with Facebook. I was hoping her mother, Susan, was still at work. I was sure Susan wasn't on Facebook and she'd probably wonder why I was considering it. I had no idea what one did on it or how to send or receive messages. I thought this site was for young people, but since Rob was on it, I guessed it was for everyone. For some reason, I was hoping Carrie would be able to come over sooner than later.

"Hey, Carrie, how're you doing? Playing basketball this season?"

"Yeah. We won every game but one last year."

"Yes, I know—I went to a couple with your mom. You killed the other teams."

"You were so cool, cheering me on."

I laughed. "Ah, thanks. I really enjoyed them."

"Mrs. Parker, my mom's not home."

"Oh, well, I actually called to talk to you. I'm sure you're familiar with Facebook."

"Oh yeah."

"I was wondering if you could help me set up an account?"

"Sure. I can come over after school tomorrow."

"That'd be great. I'll make us some chocolate chip cookies."

"My favorite. See you then."

Chapter 6

"Hi, Mom. You look nice—you curled your hair."

She looked at me. "You have to do something with yours. That color is awful."

I had added a little red to my dark brown that had gray roots seeping in at the crown. My aunt had had a friend, named Nancy, who had cherry red hair. My mother and her clashed. From then on, Mom was never fond of anyone who even had a hint of red in their hair.

"I like it, Mom. Other people like it too."

"Who?"

"Steve, for one. My friends."

"What friends?"

I took a deep breath. "Mom, let's go. The doctor is waiting for us." I ushered her out the door.

When Mom was young, before all the pain of abandonment, she was strikingly beautiful with her long, golden hair and soft blue eyes. That glow diminished, and deep lines creased her fair complexion. Her eyes looked angry and sad now, sometimes fearful.

"Where were you yesterday?" Mom asked when we got into the car.

"I was with Sara," I said, biting my bottom lip.

Mother flashed me a disgusted look. "What are you doing with her?"

My shoulders rose, and I could feel tightness in my chest. I grasped the steering wheel even firmer. "She's my aunt. Your sister."

"Who is she using now? Is she borrowing money again?"

"No, she's not borrowing money."

"She's looking for a free meal then. You going to feed her?"

I took a deep breath. "Mother, stop. Please."

"Stop what?"

I jammed on the brakes, jolting us forward. "I'm going to throw you out of this car, make you walk to the doctor's if you don't stop this."

"What are you talking about?"

"Mother, nothing out of your mouth is pleasant. You don't have a good word to say."

"I'm just telling the truth. You could never face the truth, Aimee."

As a kid, I'd detested the malicious gossipers in town, their negativity and judgment, that hung around too long. Children were seen but not heard. A cliché but true. It was like I had no voice. What I had to say was unimportant. Or didn't matter.

Maybe remaining alone was my way of surviving. I would hunker in a closet, where it was quiet and still, hoping I'd get locked in, and nobody would look for me. In the woods, I would walk and walk, not wanting to find my way back. One day far in the thicket, I found daffodils, hundreds of them in full bloom. I wondered who'd planted them and been there long before me. Why were people so far in the woods? Did they want to run away too?

Mom had given me a diary when I turned seven. "Keep all your secrets in here. And remember to keep it locked," she said as she handed me a little key. "They're no longer secrets if anyone knows."

Wednesday, September 13, 1966

Dear Diary,

Catechism ended at 4:30. Father told Mommy he would take care of me until she could come and get me. He was so nice and took my hand. He brought me to his house and the smell in there tingled my nose. We sat on the sofa, and he gave me cookies and milk. The cookies were yummy. I remembered to say thank you. He said, I was one of God's favorite children. I am special. When reading a children's bible book to me, he patted my hair and rubbed my back.

***

Mom's young doctor sat with a stethoscope dangling from his neck, staring into his laptop, reviewing her stats as my mother blathered nervously, wearing an uneasy smile. Her obvious fear of the doctor kept her displaying her best behavior. Her sweetness was almost sickening. "How is your family—your children must be getting big."

He looked up at her and nodded. "Yes, they're growing up fast," he said, his eyes back onto the screen.

"Well, everything looks good," he said. *Good?* He looked up from his computer and asked Mom, "You still taking Proventil and Advair—the Spiriva inhaler?"

Staring at him, dumbfounded, it was clear Mom had no idea what he was talking about. "Yes, she is," I spoke up.

"Do you need a refill?" he asked, glancing up from his laptop.

"No, she's all set for now."

It appeared he was getting ready to leave the room. "Aren't you going to check her oxygen level? She has COPD." I wondered if he even remembered.

"Oh, well we don't have a pulse oximeter..."

I shook my head. "What about her blood pressure—you wanted me to monitor it since it was high." He was young and didn't seem to care, but one day, he'd be old and in her place—then it would be different.

"Oh, yes."

He didn't have a nurse or an assistant. He struggled with trying to figure out how to use the blood pressure machine.

"It's okay—forget it," I tried to say nicely. I rolled my eyes. What a waste of time, I thought. I didn't want to get into a confrontation with him; it would be too difficult to change doctors at this point and especially hard to find one who took both Medicare and Medicaid. Anyway, I think a fatal heart attack would be the best way to leave—fast and painless.

While we were sitting there, he handed me the results of the neuropsychological evaluation. At the suggestion of both the doctor and her insurance, I'd taken Mom to a specialist a few weeks prior. The childlike testing was drawn out and traumatic for her, totally senseless. She was obviously frightened and visibly shaken seeing that she couldn't do simple tests and cognitive tasks. I wished I had never put her through it. "I didn't understand all of it," she whispered to me, while sitting in the lobby.

"That's okay, Mom. I probably wouldn't either."

I skimmed over the first few pages of what resembled half a manuscript and then put it aside. It only increased my anxiety. I didn't need to know or be instructed as to how Alzheimer's might affect her behavior or her daily living. I was witnessing and dealing with it—my way. I didn't need to be reminded that my mom wouldn't be coming back to us; she'd no longer be who she was.

I looked at Dr. Crane. "Why don't they take these assessments when a person's brain is healthy, then compare?"

"Yeah, you're right," he said.

I wondered if he'd ever been to medical school.

I took Mom home and told her I'd be back later to make her dinner.

***

When Carrie arrived, I'd just removed the cookies from the oven and the smell of chocolate and cinnamon permeated the house. Before we sat down at the computer, I poured us both a glass of milk and placed the warm cookies on a platter and set them in front of us on the mahogany coffee table.

"Thank you, Mrs. Parker," she said, grabbing one and taking a bite. "Yum, these cookies are so good."

"I'm glad you like them." I was pleased someone appreciated my efforts.

I never expected Carrie to be able to assist me so quickly considering all the after-school activities of a teenager. She sat with me for nearly an hour, teaching me how to use Facebook and Messenger, how to post—and the kinds of things to post. How to accept Friend requests. How to find people. I asked her twice how to find friends, so that I could look up Rob. My head tried desperately to absorb it all, knowing I might not get help so quickly again. I scribbled notes and put the password in my address book, so I wouldn't forget. The young people moved so fast; they were born into this technology.

I studied the profile questions. What town was I from? What schools did I attend? What did I do for a living? It was like I was filling out an application or a resume for a job.

"They ask a lot of personal stuff—even my email and phone number?"

"That's for your protection—so nobody can say it's you when it's not."

"There're so many options. Should it be only friends or public?" I asked.

"It's up to you—though you probably want to keep your postings to friends only. That's so you don't get weirdos making comments and trying to friend you. Being public means everybody on or off Facebook can see your posts."

"Ohh. Yeah, let's keep it to friends only." Except I didn't have any "friends" yet.

"Okay," she nodded. "Then you want to indicate that here," Carrie said, pointing. "It's pretty easy, Mrs. Parker, once you get the hang of it."

I nodded. "I'm sure it is."

"Do you have a picture of yourself?"

"Umm... no, nothing recent."

"That's okay—you don't need one to open an account."

"Wait. I do have one. One from my class reunion a few months ago."

"Perfect."

Carrie then uploaded it from my camera onto the computer. She made it look easy.

"Is there anything else?" she asked.

I looked into her valley-green eyes, against her locks of chestnut brown hair, now pulled back in a ponytail, imagining she had many boys who wanted to date her, and hoped she'd learn to be picky. "No, you've done enough. Please take some cookies home."

She grabbed a few and slipped them into her sweatshirt pocket.

"Do you want me to wrap those for you?"

"Nah, they'll be eaten before I get home."

"Thanks for your help," I said, escorting her to the door.

"Anytime, Mrs. Parker."

After she left, I ran back to the computer and tried to find Rob on FB, but there were so many Rob Stones, I couldn't tell which one was him. I couldn't find a resemblance anyway. At least what I could remember of him. I was disappointed, but for some reason I was sure he'd find me.

Walking through the kitchen, I snatched the *Cape Cod Times*, the local daily, lying next to Steve's place at the table. Before tossing it, I glanced through, stopping at the local crimes. Having worked as a paralegal in a prosecutor's office for twenty-five years, I realized that about seventy percent of assaults, domestic abuse, rapes, and drug cases never reached the newspapers—too many to mention, I assumed. After a while, people became immune to these events. Even the mass shootings elsewhere weren't getting the attention they once did. It was like the whole planet had become desensitized in the last decade. The world was changing rapidly.

Who do we trust?

Are we safe from anyone?

I saw: LOCAL PRIEST ACCUSED OF SEXUAL MISCONDUCT, accompanied by a picture of an elderly Father Maxwell Wallace. "Another predator abuses the trust and faith of his victims by taking advantage of his position in the community...."

Suddenly, the walls were closing in on me. My head started spinning; nausea rolled up like an ocean swell. I dropped to the floor. Curling into a ball, rolling back and forth. Gasping for breath.

Wednesday, November 15, 1966

Dear Diary,

Today, that smell tingled my nose again. I guess it's there every day. After cookies, Father told me I was God's angel and he said, "This is between you, me, and God. You don't tell anyone." I nodded. Then he took my hand and put it on his pants. He pushed my hand up and down on his zipper. A mountain grew under my hand, and he made weird noises. Then his pants got wet. I was so scared. And I can't tell anybody. I promised.

Chapter 7

Mom was dozing in the recliner when I arrived. I glanced at her ankles; they seemed okay. All those years of smoking had caused COPD, and I was worried about her congestive heart failure.

"Hey, Mom," I said quietly.

"Hi," she said groggily.

"Do you want to rest? I can come back later."

"No," she said, trying to sit up straighter.

"You hungry?"

"No."

That response was becoming far too common lately, which concerned me.

"I brought some groceries," I said, walking into the kitchen, placing the paper bag on the counter, and unloading. When I opened the refrigerator door, I smelled something foul. All I saw in there was a quart of milk, a tub of butter, and two yogurts. Then I opened the drawers and inside one was a pound of clear-sealed hamburger that had turned bad. *Another sign of cognitive decline.* I chucked it and put in the eggs, vitamin water, and jelly. After folding the bag, I saw that there were no dishes to wash; either she'd cleaned up or hadn't eaten anything.

I dropped on the sofa I'd bought her five years earlier, that still looked brand new, another piece of furniture that had never been broken in. I looked around. As usual, her little place was spotless. There was nothing for me to do but keep her company. I only wished she had made friends through the years, real friends. Other than a few phone calls and an occasional drop-in, usually a neighbor, she basically sat alone day in, day out.

"Where have you been?"

"Oh, you remember Carrie Greene—our next-door neighbor's daughter?" Mom stared at me blankly. "She came by to help me with an account on the computer."

Mom had never used a computer in her life; she had no idea what I was talking about.

Feeling a bit guilty for not being there sooner and knowing

the last thing on her mind was dinner, I thought doing something *she* enjoyed would make her happy.

"Hey, let's play checkers."

"Yeah," she said, jumping up and heading to her bedroom.

After a couple of minutes, I walked into the bedroom; she was plowing through the closet.

"Did you find it?"

"I know it's here somewhere," she mumbled.

"Mom, there it is on the top shelf to the right."

She looked up and tried to reach it.

"Let me get it down for you."

We walked back into the living room, and I set up the board. "Do you want red or black?"

"Red."

"Okay."

Mom looked like a little girl all excited to play, but when it was her turn to make a move, she had no idea what to do. She looked lost.

"Mom, you can jump me. Watch," I said, showing her.

I could see confusion rising as she attempted to move my checker instead.

"Remember yours are red."

"I know," she snapped.

I watched her eyes floating from here to there, lines in her forehead creasing. She put her finger on the red checker and looked at me. I nodded. She took her move, where I could jump twice. But I ignored the chance.

Nearly two hours had passed. I knew Steve would be home from work and would have a meal on the table already.

"Mom, can I fix you something before I leave?"

"No."

I grabbed a Healthy Choice dinner from the freezer and popped it in the microwave. I knew making a balanced meal for her would be a waste of time, since she shook her head at nearly everything I suggested lately.

While waiting, I grabbed a bottle of cold vitamin water and a fork. When the microwave buzzed, I set the tray of steaming food in front of her.

Her nose immediately crinkled. "I don't like it. I told you—I'm not hungry! You never listen!"

"You always liked pot roast and mashed potato. Look," I said, pointing out with the fork, "there's mixed veggies here too."

"Yuck," she said, shuddering.

Yeah, I had to agree with her. It reminded me of those TV dinners Mom would keep stocked in our freezer growing up.

"Will you at least try a bite?"

She pushed the plate away, toward me. "You have it!"

She'd always been stubborn. And dementia was exacerbating her negativity.

"Okay, fine," I said, handing her a couple of pills. Amazingly, she took them. Maybe if I avoided badgering, she'd be more compliant. I just wanted her to stay healthy. Physically anyway.

"I gotta go now. I love you."

"You coming back?"

"Tomorrow."

Her sullen look tore at my heart.

I was holding a lot of resentment. Not so much because she'd become ill; she couldn't help that. I'd always felt it was my obligation as her daughter to be there for her in every way I could. The way I expected she had always been there for me. But, sadly, through the years, I was her everything. I would never abandon her; I just wanted to be free. Free. Free!

Chapter 8

"Let's go," Steve said, holding the front door open.

We walked out to the driveway paved with stone and got in the car.

"What are you getting in Hyannis?" I asked when we were settled in.

"I have to pick up a few tools for work."

"Oh. Do you think we can stop at the mall?"

"For what?"

"Macy's is having a big sale."

"I want to get up there and get back—I've got things to do."

"Okay." I was happy to take a ride, break up the monotony.

I remained in the car while he went into the tool store. He knew there was nothing of interest for me. Despite the rawness, the sun's heat penetrated the car windows, warming my face. After fixing Mom breakfast earlier I hated to tell her she couldn't come because Steve didn't want her to. In fact, he preferred that neither of us go. Oh, he didn't say that, but I'd learned to read him through the years. Mom had put on her jacket and shoes and said, "I'm ready—let's go." She just wanted to get out of the house too. The disappointment on her face when I told her it wasn't possible hung like a dark cloud over me.

Twenty minutes later Steve strutted out jovially. "I ran into Billy Slater."

I knew he'd been talking to somebody; he'd been in there too long. I was glad he was finding people to have conversations with since we never had any.

"Oh, do I know him?"

"You've met him."

"I did? Where?"

"I can't remember. Somewhere. But you met him and his wife. That's him coming out now," Steve said, waving.

"Yes, I've seen him before."

"He's a great guy," Steve said, nodding.

"I'm sure he is—you are too." But only occasionally, I thought with a sigh.

He turned toward me and flashed a smile.

Instead of going home, Steve headed toward Macy's. I hated that he felt it was his obligation as a husband to honor my request even though he resented it. Instead of just saying "no," his heightened shoulders, narrow eyes, and pinched mouth spoke to me.

While at the set of lights near the mall, I could see Steve's patience waning—his rapid eye movements, his creased forehead. "Why is this fucking light taking so long?"

"I can go to the mall another time. It's okay," I said, biting the inside of my cheek.

"Let's not make this a sermon. Go in and get what you need. Just hurry it up."

I'd lost all interest in shopping now, but I didn't dare tell him. He pulled up to Macy's entrance and I went in anyway. I took a quick look around, admiring several sweaters and slacks. I even went into the dressing room and tried on a few and liked them. But I was feeling too anxious to stand in the long, slow lines at checkout knowing Steve was outside waiting for me.

"Do you need some help?" a saleswoman asked.

"No, I'm just browsing. Thank you."

"You didn't get anything?" Steve asked, noticing I had no shopping bags when I opened the car door.

"Nah, plus those long lines—no help these days."

"Then what took you so long."

"I tried on a few things. Nothing looked good."

He said nothing.

Exiting the mall, we stopped at the red traffic light. Minutes passed; it seemed like it was never going to turn green.

"Jesus, why the hell does this light take so damn long?" Then just as the light was about to change, a pedestrian crossed in front of us. "Come on, you idiot, move your ass."

"The light hasn't turned yet. She's going as fast as she can carrying a lot," I said, noticing her bundles and a cart she was pushing.

"Yeah, she's carrying a lot all right—a lot of fat."

I shook my head in revulsion and took a deep breath, blowing out tension.

We were coming up on Trader Joe's. I knew I was pushing it, but I had to ask. "Would you mind stopping—we need to get something for supper."

He grumbled, but any time food was involved he usually agreed. He parked and got out of the car with me. Inside, we walked the aisles together. Steve packed the carriage with cereals and canned goods, and I grabbed a package of wild Alaskan salmon, fresh fruit, and vegetables. Soon our carriage was full. Though Steve appeared calmer in the market, my insides still thundered.

Chapter 9

I had time now to work on a new novel, but when I sat at the computer my mind was blank. Not even a single sentence appeared. I stared vacantly, waiting for my characters to do their thing—to take over the keyboard. But nothing happened. A friend had once told me to just show up, discipline myself, and whatever came to mind—write it. Yeah, sure. Write a bunch of nothings—every word I hesitate on. Try to find a better one, a prettier one. *Maybe I should just stick to my journal.* The whole time sitting there, I was worrying about how Mom was doing. Dementia patients were known to wander aimlessly and do the unthinkable. So, after an hour of staring at the empty screen, I got up and went to her house.

Mom was on the phone talking with a friend. I waved to her and sat quietly, cross-legged on the living room rug, and pulled out an old case of picture albums from a shelf. Opening one, I looked at pictures of Mom when she was in her teens. She was so beautiful. Even though the photographs were in black and white, I recalled how my dad described her when he first saw her. "She was walking down Main Street in this red coat, her long, wavy blonde hair blowing in the breeze. And those legs… I was with my buddy, Mikey, both of us headed for Coast Guard duty, when I slammed on the car brakes. I'll never forget those baby blue eyes and the way she smiled at me."

There were no pictures of my dad and her; she had destroyed them all after their divorce. Well, all but one she missed, their wedding day, that I had found later and kept. They both looked so happy.

As a child, I never understood why she couldn't love my father the way I adored him. He was a good man, decent and respectable with great virtues. He was a kind and loving father who was there for me on every special occasion that mattered: graduations, birthdays, Christmases; everything that was important in a child's life.

When she thought I was old enough to understand, Mom told me that she and my dad were at a neighbor's house partying, and he'd been drinking. Later that evening, Dad brought a woman home to their bed. People drinking do foolish things, things they regret when they're sober. An immoral act can't be taken back, only forgiven. Mom couldn't pardon his sin and made the rash decision of divorcing him, at a time when women didn't do those things.

She fell in love once more when she turned thirty-two; I was almost eleven. Irving was divorced and had children from his marriage, but he wanted no part of his own flesh and blood. So why would he want anyone else's kid? I wondered how my mom could have loved someone like that when I had meant everything to her. She wanted him so badly that one time the words that escaped her lips shocked me. "I wish you were never born."

She was implying she'd be better off without me and it felt like I'd just been stung by a trillion bees, but I knew—later—she was blindsided by this tangle of emotions. She wanted to believe I'd ruined her relationship, was in the way of what she could've had with him. Instead of facing that he was just no good. And didn't want her.

I never thought of Irving as handsome, not even slightly. He was tall and thin and dressed conservatively in drab browns and grays. His face was devoid of any feeling. He had zero charisma and his personality lacked pizzazz. Maybe Mom was attracted to the shiny new T-bird he drove. He took no interest in me. Why would he? He had given up his own children. Mom dated him for five years and convinced him to give her a diamond, hoping he'd marry her. After Mom miscarried his child, he vanished. She was heartbroken, but I was glad he was gone.

Astonishingly, one day long after her breakup, Mom shared an intimate confession. "I could just watch him walk by me and come in my underwear." Mom had never been open to any sexual discussions before, but suddenly she had this need or want to "tell" what this man, Irving, was able to do to her.

Even though I couldn't relate, I never forgot what she'd revealed. It was hard to understand how a man whom I saw as completely lacking loveable traits could turn her on like that.

Mom married again when she was in her early forties but not for love; she thought I was getting married. Once she learned that that wasn't going to happen, she immediately had her sixth-month marriage annulled. The third time, she was turning forty-five. She never divorced him, but up and left after a couple of years and moved in with us. Me. Again. Mom had other men who'd fallen for her, but the only two she'd ever loved were gone and all the resentment, hurt, and anger left her bitter toward men in general.

I always felt, in some way, responsible for her happiness—or unhappiness, I should say. I wanted her to be happy, but the only happiness she knew or thought she knew had been banished from her when the only two men she ever loved had done her wrong. The only thing she ever held on to was me. Mom believed I could provide her with something that only she could manifest from within. It was a void I couldn't fill. But tried.

Flipping through the album's pages, my eyes lingered on Mom with this cute guy, wearing a military uniform. Then I saw the newspaper announcement of her engagement to William Baker—she was going to marry someone other than my dad? She'd never mentioned him. Why? Too long ago? I held it aside.

Another photo album was filled with pictures of my grandparents, cousins, aunts, and uncles. I stared at the various relatives. Their smiles now looked forced. A mélange of brokenness. Family on both sides were divorced and the few that weren't, or so I believed, lived in pretend contentment. *Like me.* Life was simpler back then but not always easy. It saddened me that most had since passed, even ones younger than myself. But maybe on the other side they've found what was missing here for them. Love. Happiness.

Then, surprisingly, I saw photos of my sixteenth birthday party. Skimming through them, I came across pictures of the band, Beloved Townies, who played that night on stage. Staring more closely, I saw that none of them looked like Rob. Nor his brother, for that matter. I wondered if he was on break when the pictures were taken. It's odd that both would be missing. So much happened that evening, I was just grateful the band was there.

I gathered the few birthday reminiscences from the plastic sleeves and slipped them into my purse. I kept in my palm the newspaper clipping of my mother and this mysterious man, whom I hadn't recalled seeing before. "Mom, who is this guy?" I asked, showing her.

"I was going to marry him," she said, looking melancholy.

"What happened?"

"His mother broke us up."

"His mother?"

She nodded.

"Oh, that's too bad. Did you love him?"

She nodded. "Yes." She shifted in her chair, let out a big sigh, and smiled.

"How did his mother break you guys up?"

"One day, she made me clean her house."

"Clean her house—your boyfriend's mother?"

"Yup. I sat on the sofa and was all pretty when he came home."

"Like you did nothing all day?" I assumed his mother had her do her dirty work, and when Mom's fiancé arrived, she was looking unruffled and wearing her best. He'd have no clue she'd been his mother's Cinderella for the day.

"Yup."

"So, do you think it would have worked out—if his mother wasn't in the picture?"

"Yeah—she was a bitch. And he was a mama's boy. He broke up with me—she didn't like me."

But you would never have met Dad."

Mom crinkled her nose, flashing her unclean false teeth. "That was a mistake."

"As long as you don't regard me, Mom, as a mistake," I said, looking at her. "If you had married someone else, I wouldn't be who I am. Seems strange when I think about it."

I could tell she didn't understand. I couldn't help but wonder who I would be today, if my mom had married this man named William. It's weird how things turn out—how people turn out. What gives us the uniqueness of feeling, thinking, knowing? To think that we are only a speck in the universe, and just a single move, one decision, can alter our lives. Change who we could have been. Might have been. Indeed, might not have been at all. A sobering thought.

I fell in love and was engaged to marry at the age of twenty. I gave that man, named Gary, everything. Well, almost. Roof over his head, food, clothing, even an automobile. I kept hearing the priest's voice in my head, "You cannot wear the white wedding gown should you *not* be a virgin when you marry." And, oh, how I wanted to wear a beautiful *white* wedding gown like in every other young woman's dream. So, obeying the priest, the church's rules, I kept my legs closed, off limits, till that special day.

That day never came.

When I had broken it off with Gary, who betrayed me, he walked out the door calling me a "Fuckin' Virgin." I fell to my knees, looked up, put my hands in a prayer position, and thanked God. I had given him everything but my vagina.

The priests and monks, along with my family's religious and moral values, had strongly influenced my own attitude about sex. Only negative thoughts rose about my genitals, ugly and wrinkled, like a prune, instead of comparing my shape to parts of a flower, or a shell, or even a design, something nice to the eyes. I refused to learn to appreciate my genitals as beautiful parts of myself. My private parts, I'd come to believe, were for the toilet and the bathtub, not for a male to take advantage of for his own needs.

> *"Come," he says, holding out his hand. I eagerly take the hand of the man who represents God. In the rectory, we walk into a room at the end of the hallway. So high is the ceiling—so many books. I'm in awe. The moonlight beams through the dark gothic windows. Suddenly, I hear a snap and look at a woman putting clean sheets on a bed, sending wafts of lavender in the air. I say, "Hello," or maybe I just said it in my mind. The woman never acknowledges me.*

Even if I had sexual desires, my body crying out, I suppressed it. I forbade myself to engage in what I believed was a forbidden act before matrimony. I obeyed the church, my parents. God. *Him.* Always. The whole time, while feeling sexy and being flirtatious, I had no idea what I was doing to boys. To men. All I knew was that I loved them. But I refused to be fully loved by them. I could hear my mother's voice. *"Men will just use you. They won't love you. Not the way they should."*

My reverie was interrupted.

"Ooh, I have to go to the bathroom," Mom said, wiggling in her chair.

"Okay, go ahead. Do you need help?"

"No," she said emphatically, waving me off.

When she sat back down, I gently asked, "Mom, please put your oxygen on."

"I don't need it."

"Your doctor says you do."

"I don't, Aimee!"

I was so worried each night when I left that she'd remove it again. *What if she dies in the middle of the night? It will be my fault.*

"Mom, what would you like for dinner tonight?" I asked, looking in the freezer, still stocked with sodium-filled meals. I tried healthier foods, even homemade meals, but she refused to even try any of them.

"I'm not hungry."

Lasagna took precedence over roast beef and turkey. But tonight was the turkey. None of the dinners was good for someone with congestive heart failure. I hadn't shopped for her in a couple of weeks, but her preference was eggs and ice cream. Finicky and stubborn were an impossible combination. She was continuously losing weight and it was a battle trying to get her to eat anything nutritious.

"Mom, will you have just a little bit? Please?"

She tightened her lips and shook her head.

I collected a fork of food and held it in the air. "Here comes the airplane—open up."

"For God's sake, Aimee, I'm not a child."

"Fine. I will call you later."

"You're leaving?"

I nodded.

I kissed her on the forehead. When I walked out the door, we both had tears streaming down our cheeks.

Chapter 10

I got on Facebook after Steve went to bed and saw that Rob had "friended" me. There was a message from him.

Dearest Aimee,

It was so good to see you at the party. Long time, eh?

When I got home, I began thinking about your 16th birthday party. How could I forget! Just a long time ago, I guess. How are you? Are you still thinking about my son and me coming to perform? It would be wonderful! He is amazing and together we are flowing.

Keep in touch and be well. You looked great and I thought you were much younger than us, and we couldn't have possibly played at your party, but we did!

Bye for now.

Rob

I messaged him back.

Hi Rob,

Yeah, it was great seeing you too. I found some old photos from the party at my mom's house. None of the band members look like you or your brother. Are you sure you were there?

Rob responded immediately.

What year was that?

It was 1975.

Oh, I went in the army for a couple of years and got back in December of '76.

I was bummed. I had no reason to be. Why did it matter now?

If you'd like to see the pics, I could mail them to you.

Yeah, that would be great. I haven't seen any of those guys in years. Let me give you my address—I'll mail them back to you.

Oh, that's good—I'd really like to keep them.

Well, I hope you have a great night.

You too.

He was still on Facebook. He had over a thousand friends! Clearly a social guy. But no mention of marriage in his profile.

Strange. I did see women with the same last name, but none of them looked his age. A young man named Tyler Stone was one of his friends. Maybe his son. Although he didn't look much like his father. I checked out more of his women friends but other than Diane being his friend, no names or faces looked familiar.

I didn't care about making new friends or even feeling confident posting. I waited a few minutes, and when there were no more messages from him, I closed the laptop.

Chapter 11

It was harder to rise these dark mornings, and the house was chillier. I donned heavy socks and grabbed my fleece bathrobe. I hurried downstairs to fix breakfast for Steve and me. He was already up, watching the morning news, drinking coffee. I poured myself a cup. I heated the skillet, laid bacon strips. Then I took the last two eggs from the carton, broke them in a bowl, added milk, scrambled, and emptied them into the hot frying pan. While waiting, I popped English muffins into the toaster.

"It's ready," I yelled.

Henri, short for Henrietta, our calico cat, was rubbing against my leg, letting me know she was hungry. "I got something for you too, girl," I said, filling her dish. We kept Henri's name when we adopted her at eight months old from our elderly neighbors, who both became residents of a nursing home—nearly thirteen years ago now.

"You're overfeeding her," Steve remarked, walking past me, taking a seat at the table. I dished out Steve's plate first, bringing it to him. After tending to Henri, I grabbed mine and sat down.

"I only give her what the vet suggested."

"Well, look at her. She looks like a fat toad." *And you croak like one.*

While Steve was reading the paper, I jotted a few reminders on post-it notes.

Call doctor for Mom's eye exam.

Get Mom more milk and coffee.

Do laundry. Mom's and ours.

Take the cat to the vet on Thursday for a checkup.

Steve glanced at his plate, then over at me. "What'd ya do to the bacon?"

"I guess I overcooked it. Sorry."

He wolfed the eggs. Then bit into one strip. "I can't eat this," he mumbled, standing up.

"Have a good day. I love you," he said, kissing me on the forehead. *I don't believe you.*

"You too," I said, feigning a smile.

After Steve left for work, I cleaned up the dishes. Before heading upstairs, I snapped on the coffeemaker. I made the bed and scooted to the bathroom. Looking into the magnifying mirror, I applied a moisturizer, avoiding foundation since it enhanced the wrinkles that seemed to be increasing by the day. Lastly, I dabbed blush to my snow-white cheeks and gloss to my parchment paper lips. I could see why women considered Botox. I slipped on long underwear, jeans, and a flannel shirt. Then I whipped my hair into a bun and wrapped a scarf around my neck.

Downstairs, I went to the laptop and opened Facebook, hoping to find a new message from Rob. But no. *Maybe later.* Some names and faces looked familiar from years ago, but I wondered if they'd even want to be my friend. Besides, I really wasn't looking for a friend. Vicky was enough and they'd only be acquaintances. I logged out and shut the cover.

It was only 5:45 a.m. I yanked my down jacket from a hanger in the hall closet and dashed to the kitchen. I poured coffee in the travel mug and hurried out to my car. Before heading to Mom's, I detoured since I doubted she'd be up. At least I hoped not. I drove ten minutes in the opposite direction, and when I reached the beach parking lot, I found it empty. I smiled. Too early for locals. I laid down the wool throw on a dune and parked myself, bringing my knees to my chest, wrapping my chilly fingers around the mug. I took a sip as I watched the yellow and burnt orange rise of the new morning. I blinked at the sun; I was glad to see it. I let the moment sink in, since only a new dawn is all we are really promised.

I began reflecting on my life, Mom's life. The woman who appeared so strong, who had the courage to divorce in a time when women were afraid. Divorce was unthinkable; even the miserable ones remained in their marriages. In the 1950s and '60s, a divorcee was labeled and shunned. Worse for Mom, she had converted from Protestantism to Catholicism at eighteen. I don't know why; her other siblings were Protestant. Divorcing meant being ousted from the church she had gone to so much effort to be a part of.

As a child, seeing Mom cry made me cry. The mother I loved was hurting and I couldn't bear to see her so sad. Then suddenly—it seemed to happen in one day—she hardened like honey left too long in a jar, like she had no choice. She had to be seen as a strong woman to survive. Nobody was going to misjudge or wound her again.

I admired her.

Still, that jagged exterior never invaded Mom's generous heart when it came to helping other people. Cleaning houses for a living didn't bring in much money. Even so, she would give every cent she'd earned to someone who needed it. Once she gave a single parent all but ten dollars of her paycheck so that the young woman could feed her child.

Before Mom's driver's license was taken away by the hospital, she had enjoyed driving her neighbors to doctors' appointments and other errands. And they appreciated her generosity. But once Mom fulfilled their needs, she never heard from them again. I wondered if signs of Mom's dementia scared them off or if it was her blatant remarks. She had no problem telling a heavy-set woman in the laundry room, "You should go on a diet—you waddle like a duck." She'd said to one of my lanky boyfriends in high school, "Don't turn sideways—the wind might blow you over." She was a candid woman, maybe too honest, and had no problem saying it like she saw it.

After sitting for nearly an hour, I packed up and headed to Mom's. I stopped at Dunkin' Donuts, one of her favorites.

"Hey, Mom, I brought you a coffee."

"What else you got?"

"Your favorite—a jelly cruller," I said, pulling it out of the bag.

Mom grabbed it from me. "Thank you."

"You're welcome."

If she had her way, she would live on sweets and stimulants.

I had coaxed Mom into a golden-age program at the senior center but that lasted only a few months. I went with her in the beginning to make her feel more comfortable around strangers. The volunteer staff was understanding and caring and so compassionate. Some of the kindest people I had ever met, relieving any reservations I had about leaving her there alone. As I weaned away though, she began losing interest.

The break I was hoping for—evaporated. She was missing out on what could have been a delightful time with all the fun doings they offered each week. I kept quiet—I didn't want to upset her, but I was angry at her for not trying hard enough to enjoy new things, to be with others, instead of restricting herself—to just me. *Cut the damn cord, Mom!*

"Hey, you want to play UNO?" I asked, after Mom devoured the donut.

Mom's head bobbed up and down like one of those bobbleheads. She flashed a little girl grin.

"You'll have to teach me," I said. Mom always played with Casey and Cameron, her grandniece and grandnephew. She enjoyed the card game as much as they did.

"Okay."

We played for an hour or so; she was still amazingly good with numbers. Still had periods of sharpness.

"Mom, I have to go soon. Can I get you anything before I leave—maybe a drink?"

She shook her head. The coffee and donut had evidently packed her belly.

"Why don't you sit down and put on your oxygen?" The big, noisy, ugly tank was stationed next to her recliner, and the regulator produced an annoying humming, followed every few seconds by puffs of air.

"I don't need it."

"The doctor says you do."

"I don't listen to him."

"You do know it helps you breathe better. That way you won't get so tired."

"I'm not tired!"

"Okay," I surrendered, sticking the palms of my hands in the air.

I was so happy she'd stopped smoking after contracting pneumonia three years earlier. She wouldn't have done it if a visiting nurse hadn't asked her if she wanted to die. She quickly put down those cigarettes. She feared death more than anything. Even though she seemed miserably unhappy, she still wanted to be here. On this planet.

"Come on, sit in your chair. I'll turn on the TV."

"I don't want to watch TV."

"Okay, well fine. I have to go home."

"Can I come?"

I looked into her pleading blue eyes.

I sighed. "Sure, why not."

When we got to the house, Mom immediately began her habitual cleaning: picking up things, wiping down the kitchen counters, and washing some dishes left in the sink. She had always been like the Road Runner, racing around on Everlasting Duracell. I felt more like a ragdoll that had been siphoned through a ten-foot straw.

"Aimee doesn't do anything anymore," Mom said to Steve when he arrived home.

It was as though she was trying to impress my husband by making me look useless. I felt my mother and husband ganging up on me, or maybe I was just tired.

"Yeah, she is getting a little lazy," he said.

"Really," I said, steam surging through my nostrils. *Arm me with a lasso—I'll show you lazy.*

We cooked Mom one of her all-time favorites, hot dogs and beans. Then I opened the canned brown bread. It was a Saturday night staple growing up. I watched Mom examine her plate. I wondered if her taste buds would remember. I thought if she watched us eating, she would follow.

"Evelyn, would you like mustard and relish?" Steve asked her.

She nodded, flickering a smile as though he was giving her the world on a golden platter. Or maybe deep down, or in another mind, she still had a tenderness for men, an ache she constantly fought yet continually felt.

He took her plate and lavished her hot dog with the condiments, then handed it back to her.

"Could you cut it up for her, please?" I asked, since she seemed suddenly smitten with him. When Mom first met Steve, she told me he wasn't my type and that he dressed like her father. I wondered how she thought she knew my type—when I didn't even know. *Why do we even need a "type"? Why can't we just connect?*

Surprisingly, Mom ate every morsel of her meal. Maybe it was the presence of a man that gave her an appetite. Mom had snubbed men for years though, finding fault with them. Was she viewing men in a different light now?

After dinner we went into the living room to watch TV. I saw my mother's eyes wandering, fixating on the items in the built-ins at the far end of the room. She got up and began rearranging pictures and knickknacks. "You've got too much on here."

"Everything is fine, Mom. Please leave things alone and don't remove anything."

She didn't listen; not that she did before dementia.

Mom grabbed my dad's eight-by-ten senior high school picture and stuck it in the far corner, moving the one of herself up front, where everyone could see it. I didn't blame her; Mom looked beautiful back then. After Mom divorced my dad, she would never allow anyone to take her picture; if there was one, it was only by accident—a random shot when she was unaware. She'd never look at the camera. It was like she knew all her pain would be revealed if she did.

"Mom, I think it's time for you to go home. Sit down—I will help you put your shoes on."

"Where's my pocketbook?" she asked, looking around.

"It's right here," I said, picking it up from the carpeted floor and handing it to her.

I drove her home, walked her into the house, stayed until she was ready for bed, and made sure her oxygen was on her. I felt sad leaving her alone. She had to be frightened knowing that her mind was off, becoming illusive. Her thoughts were no longer hers. I understood that.

May 1972

Summer was approaching. I had just turned thirteen a couple of months before. I was alone in the house; Mom was at work. I woke up out of a sound sleep, feeling this urge. Something was pulsating between my legs; it was like my private parts were speaking to me. I hurried to the bathroom and grabbed a towel. I brought it back to the bed and folded it into a long, thick log. I lay on the bed with it and turned on my side, wedging it nicely between my legs and squeezing my thighs tight around the cloth. I humped and humped, rubbing it against my clitoris until my body quivered and released this warm liquid that saturated my underwear. I wasn't sure what it was about. The only thing I knew: it felt good. Afterward I felt ashamed—I immediately took my underwear to the bathroom sink and washed it. Masturbating was once considered evil, a sin. I'm not sure if I knew that then or had even heard the word masturbating.

Suddenly though, after the release, my heart began to race, and this strange feeling came over me. I lay in bed waiting for it to pass and when it didn't, I began praying. Is this what it feels like before we go to heaven?

Stepping outside, the world seemed distorted, skewed. I knew I wouldn't even be able to describe it to anyone. It was a warm and sunny day, and everything seemed heightened. The sky—more blue, brighter. The birds were louder. The greenery fluorescent. The earth's fragrance was new to me. Exotic. I felt disconnected—like I was having an out-of-body experience.

I walked fast; I had to find my mother. I needed to see her so I could say goodbye for the last time and feel her comforting embrace, soothing me, and making me feel less alone when I died.

I searched the grocery store, where she was a cashier, and there was no sign of her. Without an automobile, I knew she had to be with my aunt, who was only a couple of miles away in the little village. I upped my pace in fear I would not make it in time.

When I, at last, opened the front door of my aunt's house and stumbled through, I heard her voice. "Mom," I cried, running down the hallway into the kitchen, falling into her arms, "I think I'm dying."

"What? You're not dying."

"There's something wrong—I need to see the doctor," I cried.

"But you just went recently—you are fine."

"Mom, please, no I'm not. Call him," I pleaded.

I was afraid she was thinking I was overreacting. But somehow, she believed me.

"Okay, I'll give him a call."

Unlike my dad, hugs and kisses were rare with Mom, but she would lie at the end of my bed if I was extremely sick with the mumps and measles, running high fevers. It was obvious how much she loved me. But now I wasn't lying on a bed running a temperature—although I wished I were. Mom always got the fever to go away.

Although I had her attention, her support, I had this dreadful concern that this, whatever it was, was never going to go away. When my doctor came closer, a familiar foreboding came over me. The white coat turned black. The big silver stethoscope hanging down on his chest, reminding me of Father's cross, suddenly turned gold and so bright, it blinded me. It was frightening. My serene surroundings were collapsing around me—something terrible was happening. It was as though a distorted evilness was entering me, leaving my mind and body out of sync.

I didn't die but my mind was altered and had been thrust into what I referred to as a "living death." Weeks led to months and then years passed, as more anxieties were born and snowballed. That calm little mind no longer existed; there was a new meaning to my normalcy.

I became silent. And alone in my dread.

Chapter 12

Before heading out the door, I grabbed the ringing landline phone on the kitchen wall.

"Hi, Margie, how are you?"

Mom was Margie Smith's housecleaner, and they'd become good friends despite the age difference. Margie was young enough to be Mom's daughter. Margie said my mom had reminded her of her own mother with their similarities. I wondered what parallels Margie was referring to—perhaps my mom's old-fashioned values.

"I'm doing fine. I don't know how to say this..."

"Please, it's okay—what is it?" I asked, twirling the phone cord around my fingers, holding my breath.

"Your mom," she hesitated. "Borrowed money from me."

"Oh?"

"She said she had no money to pay her rent."

"Her social security check covers that."

"Maybe she gambled it away?"

Local casinos were over a hundred miles away, so gambling meant she'd stopped at every convenience store or market in the village and bought Lotto instant tickets. She'd spent more than she gained. Even if she won big, we knew she'd give it away to someone who needed it.

"She's always been conscientious about paying her rent," I said, shaking my head. "This really concerns me."

"I'm sorry I had to tell you this."

"I'm glad you did. I'll pay you back...."

"No, don't worry about it. Besides, I wanted to help," Margie said.

"She never said a word."

"She probably didn't want you to know."

"That's not like her to do something like that," I said.

"Maybe it's, you know, her illness."

"Yeah, I'm sure that's it."

Now I knew I had to convince Mom to sign papers for me to become her power of attorney. It was time to manage her finances; I had no choice. I couldn't have her thrown out on the street; I sure couldn't go back to having her live with us. I thanked Margie, bid her good-bye, hung up the phone, and took a deep breath.

Day and night, I was there for her and still it didn't seem like enough. I was unsure how much longer Mom could live alone. No way I wanted her to go into a nursing home, but I wasn't sure I could handle taking her back to our house. The stubbornness. The OCD. The negativity. At least with her in her own place, I still had my space, even if I was constantly worrying about her. Just the thought of her coming back, my life being disrupted like that, caused me to hyperventilate. I ran and got a small paper lunch bag out of the kitchen drawer, bunched up the ends, and blew into it. *Deep breaths, deep breaths. Let it go, let it go.*

I grabbed my long down parka, woolen hat, scarf and gloves from the closet and drove to the beach. I walked for miles along the shore. The cool wind slapped my face as I trudged the damp sand in my boots. Squawking seagulls flew overhead, and plovers and terns raced along the shoreline. Clouds began filling up the sky like vaporous veils intent on causing mischief. I welcomed any distraction to alleviate this heaviness. And I felt a sense of freedom here.

***

"Hey, Mom—what's going on? Having a good day?" I asked when I walked in.

Her nose crinkled up. "It's all right."

"The house looks great—you always keep it nice."

"Never know who's going to come," she said with an anticipating smile.

Trouble was, nobody came, aside from a plumber or carpenter repairing something. It seemed, though, like enough interaction and excitement for her. The workmen's pleasantries, their seeming interest in what she had to say, made her day.

"Can I fix you breakfast?" I asked.

"Where's Margie? She told me she was coming today."

"She couldn't make it."

"Why?"

"Peter got sick, and she had to pick him up at school," I fibbed. I didn't really know if Margie called Mom and told her she was coming. Margie did visit Mom often; she was a stay-at-home mom. Her husband, an electrician, preferred that since he made enough money to support the family comfortably. Even enough to hire a housecleaner.

"Oh." I saw the disappointment registering across her face.

I pulled out the small frying pan from the lower cabinet and grabbed the bacon and eggs from the refrigerator. When everything was ready, I dished it out for the two of us and set it on the table.

"You're eating with me?"

I nodded.

"Good."

The kettle whistled, letting me know the water was ready for instant coffee. I filled our mugs and brought them over to the table.

"We're going to see your old friend, Cyrus Horton."

"Today?"

I nodded. "Yes."

"Why?"

"Remember I told you—I want to be able to help you manage your bills?"

"I think so."

"To be able to do that, we need to sign some legal papers. Meaning that you're giving me permission to be your helper. They call it 'Power of Attorney.'"

"Ohh," she said in a deeper voice.

After breakfast, I helped her bathe.

"What should I wear?" she asked.

"Something casual—we're just going to his office."

"Will you help me pick out something?"

"Of course."

We rummaged through her closet, searching for the right outfit.

In Mom's younger years, if she had an appointment or anywhere special to go, she'd always dress nicely. Her clothes were spotless and ironed, if needed, as well as matching and well-fitting. She'd go to the hair salon every week, even if she had to barter with the hairdresser by cleaning her house. She made sure her fingernails and toes were manicured perfectly and painted the color of her lipstick, which was usually red and stunning against her smooth fair skin.

As Mom grew older into her late forties, she rarely dressed up, just on a few occasions. I used to be embarrassed at the way she looked. Her clothes were sloppy, unmatched, and sometimes stained, usually from her housecleaning jobs. She would justify it by saying, "I just got through work." "But you're going to the store and people who know you will see you." She'd respond with "So what?" *You always wanted me to be perfectly groomed.* It was like she had given up on herself, as if she was too old to worry about what others thought.

Mom chose one of her newer black blazers and matching polyester slacks. She liked and respected Cyrus and wanted to dress accordingly. Her dress clothes still looked good, like new, even after twenty years. She rarely went anywhere to wear them. I found black unsuited for her complexion. Yellow was, without doubt, her color, but she never recognized that. The wardrobe in her closet and bureau was of neutral colors, black and navy. An occasional white. I opened one drawer and discovered a scarlet red sweater. I assumed it was a gift or a hand-me-down.

"Hey, Mom, this red will complement those black slacks and blazer."

"Yup," she said, grabbing it from me.

Mom had no trouble dressing and coordinating her outfits. Still, she liked getting my approval. She always said, "A woman values another woman's opinion, even if they disagree."

***

I'd chosen Vicky to be a witness on the document, but since it required two signatures, I'd also asked Margie. However, the way Mom was feeling, like everyone was robbing her—of the little she had—I knew this could pose a problem.

Pulling into the parking lot, I saw that Margie had already arrived.

"Why is she here?" Mom asked, wrath in her tone, after noticing Margie's blue Toyota.

"Mom, the contract requires two witnesses."

"Who's the other one?"

"My friend, Vicky. You remember her." Mom didn't like any of my friends. Probably because she never wanted me to have any.

"No. Take me home."

Mom was noticeably distressed.

"Let's go in and see what Cyrus has to say. Okay?"

Right away I knew this was going to be unpleasant. My mom had great respect for Cyrus, so I hoped she'd be on her best behavior and trust him. I fully understood Mom being upset, first losing her license, now all access to the little money she was receiving from social security. Her whole life she was strong and independent, and now everything she owned, even if it wasn't much, was being taken from her. Losing all control had to be devastating.

No colleagues or secretary to greet us in the entryway, only two small dogs—a Boston terrier and a pug mixture. I knew their names once but had forgotten; it had been so long since I had been in his office. Cyrus's dogs were like his children. He married later in life and his wife had already passed the child-bearing years. Cyrus reminded me of Jed Clampett from the old TV show *The Beverly Hillbillies*, minus Jed's hat, that is. Cyrus never flaunted what he had. Quiet and reserved, yet intelligent and well-respected. Cyrus was also patient and generous. Rich or poor, he charged everyone the same. Chicken feed.

His bland office of gray walls displayed only a few photos, one of each dog, and an old map of the town. A framed degree hung on the wall directly behind him. Clients' folders stacked his large, particle board Staples desk. He dealt mainly with property, land, wills, and things of that nature.

He was wearing simple khakis and a V-neck brown cashmere sweater, a striped beige dress shirt beneath. No tie or blazer. He spoke like a hick, and sporadically his pearly whites would beam, and jolly dimples would grace his cheeks. Then a blooming chuckle would emerge. The client usually had to initiate a conversation or a request before Cyrus would tell you what he knew or thought.

"Hello, Evelyn," Cyrus said. "Good to see you again."

"Did you hurt your hand?" Mom asked him, noticing a bandage on his right hand.

"No. It's carpal tunnel," he said, rotating his thumb. She looked at him, puzzled. "Too much work, Evelyn."

Mom nodded. "Oh."

Everyone turned when Vicky stumbled through the door, nearly tripping over her long, chiffon, pale-blue skirt. She had a knee replacement the year before and at times had difficulty when walking. "Here she is now, Mom."

"Hi, Evelyn. It's good to see you," Vicky said.

Mom glanced at her and turned away.

I was looking over the paperwork and trying to explain it all to Mom. But she wasn't comprehending or even trusting what I was saying to her. In her mind, she feared that Margie and this stranger were going to take over her business affairs, rip everything from her.

"I don't want her on this," Mom said, gesturing toward Vicky.

"She's not going to be. We need two witnesses—that's the law. Do you understand? Ask Cyrus if you don't believe me."

"I don't want them to have anything." Not that Mom had anything of real value, but the point was, she was adamant about Vicky and Margie getting nothing of hers.

"Mom, please listen to me." Her angry blue eyes glared at me. "I'm the only one taking care of your finances. Nobody else. I promise you," I said, wrapping my arm around her shoulders.

Cyrus intervened, "Yes, Evelyn, your daughter is telling you the truth. She will be the only one in charge here. We've known each other for a long time. You know I wouldn't lie to you, Evelyn."

After much persuasion, Mom nodded. "Okay," she said, reluctantly, taking the pen from Cyrus and signing the contract.

I thanked Cyrus, Margie, and Vicky for their help and time. We said our goodbyes and left.

I could tell Mom was tired, more emotionally than anything, so I took her straight home.

Chapter 13

I checked Facebook and saw that a couple of old classmates had sent me friend requests. I accepted. But I found no message from Rob. I prepared dinner for Steve and me, and then I fed Henri. Henri rubbed up against my leg, purring in gratitude. I held her in my arms. "I don't know what I'd do without you, Henri—you're such a love."

"Hi, how was your day?" I asked Steve when we sat at the table.

"Crazy. Paul is so fucking slow." I had met his employee, Paul, and even had him over for dinner once. He was pleasant and likable. I had also seen his impeccable work.

"Not everybody is as quick as you," I said.

"He's got to analyze everything. I'm going to have to get rid of him."

"He does decent work though, doesn't he?" I asked.

"What he does is good, but he's costing me money."

"Did you talk with him—tell him what he needs to do?"

"No. It won't change his pace. He's like a fuckin' turtle," Steve said heatedly.

"It might help if you put a little bug in his ear. Can't hurt. Or what about charging the builder by the hour—then it wouldn't matter how long it took him."

"No, Aimee—we charge by the job."

I got a scalding glance, so I dropped the subject. Steve didn't ask about my day with Mom, so I didn't bother telling him. Steve picked up the newspaper and mouthed off about nothing being done about the nuclear plant. "Why the hell don't they close that place down before it kills us all?"

"I don't know. They were offering nuclear pills—I forget what they're called—at the town offices in case there was leakage."

"Yeah, for people forty and under. They don't give a shit about us. What fucking good is a pill going to do anyway if the plant blows."

I didn't respond. I finished eating, what I could, and brought the dishes to the sink.

"Aimee, come here."

I walked over to the table. Steve was on his phone. "Do you know who this is?" He started the video where there was music and someone singing.

"No, who is it?" I asked.

"Come on, you know."

I glanced again and rolled my eyes. "Michael Bolton."

Steve smiled. "Wow, honey, you got that right. Good guess," he said sarcastically. *I didn't guess; I knew.* I could feel my eyes welling up and my chest tightening. I slowly walked out of the room, climbed the stairs with a heavy heart, and reached my pillow… and the tears flowed.

"*Tell me, how am I supposed to live without you?*

Now that I've been loving you so long."

How am I supposed to live with you—when I've been hurting so long?

"*How am I supposed to carry on,*

When all that I've been living for is gone."

Chapter 14

The next day I took Henri to the vet in the small carrier for her annual. "For an old girl, she's in good shape," said Owen, the vet, rubbing Henri under the neck.

"My husband thinks she's overweight," I said.

"Maybe a pound or two, but I wouldn't change her diet. If she's not getting enough exercise, just cut back on the food."

I was relieved Henri was healthy. No old age issues creeping in. Not yet. On the ride there and back Henri fell asleep. After I took her out of the carrier, she purred and rubbed against my legs as if to say, "Thank you." Thank you for the ride and getting me out of the house. "I love you too, Henri," I said, giving her a peck on the cheek.

When I got to Mom's and found she was napping, I put left-overs from my and Steve's dinner the night before in the fridge. Then, I gathered her dirty clothes from the hamper. I grabbed my purse and headed to the complex's recreation center, where there was a laundry room. A pleasant-looking white-haired lady, with obvious class, was folding her clean garments on the long counter. I could tell she had been incredibly attractive in her youth. "Beautiful day," she said with a sweet smile and a sparkle in her cloudy blue eyes.

I nodded. "Yes, it is," I said, turning to stuff the clothes in the washing machine.

"Are you Evelyn's daughter?"

I smiled. "Yes. Yes, I am. I'm Aimee."

"I'm Rose. I've seen you several times with your mom. She's such a nice lady. How's she doing?"

"She's hanging in there. She has dementia," I volunteered quietly.

"That's what I gathered. I praise you for being such a good daughter. She's lucky to have you."

"We're lucky to have each other. Thank you—you're very kind. Nice meeting you, Rose."

"So nice to meet you too, dear."

Mom was awake, watching TV, when I returned with the basket of clean clothes.

"Mom, I'm going to eat with you tonight—look what I brought," I said, opening the refrigerator, pulling out the Corning Ware and showing her. A clump of lemon boneless chicken, roasted Brussels sprouts, carrots, and red potato. Leftovers from the evening before. She ignored me and went straight to folding the laundry. So, I popped the food into the oven to warm it.

I watched how she carefully folded the towels, pants, tops, even her underwear with such patience and precision; she could have been a surgeon. Well, that was a little exaggerated. Something other than a housekeeper anyway. A position that carried more respect. More prestige. I believed she had many capabilities, but never utilized them. "Mom, you do a great job. I can't fold like that."

"I know." I wasn't sure what she was referring to—that she did a great job or that I couldn't fold like her. Or both. Mother had had a habit of letting me know I wasn't capable of too much—making me believe I needed her, because she could do anything and everything better. Steve had adopted her role. *You don't own me. Neither of you!*

The timer on the oven went off. I grabbed a potholder and removed the dish, placing it on top of the warmer in the middle of the table. Lately, I hadn't felt much like eating, but I knew I had to keep my strength up to care for her. Mom was already sitting down. This felt like a good sign. I took a seat across from her. I lifted the glass cover and dished out for the two of us. I dove in, but I noticed she didn't even lift her fork.

"Mom, why aren't you eating?"

"I don't like it."

"How do you know? You haven't tried it."

Like a needle playing over a scratched record, every day I kept repeating the same lines over and over. I just wanted to keep her well and content. Although, it was unlikely that either of us would ever be again.

I want you well. I don't want you to die.

She pushed her dish away. "I want some ice cream!"

"Yeah, sure," I said, picking up our plates. Then I grabbed an ice cream sandwich from the freezer and brought it to her.

"Thank you," she said, taking it from me.

"Mom, your favorite shows are coming on. *Wheel of Fortune* and *Jeopardy*."

"Stay and watch with me."

I sighed. "For a few minutes, then I have to go home."

"You can stay here."

"I can't, Ma. Steve is waiting for me. I need to spend time with him. He works all day." *Steve. Mom. Steve. Mom. It's all one way.*

Her pouty face and sad, sunk-in blue eyes almost held me there, but I knew this would go on every night. She wanted me to be with her all the time. But she'd wanted that since I was first placed in her arms.

That night at 3:00 a.m. I sat up in bed. Vision. Dream.

Pink illumination
Angelic child with white wings
Cutting a rose
Beautiful woman
With wavy golden hair
Goddess gown flowing
Holding an open prayer book
Glancing toward cherub
An insurmountable stone wall dividing the two

I am losing my mom.

Chapter 15

I opened my email and there was Rob. I'd never known an email to bring such elation.

Subject: *Hey there!*

I'm back from my trip and I wanted to say hello!

I smiled and wrote back.

Hi!

Surprisingly, I got a return.

How are you?

I'm good.

How's the weather there?

The sun is partially out, and the air is still and warm.

It's raining here; it rains a lot here.

Oh wow. I didn't know that.

Yeah, it can be pretty dismal at times, but you get used to it.

I can't imagine getting used to it.

That's when you appreciate the sun even more and you can't help but smile from ear to ear.

Never thought about it that way. But you're right—I think you appreciate something more when it's not always there.

So, tell me something about yourself. Do you have a middle name?

Yes.

What is it?

Marie.

How many people ask your middle name? I mean, sure, when you're applying for credit, insurance, or a loan. But nobody I knew personally had ever asked me what my middle name was. Middle names might not have much significance to most, but it meant something to me, and obviously to him.

Aimee Marie. I like that—that's very pretty.

Thank you. Do you have a middle name?

Yes, Edwin. That was my grandfather's name.

That's nice too.

I have an appointment, so I must get ready to leave. Can I call you sometime?

I guess. Sure.

I want to get to know you.

Why? Why does he want to get to know me? I guess there's no harm; I do have male friends I talk to occasionally.

Are you still there? he asked.

Yes, I'm still here. I was staring at the computer.

I don't have your number.

Oh. I gave him my number.

When's a good time to call?

Doesn't matter—anytime, I guess.

Is daytime better? I'm three hours behind you.

Oh, of course. Not that I paid much attention to time zones. I rarely traveled, but he *was* on the West Coast. *Yes, day is fine.*

We'll talk soon. Have a great weekend.

You too.

***

A giant jigsaw puzzle covered the entire kitchen table. Mom had assembled a thousand pieces of countryside. How can a mind like that get dementia?

"This is great, Mom."

She nodded.

"How was your day?"

"All right."

"What did you do?"

"Nothing."

"Looks like you've been working on the puzzle."

She shook her head. "No. That was last night." Nights melding with days. She couldn't discern the difference. There was no one or the other—dark or light. It was all the same to her.

"Do you want to go to the store?"

She nodded, with a smile. "Yeah."

"Let's get your shoes on."

I grabbed her low-heeled flats and when I slipped them on her feet, I noticed her ankles were slightly swollen. With socks, she struggled getting the shoes on, so I removed the socks.

"Are we ready?"

"Yup."

We drove to a 7-Eleven, a mile down the road. It was a place she often went when she could drive herself there. Mom always stood at a side counter eating a pastry while scratching her instant tickets, and any winnings she would turn in and scratch again. This had become a daily obsession for her; I don't know why this bothered me so much if she was content. Granted, the gambling got out of control when she spent her rent money, but that was the first time she'd done such an irresponsible act. The cognitive decline was likely the main factor rather than her gambling addiction. Unless one of her lucid thoughts was—who gives a damn at this point.

Locals would see her and say hello, but she'd never remember their names. "I saw a friend of yours— you went to school together," Mom said.

"What was her name?"

"I don't remember."

Walking in, two young girls at the counter greeted Mom in unison. "Hey, Evelyn."

"Where have you been?" the older of the two asked.

"Home."

"We missed you. Buying some tickets today?"

Evelyn nodded and smiled, as she pawed through her purse for money.

She looked up at them. "I don't have my wallet," she cried.

"It's okay, Mom. I'll buy them for you."

I looked at the older girl, who was wearing a name tag. "Jean, five two-dollar tickets, please."

When she pulled them off the roll, I gestured for her to hand them to Mom. I hated contributing to her addiction but what did it matter now? Besides, buying Lotto tickets had been and still was one of Mom's only pleasures. She immediately began scratching the cards on the counter, her thumbnail already blackened with residue from previous visits.

"Mom, we can do this in the car."

I paid the girl for the tickets and the honey rolls I had grabbed from the glass cabinet, and guided Mom out of there.

Chapter 16

Around noon on Saturday, Steve and I arrived home at the same time. He gaped at me through the van's windshield, *angry ape* wondering where I'd been; he knew I'd gotten a respite from taking care of Mom. I'd checked on her in the morning, and Margie offered to go to Mom's place in the afternoon and promised to stay through dinner.

"Where did you go?" he asked while we were walking in.

"I went to the beach, and I had to get some things at CVS."

Steve dropped the bag of groceries on the kitchen counter and sauntered into the living room. I heard the TV come on. After putting everything away, I joined him, parking myself next to him on the sofa.

"I am afraid Mom will take off her oxygen mask. She was fighting with me over it this morning."

Steve stared straight at the TV.

Good seeing you too.

"I want to make an apple crisp for dessert. I think everyone would like that. Don't you?" Our neighbors, Scott and Katrina, and our friends Diane and Joe were coming over for dinner. I hadn't seen or heard from Diane since the Oktoberfest at her house.

"Shh. I'm trying to listen." *And I want to be heard!*

I waited for a commercial. "Could you show me how to use the apple corer?" I asked.

He got up grumbling and strode to the kitchen with me. He showed me quickly, and the look on his face made me so nervous, I hated to, but I had to ask again.

"Show me one more time, please?"

He stared at me. "Are you fucking stupid?"

"Yeah, maybe I am," I mumbled, avoiding his eyes.

He walked away. I finished peeling and slicing the apples without using the tool. Then I combined the rest of the ingredients: the oats, brown sugar, flour, cinnamon, and salt. I cut in the butter, the size of coarse crumbs, placed them in the glass baking dish, then sprinkled the flour over the fruit. When the oven was preheated, I set the timer for forty minutes.

I am capable whether you want to believe it or not.

Instead of parking in the living room with Steve, I went upstairs to our bed and read. I must have been tired; minutes later I lapsed into a dream. A dream of Rob and me; he was taking me to a faraway land. I remember smiling, thinking I couldn't be happier. The illusion vanished when I heard Steve yelling that the timer on the stove was buzzing. Not sure how long it had been whirring before he heard it. Groggily, I hustled downstairs to remove the apple crisp from the oven.

"I smell something burning," he said, getting off the sofa. He marched into the kitchen. "Can you ever do anything right?" he barked, opening a drawer, grabbing an oven mitt. Then he snatched the apple crisp from the oven, slamming it on top of the stove.

"It's only slightly burnt on the top," I said, examining my creation.

"Slightly?"

"I'll do another one," I said, not looking at him, my eyes watering up.

"No, you won't. I'll take care of it. Go get ready."

"It's still early—they won't be here for another hour."

"I know how long it takes you."

I disappeared until I heard him yelling for me to set the table.

He studied me, but never said anything. I assumed he thought I looked nice because he didn't make a derogatory comment. I had on a pair of flare-leg jeans and a beige, scooped-neck jersey adorned with a jade silk scarf. I had enhanced my fair face with a light foundation, mascara, and rose blush. The curling iron helped add more fullness to my hair. Lastly, I had decked my ears in large silver hoops.

Diane and Joe arrived before our neighbors. We embraced with smiles and flattery; it had been a couple of months since we'd seen each other. Steve and Joe had been good friends growing up. Diane and I had attended the same school, but we'd rarely crossed paths, hardly knew each other. She was a grade behind me. Still, our gatherings, though few, were always fun and entertaining. We would catch up on what'd been happening with each other.

Joe handed me two bottles of wine. "Thank you," I said, taking them from him, looking into his mirthful eyes. Joe was a tad taller than my five-foot-seven, with atlas shoulders above a six-pack. "I guess we can enjoy this with our dinner."

"It's a French wine. A William Fevre 2005 Chablis. One of the best." Joe smiled, running his hand through his swirling lion's mane of gold hair.

"I'm sure it is." It was an alien brand to me like most—but I knew good wine always accompanied their dinners. Their social outings. The only way I could differentiate between a cheap and expensive wine was if I were spared nausea or a headache.

"Did you get Rob's CD?" I noticed Diane bubbled, her champagne-brown eyes sparkling and those silicone-enhanced lips looking more sensuous and velour soft when speaking his name. Maybe it was my imagination humming. I knew they were friends and had been conversing back and forth through emails; Diane had planned with Rob to play at her party. Other than that, I had no idea how close they really were.

"Yes, thank you. I meant to call you…"

"What'd ya think?"

"It was great—he's got an awesome voice. We listen to it all the time," I said, gesturing toward Steve. I chose to save my intimate thoughts, and I hoped I hid them well.

"He's been singing and playing for a long time now."

"I know—I asked if he'd come and play at one of my parties."

"He just can't come when he feels like it—what would his wife think?" she asked, holding a scowl. *He is a musician; this is what he does for a living.* I'd hit a sore spot with her. I wondered what that was all about.

"Maybe she'll come with him?"

She ignored my last remark.

The subject was dropped when Katrina intervened. "Oh my, look at this," she said, walking through the door as she watched Steve remove a pan from the oven. Steve beamed. "Sorry we're late. My daughter didn't pick up the kids till a few minutes ago.

She got tied up at work."

"No problem," I said, admiring her new bob haircut. The ebony color looked stunning, complementing her galaxy-blue eyes. "I'm just glad you could make it—and just in time."

Steve set the beef and broccoli dish he had concocted with egg noodles on top of the stove. He had bought baguettes from the local bakery. It was a hit with everyone.

"Where did you get this recipe, Aimee? It's delicious," Katrina remarked.

"I didn't. Steve made it."

"I don't use a recipe—I make my own up. You know a little of this, a little of that," Steve said, smiling.

"Well, it's very good. Incredible flavor."

"Thanks, Katrina. See that, honey? Somebody appreciates what I do."

"I do too," I said quietly. I don't think anybody heard.

During dinner, Steve, Joe, and Scott exchanged guy talk while we women swapped our sentiments on books, movie ratings, store sales, even Amazon bargains.

After dinner, I rose to remove everyone's plate, before dessert was served.

"Can I help?" Katrina asked.

"No, I'm fine. You're our guest."

"I feel guilty sitting here watching you," said Diane.

Steve spoke up. "Don't. Aimee loves cleaning up. Don't you, honey."

Yeah, it's what I live for. "Yup."

Steve pulled the apple crisp from the oven and was placing warm squares on dessert plates. All eyes watching.

I could tell them I made the apple crisp, at least the first one, and burnt it. Steve came to my rescue. Steve does everything—perfectly. Aimee can't do anything right. So, I'll just sit and look pretty like I've done nothing to contribute, recalling my mom's story of the time her fiancé came home, finding his bride-to-be looking pretty and unruffled like she'd done nothing all day when his mother fashioned a Cinderella out of her.

"Aimee, get the whipped cream," Steve ordered. I grabbed the bowl from the refrigerator. Instead of buying a can of whipped cream, he had made his own.

"You are a very lucky woman, Aimee—your husband is so talented," said Katrina.

"Scott is too." Her husband, Scott, was a retired fireman from Quincy. At fifty-two he still looked debonair with his silver-gray hair and tidy military mustache. I think it was his debilitating arthritis that forced him to leave the job he loved sooner than he would've liked to.

"I know. He can't cook like this though," Katrina said.

"But he saved lives." Remembering how he saved a little girl from a four-story burning building, "I think that counts for much more," I said.

"If you ever want to swap let me know," Katrina said with a wink.

I laughed. "You watch that swapping of spouses reality show too?"

"A few times. We always think the grass is greener. Once you try it though, you appreciate what you have," she said, looking admiringly at her husband.

"Or don't have," I said under my breath.

"What?" Katrina asked.

"Oh nothing."

"How's your mother doing?" Diane asked.

"She has good days and bad days. More bad than good lately."

"It must be hard—I can't imagine what you go through," Katrina piped in.

"It's not easy, but you do what you have to do."

"Yes, that's what we do for family," Diane said. "Now that people are living longer, many of us will end up caring for our parents."

"Okay, let's get off the subject," Steve intervened. "It's depressing."

I turned toward him. "It's part of life."

"We don't need to talk about it now."

I understood what he meant; we wanted to have a good time

with our friends. Not dwell on the irreversible. Still, it felt good that somebody took an interest.

We stayed at the kitchen table chatting. By nine o'clock, our guests were ready to leave; everyone was getting tired. The wine had made me sleepy. We hugged and said our goodbyes. Steve went ahead of me to retire, and I stayed up washing the wine glasses. In bed, Steve was looking for some relief, and I was searching for dreams. I reluctantly satisfied him and lay awake as he drifted off.

Chapter 17

My phone rang, an out-of-state number. I was anxious to answer but waited till after the third ring. Praying I hadn't waited too long.

"Hello."

"Aimee?"

"Yes."

"This is Rob."

"I know. I mean, I didn't really know..." I trailed off.

"How are you?"

"I'm good."

"It's nice to hear a voice after all your writings," he said.

"Thank you."

A pause.

"So, tell me something about yourself."

Why?

"Umm—I have a cat."

"What's its name?"

"Henri. Short for Henriette. She's calico."

"They're beautiful cats—aren't they mostly white with multi-colors?"

"Yes, Henri's got one ear that is black and the other is brown. Her little paws are all white."

"I bet she's beautiful."

"Yeah, she is. Do you have animals?"

"I love animals, all kinds, especially dogs and cats. But we can't have any here—where we live, that is."

Where "we" live. Must mean he and his wife, I thought.

"Do you have just the one boy?" I knew about the one he had mentioned, the musician.

"I have two boys—and four grandchildren."

"That's nice," I said quietly.

He didn't bother to ask if I had children—for some reason I felt he already knew. Either by my quietness or maybe Diane had told him. Almost instantly though, I felt comfortable talking with him.

"Yeah, they keep me pretty busy," he said.

"I don't have any."

"Children. Grandchildren?"

"No. Neither," I said, suddenly feeling this huge void, sadness.

"Your cat's your baby."

"Yes, Henri is my baby—I don't know what I'd do if something happened to her."

"Cats have nine lives—they can live a long time."

"I hope Henri will be around for that long."

"I'm sure she will."

There was a brief silence.

"So, tell me something else about you," he said.

"I was a paralegal."

"Wow. That must have been interesting."

"Yeah, lots of crazy stuff."

"You're not still doing it?"

"No, I quit recently. I'm taking care of my mom." I paused, debating whether I should mention it. "She's got dementia."

"I'm sorry to hear that," he said, sounding sincere.

"What about you? Have you always been a songwriter and musician?" I wondered what he had done for a living or if he was successful in the music business, after that one big hit.

"I was a landscaper for twenty-five years, until I tore some psoas muscles."

"Psoas muscles—I've never heard of them."

"They're in the vertebral column and in the pelvic area and the pain goes right down the lower back to the legs."

"Oh wow. Sorry to hear that. Landscaping is hard work. I'm sure it kept you in shape though," I said, recalling he had no noticeable roundness in his middle section.

"Yes, it's hard work. It's rewarding too—planting trees and flowers and seeing them grow and blossom. It's a beautiful sight."

His sultry voice made me want to do headstands, cartwheels. All I could hear in my head were his love songs on his new CD he'd sent me, remembering those brown eyes staring into mine, like he was staring into my soul, that night of the Oktoberfest party.

"I love flowers. Plants. But I kill them." *Why would I kill something I love?* "Either I overwater them or forget about watering them."

"Maybe you're busy—it has to become a habit. You know, like brushing your teeth."

"Yeah, that makes sense." I changed the subject. "Do you and your son do a lot of gigs?"

"We've done quite a few. We usually do one or two on weekends. My son and I sang at a local park recently and about two hundred people showed. This weekend we play at a gallery opening. The weekend after, we will perform at the Farmer's Market in Seattle."

"I don't know much about the industry, but I think everybody loves music. It's like a universal language."

"Yeah, sure is. And it brings out so many emotions. Happy. Sad. Even gets people up dancing, shaking their booty."

I giggled heartily. "The songs on your CD are so romantic. I can't stop listening. I think it's the combination of the lyrics, music, and, of course, your great voice."

"Thank you. That's so kind."

"I'm just being honest," I said.

"A local radio station wants my CD to play."

I detected a kick in his voice. "Oh, that's so awesome!"

"Thanks. I'm looking forward to it."

We were both quiet for a moment.

"I think we can help each other," he said. *Help each other?* "Us both being artists."

"Well, I can write but I'm not a musician."

"You don't have to be—I can teach you."

"Really?" I asked quietly.

"Sure—I'd be happy to."

"I'd like that."

"It's funny how things happen, huh? I was hanging outside with a few guys staring into the fire that night, half listening to their conversations. I turned around and through the glass door, I saw you standing there. I couldn't help but stare. You were the best thing I'd seen all night."

"What?" I responded, like I didn't hear him.

"Yeah," he said. "I liked the way you carried yourself—so confident, so sure."

My head began whirling with the *whys. Why did that matter to you? Why do I matter? Why were you looking for... at someone... you're married!* Then I quickly dismissed them, relishing the kudos.

"Thank you—I guess."

"What do you mean, you guess?"

"I don't know—I never saw myself that way."

"Well, that's what I saw, and I liked it."

And I'm liking that you're telling me this. Any guy, though, who's married and is uttering these words to another woman—something's missing at home.

"I wonder if we ever met—we grew up only a couple towns away," I said.

"It's possible." The community was smaller in those days.

"Your band was so popular—everybody knew you guys. We had to meet, even if it was briefly."

"I wouldn't forget a girl like you." *He talks like he's single.*

"Come on, you guys had hundreds of girls swarming around..."

"The universe works in strange ways—maybe it wasn't meant to happen then."

Why is it happening now?

"I was pretty messed up in those days," Rob revealed.

"Messed up?" I asked.

"Yeah, a lot of alcohol and drugs."

"Many kids did that stuff back then."

"That's no reason. I'm ashamed of it."

"You shouldn't be—that's your past. Not who you are now."

"Did you?" he asked.

"Did I drink—do drugs? No. I mean I drank, maybe a whole lot at parties, but no drugs. I had friends—*boyfriends* who did."

"I bet you had a lot of boyfriends?"

"A few," I said. "It doesn't matter."

There was a silence.

"Your group became pretty famous," I said.

"Ah, that was a dream. That one big hit helped a lot. And we did open for big bands. Artists—Four Tops, Aerosmith, the Lovin' Spoonful, the Drifters. The Commodores…" He trailed off.

"I don't know if I'd really want to be with someone famous."

"I'm curious. Why?" he asked.

"Well, the idea of it is thrilling—knowing that this person who is loved by so many loves you. But you never really have that person—not fully."

"What do you mean?"

"You share them with the fans. Being on the road all the time must put a strain on a relationship?"

"Yeah, you're right. The separation could be hard on each other," he said.

I wondered if that had ever happened to him—with him and his wife. Or with someone he had met before her.

"It's getting late—I really have to go," I said after glancing at the clock.

"It was nice talking with you—maybe we can talk again soon."

I'm not sure if it was a statement or a query. "Yeah, you have my number."

"Is this time best for you?" he asked.

"Yeah, sure. If for some reason I can't talk, I'll tell you."

"Sounds good. Bye."

I hung up and Steve called.

"Hi."

"Hey, I'm running late tonight—do you think you can fix dinner?"

"Sure—what do you want?"

"I don't care."

"Okay, I'll run to the store and get some hamburger, and I'll throw together a salad."

"Thanks, honey." I hated when he called me honey. Though he meant it, it seemed so fake to me.

"You're welcome."

I glanced at the clock after he hung up. Even though it seemed short, Rob and I had talked a long time. I had an hour and a half to tend to Mom, run to the store, and get home to make dinner before Steve arrived. Mom, thank goodness, was in good spirits and willingly ate the dinner I had popped into the microwave.

"You going to stay—we can play a game?" Mom asked.

"I wish I could—but I have to go home and cook tonight. Steve's going to be late."

"Where is he?" Mom asked.

"I think he got tied up at the job," I said. The disappointment registering across her face killed me. "See you in the morning."

Chapter 18

At home, I turned on the radio and prepared dinner. Listening to the oldies station made me think about Rob. I wondered if there was a popular artist that had a similar voice. No one I could think of. There was this uniqueness in Rob's voice that mesmerized me. It was calming and smooth. I could only describe it as a "pretty" masculine.

I got a text. I checked my phone. It was him. *Nice talking to you today.*

I smiled and wrote back. *Same here.*

The phone pinged again. He sent me a smiley emoji.

I preheated the oven for waffle fries. I mixed the salad greens in a large bowl, adding a cuke, tomato, scallion, and carrot shavings, and set that aside while I boiled water for cauliflower and broccoli. I cleaned up everything during the process.

Steve arrived when everything was ready. I dished the food onto the plates and brought them to the table.

"Where's the burgers?" Steve asked as I was about to take a seat.

"Oh my God—I forgot."

"You're losing it—you're fucked."

Thank you. You have a way of making me feel appreciated. "I'll make the patties if you want, but we have plenty here. We can have it tomorrow night. Besides, too much red meat isn't good."

He shook his head. "Whatever."

Since it was getting late, I took our plates to the sink and just rinsed them. I hated leaving things undone, but tonight we were going to Walmart in a town twenty miles away. Walmart had better prices than CVS or Rite-Aid, even if we had to travel out of our way. It was worth it.

"Are you ready to go?" he asked me.

"Yeah, I'll finish cleaning up when we get back."

Steve insisted on driving. I got in the car, strapped on my seatbelt, and leaned back. On the highway, he merged into the fast lane to pass a few cars and then pulled back into the slower lane. Suddenly, I felt the car jerking; Steve was tapping the brakes. He thought the driver in the car behind us would get the hint.

"I know what you're doing. Stop it!"

"Shut the fuck up—those headlights are hurting my eyes."

"Cause you keep looking at them—keep your eyes focused on what's ahead of you. Stop looking in the mirror. That's what you've always told me."

My body tensing up, I prayed Steve would stop aggravating the car behind us. I was relieved when the car passed us—until it pulled in front of us, giving us a brake job.

"Son-of-a-bitch."

"Just pass him," I pleaded.

"I'll fix that asshole."

Oh God. Steve went to pass him, and the driver sped up. Steve stomped on the gas pedal. I knew we were going at a high speed; I was afraid to look. My right hand was clenching the door; my right foot pressed firmly on the floor mat as if it were on the brake. My body stretched and stiffened, my heart racing. I closed my eyes.

"Put your blinker on—get off at the next exit," I yelled. Steve kept going; he was enjoying this.

Five miles later, Steve finally turned on the blinker to indicate our departure from the highway. The driver, now in front of us, saw this and veered off the same exit. The old Oldsmobile halted in the middle of the off ramp, blocking us. We were inches from his bumper with no room to get by him.

"What do we do now?" I asked.

Before Steve could answer, I watched the driver's door open. A large man with long curly hair got out. He stood legs apart, his bare arms crossed, staring. Daring us to mess with him. "Oh my God," I cried. He had to be over six feet tall and weigh three hundred pounds.

"What are we going to do?"

"Sit there and shut the fuck up."

"Stay here—don't get out," I begged. "He might hurt you."

"He doesn't scare me," he said, reaching beneath the seat and pulling out a baseball bat.

"He might have a gun."

"I'll kill the motherfucker before he can pull the trigger!"

My sweaty hands clutched my purse. My head bent, I closed my eyes and began praying. When I opened them, the guy was getting back into his car. I turned around and saw a Chevy pickup behind us; the creep was challenged and decided not to tangle with more than one.

"Chicken shit," Steve barked.

***

He nudged me as soon as we got in the store. "Let's get what we need and get the hell out."

I yanked my long list from my purse and hurried down the aisles. I had no idea where anything was. And I was shopping not only for us, but for Mom too.

Scanning the aisles, I grabbed Tylenol and vitamins, toothpaste and cough syrup. When we reached the feminine aisle, perusing the variety of sizes and shapes of Depends, Steve rolled his eyes and vanished. I imagined him scouting the automotive section. Once I crossed everything off the list for Mom, I concentrated on what we needed, trying not to get distracted by sales or clearances on the already low-priced items. Passing the kids' clothing section, I stopped and fell in love with the cutest outfits for babies, boys and girls. I was tempted to buy, even though I had no one to give them to.

Then I saw a child, around six, begging her mother for an adorable Minnie Mouse birthday dress. It had a glitter waistband and a tulle lace skirt full of cupcakes. It was so adorable and reminded me of the time I had begged Mom for a poodle skirt in Zayre's department store when I was six.

"We can't afford it," the mother said. The same response I had gotten. The little girl was in tears. "Please, Momma."

The child noticed me and looked down shyly. "Hi," I said. "How are you?"

"I'm good," she said sadly, looking back up at her mother.

I moved closer to them. Bending down, I pretended to be picking up something from the floor. Then I stood back up. "Miss, I think you dropped this," I said, showing her a twenty-dollar bill. She shook her head. I nodded, glancing at her child.

She hesitated. "Thank you," she said, taking it. Then she lifted the dress from the rack. I smiled.

Steve suddenly appeared holding two pairs of Wranglers. "Ready to go?" he asked.

"Almost. Could spend hours in here."

"Yeah, but we don't have all night—so move it."

"Well, I guess I'm done."

"Good. Let's get to a register," he said, grabbing my shoulders, pointing me in that direction.

I knew he was getting tired; he had to work the next day. Some days I wished I were back in the office, a routine that gave me a sense of purpose. Belonging. *Why would I leave a job I loved for abuse at home? I was treated with respect by my peers and was loved at work. Now I walk on eggshells with a trembling heart. Between Steve and Mom, I am going crazy. Mad maybe. I need to talk to someone soon, or I will lose it.*

On the way home, Steve flicked through the radio stations. He stopped when he heard one of Willie Nelson's songs playing. Crooning with the artist, Steve took my hand and gently held it in his. I wished I could feel in my heart all the words Steve was chanting. He had tender moments, but too few and far between to make an impact. So much had already been lost.

Chapter 19

The next morning, I overslept. I was surprised Steve let me sleep. Henri jumped on the bed and licked my nose—her way of letting me know she was hungry. She made me smile. I picked her up and held her close to me. "You're my sweet girl, Henri." After a few minutes I put her down, then washed up and got dressed. Then I ran downstairs and called Mom.

"Hi, Mom. Everything okay?"

"Yup."

"I'll be over shortly to make you breakfast."

Before going out the door, I checked Facebook and my email for any messages. None. It was too early for Rob; it was only 6:00 a.m. in Oregon. I wanted to write to him, but I knew I had to get to Mom's—and besides, I didn't know quite what to say. He was a stranger, yet he wasn't. Too early for best friends? We didn't have to see each other in person for that to happen.

On the way over to Mom's I listened to Rob's CD again, for the hundredth time. I could see why he became famous; his beautiful voice was penetrating. Soothing.

"You hungry?" I asked, taking a seat on the sofa, next to her chair.

"What's in the bag?"

"Look, I got stuff you need," I said, handing it to her. I went into the kitchen. "How about toast with peanut butter and jelly to start?"

"For God's sake, Aimee, you know I don't like toast."

"Then how about a waffle with maple syrup?"

"Okay."

I heated up sausage links too. She ate a decent portion of the waffle, but after taking a bite into a sausage, she spat it out onto her plate and pushed the rest aside.

"That's terrible—what's wrong with you? You know I don't like toast—you know I don't like sausage—are you trying to kill me?!"

"Well, next time I'll make bacon."

"Good."

I washed the dishes; she dried them. We watched TV for a while and then we played a few card games. Afterward, I looked around the house for something to do but as usual all was "spic and span," Mom's favorite saying when I was growing up. Mom would emulate Lucille Ball, wearing a pink scarf turban, and get down on the kitchen floor on her hands and knees and scrub that linoleum till it sparkled. She never asked but while she was at work elsewhere, I would get down on my little hands and knees, wearing that turban, and scrub that floor for her with hopes it would make her happy, and she would be proud of me.

It wasn't long after I arrived home that my phone rang.

I took a deep breath. "Hi, Rob."

"I hope this is a good time."

"Yes. I just got home from taking care of my mom."

"How's she doing?" he asked.

"She's hanging in there. It's all up to God..."

"Yeah, the Man upstairs has the final say," he said.

"I think my Catholic upbringing instilled too much. I even wanted to be a nun when I was little. I had this porcelain nun doll in full habit that sat on top of our TV console. And I swore that when I grew up, I'd wear one of those habits too."

"So why did you want to be a nun?" Rob asked.

"I don't know really—maybe I just liked the attire. Or the concept of it. What it represented..."

"What changed your mind?"

> *Wednesday September 13, 1967*
>
> *Dear Diary,*
>
> *I don't want to go back to Father's, but I must keep my promise. I don't want to go. Please God.*

"Boys. Wanting to have a family of my own."

"I was an altar boy."

"You were?"

"Yeah, and I even thought about being a priest."

My hands began to sweat and tremble. I ignored it.

"Really? What changed your mind?"

"I don't know—maybe the dysfunction in our family. My dad would leave for weeks at a time."

"Where do you think he went?"

"I think he was having affairs—I'm sure of it."

"Oh."

"And every time my dad came home drunk and started beating on us, my mom would take out her rosary beads and start praying. I guess she thought that would help."

"And did those rosary beads help?" I asked, already knowing his answer.

"No. I think I blamed my mother for not protecting us," he said with a sigh.

"Do you still feel that way—blame your mom for not protecting you boys?"

"No. I understand now—although it took me a long time. She was frightened and didn't know what else to do. She didn't have a good childhood. Mom had been tossed from one foster home to another."

"Oh, that's too bad. Maybe she didn't know how to be a mother because she never really had one."

"Yeah. She said to me once, 'I wish *you* could be my husband.' I don't know, but that always bothered me."

"Because you were the opposite of him. I don't think she meant it the way you interpreted it. She was suffering from abuse. Parents can really mess up kids," I said.

"Not intentionally—they only do what they know."

"Yeah."

"Is your dad still alive?" he asked. I thought I'd told him when we first met that my dad had passed. But maybe not.

"No, he died ten years ago. Heart attack."

"I'm sorry," he said.

"It's okay." I still missed him. Very much.

I was afraid to bring up his dad, knowing he'd killed himself.

I still wondered what had made him do it. Guilt? Or was he just a lonely old man with lots of regrets? Moreover, I wondered what Rob felt about it. Suicide is a sin for Catholics. Maybe his father didn't care after losing his wife to cancer. He probably thought she'd always be there, and when she wasn't anymore… Whatever his reason, it was a courageous doing; it takes a lot of guts to end your life.

"Where did you get that beautiful voice of yours?" I asked.

"I got my voice from myself. Although I was afraid to sing for years."

"Why?"

"Because a priest had told me, 'Don't ever sing—save the world some pain, son!'"

"Oh my god—a priest said that to you? Why would a priest say something like that to a child?"

No, Father—I didn't do anything with anybody. Just you. What is he accusing me of?

"Yeah. I used to wake up early as a kid—5:00 a.m. I would hum and sing. I'd often wake up my dad, who usually had a hangover. He would be mad as all heck. Being a kid, I thought that it was my voice that made his head hurt. I didn't know it was the alcohol. So Mom told me, 'Don't sing.' I did not sing again until I was sixteen."

"Sixteen?"

"Yeah, I was talking to myself in a room and said, 'I can't sing.' And a musician named Dean walked in and replied, 'Like Hell!' Dean then started picking me up to audition as the head singer in his group, Beloved Townies, and I've been singing ever since."

"That's a great story. Were your parents musical?" I asked, though I'm not sure I even liked his parents now.

"My mom sang jazz, and my dad sang at home, late Sunday mornings—country music."

"That's nice. Do you have a favorite genre?"

"I like all music but love R&B, soul, and the Beatles. How about you—what do you like?" Rob asked.

"I like it all too—whatever moves me."

"Are you a romantic?" I could visualize him smiling as he asked.

I laughed. "Yeah, a sappy one."

"I enjoy talking with you."

"Me too."

"I have an appointment—can we do this again soon?" Rob asked.

"Sure."

"You take care of yourself. I want you around for a long time! I have a lot more to say," he said.

"Look forward to it. Bye."

I wondered what he meant by that— "I want you around for a long time." I kept hearing that line in my head the rest of the day—it made me happy inside.

***

That night the wind howled. I pulled the covers up to my chin. Steve's snoring, for once, didn't bother me. I lay awake thinking about my conversation with Rob—how easy he was to talk to. And for whatever reason, he didn't just hear me, he listened. Listened. And it felt good. It felt amazing.

The next morning, I stared out the storm door. Fallen leaves had coated the roads. The vivid autumn colors had long vanished, and the leftovers—brown leaves—had been whisked from their trees the harsh night before, leaving the trees' limbs wintry barren. I slipped on a pair of old jeans and ratty sneakers and went outside and walked to a nearby dead-end street and shuffled through them. While walking, I saw a huge mound of leaves at the end of the cul-de-sac where nobody was living and seized the opportunity. I leaped in and covered myself. Then I splayed my arms and legs as if I were making angels in snow. I lay motionless looking up at the sky. Droplets of rain trickled down my face from a passing shower. I licked my wet lips.

I heard a low roar in the distance that sounded like a vehicle was coming this way. It didn't. Still, I jumped up, brushed myself off and walked home. If I were six years old, I'd get a smile. At this age, I'd get a concerned look and maybe even a police ride to La La Land. I felt relaxed though, more than I had in a long while.

Chapter 20

I started retreating to Vicky's place at the end of the day. A distraction. A delightful one. The strands of miniature white lights, plaited with artificial ivy leaves, strung around the living room, and the fairy figurines seated on the bookshelves and windowsills just swept me away.

Sitting on the sunken sofa, Vicky was showing me pictures of guys, young and not so young, that had been messaging her from FB, as well as an online dating service she'd recently joined. Vicky had been divorced for several years now, and she was searching for someone who complemented, paired, her new image. She had changed her hairstyle, now long and feathery, from the short, cropped style she'd had when she was selling insurance. I hadn't known Vicky back then, just from the old picture albums she'd shown me recently. Even her conservative wardrobe—gone. Replaced with gossamer fabrics and filigree detailing. Vicky had transformed herself totally. It wasn't just her appearance that had changed; she'd become who she wanted to be, unconcerned about what others thought. I admired that.

"Come on, you're holding back—what is it?" she asked.

Even though I hadn't known Vicky long, I felt I could trust her. "I can't keep this a secret anymore." She looked at me, those iridescent blue eyes of hers full of curiosity.

I took a deep breath. "I'm crazy over someone."

She put down her phone and turned toward me. "You're in love?"

"I think so. I mean, it feels like it. It's too early to really know."

"Yeah...," she said, her lively eyes, her expression, waiting for more. "So, are you going to tell me who this mysterious one is?"

"It's Rob."

"Rob," she repeated as her eyebrows creased. "You mean the musician?"

"Yes."

"He lives thousands of miles away—when do you expect to see him?"

"Oh, I don't know—but I hope soon."

"But you're married..."

"Yeah, and he is too."

Her eyes widen. "Whoa—a double whammy."

"I know it's crazy, isn't it?"

"Yeah and no."

She stopped there, and I wasn't going to ask her what that meant. I liked the way things were heating up with Rob and me; crazy or not, I wanted it to continue. As far as I was concerned, we were doing nothing wrong—just getting to know each other.

"I like hanging out with you, Aimee. You're a lot of fun. My friends were acting so old—I had to drop them. All they did was whine about their ailments every day."

Other than Vicky and Rob, I had no other real friends, so I did not have to worry about that.

"Being old and acting old can be quite different. Nothing worse, though, than a bunch of old fuddy-duddies whining over every ache and pain, letting you know how many times they pooped or didn't poop each day," I said smiling.

Vicky laughed.

I stayed with her until it was time to go home; Steve called to let me know dinner was almost ready. I hated to leave, but I knew I had to.

Chapter 21

On Saturday morning the sun was shining brightly, as brightly as possible, on this early December day. I quickly got dressed and ran downstairs to the closet in the hallway, where our coats and scarves hung.

"Where are you going now?" Steve asked.

"I have to feed Mom and make sure she takes her meds."

"Can't someone else in the family help?"

I shook my head. "One of Mom's neighbors called and said she's burning pans. She boiled water for coffee and then forgot it was on the stove."

"Not that we haven't all done that at least once or twice," he said.

"True, but she could burn the apartment down."

He shrugged and walked away.

When I got to Mom's, she was sitting in the recliner. A cup of coffee was on the end table next to her. I checked; it was cold.

"Hi, Mom."

"Hi," she said quietly. Her eyes drooped and she seemed out of it.

I looked down at her feet and noticed her ankles were blown up and bluish. I grabbed my phone from my purse. I walked outside to talk so Mom wouldn't hear.

"My God, her legs and feet are swollen badly. I'm calling for an ambulance," I said to Steve when he answered.

"What do you want me to do?"

"Nothing—I will let you know what the paramedics say. Please keep your phone with you."

"Okay." I could tell he was relieved I didn't ask for his assistance.

It was frightening enough to see an ambulance and a fire truck. But when four paramedics showed up at the door, it made me think she was dying, but I soon learned it was protocol. One of the guys evaluating her condition I had known since I was kid. He briefed me. I was so relieved to see Keith Cavanaugh, someone whom I knew I could trust.

"Looks like she's having congestive heart failure," Keith informed me.

"Oh no," I said, although that's what I had assumed was happening.

"We're going to take her to the hospital. Do you want to ride with her?"

I nodded. "Yeah I do. Thank you."

"We can't give you a lift back."

"I understand. I'll have my husband meet me there."

I had never ridden in an emergency vehicle. I watched the EMTs attend to her with an IV and whatever else they were dispensing. Mother willingly answered their routine questions. I gave them the names and dosage of her medications.

Immediately after being checked in at the ER, Mom was taken into one of the examining rooms for evaluation. She was hooked up to an IV as well as a machine that monitored her heart and blood pressure. Hours passed while a nurse and other staff members came in and attended to her. Then a sweet, young, blond-haired woman entered the room. She didn't look much older than my neighbor's daughter, Carrie.

"Hi, Mrs. Thomas?" she asked. Mom stared at her.

"Yes, this is her," I said. "You can call her Evelyn."

"Evelyn, I'm just going to take a little blood from you today—is that okay?"

Mom nodded faintly.

"Do you know your date of birth?"

Mom didn't answer, so I said, "June 7th, 1938."

The young phlebotomist siphoned Mom's blood into several small tubes, sealing them. Half an hour later, a tall male X-ray technician appeared. "We're just going to take a few pictures—is that okay, Evelyn?"

Mom nodded.

Mom shot me a slight smile and a petite wave as she was being wheeled away. I waved back. "I'll be here waiting for you."

I stayed with Mom until she was admitted and resting in bed. I turned my phone back on and called Steve to pick me up. I saw he had called a couple of times. I knew he was concerned, but I felt better being alone.

"What the hell, it's been almost five hours!" he screamed, sounding distraught.

"I'm sorry—phones had to be off."

"You could have walked outside and called me."

"I didn't want to leave her—she was scared. She's settled in a room now. They're keeping her."

"I'm on my way."

"Give me a heads-up—I'll meet you outside."

That night I lay awake. Another vision. Fragments of a dream? I felt myself slipping through my mother's arms, her fingers letting go of me.

Falling. Falling away.

Separation.

Anxiety.

Fear.

Unknown.

***

The following morning, a middle-aged doctor came in to examine her. She wasn't Mom's primary physician—I assumed the doctor worked for the hospital.

"Does your mother live alone?" she asked while checking her over.

"Yes, but I'm only two minutes down the road. I'm there every day."

"Since she lives alone, she needs to go into a nursing home."

"Nursing home—permanently?" That was like our worst nightmare. Mom's and mine. Granted it hadn't been easy, but we had managed.

"There's a rehab there. She'll be able to go home when she gets better."

"Why can't she just stay here?"

"Policy reasons."

"Oh, I see."

She'd have care around the clock. A load off my mind. Or maybe it'd be more of a load.

Mom shook her head. "No," she said adamantly. "You take care of me."

"It's only temporary, until you get better. I will come every day."

"You promise?"

"Of course." I committed myself now. I should have just enjoyed this break, but I knew how frightened she'd be—alone with strangers.

***

After a week in the rehab ward at Bellview nursing home, a hefty, dark-haired social worker, named Karen, came in and asked to talk with me privately. She thought it would be best if Mom was transferred to the Alzheimer's unit. When staff members tried speaking with Mom, they observed her ability to comprehend worsening.

"I'd be happy to show you around."

"Sure," I said, even though I had made up my mind before the tour began. The place felt inviting with its shining staff, pleasant and honey tongued. And all the daily activities— music, bingo, arts and crafts, card games—Mom would have plenty of fun things to do. As Karen walked me down the hallways, I peeked into the rooms. I saw that my mother wasn't like any of them in there. The residents were seemingly in some hypnotic state. Zombies in a chair or bed. Unaware of our presence.

Karen smiled. "You think about it."

"I will," I said.

The next day Karen called me. I was standing in line at a checkout register, about to unload my groceries onto the belt.

"I know I haven't given you much time, but a room came available this morning. I thought I'd give you first dibs."

"Umm..." I hadn't even thought about it.

"I think it would be the best for her—and you." *How does she know what's best for either of us? She doesn't even know us.*

"Lady, could you hurry up? Finish unloading your cart before gabbing on the phone."

"Okay, Okay," I said, looking up at the tall, gray-haired grump behind me. My phone, somehow, was on speaker.

"Great. You've made the right decision. You'll both be happy."

"No, I wasn't talking to you. Hello, hello…" I repeated. Karen was gone. When I left the store and got the groceries and myself in the car, I picked up my phone to dial her back.

But didn't.

I thought about the welcoming appeal the Alzheimer's unit displayed during this special holiday. The Christmas cards taped to the wall behind the nursing station reminded me of how we had displayed our cards around the door frames in the house. Draped red and gold garland dressed up the semi-circled counter at the nurses' station, like the one I'd seen on the soap *General Hospital*. The whole setting, including the warm-spirited staff, helped convince me that this place was okay for Mom.

That night, I couldn't sleep. My mind raced and my heart nearly thumped out of my chest. I hadn't had adequate time to think about this.

Early the next morning, I called the nursing home. "Have you moved her?"

"Not yet. We're waiting for the unit manager."

"Please don't. She's not like the rest of them..."

"You sure you don't want to give it a try? If you find it doesn't work, we can always move her back upstairs." I thought it was strange that they could move her back to the rehab floor if she was physically better. *Why would they lie to me?*

"You'll move her back—really?"

"Yes."

"Oh, okay," I said meekly. Knowing I had an option, I felt better about it. Somewhat.

***

I woke at dawn, wondering how Mom had made it through the night. I wanted to go immediately and check on her but decided to hold off until after breakfast. She was in good hands, I kept reminding myself. If anything went wrong, they'd call me.

After pouring myself a cup of coffee, I sat at the table. While sipping I checked my phone. I saw Rob's number among recent ones, but being so occupied with Mom, I'd missed it. Knowing it wasn't a good idea to reciprocate this early, I went to the computer to email him and found he had written to me.

Dear Aimee,

I tried calling you earlier this week. I hope everything is okay. I just wanted to say Hello; it's been a while since we've talked.

Dear Rob,

I'm good. Thank you for thinking of me. I hope all is well with you too.

I wanted to write more, tell him about Mom, but I pushed send.

I sat there staring at the screen, hoping to get a response. It was just wishful thinking.

With Mom being in the nursing home, I needed to occupy my time. I decided to give the house a thorough cleaning. I removed all the stuff from the bookshelves, even dusted the tops of the books and the picture frames. Then wiped down the radiators and used Windex on the mirrors. Lastly, I scrubbed the kitchen floor on my hands and knees. *At least I could do it as good as Mom.* Afterward, I collapsed on the sofa and dozed for twenty minutes. Just enough to refresh.

Opening my email again, I found Rob.

Hi Aimee,

How's your mom doing? I know it must be hard. I can't imagine what it's like taking care of a parent.

I have a nice prayer book. I'll say a healing prayer for both of you. I hope we can talk soon.

Your friend, Rob.

P.S. I think of you often.

I think of you often too, I wanted to tell him. It was the truth. I always tell the truth, even when it hurts. But I don't speak my mind. I should have walked away from the computer, but I couldn't. I wanted to talk to him. Something happened to me inside when I saw his name come up on the screen. I got starry-eyed like a teenage girl noticing a good-looking guy for the first time. But honestly, it wasn't his looks; he had something else. Something more.

Something I couldn't resist.

Thank you for the prayers. Mom has gone into a nursing home. Looking forward to hearing from you.

Aimee

I glanced at the clock on the stove: 10:30 a.m. It felt strange—sad, really—knowing I wouldn't be going to Mom's house to prepare her breakfast. Lunch. Dinner. Today. Tomorrow. Or ever again. I wondered how long she'd be able to keep her apartment—she surely wouldn't be returning. Only if a miracle happened, but I knew there were no miraculous recoveries from dementia or Alzheimer's. Bellview was her new home, and the staff would assist her until her heart stopped. Moving into a nursing home was like the beginning of the end.

I knew I would have to surrender Mom's key and pack up all her belongings. I had just paid the month's rent, so I had a little time. Something I wasn't looking forward to. Once the owner of her apartment complex got wind of her new residence, he'd want the place vacant for someone who needed it. Understandably. But I couldn't think about that now.

As this was all reeling in my head, I got a text message from Rob.

Can you talk?

Yes.

A minute later my phone rang. "Hello."

"Hi. I enjoyed our last talk so much. I couldn't stay away."

"You don't have to. We're friends now."

"Yes, we are. And I hope always." He had a way of warming my heart—with little effort.

I told him what had happened with Mom and how I'd found her, and then about the transition from the hospital to the nursing home. He listened with so much compassion and kindness.

"You're amazing."

"No, I'm not. We do what we have to."

"Still, you're strong. I see that in you." *You see in me what I don't see—what nobody else sees.*

"I just keep going, I guess."

"Your mom is lucky to have such a wonderful daughter."

"She was a good mother—she did the best she could." *If her negativity and criticism were omitted, she would have been the perfect mom. And maybe I would have been the perfect daughter. And would've flown the coop. Left the nest. But people aren't supposed to be perfect. Are they?*

"I wish I could've been there for you—could have helped in some way."

"That's so kind—but I'm the only one who could do this."

"It's hard taking care of mothers, fathers, isn't it?" he asked.

"Yeah, it doesn't seem right—when they've taken care of us."

"How do you feel about her being there—in the nursing home?"

"Awful."

"I'm sure it's somewhat of a relief, knowing she's safe and you don't have to worry about her so much."

"Yeah, in a way, but I vowed I'd never do it. Myself—I'd rather someone shoot me than stick me in one of those places," I said, regretting my words, knowing that his father had shot himself. "I had no choice..."

"I know. It's not such a bad place—I used to go to a nursing home every week. I'd sit and sing to so many of them."

"You did?"

"Yeah. There was this one lady named Isabel—she must have been close to ninety. She was the sweetest lady. I'd go into the nursing home once a week if only to see her—I became fond of her. I'd pull up a chair and sit next to her bed, play my guitar, and sing her a song. She would grab my hand afterward and say,

'Thank you—your voice is lovely.' Then she'd pull my hand to her mouth and kiss it."

"Aww, I bet she adored you—looked forward to your visit." I suddenly began daydreaming, seeing him singing to Mom. Singing to me.

"I don't know about that—but I know I brightened her day, at least."

"It's a wonderful thing that you did. It makes you feel good—doesn't it? I mean, making someone else feel good," I said.

"I never really thought about it. I just know I enjoy making others happy," he said. "Does your mom like music?"

"It's odd—I don't know. Although, she used to sing this one song around the house when I was young. I can't remember the name of it or even the lyrics now, but I believe it was meant for my dad."

"Sometimes songs trigger sad memories."

"Yeah, that would make sense." I paused. "I didn't mean to burden you...," I said.

"You didn't burden me—you could never burden me. I like talking to you—and hearing everything you have to say, no matter what it is. I don't care if you just tell me you're cutting a pear," Rob said.

He made me smile. I wanted to wrap my arms around him right then. *Why? Why are you so kind, attentive—so interested in me?*

"Enough about me—how was your week?" I asked.

"Quiet but nice."

"Quiet is good. It's quieter here, my surroundings at least. It's different..."

"I know what you mean. Life has its difficulties, doesn't it?" he said.

"Yeah. It's like we're being evaluated all the time."

"Maybe we are. It's okay. Your peace will come."

"Yeah," I said, not really feeling confident about that.

I glanced at the clock; it was nearly 11:40 a.m. I needed to get to the nursing home—I wanted to have lunch with Mom.

"I'm sorry but I need to head out now, to see how Mom is doing at her new place."

"Sure, you go ahead—we will talk again soon."

"Yes."

The clock seemed to zoom whenever Rob and I talked—we had so much to say to one another. So much to learn about each other. He was becoming a good friend, a supportive friend. A friend I needed. It was as though the universe had skipped over us in high school. Fate, being all-knowing, saw that we didn't need each other then as we do now and thus had waited to bring us together.

Chapter 22

I waved to the RN unit manager, Jake Gardner, who was young enough to be my son. He seemed smarter than many of the staff at the nursing home and possessed an old soul. Despite Jake being only twenty-five, it was obvious to me *why* he was the unit manager. After my initial talks with him regarding Mom and the concerns I had about her COPD and dementia, I felt confident knowing he was in charge. His knowledge of the disease and how he articulated it to me, if I hadn't seen his face, he would've convinced me I was speaking with a seasoned, fifty-year-old doctor.

Jake had a medium frame and thick, dark brown hair. Cute as all heck. His doe-shaped, clay-gray eyes were like the mirrors of his soul. He smiled. "How's it going, Aimee?"

"I'm doing okay, Jake. Thanks for asking."

"Your mom's adjusting really well."

"Is there anything you can give her to do? She was a house cleaner for years."

"We can have her working in the laundry room, folding clothes."

"That'd be great. She'd love that."

"We gave her a small vacuum the other day. She vacuumed her room and her neighbor's room too."

I smiled. "That's Mom."

"I admire her energy. She is an amazing woman."

"Yeah, she is," I said. "She could always run circles around me."

Most residents had a roommate, unless you were one of the fortunate ones who could afford to pay for privacy. Mom's roommate seemed limited to her bed, not uttering a sound. Occasionally she'd look my way, but remained tranquil and motionless. Like the others, Mom had a twin bed, a small bureau, a TV, and a comfortable sitting chair. Bright sunlight streamed in from the double windows on the east side of the room. Surprisingly, there was even a decent-size closet where Mom could put her things, though there wasn't much she had now or would even need. Still, I wasn't sure if Mom belonged here; she was mobile and energetic—how could she be restricted to such a confined environment?

To me, it was just an upgraded jail cell, only without bars.

Instead of eating in the main dining room, Mom preferred to stay in her room. She had always been a bit antisocial. She stuck mainly with family. Each week, I'd check off food choices from the paper menus sent around. She frequently refused to eat the meals. So instead, they'd bring her a peanut butter and jelly sandwich. I supposed some nourishment was better than none. After a while though, it was even hard getting that into her.

"Mom, would you like to sit with your friends in the dining room? They invited you."

"No. I don't like them."

"Why? They seem like nice ladies."

She shook her head, stuck her nose up in the air, and flipped her tongue out like a snake ready to bite. "Yuck," she said. "Pains in the asses."

"Let's take a walk down there anyway. Just you and I will sit together."

The spacious dining area was bright and cheerful. Four female residents were gathered closely at a round table eating their meals.

"Hello, ladies," I said.

"Hi," two said in unison. "Evelyn, would you like to sit with us? We can make room," said one smiley, white-haired lady.

"No," said Mom, shaking her head. "Come on, let's leave."

"Let's go sit down there," I said, pointing at an empty table near the back of the room.

We put our trays down and took our seats. Staring into my plate, the American chop suey flashed me back to those horrible school lunches. Since the meal was full of gluten, I just focused on the salad. Mom skipped it all and went straight for the Hoodsie cup.

Across from us was a kitchen countertop with a small sink and a few cabinets above. Further down that same wall, I spotted a dartboard. *Are they crazy? What are they thinking?* I stood and hustled over. After picking up a dart, I was relieved to find it had a spongy tip. I hurled one after another at the rubber board, then took all the darts off and hurled them again. And again.

Missing the bull's-eye each time. By a mile.

Then my eyes were drawn to a mural on the wall to the right of me. The painting depicted an early summer: a pond, blossomed trees, and a slope of lush grass. A couple in '40s attire, wearing hats, were lazing on a blanket, a picnic basket beside them. They looked so peaceful and in love. I began daydreaming, picnicking with Rob, imagining us as a couple.

Once I snapped out of my reverie, I saw that Mom was getting restless in her chair. In her hand, she held a fork and seemingly was ready to heave it. I rushed over and grabbed her wrist. Nobody saw. Other than one gentleman sitting by himself, the place had cleared out.

"Mom, would you like to take a walk?"

She nodded. "Yeah." Her face lit up. "I gotta get my coat."

"Mom, I mean, let's take a walk inside here—the building."

"No! I wanna go home!"

"Mom, this is where you live now."

"No, I don't want to stay here. Please take me home," she cried.

Being able to feel what she felt, I asked Jake if I could take her out for a while.

"I'm sorry, it's not a good idea—let her get used to being here first," Jake said.

"Yeah, it's just really hard—for both of us."

"I understand."

I wasn't sure Mom would ever get used to being there, but the reality was that this *was* her place—her home now. Even if neither one of us wanted to face that.

When I left, the guilt laid heavy, knowing I was leaving her there—alone. I could take her out of the nursing home and care for her myself.

But could I?

Chapter 23

I was apprehensive about having Vicky over to the house for dinner; I hoped Steve wouldn't act up. She'd had me over for tea and homemade soup several times. It was time for me to reciprocate. I had made it a mission not to get too close to anyone where I'd want to have their company. I was embarrassed by Steve's impulsive actions and his crude and offensive mouth. He couldn't control himself. *Can he?*

I knew Vicky liked lobster and Steve did too. I took cash from my savings and went to the fish market and bought six lobsters and a pound of scallops. Back home, I cut potatoes for French fries and breaded the scallops. When the oil in the fryolator was hot enough, I lowered fries in first. Steve insisted on overseeing everything.

The doorbell rang at 6:00. Vicky bounced in handing me a pie. "You didn't have to do this. Thank you."

"It's not homemade—but they're pretty good."

"Especially heated up."

"Oh, I almost forgot." She dug into her purse, pulling out a plastic-wrapped brownie. "It's gluten free."

"That's so thoughtful."

We walked into the kitchen. Steve was boiling water for the lobsters.

"Steve, this is my friend Vicky." Her hair looked gorgeous. Her lilac platform shoes and dangling sun and moon earrings coordinated nicely with the violet dress. Two lush layers fluttered from the Empire waistline to the double-tiered handkerchief hemline.

"Well, finally," Steve said. I saw him scrutinizing her from head to toe.

"Yeah, I finally get to meet you."

"I hear you like lobster," he said, escorting her to the table.

"Love it," Vicky said.

"Aimee, set the table. It's almost ready."

"Okay." I got out the plates and silverware.

"What do we need knives for? Get the nutcrackers." While I was searching for them, he said, "Come on, move out of the way."

"I'm looking for them."

He nudged me and slid his hands through the drawer. "They're right here," he said, holding them up.

Steve brought the lobsters to the table and joined Vicky. I served scallops and fries.

"I almost forgot," I said while getting up. I went to seize the coleslaw from the refrigerator.

"Wow," Vicky said, looking down at her plate, then digging in. "This is like a fisherman's platter—for two."

I watched Vicky crack the lobster's hard shell. Steve noticed as well.

"See, your friend Vicky knows how to use the crackers."

"My husband used to do it for me. When he left, I had to learn," Vicky replied.

"Could you crack it for me, please?" I asked, handing my plate over to Steve. *I'd learn and crack my own lobsters if you had the patience to show me.*

"Yeah, now we just need a bib." Steve gazed my way. "Aimee, where's the napkins?"

I got up and swiped a new package of napkins from a cabinet drawer and dropped it on the table.

"You could've opened it," Steve remarked, breaking into the cellophane, handing each of us one.

"Thank you," Vicky said. "I haven't had a lobster in months. Matter of fact, not since last summer."

"You're very welcome," I said.

"It was awfully kind of you, honey," Steve said, turning to me with a smile.

I nodded. "I knew you two liked lobster."

"You don't?" Vicky asked.

I shrugged. "On special occasions—like this."

Then Vicky's phone pinged. I watched her check it. It was either a text message or a FB message. She hesitated on whether to respond. She looked at me with those playful eyes of hers and shoved the phone into her flowered, handmade bag. I smiled.

While Steve was bragging about his work and how he liked to

cook, I preheated the oven for dessert. I cleared the table. Then I served each of them a warm slice of blueberry pie, and myself the brownie, with a dollop of Cool Whip.

Later, I tagged along while Steve gave Vicky a tour of the house, showing her the dentil crown molding, chair rails, and wainscoting he had meticulously crafted. He neglected to add how he had ranted like thunder the whole time. Leaving me wondering if that beautiful detail was scarred by his negativity and lack of enthusiasm.

Afterward, Vicky and I returned to the table and had a cup of tea and talked about Mom. Steve went into the living room to watch TV.

"It's getting late—I should get going," she said, standing up. Steve's eyes popped open. "Steve, it was nice to meet you."

"Nice meeting you," he said, and turned back to the TV.

"Thanks for coming. We'll get together soon," I said, going to the hall closet to get her coat. I walked her to the front door.

"God, I thought she'd never leave," Steve barked. "Nothing like overstaying your welcome."

"She probably enjoys getting out. She lives alone. She must get lonely." *One doesn't have to live alone to get lonely.*

"That's not our problem."

"I got the impression you liked her."

"I didn't say I didn't like her."

"Then what? What is it?" I wondered if her vivacious spirit had bugged him. Or if he didn't want me to have friends? *More likely the latter.*

"She's just a little weird."

"How so?"

He shook his head, shut off the TV, and walked upstairs.

Chapter 24

The next morning at 5:00 a.m., I got up and went downstairs with Steve. I fixed us sausage and pancakes.

"Can you get the maple syrup, please?" Steve asked.

I went to the refrigerator and saw that there was only a drop left in the bottle. I took it out anyway and handed it to him.

"What's this going to do?" he asked, holding up the bottle.

I shrugged. "Do you want a little butter with cinnamon?"

"No."

"Eggs?"

"Forget it, it's too late now—I have to get to work."

I took my pancakes to the table, grabbed the maple syrup bottle, and poured out what was left.

I felt Steve's eyes on me. "You have a rough life." *Yeah—I live with you! But maybe not forever.*

I looked away. Henri was meowing at my ankles. The side door slammed, and soon I heard the squeal of tires. I drank my coffee and smiled. Steve might be miserable, but I felt happy for the first time in a long while. I had found someone who genuinely cared, cared about me—what I was going through. I didn't feel so alone anymore.

Since it was still early, I grabbed my coat and hat, filled my traveling mug with coffee, and scurried out to the car. At the beach, pinks dominated the early morning sky over the water. Terns darted in and out of waves that rolled in a steady rhythm. The sound was hypnotic. I sat cross-legged in a state of blissfulness. I wanted to remain like this for as long as I could. One's life was like a scale, an equal balance of good and bad, yin-yang. Just one little thing could throw the balance off, tip you too far sideways. Punish you. Destroy you. Forever.

When I got home, Henri was glad to see me. I picked her up and kissed her on each cheek. Then I held her closer to me. Afterward, I went upstairs, made the bed, picked up Steve's dirty clothes, and brought them down to the basement to wash them. While I was there, Rob texted me. The day keeps getting better.

Hi. I can't get you off my mind.

My smile widened. *Good. Cause you're on mine too.*

What are you up to today?

I mentioned that I'd gone to the beach and how beautiful it was. I told him I'd be visiting Mom, and that later in the day I would see my friend, Vicky.

I should be working on my new novel, but I just haven't felt it lately. I do write in my journal daily. Or before I go to sleep at night.

What do you write about?

Oh, that's secret. You know, like a diary with a lock and key.

No hints?

Okay. I write about what goes on during the day and how I feel about it.

Maybe someday you'll tell me your inner thoughts—we'll tell each other.

A few minutes later, he sent me a poem. He had told me he liked haiku poetry. Or maybe its lyrics to a new song? I wondered if this were in his own words or found online. Either way, I loved it. What is the message here? Is this what he would like—we both would like?

Come sleep next to me
and tell me all that you want to be.
Let's watch the sun come up
We'll drink from the same cup.

I texted him right back.

Wow! Did you just write that?

I did—it just came to me.

It's lovely.

You're lovely.

I shook my head. *Thanks. You're pretty nice yourself.*

Hey, do you wanna talk?

Yes.

The phone never rang.

A half hour later, I received a new text message.

I am so sorry—something came up. Can we talk later—maybe tomorrow?

Of course. Looking forward to it. Take care.

Chapter 25

The sprawling trees along the long, tapering driveway to the cottage were like gatekeepers. Squirrels searched for food beneath bristles of wispy moss. I parked in front of Vicky's house, and two deer briskly vanished. Next a rabbit scuttled beneath the vines. Critters chose to roam the quiet. It was all fairytale magical. Whisking me away from reality, rendering a calm.

I sat at the table watching Vicky finish a necklace. Once or twice a week, Vicky would wander the beach collecting sea glass from broken medicine, soda, and beer bottles, even making use of the necks, caps, and bottoms. She took sterling silver wire and wrapped it around several times until it made a design she liked. Then she would put a loop in the wire to run a chain through.

"I'm going with you next time."

Vicky looked at me.

"To the beach—this glass is beautiful," I said, picking up a blue piece. Feeling its smoothness.

"Blue is rare—it's hard to find. But yes, it is beautiful—makes desirable jewelry. Would you like to try?"

"I'd love to—just guide me."

I struggled with the wire. Wrapping it was tricky and it took a lot of patience.

"I think I'm getting the hang of it," I finally said after an hour, showing her.

Vicky smiled. "You're catching on. Let's take a break. How about a cup of tea?"

"Yeah, that sounds good right about now."

"Thanks for having me over for dinner," she said, handing me a saucer. Your house is lovely."

"Thank you."

"Can Rob give you what you have now?"

"No. I don't think so. But I'm okay with that."

"Are you?"

"Yes, I truly am. Material things don't give you real happiness—you know that. Maybe if I were twenty years younger, I'd feel differently. But now I just want a peaceful life—with someone I love."

"When the heart's involved, rhyme and reason go out the window. Steve does everything for you—he's very talented," Vicky said, sounding envious. I knew she was referring to the detail work in the house he had shown her; it *was* quite impressive.

"Yes, he has skills most guys wished they had. But that's not everything."

"That's enough for most women."

"But I'm not most."

Vicky grinned. "That I know."

"You don't know it all."

Vicky looked at me. "You heard the way he spoke to me the other night. And that was actually nice. He constantly puts me down. Screams at me—swears profusely. His road rage makes me tremble. He belittles me in public and pushes me around. And at home, sometimes it's even worse!"

Vicky grabbed my trembling hands and said, "I'm so sorry, Aimee—I had no idea. Whatever I can do to support you in any decision you make, I'm there for you."

I broke down and cried. "He hurts me down to my very soul."

Chapter 26

For the first time in all the years I'd been alive, I wouldn't be having Christmas at home with Mom. There would be no big turkey dinner. Mom always did the fixings for the holidays. Steve wasn't satisfied with what he saw and sampled, so he took over the task. Holidays were never pleasant with Mom's negativity and Steve's wrath. They were filled with crass and hostile comments. What we tolerated to be together.

I woke to the robust aroma of coffee. Stretching, I inhaled deeply. I just wanted to lie here. Didn't want to see his face. I reluctantly threw on my bathrobe and slipped into my slippers and went hesitantly downstairs.

"Morning, sleepy head," he said with a smile. "Merry Christmas, honey." Steve was preparing a gourmet breakfast: eggs, sausage, bacon, and blueberry pancakes. He had a big heart and meant well; he just ruined things sometimes. Like taking a pickle from a non-labeled jar, you weren't sure what you were going to get—sweet or sour.

"Merry Christmas," I said, half asleep, getting Henri's food from the closet. I opened a can of wet food and mixed it with dry food. Then I replenished her water.

"Sit down and I will serve the Queen." Was he being sarcastic or sweet? And this time it seemed to be the latter. And he wasn't stressing himself over preparing the big dinner—because there wasn't going to be one.

"I'll go get the newspaper," I said, heading toward the front door.

"You're going out like that?"

"It's Christmas—nobody's going to see me."

Steve stuck his nose in the paper and relayed to me anything he found of interest: local and world news, obituaries.

Then he handed me the flyers, knowing I liked the post-Christmas sales, saying, "Hurry up, get upstairs, and get dressed."

Aunt Sara's kids—my cousins, Jeff and Amanda—would be meeting us at the nursing home in an hour. Even though Mom and Sara never got along, Mom had always been close with Jeff and Amanda and their two little ones, Cameron and Casey.

I picked up my phone after charging it through the night and saw that Rob had left a message.

Merry Christmas!

I messaged him back. *Merry Christmas.* If only I had time to talk to him right now.

He immediately sent me back a smiley face with a couple of kisses and hugs. I returned the same.

***

Bellview gave us a conference room for privacy. One of the best-looking rooms in the building. It was fully carpeted and lined with a new-looking, traditional tapestry sofa, where we parked with Mom. And in front of us, to our left, was an artificial blue spruce, striking and full, lit with white lights and decorated with handmade ornaments.

I had overdone it with gifts for Mom; we all had, not knowing how many more Christmases we'd have with her. But also, she was in a different holiday environment for the first time. Most of the presents were clothing, which we learned after could vanish in a flash—either taken by other residents or even lost in the laundry room. I also bought her an inexpensive comforter and sham—in her favorite color, blue, and a pattern similar to the queen-size one she had on the bed in her apartment. I wanted her to have some sense of home.

We snapped phone pictures of Mom opening her gifts. Then we gathered to take group pictures. Enough to fill an album. I had Steve take one of her and me alone. Mom smiled a lot, seemingly happy that everyone she cared about was there. After an hour though, Cameron and Casey cried because they wanted to go home and play with their new toys. We ended up staying a little longer. I would have spent the entire day with Mom, but Steve was obviously restless too, giving me eye signals that he was ready to leave.

"Let's go put your gifts away."

"Okay, let's go," Mom said, rising from the sofa.

We carried her presents to her room, placing some clothing in bureau drawers and hanging up the rest. I placed the bouquet of flowers on her nightstand and the box of chocolates in the drawer. Then we hugged and kissed her goodbye. "I love you so much. Merry Christmas, Mom," I said.

The whole scenario felt displaced. One we were unable to foresee or imagine. *Wake up, Aimee. Face reality.*

When Steve and I walked outside, the grounds were covered in a deep layer of white fluff. It stood out brightly against the dark sky. I just wanted to bury myself beneath it.

Chapter 27

I finally got to talk to Rob after the holidays were over. I told him how sad I felt celebrating mine at the nursing home.

"I just never thought it would come to this. You just never think it's going to happen to you or your family. I'm sorry for the self-pity."

"Please don't worry—it's okay. I understand."

Then he briefed me on his day with his boys and grandchildren. Never a mention of our spouses. Afterward, he popped the unexpected.

"So, tell me, Miss Aimee, where do you find your happiness?"

"I don't know—dancing barefoot in the rain. Even just watching rain against a windowpane. I like the feel of soft snow falling on my face too, and sticking my tongue out, catching the wet flakes."

"I like that—all of it," he said quietly.

"What about you—where is your happiness?" I asked him.

"Happiness for me is—my hands in my garden, feeling its new soil and letting it slip through my fingers."

"Flowers?"

"Yes, easy-to-grow perennials, ones that come up every year and support nectar and pollen. We have clusters of fragrant small flowers: peonies, California poppy. And checker mallow that are so pretty in that lilac pink."

There's that *We.* "It sounds lovely."

We were both quiet. Then Rob asked, "Are you happy?"

"Yes, I think so. I mean, besides the situation with Mom. What are you really asking—am I happy with my husband?"

"Are you?"

"Honestly. I mean he's good in so many ways..."

"Something's missing?"

"Yeah."

"You want to talk about it?"

"No, not really," I said.

"If you ever do, I'm here. I don't judge."

"Thanks—I appreciate that."

"I'm so glad we became friends," Rob said.

"Me too."

"I think we're more than just friends—there's something very special about you."

"I feel like I've always known you. That I could tell you anything," I said.

"You can—and it will always be safe with me."

"I know," I said quietly.

I am usually cautious in what I say to most people, but it was like he was the other half of me. Through the years many friends came and went; I never had the kind of closeness I was already experiencing with Rob. I could finally utter my thoughts and feelings to someone and not be judged, and he wasn't going to run away.

At least I didn't think so.

Chapter 28

The sliding doors opened as I approached.

"Hey, Aimee."

"Hi, Stephanie." The well-dressed, heavyset receptionist greeted everyone with an infectious smile, colorful and vibrant. She had shoulder-length, wavy black hair and big onyx eyes in a pretty and clear complexion. Her desk was always brimmed with a bouquet of flowers and a bowl of candies. Seeing the bite-size Milky Ways left over from the holidays, I dipped in.

"My mom's favorite."

"Take a few."

One of my favorites too, so I took a handful, stuffing them in my purse. *Chocolate helped.*

I walked over to the small corner table and signed the guest book, marking the date and time I arrived and who I was seeing. Afterward, I slunk down the sea-green corridors, peering in the open-door office rooms: Financial, Director of Social Services. Administrator's Office. Another for the Activities Director.

Further down, I passed the entertainment room where musicians contributed their time once a week strumming their guitars. Pianists would come and play the old grand Steinway. If Rob lived here on the Cape, I was sure he would give a little of his time singing and playing for them. It amazed me how the full-blown Alzheimer's residents remembered lyrics to old songs they grew up with. Even Mom's spirit rose when she heard the music, and she'd sing or hum along too. Some residents would sway in their wheelchairs, while others would tap their feet, feeling the rhythm of the music. Music was like their magic; it never left their souls.

I waved to Jake.

"Aimee, can I talk to you for a moment?"

"Sure. What's up?"

"We have a problem."

"What kind of problem? Is Mom okay?" I asked, feeling panic rising in my chest.

"She's fine. But she's been making out with Jim Smith in her room."

"What?" I asked, astonished. Jim was a resident there. He was a good-looking man, and quiet. Kept to himself. The few conversations with Jim had me wondering why he was even in this unit. He spoke eloquently, and he was lucid and coherent. He chatted about his job working at Sears and Roebuck for fifty years in the automotive department, and about the time he served in the Marine Corps. I couldn't detect any sign of dementia. I wondered if he'd been admitted too early.

"Yeah. His wife came to visit him and saw them. She was terribly upset."

"You're kidding me?" *Maybe she shouldn't have stuck him away so soon. Dealt with it—through sickness and health. Till death do you part.*

"No, I'm not and something has to be done about it."

"Wait a minute," I said, raising my palm, indicating to him to stop. I needed to digest this. "Are you saying my mom was kissing someone?"

"Yes, that's what I said."

"Oh my God," I said, covering my mouth with both hands, stifling a chuckle.

Jake flashed me a bizarre look.

Just the look on his face made me burst into a fit of laughter. I bent at the waist, tears running down my cheeks. "I'm sorry."

"I don't find this funny," Jake said.

"My mom hasn't kissed a man in at least twenty years—that was when she had too much to drink one night."

"Well, his wife didn't appreciate it when she walked in and found them. We have to keep your mother away from Jim. It's causing problems."

"How can she be jealous? Doesn't his wife realize they both have dementia? Does he even know what he's doing?" I asked. *Or maybe he did know.*

"Probably not, but we're going to have to keep them apart." *I might be here often but not around the clock. That's your job to keep them apart.*

"All right," I sighed. "I'll try and talk with her."

Bravo, Ma. Not so good, though, picking a married man.

***

"Mom, I want to talk to you for a minute. Can we sit down?" I sat on the edge of her bed.

"About what?" she asked.

"Mom, have you been kissing Jim?"

"Yeah… So what about it?"

"Well, first of all, he's married."

"Who cares?" she said while standing up, giving me a "whatever" look.

"His wife does. She was very upset about it."

"I don't see any wife here. She doesn't live with him."

"No, not now but she did for many years."

"That doesn't make sense," Mom said.

"A lot of things don't make sense—but it doesn't mean it's right."

My phone pinged—it was Rob.

"Who's that?"

I smiled. "A friend."

She smiled back. "Who is it?"

"Oh, you don't know him, Mom. But I think you would like him."

"Yeah." I had this gut feeling she knew I'd fallen for someone, and here I was lecturing her to stay away from Jim. The only one she'd found any pleasure with—in years.

"Mom, will you stay away from him?"

"Why should I?"

"Because we don't want to hurt people."

She just looked at me. Those eyes of hers disclosed a lot: No one's going to take away the best thing I've had in years.

Am I a hypocrite?

***

Later that afternoon, Rob sent another text.

Hi. Do you have a few minutes?

Yeah.

A minute later my phone rang.

"How are you?"

"I'm okay," I said.

My tongue poked the insides of my cheeks while I wrapped strands of my hair around my left index finger.

"What's that mean?" Rob asked.

"Well, most say 'great.' And that's overrated. Plus, they know that it's really just a friendly greeting—nothing more."

"Except for those who *do c*are—and want to know more. Like me."

A warm sensation flooded my insides. "I care too," I said quietly.

"So, tell me—what's on your mind?"

Other than you? "I'd just been thinking about how life is. How unpredictable it can be. Things happen—good and bad. We think we have control over it all, but we really don't. Do we?"

"No, I don't think so."

"I mean like Mom getting dementia—us meeting each other. And not leaving before you came to the party."

"You were going to leave?"

"I was getting bored. I only came because Diane told me you guys were going to be there. I thought it would be nice to reconnect with someone who played at my party."

"And I wasn't even there—at your party." I heard him sigh.

"At least you were at this one."

I told Rob about Mom kissing Jim and everybody's reaction to it.

"I met the man, and I can see why she might be attracted to him—really nice person. But Mom hasn't kissed a guy in a long time. I mean, it's been years since she's made out with anyone."

"When we were walking out that night, side by side—I wanted to kiss you."

What! "You did? You wanted to kiss me?"

"Yeah, but I didn't. I wish I had."

I was speechless. *Why would you want to kiss me?* I wanted to ask but didn't.

"I'm sorry, maybe I shouldn't have said that."

Things just flew out of his mouth at random times. But I liked that about him. It made him different. "No. Don't be sorry."

I heard him taking a deep breath. "Well, my dearest—I have to go. Write to me. I will look for your words."

I wanted to go to the computer right away and tell him all that I was feeling—about everything. My husband. My mom. Meeting him. But instead, I dressed warmly and went for a long walk through the woods. I trudged along in my boots through the dried leaves and pine needles sheathed in snow. The flogging squalls of winter blew fiercely. My face flushed from the cold; my teeth chattered. Suddenly it all stilled. A gentle hush cloaked the forest. The long-limbed trees stared at me like silent sentries, providing a sense of protection. And the moonlight was now glowing through the pasty sky, lighting my path. I walked for another mile or so and then reluctantly turned around.

Chapter 29

Mom was not in her room. She had too much life left in her to waste it in bed or even be restrained for too long. So, surprisingly, she began socializing, venturing from one room to another. She gladly volunteered rides to those stuck in wheelchairs, trundling them up and down the nursing home corridors. Even her friend Jim, who was now confined to a wheelchair too. He seemed to be failing fast; his dementia appeared to have heightened quickly. Residents and staff smiled and waved at Mom and her passenger as they traveled past.

But today nobody had seen her. I began peeking in one room after another. At last, I found Mom in a resident's private room at the far end of the corridor. She was trying to console a woman named Ruth, who was in tears. Ruth said she'd been waiting for her husband to come and visit. Though Mom rarely exhibited it, she did have a lot of compassion. Mom always had a tough time opening up, expressing her own feelings, but she often offered advice and expressed kindness to anyone she saw hurting, blue, or brokenhearted.

"He'll come soon," Mom said to her. Mom didn't know that this lady's husband had died three years earlier, which I learned later after speaking to one of the aides. I glanced around the room at the old photos Ruth had of her husband and her together.

"I don't know—I've been waiting all night," Ruth cried as she cradled his picture in her hands.

"It's okay, dear—he's probably busy doing something. He'll come. You'll see. He loves you," Mom said, patting her shoulder.

There was nothing I could contribute; I just stood there.

***

I opened Facebook and began reading others' posts and accepting new friend requests. Occasionally, I'd post a photograph of the beach or my walks through the woods and I'd get likes, which was nice. I didn't feel comfortable interacting with too many. Or maybe I just didn't care to.

Then I saw a message from Rob.

I lose all sense of time and space and float above the floor of my apartment in ecstasy, dazzled by your picture and how wonderful you look to me, and I forget my purpose of being on FB to begin with. Then I go about my day with this lovestruck grin upon my face which no one dares to approach. But that's okay because I love being in this state of complete Aimee.

I smiled. I knew he was staring at my profile picture on Facebook. I loved the way he described his thoughts. I loved the way he made me feel. I'd never met anyone like him; he was far from the typical romantic. He was just him. He never tried to mimic another. I think it was because he was a true Romeo. He saw things differently and expressed them his way.

You make me smile, I wrote back. Even though I wasn't sure when he wrote this, or whether he was on Facebook now.

He was.

That's my job to make you smile. I stared at his words; I heard his voice when reading them.

I sat for a minute and reread our writings to each other, then I logged out of Facebook. Rob was becoming a major part of my life—and quickly. There was no reason to move slowly, not at our age. It wasn't like we were rushing it; it was coming naturally. As if he always belonged there.

Chapter 30

When I got to the Alzheimer's unit, Celia, the night nurse, buzzed me through the secured doors. "Can I talk to you for a minute?" she asked.

"Yeah sure—what's up?"

She backed me into the gray-tiled wall and stood in front of me. Practically barricading me with her heavyset frame. I figured she was around my age. Her blonde hair was dyed and was hanging straggly to her shoulders and her breath reeked of cigarette. That was a habit I didn't miss; it had been ten years and even the smell of it now, nauseated me.

"Do you work?" she asked quietly.

"No—I mean I did.... Why?" *It's none of your business what I do. Why do I owe you an explanation?*

"Well, you come here every day."

"Yes, I do." *What does she care whether I go every day? That's my mother. She's frightened to be there alone. She never socialized much and never had any real friends. All she had was family—now only me.*

"You don't need to do that. Do you see anybody else's family come like you do?" Celia asked.

I looked at her. "This is my mom! I don't care what others do or don't do."

"I know, and I understand that. I think that's good but don't feel you have to come every day."

"I want to. She's my mother," I repeated.

"I'm just saying, you don't have to worry. She's in good hands. She's being well taken care of."

"I'm sure," I said. Although I had my doubts. "I won't be staying long."

Who was she to tell me? The more I thought about it, the more suspicious I became. *Why doesn't she want me here? Is she afraid I'm spying on her? On them? Am I overdoing it, coming too often?* If I thought for one moment that my mother didn't know I was there, I wouldn't have come as often. But I knew she knew, and I knew she waited for me.

***

"Can't anyone else go to the nursing home?" Vicky asked, when we were sitting at her table having tea.

"I talked with Amanda, her niece, and her kids are sick."

"Like that nurse told you, maybe you should take a break. Go every other day."

"But I'm not working anymore. I'm not writing..."

"Your mom needs to learn to adjust in her new environment—you can't be there all the time."

"I know. You're right. It's just that she's been a certain way all her life—she can't change. Not now." *I know her so well—it's like I know what she's thinking. Her fears. Her anxieties.*

"You need a break—you're going to drive yourself crazy, worrying about her." *She worried about me—always. If the situation was reversed, she'd never leave my side.*

"At least if I was still working, I'd have a legitimate excuse."

"Ah, the Catholic guilt. What it's done to us."

"Yeah, it sure made me feel guilty about a lot." *You have no idea.*

"Don't get me started."

I laughed. "You brought it up."

Chapter 31

Every Sunday I took Mom out to breakfast, but it was getting harder to handle her by myself. I was afraid that she might open the car door while I was driving. Either jump out or fall out. Her stubbornness and her inability to comprehend reality were becoming more of a challenge.

Steve reluctantly agreed to come with me. It was seemingly a chore to him; one he preferred not to do. But I was tired of doing it alone, day after day, week after week.

"Are you ready, Steve? Mom is waiting."

"I have to change the oil in the truck."

"Can't it wait till we get back? It's almost lunchtime there. And if she gets something to eat, she won't touch her breakfast."

"Give me ten minutes."

Between Mom's fragility and unsteadiness, we began retrieving Mom from the back entrance of the nursing home, where the employees parked. Fewer steps. We figured it would be easier getting her in and out of the car, especially during the colder months with the snow and ice.

Steve waited in the car, while I went in to get Mom. I saw the aides already escorting Mom's neighbors into the elevator to the main dining room upstairs. When I got to Mom's room, she was dressed and waiting; it was an outing she looked forward to every week. "Let's get your jacket," I said. Mom scurried straight to the closet and pulled it from the hanger. I helped her slip her arms into the sleeves and buttoned the coat. Then I handed her a hat and gloves.

After becoming Sunday regulars, the staff at the Hearth & Kettle restaurant got to know us well. I was partial to one young server, named Graham. As we walked in, I waved to him, beckoning we wanted one of his tables. The hostess noticed and seated us, handing us menus. Mom always cozied up to me in the booth; she'd lay her head on my shoulder. It felt odd, but good.

"What would you like today, Evelyn?" Graham asked.

Mom shrugged and smiled sweetly.

"How about a blueberry pancake?" Graham suggested.

Mom kept smiling as she stared at him. I wondered what she was thinking; I could only guess. He was tall, handsome, and young—friendly and compassionate. Exactly what every woman coveted, young or old—Graham was the whole package, maybe the real deal in her mind.

"Yes," I said. "Mom loves pancakes. Some bacon too, please. Well done," I added as he walked away.

"Well done it is," he said while turning around. He soon came back with silverware and took the rest of our orders. "I'll bring the coffee right over."

"Great. Thank you."

Mom seemed content being with us and even just being in the restaurant, somewhere different. Away from the pen. Or maybe she recalled the pleasure she got from dining out. Which wasn't often.

Ten minutes later, Graham brought our meals; Mom's first.

"Here you go, Evelyn."

Mom smiled. "Thank you."

"My pleasure, Evelyn. You enjoy now."

Just as we began eating, Mom let us know she had to visit the restroom.

"I gotta pee," she announced loudly.

"Jesus Christ," Steve bellowed.

I got up to assist her. "Where are you going?" Steve asked, looking at me.

"She needs help," I whispered, glaring at him.

When Mom and I got back to the table, Steve was finished with his breakfast. Mom refused to eat anymore. I stuffed in a few forkfuls of cold egg and home fries.

While we were waiting for the check, I could see that Steve was getting antsy.

"What the hell is taking him so long?"

"Look how many tables he has—if a customer's food gets cold, they will complain."

"If he can't handle it, he shouldn't be working here."

"He's doing the best he can. Be patient."

"I got things to do at home."

"I understand."

"How can you understand? You don't do anything."

I felt my face heating to bright shades of red. "Right." Some days I just wanted to punch that mouth of his. *Breathe.* Maybe his anger was his way of concealing his own anxieties.

I took Mom out to the car while he waited to pay the bill.

Chapter 32

On Monday morning before doing anything else, I opened my laptop and went straight to my email. I knew Rob probably wouldn't be up yet, but I wanted him to see my message as soon as he opened his email.

Hi Rob,

Hope your weekend went well.

It's weird—here I am, and I don't know what to say—I mean I want to tell you so much. But I'm scared. It's not that I feel uncomfortable talking to you—just the opposite. I love talking with you. You make everything in my life feel meaningful. Worthwhile. I just don't want you to get tired of me. Sometimes I ramble about things that probably should be kept to myself. But you always listen with so much compassion in your heart. I appreciate you helping me to lighten my burdens. But it's not right for me to keep unloading everything on you.

I just want to thank you for being you.

Aimee

After I wrote to him, I filled the car with cardboard boxes, trash bags, and old newspapers. Then I went to Mom's apartment to pack up her belongings: clothing, loose photos and albums, framed prints, knickknacks, dishes, pots and pans. After cleaning out the medicine cabinet, I went into the bedroom. In a bureau drawer was a rectangular wooden jewelry box. Inside, a strand of faux pearls, an old Timex watch, and several clip-on earrings and pins she'd wear when going out on a date or attending a christening or wedding. I remember how pretty she always looked dressed up. And then I uncovered a smaller box beneath more clothing. I recognized it immediately. I couldn't believe she'd kept it. I was eleven. In Kings department store with my girlfriend and her mother; I bought it with my babysitting money. I had to. *It will help. She will love it—won't she, God?* The perfect gift for Mother's Day.

I sat on the bed, rivulets of tears sliding down my face. Trembling, I slowly opened the light gray box. Staring. The play of light on the multifaceted rosary beads lying in white satin was almost spellbinding. The way I felt that day in the department store when I first saw them.

I gently picked up the chain and closed my eyes, feeling each bead. Praying. For Mom. For Steve. For Rob—I remember him telling me, "Every time my dad came home drunk and started beating on us, Mom would take out her rosary beads and start praying."

I kept a few other things I had given her over the years. Amanda and Jeff didn't want anything. A couple of neighbors came by to see what they could get for nothing. But I didn't mind since I would be donating a lot of the stuff and heaving what was left into the complex's dumpster.

I sat on the living room floor and looked around—waiting for Mom to walk in. Twenty years she'd been here. *My God, I'm nearly the age she was then.* But now she was never coming through that door, back to her home again. I just sat there unable to move, tears falling. Thinking about how one's life can sail smoothly for a long while, then in an instant it can all change, be turned upside down. Change was constant; it might not be what you expected or wanted, but you could rely on it.

My phone pinged; it was a text from Rob.

Hey, you okay?

Yeah, I'm exhausted. I'm at Mom's apartment—cleaning out.

I'm going to leave you alone—if you need me—I'm here.

Thanks.

I wanted to tell him I did need him—but I also needed this time alone.

After a few hours of sorting, making piles of things I planned to discard, and wrapping the things I planned to keep, I went home and made dinner. I was feeling melancholy and wanted to make Steve something special, something I hoped he would really like at least. *I have to try.* I had called Steve to let him know, so that he wouldn't have to stop at the store.

"What are we having?" he asked.

"It's a surprise." Something to lift our spirits.

"Surprise? Oh boy," he said.

I took the plates of salad I had fixed from the refrigerator.

"A healthy start," I said, setting one in front of him.

I seasoned pulled pork with onions and barbeque sauce. I grilled the gluten-free submarine rolls, melting mozzarella cheese. Then I made homemade sweet potato fries, adding a dash of sea salt and pepper.

"What's all this?"

I smiled. "Comfort food."

I watched Steve take his first bite into the sub, waiting for his reaction. "Not bad," he said.

That was a compliment from him. "I'm glad you approve."

"The French fries are a little soggy. You should have kept them in longer."

"Do you want me to stick them back in? It won't take long."

"No. But next time—pay attention, honey." Never a kiss or a hug or a "thank you." It had been so long since I received any of those gestures, I wondered if I ever had. But I knew in the beginning of our marriage it was different. It was sweeter. He was kinder. More loving. What went wrong?

Till death do you part.

"Okay." I did what I could to avoid confrontations; I just wanted to live in peace. Tired of the degrading. *Why is he always angry? Why can't he talk about what he's feeling?* He buried his head in the newspaper. I finished eating and took my plate to the sink, wondering what it would be like to sit at the table with Rob each evening.

"Hello—I am talking to you," Steve yelled.

"I'm sorry—I didn't hear you."

"How the hell can you not hear me? You're right there!"

"I don't know. What is it?" I was drifting elsewhere.

"I am waiting for dessert."

"There is none."

"What do you mean—you didn't think of that?"

"No, sorry."

"Now I have to go to the fucking store."

Why did he have to spoil it all?

I finished up the dishes while Steve was gone and went to the computer. I found five more friend requests from people I had known either from school or had worked with. I accepted them. Rob must have seen me on there and messaged me.

Hi, how are things going?

I wrote back. *Good. Just finished up dinner.*

I waited to hear back. Then I realized it was an old message. I still hadn't gotten the hang of how Facebook or Messenger worked. I closed out and went to my email.

Dear Aimee,

Please don't you ever feel afraid to talk to me or feel that you are burdening me. You are my friend, and I want to be there for you. Always.

I wish I lived near you—I'd have you here with me all day and into the night, if that was possible. And we'd talk about everything. Our feelings, emotions flowing. All the pain, sorrows, joys and happiness. Sharing with each other all our frustrations and fragilities. Our imperfections and our strengths. Things we have never shared with another. This is what is—in this moment tonight.

I could go on—but I think it is best that I stop for now.

XO Rob

I smiled, wiping a fallen tear.

I closed out of my email. Then I went upstairs to wash up and put on my night clothes. Downstairs, I joined Steve on the sofa. And dreamed about Rob.

Chapter 33

In her room, Mom's bed was made, but she was not there. I sat in the chair by the bed and waited. I glanced at her roommate, Katherine, who was not moving a muscle. She seemingly looked back at me with her beautiful powder blue eyes in a soft, round face. I smiled and said, "Hello, Katherine. How are you doing today?" Of course, I didn't expect a reply. She never spoke. I saw her blink though. I wondered what her mind was saying. If anything. *How the heck do you think I'm doing—stuck like this? Trapped.* None of this seemed real. I kept thinking I was going to wake up and find this to be just another bad dream.

Mom came in looking right past me, holding a doll. "Where is it? Where'd you put her?" she cried.

Two lifelike dolls, that once belonged to a resident who had passed, had become my mother's obsession. Her world. Mom carried them everywhere. She'd feed and dress them and keep them in bed with her at night. This morning, however, one was missing. I could see she was frantic.

"Mom, we'll find your baby. She couldn't have gone far."

But she didn't hear me. Or believe me. Her face full of distress, she kept searching. Under the beds. In the closet. Bureau drawers. No success. She headed down the hallway to neighboring rooms.

I spoke to one of the older aides, named Sally, and told her what had happened. She said she'd look in the storage area; it was like a lost and found room. I prayed the doll was there. I'd never seen Mom so emotional; she saw these dolls as her children. I wondered if she regarded these babies as me—and the one she had miscarried.

I walked with Sally to the storage room and waited outside the door. A few minutes later, she came out. "Here she is," Sally said, smiling with the doll in her arms.

"Oh, thank goodness. You're a lifesaver—Mom's been so upset."

"I've seen her with these dolls everywhere," she said, handing it over to me. "Your mom is so sweet—I sit and talk with her whenever I can."

"Thank you. I appreciate that."

"No problem. I don't mind—she's a nice lady."

I walked into Mom's room; she was holding the other doll against her chest. "Mom, look who I have."

She looked, stood up, dropped the doll she was holding, and reached for the one I had. "Where'd she go?" Mom asked, grabbing the doll from me.

"She got lost—but she's fine."

"I have to feed her," she said, sticking the doll's plastic milk bottle in her mouth.

"She's happy to be back with her momma."

Mom nodded gratefully. "Yup."

It was so hard seeing my mother, an old woman now, who'd always been my rock, my protector, reverted into this child-like state. Part of me wanted to shake her and say, "Stop it—you are my mother." It's not supposed to be this way. *Aimee, you need to face reality.*

***

I found this sense of peace whenever I went to Vicky's; I was whisked away from my troubles. While walking in I wanted to free the rooms of dust and the wispy cobwebs, like those in a haunted house. Yet it gave the home unique character. *How does she ignore the pile of dishes in the sink?* I wished I could be more like her in that respect. Be able to let go of it all. Vicky had told me she was her mother's housekeeper as a child while her mother was a socialite. That is why she despised maintaining a house.

Maybe it was selfish of me, but I liked that she had no husband or grandkids running around; it was always just her and me. No noise, no interruptions. Vicky had a TV. But she kept it in her bedroom. Sometimes she'd listen to jazz or classical music on her stereo in the living room. Peacefulness here, never yelling, nor fighting. Just two women who respected each other and were able to pour out to one another what was inside.

Even though Vicky and I had only met recently, not long before I met Rob, she'd become a good friend fast. She was the only girlfriend I had really, and I knew I could trust her—and she was there when I needed to vent. She had gotten to know my husband better, witnessing his erratic behavior after coming over to our house more. She was even learning more about the other man who was becoming an important part of my life. Although I kept much of this new relationship with Rob between just him and me.

"It's so weird how life works, how people come together, unexpectedly. Meeting Rob—even how you and I met. I wonder if it's all in a plan."

"Plan?" Vicky asked, frowning, as she looked at me.

"You know, God having something to do with this?"

"I'm spiritual, you know. I do believe the universe brings people together," Vicky said.

"I believe that too. You know, Vicky, even though I don't go to church anymore, I still regard myself as being Catholic."

"It's been implanted in us. That's why."

"Yeah, I guess."

I became quiet.

Vicky stared at me. "You can't stop thinking about him, can you?" she said with a smile.

"Vicky, I never thought...never dreamed... I never had this kind of connection before—with anyone." Was I becoming obsessed or desiring a relationship that didn't really exist, like Scarlett O'Hara pining over Ashley in *Gone with the Wind*—wanting someone I could never really have?

"And Rob felt something that night too."

"Yes, he did, and that's what makes it so amazing."

"What are you going to do about it?"

"I don't know yet," I said, changing the subject. "Tell me about your date with this Egyptian guy—what's his name?

"Rashida. He brought me a gift."

"Oh, how nice. What'd he bring—flowers?"

"No."

"Perfume?"

"No. You won't believe it."

"Tell me for God's sake," I said.

"He brought me wrinkle cream!"

"What! Cut the crap," I said. "The gall of him..."

"I guess he thought I needed it."

"Well, first of all—you don't. You take care of your skin. It's beautiful."

"Thank you. What was he thinking? I'm not thirty years old. Or even fifty, for that matter."

"He's just a weirdo," I said.

"He couldn't even hold an erection."

"What! You had sex with him after that? You should have used the cream on *him*."

"Seriously."

We laughed till we ached. Then Vicky was distracted by a ping on her phone.

What we can overlook when we are lonely. Hungry. Starving for affection.

"We had a good time together though," Vicky emphasized.

Before the sex?

"That's good—what'd you guys do?"

"We took walks on the beach—I couldn't go too far with my leg. I lost my balance once and he helped me up." I wondered if he was attentive—took her hand when she fell. "We went out to eat. A lot," Vicky added.

"Nice," I said, wondering if he'd treated. She must have read my mind.

"It was Dutch treat." *I am not surprised.*

"Oh," I said.

"We barely know each other." *But you had sex with him, and he stayed at your house...*

Eventually I went home. I set the table while Steve was preparing dinner and then fed Henri. I sat in a chair at the table, thinking about Rob and all the things I wanted to share with him. I wondered what it would be like if he were here instead of Steve. Sweeter. Pleasant. Calmer. And I know I'd be appreciated. *Would I?*

Henri purred against my leg. I picked her up, laying my face against her. Her fur felt soft and smelled clean, from the oatmeal bath I had given her the night before. "Henri, you're a beautiful girl."

Steve barged into the kitchen. "Put her down—I don't want cat hairs in my food."

"She's not even near you." Henri jumped off my lap and ran.

"Look," he said, picking up a fur ball. "This is what I'm talking about."

"That's because you scared her."

"Scared her, my ass. You should comb her more."

"I comb her every day," I said.

"How come you didn't put the vegetables on?"

"Sorry—I didn't realize the time had gone by so quickly."

"Can't you hear the damn buzzer?" Steve grabbed the frozen broccoli and carrots from the freezer.

"I can do it," I said.

"No. Just sit there—like you always do."

Even though his remark hurt, I wasn't in the mood to fight. I felt happy. For the first time in a long while.

I guess it showed. At the dinner table, he must've glanced over at me while reading the paper.

"What're you smirking about?"

"Nothing. Just thinking."

"About what?"

"Something Mom did today," I lied. *When did I start becoming a liar?*

He didn't bother to ask what—he didn't care.

Steve went to bed early. I finished the book I was reading and went to write Rob.

I saw his email and smiled.

Dear Aimee,

There's so much I want to say to you—when I hear your voice, though, sometimes I just go blank. I'm mesmerized by you—it's not just what I see on the outside of you that dazzles me. Your beauty goes beyond that. You give so much of yourself to everyone around you. You're kind and generous and loving. And so thoughtful. Everything you say matters—matters to me, and I will always care about you, wherever this friendship takes us.

I don't know what this connection is all about—all I know is that I get these deep feelings whenever I think of you.

Sleep well, Aimee. You'll be in my dreams.

Love, Rob

Dear Rob,

Thank you for this beautiful email. I don't understand what's happening either—only what I'm beginning to feel. I think about you a lot, and sometimes I feel like our friendship is like a Christmas present under the tree.

I know what it is, and I know it's really special.

But I feel like I'll never be able to open it.

Do you know what I mean?

Aimee

I waited for his response.

Yes, I know. I understand. Maybe you will get to open that present. Soon.

XO Rob

Chapter 34

Once a month, I'd get an invitation to the Care Plan meeting at Bellview, where I'd enter a small office room. Waiting there was Jake Gardner, along with a social worker, an activities director, and whoever else was associated with Mom's care. Sometimes a physical therapist would join us, for whatever reason. Mom didn't need that service—yet. Each one would give me an update, an evaluation on how Mom was doing. Progressing or regressing. More the latter. Everyone was pleasant and always had something positive to say about Mom. Then they'd ask me if I had any questions or concerns—I'd always answer with a "No, not at this time."

Before leaving, I would sign papers, acknowledging I was there and stating what I wanted for my mother. Vitamins were okay but no medication. And I specifically emphasized that to them each time.

They weren't listening.

Without my permission, they had begun giving her Xanax or Ativan. One of the nurses had requested the drug from the doctor after hearing the aides' complaints; they couldn't handle Mom's excitability and nervous energy. They wanted to calm her down to make their job easier—make her as oblivious as the rest of the residents. I was upset about it and made it clear to them. But I had no control over what they did when I was not there.

On Wednesday morning when I got to the unit, I was informed that Mom had punched one of the young aides in the face, sending her to the hospital. I wondered where Mom's strength came from, being so thin, so frail. I questioned if the aide had irritated her in some way. Something had to set her off.

"Who is this girl—I would like to talk to her," I said to nurse Cathy Stiles.

"Her name is Stephanie. She usually works evenings."

"Is she new?"

"No, she's been here for a while—maybe a couple of years."

"Could you have her give me a call? I'd like to find out what happened."

"Your mom didn't want to get ready for bed. She was socializing and it was getting late."

"Mom was always a night owl. Just have her call me, please."

"I will leave a message with Stephanie."

"Thank you."

Mom was abusive verbally growing up and beyond, but she rarely spanked me. I gave her no reason to. Other than that one time when I was eight; I had misbehaved for a babysitter and ruined Mom's evening with a date. I refused to put on my pajamas. I refused to go to bed. I just wanted my mother home. I needed her. I pretended to be sleeping when Mom returned; she pulled away the covers and whipped my behind with the paddle till it split in two.

Later that day, I got a call from Stephanie, the nurse's aide.

"Yes, this is Aimee, Evelyn's daughter."

"Aimee, I got the message to give you a call."

"I just wanted to hear from you about the other night. I'm sorry you had to go to the ER. What happened?"

"I was trying to get your mom to leave a neighbor's room to get her night clothes on. She wasn't happy about that. I went to grab her hand and she pulled away. When I tried again, she made a fist and socked me one. It took me off guard."

I had to restrain from laughing—because it was so out of character for Mom. "I'm really sorry about that—I hope you're okay."

"I didn't make a big deal about it. I got a little bruise but I'm good. These things happen with Alzheimer patients."

"Yeah, I know they can be aggressive. If you have any more problems with Mom, please give me a call."

"I will. Have a good night."

"You too."

***

After I hung up, I immediately opened my laptop.

I've been sitting here working on writing a song. For you.

It starts out like this:

From the moment I met you, I knew in my heart—we couldn't be apart
Because there is only one—only one of you.
I wish we met long ago,
I would've brought you to every show
Let the world know how much I cared
And smiled while all the other boys stared.
Things happen for a reason—we don't know why
Love is promised in every season
So, my lady, take my hand, don't be shy.

I have not finished. Meter is off—need to get that right. Smile.

I put an open hand to my chest—patting it, my eyes watering up.

Chapter 35

"You ready?" Steve asked.

"Almost," I said. "I just have to grab a sweater." I was always chilly in his brother's house. I think he liked to conserve on heat, even though Harold didn't need to; he was a multimillionaire. The small mansion with its marble floors possessed a cold atmosphere. Or maybe it was just the occupant that made me feel that way. Unwelcome. At least when he was married, his wife Claire brought in warmth with her amiable personality.

"Hurry it up. I'll be in the car."

Running downstairs, I stopped and filled Henri's bowl. "Be a good girl—I'll see you later," I said, patting her head.

When I walked outside to get in the car, I saw Steve through the windshield. He had both hands up in the air; I glanced downward.

"What took you so long?" he asked when I got in.

"I had to fill Henri's bowl—it's a three hour round trip and that's if there's no traffic. We'll probably have dinner with Harold. So we'll be getting home late."

"She'll survive."

Even though I was already feeling anxious, it was a quiet drive. The traffic was light, and the sky was clear of any precipitation. And I was relieved when Steve's driving was non-aggressive.

Steve turned on the radio, keeping the volume low.

He turned and looked at me once we got on the highway. "Honey, it's nice of you to come with me."

I smiled. *Did I have a choice?*

After driving through Boston and another twenty minutes north in the town of Winchester, Steve pulled into the long, paved driveway and parked behind Harold's Lamborghini.

Steve walked through the door first. Harold quickly greeted us, holding three pieces of wood in his hand. He asked Steve which one he wanted to use for the crown molding in his dining room.

OMG! This is about a job. Not a social visit.

Steve and Harold wandered off while I stood in the foyer.

Steve turned around and said, "Aimee, you coming?"

"That's okay—I'll wait."

"Why don't you go sit on the sofa?" Harold suggested, lifting his bushy black eyebrows. That deep voice of his sounding more like an order.

"Sure."

I parked myself on the cold, black leather sectional and looked around: the fancy window treatments were gone. I thought how empty the house seemed without Claire's zealous flair for embellishing. The mantel above the fireplace was bare of the family photos; Claire must have taken them. Harold and Claire had been married for forty years. Friends and family were stunned when she woke up and left him. I wasn't surprised. She never looked happy to me—I just wondered why she waited so long. *Maybe she found someone too?*

Steve and Harold eventually returned. "Would you like a Coke or a ginger ale?" Harold asked, looking at me.

"Water is fine."

"There's bottles in the refrigerator—help yourself."

Harold had a couple of antique cars that he'd recently purchased in his four-car garage. He seemed eager to show them off. Steve was just as excited to see. I tagged along. I admit I loved the '56 white Corvette and '75 black Jaguar, but when they got into a lengthy conversation about them, I got bored. I went back into the house. When I saw the French doors leading to the backyard, I was drawn outside. The in-ground pool and hot tub had been drained and covered for the season. I imagined their grandkids laughing and splashing around in their inflated duckies and dolphins.

Every summer Harold and Claire had hosted a pool party for family and friends. Steve insisted on attending, even if it was the only time we'd been invited, other than a couple of Christmases.

"Well, I have to get ready to go soon. Going out to dinner with some friends," Harold said.

That was our cue—it was time to leave. Harold had never asked his brother out to dinner all the years we'd been married.

We'd come all this way for what?

"We have to get home anyway," Steve said. "Aimee has to feed the cat. Don't ya, honey?"

"Yeah."

After an hour at Harold's, we were back on the road.

I knew whatever Steve was feeling was going to come out. I buckled my seatbelt and braced myself. Harold's ways bothered me; I never saw any love expressed between him and his brother. They were more like acquaintances than siblings. Steve jumped at any of his brother's requests, but Harold rarely reciprocated.

Steve crawled up behind vehicle bumpers, looking to antagonize someone. I could feel my body tensing. As we approached the Tobin Bridge, signs indicated the left lane was closed. A car tried merging in front of us. Steve refused to budge. He inched even closer to the car in front of him, leaving no room for another to enter.

"Steve, let her in."

"Bullshit—who the hell is she? She's not cutting in front of me. She saw the damn signs."

"You don't have to be a prick." Steve was acting out like a child who was hurt; his way of staying tough, in control.

As the woman tried to edge her way in, Steve blew the horn. "Can't you read?" he yelled, raising his open hands.

She rolled down her passenger's window. "You must have a little dick," she yelled back. I smiled inwardly. Then she looked over at me. "I feel sorry for you." *I feel sorry for me too.*

"Ooh, that bitch—if she only knew. Why don't you tell her, honey." I rolled my eyes.

I hoped this would be the last incident; I just wanted to get home—in one piece. I sat in the passenger's seat like an anxious dental patient waiting to go in for a root canal. My nerves were high, anticipating the worst.

"I'm hungry—let's get something to eat," Steve said.

"Yeah, sure. Sounds good."

He stopped at Longhorn's in Hanson a half hour later. We both ordered a steak strip. While he was in the bathroom my phone pinged, letting me know I had a notification from FB or an email. I checked it and I had several, mostly junk mail, but after scrolling down I saw there was a message from Rob. I didn't have time to open it; Steve was already heading back to our table.

Chapter 36

On Tuesday morning I got a call from Kelsey, one of the social workers at the nursing home, informing me that they were shipping Mom to a psychiatric ward.

"What?! Why?"

"Her energy has spiked."

"But why—why would that happen?"

"We don't know," Kelsey said.

"Is she having an adverse reaction to the meds you're giving her?"

"Oh no, that's not it."

Okay, I'm taking your word for it.

They were in the medical field—I wasn't. I assumed they would know if that was the case.

"There are two places we can send her, Hewitt Hospital in Rhode Island or the Ellsworth Hospital in western Mass. We recommend Hewitt. It's closer. In case you wanted to visit her. But you can choose which one you want her to go to."

"How much time do I have to decide?"

"A couple of days—we will need some time to make the arrangements," Kelsey said.

"Who will be taking her?"

"An ambulance will transport her there."

"Ambulance?"

"Yes. A private company."

"I don't understand—can't they do something else besides sending her there? There's no other alternative?" I asked Kelsey.

"I wish there was."

I still wasn't seeing what they were. What was Mom doing differently that made them suddenly come to this decision? Other than a spike in energy, Mom seemed the same to me.

"Okay, I'll get back to you," I said.

I was furious, yet I didn't know how to fight back, try to get them to reconsider. I couldn't see their reasoning; Mom wasn't the type of person to sit quietly all day and do nothing. But they knew that. And where was this epic burst of energy emerging from when she was barely eating or drinking? Maybe she was acting out because she thought I was deserting her. *Was I spending more of my time emailing and talking with Rob than focusing on her?*

I called Steve to tell him. "Can you believe it?" I cried.

"Well, they're seeing something you're not."

"Like what? Mom's always been the get-up-and-go type—like you. I think they just want to get rid of her—they can't stand it 'cause she's so full of life. They want everyone sedated to make their job easier."

"I don't know—there's nothing you can do about it."

"I know that—it's just not right."

"I have to get back to work—we'll talk about it tonight."

"Okay," I said, even though I knew we wouldn't.

I wanted to talk to Rob. If anyone could make me feel better, he could. Still, it was not his worry.

Rob texted me ten minutes later.

Is everything okay?

A tear fell from my eye. *How does he know things?* I was embarrassed to tell him—like it was a horrible thing. But I did.

They want to send her to a psychiatric hospital.

Oh, my sweet lady I'm sorry—do you want to talk?

My eyes filled with tears. *Yes.*

My phone rang.

"Hey, what happened?" he asked.

"I don't know—they just decided, out of the blue."

"Did they give you an explanation?"

"No. They didn't say she hurt anybody again or anything like that. Just that she doesn't behave or do what the staff asks of her."

"That's it?"

"Basically, yeah. That's what I don't understand. Rob, I don't know if Mom can take the transition. Just getting used to the nursing home was tough. Going into another environment with more new faces—she'll be frightened."

"I know it must be hard, but I'm sure she's a strong woman—

like yourself. She'll be okay."

"Yes, she's always been strong—I hope so. I just wish I could change their minds."

"I understand how you feel, but sending her there could help."

"I don't see how—but maybe there's something I'm missing. I don't know."

"I'm gonna pray—for both of you."

"Thank you."

"I'm here if you need me. Always."

"I appreciate that. Thanks."

After talking with Rob, I did some research. Later, when I was grocery shopping, I ran into our neighbor, Scott, the retired fireman. When I told him about Mom, he said, "Aimee, I wouldn't recommend Hewitt for a dog. My dad was there—but not for long!"

Scott helped make my decision easier. I chose the Ellsworth institution, farther away. I was given only two choices, so all I *could* do was pray. At least the write-up online about Ellsworth was encouraging. Of course, anybody could have something written up that would make them look good.

Chapter 37

Vicky went with me on Friday to visit Mom during her stay. I asked Steve first. "I can't—I have to work," he said. *But Steve was the boss—why couldn't he take the day off and go with me?*

I thought it was best not to rush there knowing that seeing me might complicate things; Mom needed to get situated. I was apprehensive about the institution—I had no idea what to expect. What would I walk into? I just imagined a bunch of crazies, out-of-control screaming and misbehaving. And strapping men pinning patients down, fitting them in strait jackets while nursing staff administered a calming sedative into their veins, the way I had seen it being done in old movies.

My worst nightmare. My insides trembling. My fears escalating.

I had overheard Mom talking with a neighbor when I was fourteen. "Mrs. Williams's anxiety was so bad, they had to give her shock treatments. She's never been right since. I think she's in an institution now."

As we entered the large parking lot, a two-story, brick building appeared before us, new and clean. Inside, we found the same. And the staff looked just as fresh and bright. I was already feeling good vibes from this place.

I told the receptionist who I was, and she directed me to the nearby waiting room. Vicky and I found comfortable upholstered chairs next to a coffee machine. To the right of us was a table covered in magazines, and nearby was a water bubbler. Two framed prints of landscapes, an illusory façade of Jean-Baptist Camille Corot or Vincent Van Gogh paintings, hung on the light beige walls, giving the room a warm vintage feel. Calming me.

Minutes later a social worker greeted me, introducing herself as Susan Simpson. Vicky remained in the waiting room as I was escorted out to meet the rest of the team before seeing Mom. I knew Vicky would keep herself occupied if her phone's battery stayed charged.

Knowing this hospital's expertise was in Alzheimer's patients, I felt a sense of relief. I read online that the hospital had a team of great clinicians and support staff. And after meeting with them, it was evident. Everyone expressed countless pleasantries regarding Mom. Only positivity was emanating from Ellsworth. Thorough diagnostic and medication evaluations had been done on Mom. And after an in-depth analysis, the doctor confirmed my belief; this action was unwarranted.

"Hey, Mom," I said, walking into her temporary quarters. It looked like she was ready to venture somewhere. She was carrying a stuffed bear and headed toward the door.

"Hi," she said.

"Where you going?"

She shrugged. "Wanna come?"

"Sure."

We walked the corridors and ended up in a small sitting room with a nurse behind a desk. Mom plunked into a chair and began socializing.

"Mom, the nurse is busy," I said, grabbing her hand.

"No, she's fine. Evelyn and I always have nice talks," she said, winking. "Don't we, Evelyn?"

Mom nodded.

"Thank you," I said. Mom was happy and content. Resembling a pure and precious child. So I felt comfortable leaving her.

Mom would be monitored for ten days and then they'd be sending her back to the nursing home.

"Thank you for coming with me, Vicky," I said after getting into the car.

"That's what friends do," she said with a smile.

"I have to admit, I was apprehensive going in. I just didn't know what to expect—what we'd be walking into."

"Yeah, neither did I. I'd never been in a psychiatric hospital. Although, it didn't seem any different from any other hospital. In fact, better, even pleasant."

"Yeah, and I'm grateful for that. Took off a lot of stress for me."

I stuck the key in the ignition and turned and looked at Vicky. "Hey, let's stop for lunch somewhere. My treat." It was the least I could do—Vicky had been so patient and supportive; I couldn't have imagined the trip without her.

"Sounds good. I am getting a little hungry—since now it's

nearing the supper hour."

"Oh God, it *is* late," I said, glancing at the time on my dashboard.

"I didn't even notice." I knew she'd been busy texting.

"Would you mind asking Siri what restaurants are in the area?"

"Already have. It's called Zack's Place. It has a big menu with gluten-free options."

"Awesome." I put the restaurant's address in the GPS, and we were off.

I called Steve to let him know. He was pleasant for a change. Maybe he felt bad for not going with me. *Wishful thinking.*

"Okay. I'll see you when you get home."

Zack's Place had every dish imaginable from Italian food to Asian to just a plain old hot dog. Vicky chose an Asian dish, and I went for gluten-free steak tips, chow mein, and rice. It had been a long day, and it felt good to relax with good company and a plate of comfort food.

Chapter 38

It was raining heavily. I stayed in bed a long time. Henri joined me. She burrowed herself into my chest. I petted her, soothing her. And me. I'd heard Steve leave earlier. Being a Saturday, I assumed he was having his usual breakfast at one of the local coffee shops. Rob was on my mind; weekends, I figured, were family times for him. We never talked much about our spouses or their livelihoods—but I knew his wife was an elementary teacher, second grade, he'd said. And I knew his children and grandchildren meant everything to him, so I gathered that was where most of his time would be spent.

After I tended to the household chores, the rain subsided. It seemed weird not having to go to the nursing home. Steve had been gone for hours now, so I decided on a walk. I wanted, though, a change in scenery—a new adventure. I drove east along Rte. 6A until I reached Rte. 6 in the town of Eastham. Eventually, I turned right onto Governor Prence Road. At the end of the road there was a parking lot on the left with half a dozen vehicles—others had the same idea. However, I saw no one in front of me along the trails.

I briskly walked the one-mile loop that connected to the Red Maple Swamp. A large oak had uprooted, and a robin was perched on one of the fallen branches, singing happily. It made me smile. A light breeze ruffled my parka as I trekked the clear path of the open field and stopped at the split-rail wooden fence surrounded with tall grass and gazed at the ocean view beyond. The sun shone bright in the sky and was enveloped by several cirrus clouds. I took deep breaths. Walking in nature always renewed me; a silent communication between us.

When I got back into the car, I grabbed my phone from the passenger's seat. I'd purposely left it, so I wouldn't be disturbed. Steve had called three times, leaving voice messages. "Where the hell are you? Why aren't you answering the phone?"

I could feel my tranquil state waning. I'm sure he was concerned, but he had a coarse way of expressing it. Reluctantly, I called him back and told him where I was.

"You should have left me a note."

"You're right—I should have."

"I was worried, honey."

"Sorry."

"Well next time, let me know." *You take off for hours—I don't question your travels. And you don't offer me an explanation.*

After hanging up, I noticed a text from Rob. *Hi, I just want to wish you a great weekend,* he wrote, adding a smiley face.

I wrote back, leaving a smiley emoji. *Thanks. I wish you a great weekend too.*

He helped offset the phone call with Steve. I started the engine and drove slowly home, appreciating the sights along the way and the alone time.

Weekends dragged more so than the weekdays for me. I dreaded Sundays—they were for families. I had felt that loss as a child without my dad on Sundays—the family drives, dinners—family togetherness was not there. And living with Steve felt no different. He couldn't fill that abyss for me.

Chapter 39

Monday morning went as usual. After Steve headed out for work, I did my morning duties, grabbed another cup of coffee, and opened my email. Finding nothing from Rob, I opened Facebook. Again. No message.

I read some of my Facebook friends' posts, even "liking" a few. The positive ones. I was amazed to see how friends ranted on about their problems, past issues. One friend was battling an online store who had sent her the wrong order; another was angry that her kids' school had just banned peanut butter in school lunches. One announced she had been married to her high school sweetheart for thirty years. *Lucky you.* I am now ten years sober of hard drugs and liquor. *Congratulations.* Another was angry that her kid's coach had him on the bench two games in a row, sure they would've won if he was in. I wondered if they had no one to vent to and felt alone in their crises. Or maybe they just liked reaping attention. Either way, it was just another human need. One I was looking to fill as well.

At nine o'clock I called Vicky to see what she was up to, knowing I wouldn't be going to the nursing home for a while—until Mom was brought back from Ellsworth.

"You sound groggy—are you still in bed?"

"Yeah. I was up all night texting back and forth with this new guy."

"I'll let you go back to sleep."

"No, it's okay—I should get up. What's going on?"

"Just wondering if you were busy today?" I asked.

"I've got a doctor's appointment at one. I'm free after that—stop by if you want."

"I will—give me a call or text me when you're back," I said.

The house was in decent shape, so I went to my laptop and pulled up Word to begin drafting my story. Book. But when nothing came to mind, I resorted to my journal.

Today I have this extra time to do what I please, but I have no idea what that is or how to use this free time. Things in my life are changing. It's all coming at once but not together. Things I have no control over—and even the ones I do, I let happen.

Since quitting my job to care for Mom, I can see now how bad my marriage truly is. And without the emotional support from Steve, falling for Rob is becoming easier.

I was interrupted by the phone. It was Vicky.

"Hey, I should be out of the doctor's office by two. Wanna go to Provincetown afterward?"

"Yeah, I'd like that—it's a beautiful day for it."

"Okay, see you at my house around 2:30."

I hung up and went back to my journal, then heard a text.

Hey, I got a few minutes—you busy?

No.

My phone rang.

"How's your mom doing at Ellsworth?"

"Vicky and I went to see her. She'll be there for a few more days. But she's doing quite well, and they love her. Thanks for asking."

"You know I care."

"Yes."

"So, what are your plans for today?"

"Well, as you know, I usually spend most of my time at the nursing home, but this afternoon Vicky and I are going to Provincetown."

"That'll be fun."

"Yeah, just the change will be nice. Is your day busy?"

"I have a couple of appointments this morning, and later I'll be watching two of my grandchildren. But I wanted to say hello before I left."

"I'm glad you did."

"I like what's happening between us."

"Me too," I admitted.

"You're different."

"Different?"

"I've never known anyone quite like you."

"Is that a good thing?" I asked.

"Oh yes. And I am especially attracted to your empathic way. You are so tuned in to people and things."

"No one has ever said that to me before. A lot of things you say to me—no one has ever said."

"I'm sure they were aware, even if they didn't tell you."

What I liked about Rob was that he didn't hold back. Whatever was on his mind he let me know. And what was on his mind I loved hearing.

"I had this dream," he said. "I was on the Cape, maybe Chatham, and I walked into this fishing shack. Nothing was in there except this huge chair. I went and sat in it. Then you walked in and said nothing but came and sat beside me."

"And?"

"Then I woke up."

"Hmm." I wondered what that represented. I had to be on his mind. A lot. "That's so bizarre because I was in this art gallery a few weeks ago with my friend Vicky, and I was drawn to a painting of colorful fishing shacks."

"We connect soulfully. Don't we?"

"Yes. Yes, we really do. I don't understand it though."

"We don't need to try and understand. Let's just enjoy each other."

"Yes."

"I'll let you go for now. If you have a chance, write me later. Bye, my sweet lady."

After we talked, I sat for a while unable to move, tears falling, thinking how happy he was making me feel.

***

I picked up Vicky and drove to Provincetown. The ride was peaceful, beautiful, and other worldly, especially as we passed through stark, desert-like Truro on Rte. 6A. I parked in the large paid-parking lot near the wharf. Provincetown streets were desolate, and some stores hadn't re-opened for the new season. We liked it; it was easier to stroll the narrow sidewalks and browse in shop windows, unlike summertime when you nearly collided with dog owners and felt their breath on your neck.

Vicky wanted to replenish some healing stones and crystals; she had a huge collection. She told me they were great for enhancing meditation and the healing of body and mind—educating me on each stone's purpose.

"Pink quartz is known to remove negative energy. Right?"

"Absolutely."

"Good. Pick me up the largest one you see," I said.

"You going to give it to Steve?" she grinned.

"I should."

I crossed to the opposite side of the street into a jewelry store, and after poking around I bought a silver Claddagh bangle bracelet, handcrafted by a local artist. I felt a little guilty since I was no longer working, but I hadn't bought myself anything in months. As I left the store, an older woman was entering. She smiled as I held the door. "Thank you." She reeked of lavender. I quickly covered my mouth and nose and hurried out. I could feel bile coming up in my throat. After heaving, I sat on the edge of the sidewalk, recovering.

> *March 1, 1968*
>
> *Dear Diary,*
>
> *I hate going to Father's house! That smell that is always there makes me sick. Today after cookies and milk, he pulled a snake from his pants and said it was a gift from God. He made me lick it. Father made those weird noises. Then the snake spit in my mouth. I had to run to the bathroom and throw-up. I hate it there!! I have to keep my promise. I don't want to!*

I saw Vicky headed my way and stood up.

She looked at me. "You all right?"

"Yeah. I'm fine. Let's go."

Vicky and I explored a few more stores, then walked on the wharf to the end of the dock. The air was chilly but refreshing. We stopped a couple of times to take a closer look at the big fishing boats. Afterward, we got a bite to eat at Fanizzi's on

Commercial Street, a popular Italian and seafood restaurant that offered beautiful bay views. I knew Steve would be mad, but I was having a good time with Vicky. And I had no desire to rush back. I called Steve to let him know where I was and told him I wouldn't be home for dinner. He wasn't pleased. *Mad, mad, mad… breathe.*

"Why didn't you tell me sooner?"

"This wasn't planned. I'll be home as soon as we're through eating."

Vicky and I both opted for shrimp cocktail. She had a scallop plate with mixed greens and mashed potato, and I had chicken piccata with gluten-free linguine.

"Vicky, why can't I love my husband?"

"Look at the way he treats you."

"It's not like he's beaten me or anything like that."

"Do you hear yourself? That's what abused women say. He hasn't been a good husband."

"But maybe I haven't been such a good wife either."

"I'm not behind your doors—but I don't believe that for a minute."

"I don't think he wants me to be happy."

"He'll always be miserable—so probably not."

Just the way she said that as her lashes fluttered made me laugh. It was far from funny, more like sad. But we couldn't stop laughing.

The waiter came to take our plates.

"Are you ladies considering dessert tonight?"

I looked at Vicky and grinned. "Let's do it."

The tall, handsome man handed us the dessert menu. We shared a flourless chocolate cake, and each of us had a crème de cacao.

"Great choice, ladies," the man replied with his gorgeous smile.

Vicky bent forward at the table, nearly knocking her head against mine. "Why are all gay men so damn good-looking?"

I smiled, shrugging.

Chapter 40

The text came promptly at 11:00 a.m. *Hi.*

I took a deep breath. *Hi, how are you?*

Great. I had this dream about you and me.

Hmm. Another one.

Tell me about it.

I had this dream we were making love at the beach. The sky was pink as the sun was going down. The water was calm. We were wrapped in this blue blanket. He dreams in color.

He said no more. I knew he was waiting for my response; I didn't know what to say.

We hardly knew each other, at least in that respect, and he was already dreaming about making love with me—in a beautiful setting. I should have been appalled with this impulsion of his, but truthfully, I was flattered. It was not like I was a young woman; at this age I found it a compliment.

He sent another text.

Are u still there?

Yeah I'm here.

Maybe I shouldn't have said that.

Maybe not, but I'm glad you did.

Are you sure?

Yes.

Can we talk?

When my phone rang, my heart pounded faster. "Hello, Rob."

"Do you know what your voice does to me?"

"Probably what yours does to me."

"I want more than just your voice. I wanna hold you in my arms."

"That would be so nice." But was it realistic, knowing the circumstances?

"My sons and I were together this weekend and we got talking. They asked me about my relationships when I was younger. And all I wanted to tell them is how we come together—how you make me feel."

"But you didn't?"

"No, but they did say I seemed happier lately."

"Do you think they know something?" I asked.

"I don't know. Kids are smart."

"I know they're not kids anymore, but they know you well enough."

"Yeah. I just wanna tell the world how I feel," he said.

"I know—I do too. But the people in it wouldn't understand."

"The world can judge us all they want. We can't worry about them—they can't feel what we feel."

"It's crazy. It just seems like it happened so fast," I said.

"Because it was there—right away."

I couldn't argue that. If something feels good and right, it must be.

Chapter 41

On Sunday, I decided not to ask Steve to go with me to pick up Mom. Whatever is to happen—will happen. I wanted to be alone with her; I needed to be alone with her. Besides, Steve didn't get our bond—our closeness. Even if it had been dysfunctional.

"Where are you going?" Steve asked, seeing me put on my jacket.

"To see Mom."

He didn't ask to come, and I wasn't surprised. In fact, he seemed almost relieved that I didn't ask.

"Have a nice time," he said.

***

"Come on, Mom, it's just you and me today," I said when I got to her room. She was dressed and ready to go.

"Oh good," she said.

I signaled to the head nurse to buzz us through the locked doors. Hand in hand we strolled down the corridor like best friends. Parts of her mind, I believed, knew where she was and where she preferred to be, but she was unable to convey that.

Suddenly, Mom stopped and looked my way and smiled. "I'm so happy to be with you."

I pulled her close to me. "Me too, Mom." It was those tender moments I will always hold close to my heart.

Passersby, visitors, and staff alike stopped when they saw Mom and greeted her with a warm smile and a friendly "Hello." Many even addressed her by her first name. Mom seemed to have become quite popular since she arrived. And she could be vivacious and certainly bold when expressing herself. People admired that fearlessness, I think—some wishing they could speak their own mind that way.

"Hi, Evelyn," said a tall, middle-aged woman accompanied by a shorter, burly, gray-haired man. Her husband, I assumed.

"Hi," Mom said back.

The couple stopped walking. "Is this your daughter?" the woman asked.

Mom nodded.

"Yes, I am," I said, my hand held out.

She took it. "Nice to meet you. You look like your mom."

"Thank you." Other than a similar stature, I had never noticed a resemblance. I had my dad's green eyes, his nose, and his wavy hair. But I was sure Mom liked hearing that.

"I'm Erin and this is my husband, Philip. Your mom is in the room next to my mother's."

"Oh, your mom is Dorothy. She is a sweet lady," I said, even though she never spoke, oblivious as most of them. But Dorothy's twinkling eyes and her strawberry lips always made me smile.

"Yeah, she is. Thank you. Have a wonderful day."

"You too."

"Bye," Mom said, as we walked away.

"Bye, Evelyn."

It was a beautiful afternoon, and the sun was glowing in an azure sky. After Mom and I had brunch at Hearth and Kettle, I drove around areas that Mom might recognize. I slowed the car to a crawl as we approached the old farmhouse. "Do you know this house?" I asked her.

She nodded. "Yup. It's my daddy's." The property had long been sold, when her stepmother died, but Mom had forgotten.

"Yes, it is. It's where you grew up."

"Can we stop?"

"Nobody's home right now."

"Oh," she said sadly.

I continued down the road to a beach Mom took me to often when I was little. She didn't seem to recognize it. Or maybe she had seen it enough. Places and memories that no longer seemed to matter. However, it amazed me how some things are never forgotten, never lost. Things that have a lifetime impact on us—like love. How wonderful love is when it is present.

Afterward, I pulled up at Sesuit Harbor and parked. The blue sky now had a few stationary clouds. But the sun's rays streaming through the windshield swaddled me in a warmth. "Mom, look at all the boats, the yachts." She glanced at them but seemingly never saw them. Focusing seemed too taxing for her until she turned to me and looked lovingly into my eyes. She reached her hand over and gently wrapped a tendril of my hair that had escaped my braid around my ear and said tenderly, "I just want you to be happy."

Mom, that's all I ever wanted for you—to be happy. Where did that come from? How could she have known? A mother's instinct. She was gentle and sweet. Even her deep voice took on a softer side. The soft side of her that she had kept locked up. Maybe in fear that people would find her sweet side a sign of weakness.

I reached over to the passenger's seat and wrapped my arms around her. "I know, Mom."

"That's good."

"I love you, Mom," I said, searching her watery eyes.

"I love you."

I turned away as my own eyes filled with tears and started the engine.

Chapter 42

I picked up Henri and held her close to me and stared out the window above the sink. The morning sky was leaden with bleak clouds. The gloom didn't faze me; I had plenty to do inside. Besides, a good portion of my day would be spent with Rob, and that always made me happy.

The first text came when I knew it would, 11:00 a.m.

Rob and I were able to talk more freely about so many things. We talked about movies we'd seen and liked or didn't like and why. We both liked plays and nature and art galleries. I was letting myself be vulnerable, letting him into my heart and soul. We were learning even more about each other, even stuff from our past that we had kept secret.

"As a child I was accused of being too lovable," he said.

"There's nothing wrong with that."

"My family thought so—they called me a faggot. When all I knew was, I saw wonder in everything. I loved all people. Birds and animals. Trees and flowers..."

"They didn't know how lucky they were—to have a child like you."

He was quiet.

"When I was young, I sent an older woman a greeting card, signing it with love. Which I always did with anyone I cared about. And I meant it. Do you know what she told me?" I asked.

"No. Tell me."

"She told me I used the word 'love' too freely. That made me wonder if I did—maybe I was cheapening its meaning?"

"Never feel that way. You can never have too much 'love' inside you. More love is what we all need."

"Yeah, for sure."

"When I was a toddler and my parents went out for the evening, one of my dad's brothers would babysit me and fill my bottle with alcohol."

"Oh my God—that's awful. Did you get sick?" *Why would someone do something like that? Did it intoxicate him?*

"I don't know."

What kind of brain damage would that do—when a child's mind is not yet developed, I wondered. Obviously, this still bothered him. It made me wonder what else had happened to him when he was young. *He suffered too.*

He seemed reluctant to talk anymore about it and changed the subject.

"Do you like art?"

"I do. Most art, that is. I'm not a fan of abstract art—maybe because I don't get it. It looks sloppy to me—like anyone could splash paint on like that."

"Yeah, I understand why you'd feel that way. I went to an art school in Boston in the Back Bay. A studio for pen and ink."

"Wow," I said. "Do you have anything you could show me? I'd love to see your work?"

"I do. I can send a few pics later today that I have here on my computer."

"That'd be great. Can't wait to see them."

"So, Miss Aimee what else do you like to do?"

"I like a roaring fire in a fireplace. We had one the other night—I pretended you were the flame." I wanted to tell him how Steve had acted but opted otherwise. What was the sense of bringing up negative when everything between Rob and me was positive? Pleasant. Wonderful.

"Don't have to pretend. I *am* the flame—that will always keep you warm."

I took a deep breath, feeling like a melting marshmallow beneath that flame. "Oh."

"I'd love to sit by a fire with you—in a cabin on a cold, snowy night—you and I sipping hot chocolate with whipped cream, blanket around us, watching the fire till it was just embers burning," he said.

"That sounds perfect."

"I know it would be perfect with you."

"Yeah," I said, taking a deep breath. "I really should get going." Even though I never wanted our conversations to end. We were tantalizing each other, whether intentional or not. My adrenaline was climbing so high with desire for him that I was getting even less sleep at night.

Later that day, Rob sent me some of his work. One of a wolf, a deer, and a bird, and another of a fisherman. I had seen pen and ink drawings but not as good as this. He had an exceptional eye for detail. I couldn't wait to tell him; I wrote him an email and a text.

You're so humble—you have so much talent. Have you sold many—you must get a lot of requests.

He texted back.

Yes, I've sold quite a few. I have them in several local shops—even in a local gallery. And I have sold to friends too.

That's great!

It takes a lot of time.

I'm sure it does. They're amazing!

Thank you. xoxo

I forwarded his work to an artist friend of mine, named Heather—I valued her opinion. With his permission, of course. She was a well-respected art teacher and a talented artist herself. I could barely wait for her thoughts.

***

When Heather responded, the following day, I realized I wasn't biased because of my feelings for him. She verified what I saw; she thought Rob's work was exceptional and should be displayed at local galleries.

I wanted to tell Rob right away. I messaged him.

I got an email back from my artist friend I told you about. She loves your work!

I waited anxiously for his response.

Chapter 43

At the end of the narrow driveway, Vicky was getting out of her car. I parked behind her. She was stunning in her purple parka and scarf. A gust of wind blew her long, wavy hair. At noon it was in the high forties and felt like a heat wave after the low temperatures. New England weather was unpredictable. *Like people. Who can we depend on? Trust?*

"Can I help?" I asked, after seeing her pull a grocery bag out of the car.

She reached into the front seat of the car and handed me a beautiful bouquet of daffodils, lilies, and peonies with baby's breath.

"You bought me flowers?" I asked, grinning.

"Yeah right."

While she was putting away her groceries, I clipped the ends of the flowers and stuck them in a white vase, then set it in the center of the table. Vicky boiled water for tea and brought out a plate of lemon cookies.

"You must be in love," I said.

"What makes you say that?"

"You're glowing—your eyes are sparkling. You look radiant. Flowers…"

"I don't want to jinx it." Then she gave me this slow smile. "There is this one guy. He's spiritual—and single."

And young, I assumed.

I gave her two thumbs-up. "You going to show me a picture?"

She seemed reluctant but did.

He looked younger than her, but his beard and mustache along with slivers of gray throughout his dark hair made him look older. I guessed mid-forties. Handsome, of course. I knew there were men out there who liked older women, but I was certain it was either for sex or their money. Some even searching for a mother who was never there.

"He's very nice-looking. Where does he live?"

"Arizona."

"You could fly there in no time—or even drive." Vicky had

gone more than once to meet guys who lived in various parts of the United States. She preferred the drives; she was fearless. She'd stay in low-priced motels where all walks of life would come and stay. I'd feel safer camping in the woods with *four*-legged animals.

I just hoped this new guy could fulfill her more, her every need.

"Tell me—what's happening with you and Rob?"

"Vicky, Rob has no idea how much of an effect he has on me—well maybe he does," I said, rolling my eyes. "He evokes these feelings in me… His voice alone and just the anticipation of his next text, my heart speeds like a race car."

"That sounds like love to me."

"Yeah, feels like it." *Or desperation.* "But how could I ever trust him though, knowing what he does behind his wife's back?"

"Maybe it's not behind her back. Maybe she knows. Maybe they have an open relationship."

"Unless she just doesn't do anything with him."

"She had to do something—she had two kids with him."

I sighed. "Yeah, you got a point there."

"He could feel the same way—about you. You're married."

I twisted my mouth. "You're right—I'm no different. Why do some women stick with their men when they know they cheat on them?"

"It's sad if you ask me. I guess they're just insecure."

I shook my head. "God, I don't ever want to be that insecure. At least not in that way…"

"Hey, I made some homemade chicken soup last night—want a bowl?" Vicky asked.

"Sure—that sounds really good. I have this scratchy throat."

"You're not getting sick, are you?"

"No, I feel fine. Probably just an allergy to something."

"Yeah, maybe your husband."

We laughed.

We sat in front of the fireplace in rocking chairs with our soup, staring into the fire. Vicky amused me, filling me in on a couple of guys she'd been pursuing on Facebook, but she now had no more with them than a friendly connection. Vicky still had fun with the chase and took pleasure in any attention they gave her—no matter how diminutive. She never picked an ugly man or an old one. And, of course, they had to be spiritual. Even better if they believed in fairies and lived in that fairyland that she was fervent about.

"When do you think you and Rob will see each other?"

"Well, we haven't made any real plans yet. But I'm sure we will soon."

"But you're both still married," Vicky said softly.

"I know," I said quietly, exhaling deeply. "Did you have to remind me?"

"Steve is never going to let you leave."

"It's not what he wants."

"I am afraid I'll see you on *48 Hours* someday."

"I hope not. His temper does scare me though at times."

"It would scare me too," she said, shaking her head. "If it was me, I would've left him long ago."

"It's not always easy, you know. So many things I need to consider. I don't even know if I can make it on my own. And I'm so stressed out lately—half the time I can't think straight. Sleep would help."

"Have you tried a sleeping aid?"

"They don't work."

"I know you have a lot going on, but if you're not happy with Steve..."

"How many married couples do you think are truly happy? Some are afraid to leave—for whatever reason."

"You have a choice..."

I sighed. "I just don't want to end up like the rest of my relatives either. Copy their actions. *Till death do us part.* Divorce isn't always the solution. None of them seemed any happier."

"Living in hell isn't right either. I'll never get married again," Vicky said.

How long WILL I remain in this perdition?

"Really? You might feel differently someday. You just haven't found the right one yet. One that makes you feel so wonderful you want to rush to the peak of a mountain and shout his name."

Vicky's eyebrows lifted. "I know you're not talking about your husband."

My phone rang. "It's Steve," I mouthed.

Chapter 44

As soon as I walked through the locked doors, I caught a strong whiff of urine. Indicating a shortage of aides. I noticed a new bouquet of flowers in a fancy vase. It didn't help. Just another contribution, after a resident's funeral. I glanced up at the video camera and waved. After looking for Mom in her room, and neighboring ones, I went back to the nurses' station. A short, heavy-set nurse I hadn't seen before appeared from the small room behind the counter where the medication was prepped.

"Hi," I said. "Is nurse Betsy here?"

"She's off today. I'm filling in. I'm Cynthia Crane," she said, her silky eyelashes fluttering over her cute button nose.

"Nice to meet you. I'm looking for my mom. I checked her room, the cafeteria. The activities room."

"Who's your mom?"

"Evelyn—she's in room 103."

"She's right over there," Cynthia said, pointing.

I shook my head. "Where?"

"Right there—in the chair."

I had looked straight at my mom and didn't recognize her. I rushed over, finding her incapacitated in a geri chair—slumped over, eyes closed.

I kneeled beside her. "Mom… Mom. Do you hear me?" Nothing. Unresponsive. I picked up her hand; it was lifeless. I looked to see if she was breathing; it was hard to tell. I put two of my fingers to her mouth and watched her chest to see if it rose. Barely.

"Oh my God, oh my God! What's wrong with her? She's hardly breathing. She looks like she's dying."

"Maybe you should call hospice. I'm sorry."

"Hospice? What are you saying? She was fine yesterday."

"I don't know—I'm just filling in. This is the way she was when I came in this morning."

"And nobody checks her out to see what's wrong?" I said, glaring at her. The nurse looked afraid of me. *I wouldn't hurt a soul, but then again, don't hurt anyone I love.*

"Is she dehydrated?" I asked.

"She's not. I gave her a few sips of water."

"A few sips? Are you serious—what the hell does a few sips do? I'm not even in the medical field and I know better."

I pulled my phone from my purse and called Steve. "Steve, get over here. Now!"

"Where—where are you?"

"I'm at the nursing home. They are fuckin' killing her!" I yelled. I didn't care who heard me.

"Coming—"

Steve arrived in a matter of minutes.

"What's going on?" he asked the nurse. "What did you do to Evelyn?"

"I didn't do anything. She was just given a little medication to calm her down."

"What medication?" I asked. "I told them no medication. What's wrong with you people—doesn't anyone listen?"

She looked at me defensively. "I'm just following orders."

"You overdosed her!"

"No. I did not."

"Call in the doctor who approved this drug," Steve demanded.

Nurse Cynthia looked bewildered. "I don't think I can do that."

"You better or I'm going to call the police," Steve said, glowering.

The doctor happened to be in the building and came right away. She came down the corridor toward us and nodded.

"Why did you allow this? I specified over and over not to give my mother any medication."

"The staff was having a hard time managing her. By law, the dosage we gave her is acceptable—just enough to calm her."

"Calm her? She's practically dead! This is not acceptable—I don't give a damn what the law says."

"Doctors are supposed to try and save patients, not try to kill them," Steve snapped.

"She needs to go to the hospital. Like now! If something

happens to her, you'll never hear the end of me. Do you understand?" I asked.

"I do."

"Good. You better."

"Are you threatening me?" the doctor asked.

"No, I don't threaten anyone."

The doctor had the nurse take her blood immediately; Mom was dehydrated. An ambulance took her to the hospital. Hallelujah.

"This is proof," I said to Steve when we got home. "Everyone needs an advocate, someone watching out for them."

Steve shrugged. "It's done. There's nothing you can do about it now."

Steve stormed upstairs.

I stayed up, replaying the events in my head. It hadn't been long after Mom returned from Ellsworth that the nursing home staff wanted to send her back there because she wasn't behaving, following their orders, but Ellsworth refused their request. And since the small amount of Ativan they were giving her wasn't working, they obviously increased the dosage. It was the only way, they believed, to get her under *their* control.

I fell asleep on the sofa.

***

"Why are you sleeping here?" Steve asked, nudging me.

I opened one eye. "I didn't plan to."

"Well, get up and make breakfast." I knew he was upset because I didn't sleep with him. *I am more than just a body in our bed.*

"Go to the coffee shop and get breakfast," I said as I walked away.

The house was quiet when I came down after my shower. I poured myself a cup of coffee and called Vicky, filling her in on what had transpired in the last twenty-four hours with Mom at the nursing home.

"Can you believe it? If I hadn't gone in yesterday—she'd be dead now."

"That's why that nurse didn't want you visiting so much. You were right about them."

"I had this gut feeling—you know what I mean?"

"Oh yeah. I've heard several stories about nursing homes—never knew if they were true."

"I have seen cases come across my desk through the years. And I thought these clients were exaggerating. Now I know they weren't."

"So now what's going to happen to your mom?" Vicky asked.

"She'll be recuperating at the hospital for a while. At least I feel relieved that she's there—even if it is for a short time."

"If there's anything I can do, let me know."

"I will. Thanks."

Chapter 45

"When I walked into the hospital room, a nurse's aide was sitting with Mom, holding a notebook and pen. I quietly sat in a chair nearby. "Six and six is twelve," Mom told her.

"Your mom and I have been doing math equations. She's amazing with numbers," said the pretty young woman.

Mom looked my way. "Aimee, come sit by me. I have something to tell you."

The aide stood up. "I will leave you two alone. I'll come by later, Evelyn."

"What, Mom, what is it?" I asked, sidled beside her on the bed. She seemed quite lucid today. I hadn't seen signs of that in a long time.

"When you were a child, I left you in the hands of the church."

I nodded. *"I'm to watch you, while your mother is at work." Cross. Gothic windows, tall ceilings.*

"That was wrong of me. Very wrong. The biggest mistake of my life. Watching your behavior brought back memories of me being abused—by the pastor."

"Pastor? Abused?"

"Yeah. That's why I left the Protestant church and became Catholic. But the kind of faith didn't matter. They're just men. I am so sorry," Mom said. "Will you forgive me?"

"You're a good girl—an angel. And never tell anyone—it's between you and me. And God."

"Aimee, you do forgive me, don't you? Aimee?"

I was shaken out of reverie.

"Yes, Mom. Of course, I forgive you. It wasn't your fault." *Was it my fault?* I took her hand in mine, holding it securely but gently, and looked into her eyes. *You suffered too. I know that now.*

While Mom and I were eating ice cream, which I'd ordered from the cafeteria, I checked my messages.

Hey, I miss you. Where are you?

I'm at the hospital.

Hospital? You okay? No.

Yeah. Whatever okay is. *Mom is here.*

Call me when you get a chance.

I left the hospital an hour later. When I got in my car, I called Rob and filled him in. Omitting the surprising factor Mom had revealed. I couldn't wrap my head around it. Is this why she exposed herself to those injuring relationships? *Love me and I will hurt you.*

"Oh, my sweet lady, I wish I was there."

"I wish you were too. I just want you to hold me."

"Right now, I'm holding you in my thoughts. I'm wrapping my arms around you. Can you feel that?" *"Don't be afraid, Angel."*

I laid my head back against the seat and closed my eyes. "Yes. Yes, I can."

I was listening to him breathe when I was startled by someone slamming a car door next to me. I opened my eyes and sat up more aware.

"Hey, are you still there?" he asked.

"I'm going home now. I'll text you later."

I tried working on my new book. But didn't get far. *Maybe I'm just not a novelist.* All I wanted to do was to write to Rob. *Distraction.* He was the only thing on my mind. Right or wrong, he was now a big part of my life. I stood up, went to the closet, and pulled out the vacuum. Before turning it on, I checked my phone. Again. *Love or obsession?*

Hey, you feel like talking?

Yeah.

My phone rang.

"Hi, what are you doing?"

"Besides talking to you, I'm looking out the window at a sparrow that just perched on a fir branch."

"Do you like birds?"

"Yes. Some are so lovely—like the cardinals and the bluebirds—you can't help but stare."

"Lovely like you. I stare at your profile picture every day."

I started to tingle.

"Hey, will you do me a favor?" I asked.

"Sure. What is it?"

"Put the phone down, get your guitar, and sing to me. I want to hear the song you're writing for me."

"I haven't quite finished."

"I don't care—please."

"Okay."

I listened to him strum the guitar. His voice was controlled and on key. And gorgeous. Sexy. It was hard to believe that someone could make me feel so turned on.

"Thank you—that was so beautiful."

"You're beautiful."

I take a deep breath. "You can make a girl blush." Not that I'm a girl anymore—but he made me feel like one. *And a woman too. His.*

"Well, you are, you know. Has your husband ever told you?"

"Maybe—not lately anyway."

"I'm sure he knows you are—and afraid of other men looking at you."

"He gets angry if he thinks another guy is looking at me. I don't know why he feels this way—I've never cheated on him… ever." *Until now. But am I cheating?*

"I think he's just a little insecure with a wife so beautiful. So wonderful."

Rob would continuously build my self-esteem, my confidence. My self-worth. He brightened my days. And lightened my burdens. I was convinced someone up above brought him into my life at the perfect time. Despite our situations. He'd entered my life with impeccable timing.

"Does your wife know how lucky she is—to have you?"

"I don't know. We check in with each other at least once a day to see how the other is doing. Her working, I do the shopping and prepare dinner."

"How sweet," I said, biting my tongue, trying hard to hide my jealousy. It killed me to ask, but I needed to know. "Do you love her?"

"Yes. She's a good woman."

"That's nice."

"She sweeps everything under the carpet though."

"What do you mean—like what?"

"Lots of things. Once I tried talking to her about different ways of making love. She told me to go find a whore."

"Oh wow."

"She was sexually molested when she was young by her uncle—maybe that's part of it."

"I always heard that an abused person is promiscuous."

"Sometimes they go the opposite way—refrain from sex."

"Oh," I said, as I pondered the scenario. "That makes sense."

"What about you?" he asked.

"Me?" *No, I haven't been abused—not in that way…*

"Do you love your husband?" *Please don't ask me about our sex life.*

"I love him. But I'm not *in* love with him anymore."

"What happened—do you want to talk about it?"

"Not really. Not now."

"Okay," he said quietly.

"I should get going," I said.

"Sure, I know it's getting late for you. Talk later?"

"Yeah."

Rob seemed to have this infatuation with me, but he loved his wife. At least that's what he claimed. Unless he felt for her the way I felt about Steve. How can we not love our spouses? They have been a part of our lives for many years. Though I was enjoying this relationship with Rob, it was beginning to take a toll on me emotionally. I don't know how people lead a double life. Rob seemed sincere. The excitement was there, the chemistry too, but I wasn't sure if it was all real. Maybe our marriages had become stagnant, and we needed something new. Refreshing. Tantalizing. To wake us up. Or maybe we had just married too soon—the wrong one.

Chapter 46

At the hospital, a woman came into Mom's room and introduced herself as Elizabeth, head of registration. She asked me to meet her at the nurses' station on that floor. My curiosity was piqued. What could she possibly have to say? Were they going to send her to a psych ward too? I hustled down the hallway.

Elizabeth suggested I take a seat. "I'm fine—I prefer to stand. Thank you."

"Your mom will be leaving the hospital in a few days. Do you want her to go back to where she was?"

At first, I was taken aback.

"No," I said, shaking my head. "But I can't afford—she has only Medicare and Medicaid."

"She's still eligible to be placed elsewhere."

"I didn't know we had that option."

"You do—and there are a couple of places right now with beds available." After giving me the names of the two facilities, I asked her which one she would suggest—which one had the better reputation.

Taking Elizabeth's advice with her knowledge about Saint Mary's, I concurred. "Thank you. I appreciate your help very much."

"You're welcome. I think you'll be happy with this decision."

I was ecstatic knowing Mom wouldn't have to go back to that dreadful place. If I had known I could have moved her out of there sooner. I would have. Now I was just worried about her adjusting to another new environment. Could she take the transition?

I could hardly wait to tell Rob the good news; it was like I was telling him everything lately. And he was the only one who seemed to take an interest in Mom's welfare. Steve and the rest of the relatives seemed to have bowed out.

"That's wonderful, my lady." I got chills when he called me his lady. It was probably only a salutation, but it felt special. Sometimes I'd forget that he and I were both married to someone else.

"Yes. Yes, it is. I don't know too much about this place, but it has to be better than where she was."

"I'm sure it is." There was a pause. "Hey, if you could pack up right now and go somewhere, where would you go?" Rob asked.

"That's easy—I'd come visit you."

"Maybe we could arrange something soon?"

"Yeah, it would be so nice to see you in person again," I said, taking a deep breath.

"What do you want deep down?" he asked. *I want you. And I want you to want me.* I knew what he really wanted to hear, but I held back.

"You know, this chaotic world continues to become more and more materialistic and robotic. I just want simple. The way it was when I was young. We didn't have much, but we were happy."

"Simple is good. We don't need as much as we think."

"I know that now."

"You have a lot of wisdom, my lady."

"When I was young, all I ever dreamed about was having a nice car and a beautiful home. It was like I was enthralled with these material things..."

"And now?"

"I have found a human being who's captivated me more..."

"I'm smiling," he said quietly.

"Ohh..."

"So, what do you think about you and I living together?" he asked.

What! Am I dreaming? "I think it would be wonderful—we have so much in common. And I think we'd get along great."

"I don't have much money, but I can keep a roof over your head."

"That's all I need. A roof and you," I said.

"You sure about that?"

"Yeah. Never been more sure."

"I'm getting another call. I really should take this."

"Sure. I'll talk to you later." I was inside out with desire.

***

"Haley is going to love this doll, Vicky," I said.

Vicky was finishing up a cloth doll she'd been making for her granddaughter, Haley, for her birthday. She had used art pencils and fine-tip pens for the face. Now she was adding purple eyelash yarn for her hair, and enhancing it with pink ribbon, giving the doll a whimsical look.

"I hope so—I've put a lot of time into this. She's so spoiled, I don't even know if she'll appreciate it."

"I'm sure she will—she'll always remember it came from her grandma. And it's more special because you made it."

Vicky looked up from her work. "You haven't said anything lately—how's it going with Rob?"

"We spend every waking moment with each other." I'm not going to tell her he mentioned about us living together. Even though it sounds wonderful, it's not sensible. *Aimee, you have to face reality.*

"Huh?"

"Rob and I are talking on the phone, emailing, or texting till we go to bed at night. I'm even in his dreams!"

"With your husband there?"

"Yup. Even when he's there. He acts like I'm not there anyway."

"You talk on the phone in front of him?"

"Oh no, of course not."

Steve provided me with material things and Rob gave me what I needed emotionally. I had thought I had made the right decision at twenty-seven when I married Steve, nearly twenty-two years ago. *Wow, none of my relatives had made it that far in their marriage.* He worked hard. He didn't cheat. Didn't hang out at bars. But I neglected how important communication was and having the same interests. While dating Steve, I saw only the passive side of him. It was after we married that his aggressive side emerged. The monster appeared. It might have always been there, but smoking pot mellowed him. I caught on after finding bottles of Visine in his work pockets. I insisted that he stop. It was after that this anger in him evolved. Boundless and raw.

"You're still a lucky woman—you have two men who care about you."

"I don't know if you can call it lucky. I've always been a one-man woman."

"It doesn't matter how you look at it—you're doing better than me."

Am I? Am I really?

"You are free to do what you want."

"I can't do this forever. I'm not young anymore."

"You're the youngest 'senior' I've ever met."

She smiled modestly, then looked at me. "You could be free too, you know."

I sighed. "Maybe someday. Steve brings me down. Rob lifts me up. I don't know where this is all going with Rob, if anywhere, but I can't give him up—I won't. Then there's Mom. I just don't know how to handle it all anymore. I am exhausted. I can't sleep at night. I feel like I'm losing my mind. I don't know what to do," I cried.

"Well, there's really nothing you can do for your mom. It's up to them to take care of her."

"Yeah. But look what happened last time."

She flashed a wry smile. "As far as you and Rob—only you and he can figure that out. Have you thought about talking to someone?"

"You mean a shrink?"

"Yeah. Wouldn't hurt."

"I don't know—I have to think about it."

"What's there to think about?"

"He'll ask all these personal questions—and how can I tell him about Rob?"

"That's up to you. He or she will ask invasive questions. But if you want to get better, you need to be able to open up. Sometimes it's easier to talk to a stranger," Vicky said.

"Yup, and they'll dive into the past. Starting with my childhood. I don't know about this—it's going to make me totally uncomfortable."

"You need the help—you need to get over that."

I nodded.

***

I scanned the internet for psychologists within a fifty-mile radius. I was unsure if I should choose a man or a woman; I just wanted someone I'd feel at ease with. I read a few profiles and one doctor's background really caught my attention, especially his knowledge and expertise regarding sleep and anxiety disorders. After contacting him, he set me up for an appointment the following Tuesday.

Chapter 47

I was apprehensive. *What if I become vulnerable and reveal everything to this therapist, this stranger, my deepest, darkest secrets, my fears and anxieties? Worse scenario: What if I can't be fixed—I'll always be broken?* My mind was whirling with reservations. *Even more atrocious, what if he tells me I must give up Rob, that he's only a figment of my run-away imagination.*

I parked in the large lot that had several professional businesses: lawyers, doctors, accountants. I scanned the big, white, wooden sign with black letters. At last, I saw "Dr. Bernard Bentley, Psychologist."

I held the door for a sad-looking, middle-aged woman walking out of the two-story building. I wondered what she was enduring in her life. Illness, death, desertion. Abuse. Unlikely an affair? Then I lowered my head, thinking she was wondering the same. I walked up one flight of carpeted stairs and turned right, stopping at the first door on the left. I saw his name. My hands began to tremble. I exhaled a deep breath and turned the doorknob.

I sat in a wing chair in the large, vacant waiting room. I felt awkward—I wondered what the doctor would think when he saw me. Other than I looked like hell. Whopping bags and dark circles under my eyes and thin as a twig.

"Aimee?" he asked, coming out of his office into the waiting room.

I nodded, rising.

"Dr. Bentley. Nice to meet you," he said, extending his hand. My palms were sweaty; I didn't want to reciprocate. *It'd be a dead giveaway.* Still, I took his hand. "Come in."

He nodded to an oversized chair about a foot away from his desk. *What, no sofa?* As he was taking a copy of my insurance card, I quickly surveyed his office. He had two bookcases, both filled with soft and hard covers on various mental disorders. *Am I in one?*

Dr. Bentley was a tall man with short dark hair and a mustache. His dress was casual—khaki pants, a plaid shirt, and tan loafers. I figured he was five years older than me. He spoke quietly. Even though we were only about a foot from each other, I had to lean forward in the chair to hear him.

"No drugs or alcohol?" he asked.

"No," I said, shaking my head. I watched Dr. Bentley as he scanned the intake questions that had been mailed to me prior to the visit.

He looked up at me. "You don't take any medications?"

I shook my head again. "No."

"Have you ever thought about harming yourself?"

"Sometimes I wish I had a broken leg. Or I wish I was really sick—anything but this stuff going on in my head."

"What brought you here?"

My girlfriend thought it was a good idea. How pathetic. "Sometimes, I feel like I'm falling apart—my life is messed up," I stuttered.

"How so?"

I was sure I'd overwhelm him if I told him everything at once. I saw him waiting for my response. *Where do I start?*

"I'm afraid."

"What are you afraid of?" he asked.

"I'm afraid this isn't going to work." *My last resort. My only one.*

"What do you mean—what isn't going to work?"

"I don't think you can help me?"

"But you're here—"

"Because I'm hoping…"

"Okay," he said quietly. "Tell me what you would like to achieve."

I shrugged. "I suppose a lot, but I'd like to be able to sleep," I said with tears forming. "I could think better—figure things out."

"How long has it been since you slept through the night?" I shrugged. "Days? Weeks?"

I shook my head. "Years," I said, clutching the purse on my lap. Wanting to run out of there. His eyebrows lifted. Then he scratched his chin. He didn't believe me. Who would? *He saw me as a basket case.*

He was staring. *Is he trying to analyze me?*

"Have you tried medication?"

"I've tried it all—nothing helps."

"Okay. Can you tell me a little about what's going on in your life?"

He waited for me to respond while I stared at the floor.

I looked up at him. "I don't even know where to begin."

"Start wherever you like."

"I was taking care of my mother, but now she's in a nursing home. She has dementia."

"Well, that's a lot of responsibility. And demanding. Were you getting any help?"

"Not really," I said quietly.

"I see here you're married," he said, referring to his paperwork.

I nodded.

"Has your husband been able to assist in some way?"

I shook my head. "The best he can. He works a lot."

"Are you working?"

"No, not now—Mom needed full care.... So I left my job at the law firm," I trailed off, tears falling.

"What was it like growing up in your family?" he asked, handing me a tissue. He had a couple boxes of Kleenex.

I guess we were starting with my childhood. It is said we become a product of our beginning, from the time we are in our mother's womb, and are shaped from there. *And the unborn knows more than just vibrations.*

"Umm, my mom was a good mom, protective of me. Overly protective—much of a control freak really. She divorced my dad when I was young. I was turning six."

"That must have been hard."

"It was—I missed him. Terribly."

"What was your dad like?"

"He was loving and generous and kind. And always there for me."

Dr. Bentley, still looking at me, ran a finger across his chin. His eyebrows furrowing and then releasing.

"Well, when he could be. He lived in the city and worked six days a week."

"Time is almost up here," he said as he turned to his computer. Let's set you up for another appointment this week."

"Okay," I said meekly. I was disappointed—we were just getting started. I didn't see the point of getting into the past; I wanted to tell him what was happening now. *The past is over. Over!*

"How about Thursday—same time?"

I nodded. "Yeah, that's fine."

He filled out the appointment card and handed it to me.

"Thank you," I said and left his office.

***

"How'd it go?" Vicky asked, pouring me a cup of tea.

"It's hard to say—we really didn't get far. After he went over the intake questions, there wasn't much time left. But I'm going to see him again this week."

"That's good."

"Yeah. It can't hurt," I said, staring at her collection of dangled earrings she had crafted from colored glass.

"No. It will help a lot. Help you sort things out—and see things from a different perspective."

"I hope so." *I had doubts.*

***

After leaving Vicky's, I drove to the beach. I took off my shoes and walked barefoot along the shore, the sun still high. The sand was cool, but it felt good submerging my toes into the fine grains. When I stopped to rest next to a huge boulder, I pulled the phone out of my jacket pocket and sent a text to Rob.

Hi

A minute later he sent a text back. *What are you doing?*

I'm walking the beach. I wanted to fill him in on my decision of seeing a therapist but opted otherwise; I didn't want him to be concerned.

Oh, I'll let you have your time alone.

It's okay. Besides, I want to tell you what I've been thinking about.

Tell me.

Before I could write back, my phone rang. It was Rob.

"I would love to go skydiving. I've wanted to do it my whole life, but my family talked me out of it—told me I was crazy."

"Are you fucking nuts—at your age? You could die," Steve had pleasantly pointed out.

"Why not? President Bush did it at eighty. I still have time—he didn't die. I could get killed walking across the street to get the mail."

"If that's what you want, you should do it."

"I think it'd be an incredible rush," I said as I looked into the sky, watching a helicopter soaring above.

"I had a few friends in the army who did it—their experiences sounded exciting."

"I want you to do it with me—they say you shouldn't go alone the first time."

"Oh my! I'd love to go skydiving—with you."

"Yeah, just think about it—you and I dropping from the sky… what a high!"

"Wrapped together and falling freely—hmm, sounds wonderful," he said. "Yeah, let's do it."

"Really?"

"Why not."

When? When?

I smiled as I kept walking the beach, imagining it all. The sand was still damp from high tide. Suddenly, the sky became ominous, and a fog rolled in. I could barely see two feet in front of me.

"I can't see a thing," I told him.

"I'm going to stay right here—until you are safe."

"Ow!"

"What happened?"

"I just stubbed my big toe on a rock."

"Are you okay?"

"Yeah. It just stings a little. I think I chipped the nail. I wish you were here."

"I am there—take my hand."

"Okay," I said, visualizing his hand in mine. Our fingers interlacing.

"You holding it?"

"Yes. And it's warm. Tender. I don't want to go home. I just want to be on the beach with you."

"You're always with me."

I closed my eyes and smiled. All senses attentive. On alert. His voice was clear and close, as though he was right next to me.

Chapter 48

Even though I was curious to see Mom's new home, I waited; I wanted to give her some time to adjust. Walking into St. Mary's, I smiled. Its layout and cleanliness among pleasant voices and faces were like a breath of fresh air. The first room I saw across from the nurses' station had a painted sign on the closed door: "Namaste Room." I remembered what the namaste greeting meant: the divine in me respectfully recognizes the divine in you. It invokes the feeling of spiritual oneness of heart and mind. Upon entering, I instantly plummeted into a calm, indescribable serenity. Yet, there was a tugging internal conflict I couldn't shake. I knew it was just me. I suddenly looked forward to my next visit with Dr. Bentley.

After talking with a social worker, I learned that St. Mary's once belonged to Catholic missionaries. Priests and nuns from a nearby seminary resided here if they became ill. I remembered being bussed to the seminary once or twice when I was a kid, chaperoned by monks from a catechism class. I could still recall the feeling I got when I entered that sacred place, filled with Catholic symbols and incredible, detailed carvings of religious figures. Throughout the tour I remained in a state of awe. It was as though I was transported to another world—a heaven. I could almost feel God's presence.

It had now been a week since Mom arrived. The tall nursing director, named Meredith, wanted to speak to me. I stepped into a small room. "Please have a seat," she gestured to an old Millie chair.

I sat down, my fidgety hands in my lap. Meredith was smiling so I took that as a good sign. I hoped. "I just want to tell you we took your mom off the Ativan. She's calmed a lot already. In Bellview, she had an allergic reaction to the medication that nobody picked up on for a long time. Instead of calming her, it made her more energetic than she would normally be. But that day, they gave her too much, like an overdose. Of course, they also found she was dehydrated—which made her lethargic."

"It was what I suspected right along, but you are the first to pick up on it. You're a godsend. Thank you. Thank you so much," I said, staring at her soft brown hair framing her smooth peaches and cream complexion.

After getting to know the staff and discovering this facility had a catholic history, I felt confident Mom was, finally, in a good place. A sacred place. I still visited Mom often, but not hours a day like I did at Bellview. She was now in safe hands, properly cared for. As Mom began sleeping more, I spent more of my time with Rob. Not in person, of course.

Rob and I began spending every waking moment together; all the emailing, texting, or talking back and forth lapsed into hours, eventually filling the entire day. Even the mundane stuff seemed glorious. It was as though everything in our lives was ignored or postponed, nothing else mattered, to either of us—our obligations, our friends, even our loved ones. *Love or obsession?*

When I got into my car, I stared into the mirror above the visor. I wondered who that person was looking back at me. I turned on the radio and began singing with Luther Ingram: "If loving you is wrong—I don't want to be right." I pulled my hair out of its bun and sat there combing it with my hands. I let it hang down straight. In a trance, I heard my phone pinging.

A text from Rob.

Who are you and who or what sent you into my life?

I smiled. *It's so magical!*

I don't know why these things happen. And we don't need to try and figure it out.

I shook my head. *No we don't.*

You're like a flower scent to me.

Flower scent?

Yeah—strong and sweet. A beautiful combination.

We'd make a beautiful combination, I wanted to say. I wasn't always strong nor always sweet. And I didn't feel either now.

Thank you.

The afternoon rain was whooshing off my skin, whirring off the leaves, and plinking up and out of the puddles. My hair and clothes were soaked. I didn't care who saw me; I felt wonderful. Happier than ever. I took off my sneakers and socks and skipped through the puddles like a kid.

Who decides when the inner child should stop emerging?

Chapter 49

I was beginning to feel more comfortable with Dr. Bentley, but I knew I wouldn't tell him everything. How could I? Rob was the best thing that had happened to me. And I respected my trepidations. My familiarities. Distractions. Even if they weren't normal, and if sometimes I detested them, they were still a part of me. *How can I live without them?*

I collapsed into the large chair and smiled wanly at the doctor.

"How's it going, Aimee? Nice day today," he said, glancing out the bay window. "How was your weekend?"

"I look for them to pass quickly—be over with."

"And why's that?"

I can't wait to hear from Rob on Monday morning.

I shrugged. "I don't know. I guess I've always hated weekends."

He looked at me—waiting for me to continue. I shifted in the chair and looked at him. "I dreaded Sundays more, growing up. Except when I knew Dad was coming. We had fun times together. He'd take me to the park. To animal farms. To fairs."

"And how did you feel when he wasn't there?"

"Lonely. Sad. The hours dragged. Mom would be working, and my friends were taking family drives." *Augmenting their closeness.* "I cried a lot."

"Do you and your husband... Steve, right?" I nodded. "Do you do things together on the weekends?"

"During the day, Steve is usually busy working on something in the garage. Or he's off seeing his buddies. But we often go out to eat on Saturday nights—which is nice."

"What do you do when he's busy?"

"The same things I do during the week—I go for long walks on the beach or in the woods. I see my friend, Vicky. And, of course, visit Mom."

"How's she doing in her new place?"

"Good. Really good. I feel so much better knowing she's there."

He nodded. "Would you mind telling me more about your relationship with your husband?"

"It used to be good. It's always good in the beginning though, right?" *How would he know? He's not married. Unless he just doesn't wear a band.* "Now, honestly, it's like riding a bike on a bumpy dirt road. Sometimes you get smooth patches, but mostly it's filled with ruts. I have to be careful."

"Careful?"

"You know—not make waves. I'm cautious with my words—I don't want to upset him."

"What happens when he gets upset?"

"The wildness in him is quite scary. He has the anger of a nasty drinker. And he rarely takes a drink. Even when socializing. He never drinks more than one or two—and then passes out."

"Has he physically hurt you?"

"No." *You know the worst wounds can't be seen.* He has pushed, more like shoved, me a few times, but I don't mention that.

"And you've stayed with him all these years because…"

I constantly ask myself that same question.

"Because I wanted it to work." *Better than being alone—or was it? I saw Mom struggle. I saw her loneliness.* "Truth is, I didn't want to end up like the rest."

"The rest?"

"Our family. Failed marriages—nearly all my relatives got divorced. Right down to my great-grandparents on both sides.

When I was single my married women friends, which was most of them, back then didn't want me around because I guess they saw me as a threat." *Like they did my mother.* "I wanted to be married too. Have kids. Lots of them. And obviously that didn't work out."

"We can't force things."

"I know. I still tried." *Control freak.* "Possible candidates came and went. I dumped most of them. Not their fault. I didn't feel them the way I should. I didn't want to marry just anybody for the sake of being married."

"Then you met Steve."

"I was going to marry someone before him, a few years earlier."

"What happened?"

"I think he was looking for me to support him—financially." *"Get rid of him—he's a bum. Find a rich man. Stop picking the losers," Mom had said.* Mom had a litany of failed relationships. I followed suit. But not intentionally.

"Yes—I thought Steve was perfect. Perfect marriage material, that is. And in many ways, he was."

Dr. Bentley was waiting for more. I could tell he was interested in what I was revealing—just by his rigid posture. "How so?"

"He never went to bars. He was a hard worker. He was very attentive and loving—at least in the beginning of our marriage. He was genuinely good."

"What do you think changed?"

"I don't know. But I haven't been happy in a long time. Maybe he knows that—and that's why he treats me the way he does." *Or did he begin treating me that way and I became unhappy?*

"How does he treat you?'

Like a piece of shit. "He rarely says anything nice. Mostly derogatory comments. Disparaging remarks. And they hurt."

"Have you talked to him about how you feel?"

"No," I said, shaking my head. "I've tried. But he doesn't talk to me—about anything. Anything I do say, he tunes me out or ignores me. Even gets angry. He *is* good to me in other ways..."

"For instance?"

"He always makes sure I have everything I need—clothing and food, things for the house."

He nodded and his eyebrow lifted.

"It's odd—I am always apologizing."

"What do you apologize for?"

"Everything. Like it's my fault—I'm to blame. For whatever he thinks is wrong. And I can't do anything right."

"How so?" he asked.

I tilted my head, giving him a questioning look.

"Can you give me an example—of how you treat one another?"

I couldn't think of one scenario, even though there were hundreds. I tended to block them out to avoid the pain. Forget them quickly. "He swears at me and calls me stupid. Tells me I'm worthless. I keep quiet most of the time," I said in tears.

"Do you tell him how you feel when he does that?"

I shook my head. "No, I don't think it will change anything. He's been doing this for years." *If anything, it would probably fuel him more.*

"You have to let him know this is not acceptable. And don't lash out when you're upset. Wait until things settle down, then tell him how you feel."

Sounds like something someone would say to a child. If anything, the words "this is unacceptable" would make him nastier.

"That's hard when someone is constantly yelling and swearing at you. He has a lot of anger inside him. He needs therapy—anger management. Something."

"I could split up the time—give him a half hour?"

"I'll mention it to him. Thank you."

I couldn't speak for Steve, but I doubted he would even consider it. Besides, I wasn't ready to share my therapy time. All I really wanted to do was talk to Dr. Bentley about Rob and our relationship; I wanted a man's thoughts about the situation. I wanted to know if everything about Rob and me was real. But I was embarrassed to tell Dr. Bentley about Rob. Even more, I worried that he'd tell me this was wrong, or to end it.

***

Steve knew I was seeing a therapist, but he never asked how it was going. Or even why I was going to one. That night, after seeing Dr. Bentley, while having dinner, even though I was apprehensive about mentioning therapy to Steve, I thought I would at least try.

After chewing and swallowing a steak tip, I said, "This has a nice flavor, marinated just right."

"Thank you, honey," he said, looking at me. "I love you."

He waited for me to respond. It was hard to return those intimate words, but I did. "I love you too." I lied to make him feel good and it made me feel terrible. I felt like a phony. But how could I love someone who was constantly putting me down? Degrading me? *Treating me like shit.*

Steve went back to the newspaper. Since Steve was in a loving spirit tonight, I thought it would be the perfect time to suggest counseling.

"Would you be interested in talking with Dr. Bentley? We could go together, share the therapy time?"

He slapped the paper down on the table and glared at me. "No. What the hell for?"

"I don't know. It's not like years ago—everybody sees a therapist today. Sometimes we just need someone other than family or friends to talk to."

"Why would I talk to a fucking stranger?"

"I don't know—because they can be impartial. Unbiased."

"Forget it!"

"What about seeing a marriage counselor then? I really think we need it."

"No, we don't fucking need it. Look the fuck around you, Aimee—there's nothing wrong with our marriage."

Yeah, there is—that is why I've fallen for someone else. But how would you know? You don't even notice me—or have seen how unhappy I've been.

Chapter 50

After fixing Steve breakfast and seeing him off, I went back to bed. Even though I couldn't sleep, I closed my eyes and just lay there. Henri joined me. I kept thinking about Rob and wondered where this, us, was all going. After an hour, I got up and opened the shades. The sun was dimmed by the clouds. After going to the bathroom and washing up, I threw on a pair of jeans and a navy crewneck cashmere sweater. Then I sat in front of the mirror at the vanity. My eyelids hung from tiredness and there was puffiness beneath my eyes. I used a concealer, along with eyeliner and mascara, to try and camouflage the weariness. I gave my hair a good brushing and wrapped it into a bun.

I received a text from Rob. It was what I waited for each morning. It was what I counted on—but didn't take for granted.

Hi. What are you doing?

I'm making breakfast.

What r u having?

A couple of soft-boiled eggs on top of toast. Did you eat—I can share.

No. You ARE my breakfast.

Wow! My thoughts were stirring, my body reacting.

My phone rang.

"I feel you in ways that I shouldn't," he said.

"I know—I do too. Is it wrong for us to feel this way?"

"No. I don't think so."

Rob could make me feel things that I never knew could be felt, especially *without* a physical presence. No one had ever had that kind of effect on me. *Am I desperate?*

"I wish we had met a long time ago," he said.

"Like in your song to me. Do you regret that we met now?"

"No, not at all. You're the best thing that's come into my life in a long time."

But you're married, I wanted to say. And so am I. That declaration lacked significance. Why did I have to scrutinize? *Just accept.*

"I feel the same way. I haven't felt this happy in—I can't even remember when."

Chapter 51

"Hi, Aimee—how've you been?" asked Dr. Bentley.

"I'm okay."

"Have you been sleeping any better?" *I know you see my bags—my bloodshot eyes.*

I shook my head. "Not really."

"What do you do when you can't sleep?"

"I lie there and watch the clock. Every hour that passes..."

"You shouldn't do that—you need to get up and read a book. Watch TV. Do something you enjoy. But not in bed—go to another room."

"I thought that would just stimulate me more." *Especially when wanting to write to Rob all night.*

"No, because you're not focused on sleep. Give it a try."

"I will." I couldn't see how that would help, but he was the specialist. I'm sure there have been others in my situation. Although, I've never met anybody who had this much trouble. I thought this was only in my world.

"How's it going with your mom?"

"I am with her every day. She looks for me. She still remembers me—even calls me by my name."

"Do you take a break when you need to?"

"Sometimes. She's afraid to be alone there."

"Are you afraid to be alone, Aimee?"

I looked at him. My eyes welled up. "Yeah, sometimes. I always liked being alone when I was a kid." *Being with just me. Until...* "It used to be so comforting."

"What happens when you're alone?"

"Depends.

"On what?"

"Where I am."

"Where you are?"

"You know. Like places that are unfamiliar. I've never been before. Out of my comfort zone. Sometimes it even feels like I'm in a foreign place. And I don't know what's going to happen."

"What do you mean? What do you think is going to happen?"

"That's the thing—I don't know. But my fears seem to know and become pinnacle. It's like I have no control over them. The harder I try to shake them, the worse they get. It's as though they have a mind of their own."

"What do you think about when they come?"

"Crazy thoughts. The worst… That I'm going to die." *The way I felt that day when I was thirteen.*

"You're not going to die. It's called irrational thinking."

"I know. But my thoughts don't get it. They are wired in this dark, seamless pattern. And sometimes I feel like I'm going crazy." Normalcy and sleep seemed uncertain. Like never again. Just in my visions.

"Have you tried meditation?"

"I have. But I can't stay focused on anything for long."

"When these thoughts come, don't fight them. They are just thoughts—they can't hurt you."

I nodded.

His face told me that he had a real challenge. But in a good way—a hopeful way. He wanted to fix me: *You have a lot of work ahead of you and maybe a lot of disappointment. It won't be me disappointing you.*

Chapter 52

Rob and I were continually in touch with each other. Then one day—I got no return message. The next day was the same. I kept checking. No text. No phone call. No email. I thought maybe he got tied up with a family matter. Even worse, what if something happened to him—how would I ever know?

I opted for another email instead of a text; I didn't want his family to see the message.

Hi Rob,

I haven't heard from you—I hope you are okay.

Please if you can, let me know. I'm really worried.

Hours went by and then I got his email.

Dear Aimee,

I'm here and don't worry. You mean too much to me. Smile! I will tell you if something bothers me. I don't shut people off and do the silent treatment; I got that as a kid, and it is not right or fun.

You know I'm easy to talk to about anything and everything, even uncomfortable things. I feel deeply about a lot of things and sometimes I get frustrated when they seem to get misunderstood. People think I'm off the wall or something. And lately, I've been trying to figure out how to talk to you about some of the work I do. Hoping you'll see it in the same light that I do.

I have studied true Yoni therapy. Yoni is vaginal therapy. And I say true because America has made it a sexual thing, as usual, because they don't know what it's all about. Women hold most of their tension within the vagina. Because it's the center of the first Chakra for grounding. Men in this world have abused women and have overpowered them for years. And for that reason, women hold their suppression within the walls of this area. Just as a massage loosens the body, Yoni loosens the tension there—it is a therapy. In the ancient wisdom this practice is essential to the health of a woman. I have practiced Yoga for years and have found meditation practices grounding and opening a whole new world for me. Years back, I decided to take courses in Tantric Yoga. I now have my own clients. Sessions with them are lengthy depending on the couple, sometimes all weekend. They learn about Chakras and letting go of blocks that interfere with their connection with one another. It is a rewarding experience to witness the love and intimacy that grows.

I know I can be free to express things with you and think you are open to most things, but it is me that holds back. I have been stung and am a little nervous. So far, I have only done the Yoni practice on one person and though she hesitated for a long while, she was thrilled at the results and never felt sexual things coming from me but only love for another human being. This woman said to me, "Of all the kinds of therapy I tried, this worked best. And I didn't feel like I was paying much for the wonderful results."

Your Friend.

We'll speak soon.

I had never heard of Yoni or Tantra before. I immediately looked it up. I was overwhelmed by the pictures of ancient statues depicting sexual acts. I'd never seen sexual acts done with such abandonment. I was full of anxiety yet curious. I could feel my heart hammering in my chest like it was going to burst through. I wondered if this was some type of ancient porn? It seemed Rob thought I'd been isolated, but I didn't think anything showed.

I suddenly got dizzy and had this painful tightness in my throat. I ran to the bathroom and heaved.

I was convinced that Rob was sexually deprived at home, unless he had the same problem as Clinton. I didn't want any of this to be true. I liked him—maybe too much.

He wrote so casually, so freely, as though this therapy he was performing was normal. Or, at least, he was hoping I would see it that way. Maybe normal for him. Obviously, he wasn't fazed by mentioning it, even though he didn't really know me. Was he looking for my approval? Did I look like I need sexual therapy? What was my body saying to him?

He practiced this therapy on women. Was he licensed? Did his wife know? Was she okay with it? Maybe they have an agreement? Maybe they're swingers? He wanted to know everything about me. Everything. Maybe that was his way of figuring on how to manipulate me, make me a victim. I didn't see myself as desperate either, needing someone like him. Or was I fooling myself?

Is Tantra acceptable in this western world? Still done in the East? Instead of running and telling the world how crazy he was, I wanted to protect him. Overlook what I now knew. And I think part of him believed helping women achieve orgasms was acceptable and that he was contributing a noble act.

I wrote back to Rob, my hands shaking, my insides ready to erupt. I was upset yet more disappointed. I was careful with my words; I still wanted him in my life. I wasn't sure why, but I needed to understand this. Him.

Dear Rob,

Since we've been honest with each other, I have to tell you I was taken aback by your email. What's your fascination with this Tantra, Yoni stuff? You're married—I believe you have morals.

Dear Aimee,

I only mentioned it because you're so important to me, and I wanted to share this with you. It's part of the work I do. But only with safe people who understand and that is not many. Just as you share what you do—I shared. Societies and cultures are different; most Americans make everything sexual. I am not caught up in that at all. It's not a moral issue for me nor do I have a fascination with it. It is healing work that is characterized in the healing arts. I am different and open to the world of many things. And you are the only one I would share this with.

I wondered why he'd picked on me if he'd never told anyone else? If he felt what he did was so right and justified, why was he so secretive?

After I wrote it, I let it go without a thought of you and me doing that. I don't even know you really. I don't go looking for it—it comes to me by referrals. I talk to you as a doctor of dermatology would chat with you.

Did he see me as a referral? Worse, did he see both of us trying this? I didn't think he was licensed, and this wasn't an Eastern culture. I couldn't understand how he could compare himself to a doctor.

His email came back to me:

While on the subject, I thought much like you, at first, about women not needing this therapy. So, I ignored it. But it was the women who I studied holistic healing with—my teachers and fellow students, who convinced me to go into this work because there is a tremendous need for it. Because I am very safe, respectful, gentle, and understanding, they thought I would be great at it. We teach our children to know where their nose, mouth, teeth, and feet are but avoid the restricted areas as taboo. They are part of us.

He needed to open his eyes. We weren't children, and he wasn't a licensed practitioner. The whole world suddenly seemed unreal, and I hated what I'd just learned about him, and yet… what he said stirred me, led me to feeling aroused. I was ashamed of myself. I wondered if he commanded respect and reverence from these women. Did he honestly believe he was the man with answers and solutions to a woman's sexual inhibitions? I suddenly felt nauseous again and ran to the bathroom. Should I trust what he was saying and allow him to touch me, because he was "safe, respectful, gentle and understanding"? Oh no fuck that—did he really think he could persuade me, like maybe he persuaded those other women?

I went for an Ayurveda massage once and when I walked in, she told me to take off all my clothes and lie on the table under no blanket. The massage was amazing. She said most Americans walk out when she says that.

Right. Yes. And what happened when she massaged your penis? I had to ask. *Do you still see her?*

No, she is now back in Mongolia.

Where she belonged, in my opinion.

I really struggle with Americans' lack of understanding of my work. I have a big, kind and compassionate heart, and I want to help others with their issues and their pain, but it is hard on me because of society. Women do need this, and the results are amaz-

ing! There is therapy for men too but done differently, of course. I don't do that…

My mind was all over the place. Women didn't need him to give them an orgasm, and why did he avoid the same therapy for men?

I picked up my phone, my hands shaking, my heart pumping out of my chest. I punched in his number. "What are you to these women?"

"I guess you could say I'm their coach. I guide them…"

"You seek weak and insecure ones. You gain their trust—you make them feel safe, and then you prey on their vulnerability."

He was like those priests, that was all. Just like those priests. I was furious. Upset. Crying.

"I'm not listening to this. Goodbye."

"You're delusional—run from the truth. You know I'm right." I think he had already hung up.

It was 3:30 in the afternoon and already dark and dreary. The rain was coming. But I didn't care, it coincided with my mood. My world had suddenly capsized like an overturned boat, me beneath. Drowning in disbelief. Sinking into an abyss of infinite darkness. I wanted to write to Rob and decided not to; I had to get my thoughts and emotions intact first. And I knew I'd be anxious to get a response from him. Right away. I really wanted to interrogate the hell out of him—find out who he really was.

I hadn't the right—this wasn't Steve.

I needed to understand this—understand him. Or maybe it was over between us. He could tell me disturbing stuff and because I wasn't in agreement with his beliefs, he wasn't willing to hear my thoughts, my feelings on the subject.

Then how could we remain friends? Or were we ever really friends? Was he just looking for a friend with benefits? But if that was the case, wouldn't he have chosen someone closer to him? Why would he want me to know any of this, if we weren't going to be together?

Once I got past my own emotions about his sinful deeds, I began wondering if he was trying to disclose something more, something sinister about himself. Rob told me his mother had been abused by her husband and likely she'd been neglected and abused by those in the foster homes she'd been in. What kind of mother was she to Rob and his brother? I wondered if he was a victim of incest. Had he been abused by his mother?

I got out a blanket from the old hope chest that was once Mom's and curled up on the sofa. Henri joined me. I didn't turn on the TV, I didn't pick up a book. I just sat there and listened. I could hear Henri purring, cars traveling past, and rain splattering against the windows. I tried not to think about anything. Anybody. I had to concentrate on breathing, on letting my thoughts tumble through my mind.

It was peaceful, sitting alone in the dark. It reminded me of how I used to hibernate in the closet when I was a kid, a place where nobody would look for me. I could block out noise. Voices. Pain.

I began dreaming. I was with a boy walking in the woods like Hansel and Gretel. We stopped at this old house; inside were two witches, dressed in long, black satin dresses—embroidered gold crosses woven throughout. Big wooden crosses hung just above their bosoms. They frightened me. The boy dropped coins into the palm of the tallest one and the other witch handed me a dozen eggs. Then the scene suddenly switched to my mom in a frantic state, dragging me away. It startled me awake.

I had turned my phone off but wanted to turn it back on. I'd hoped there'd be at least a text from Rob if not a phone call. My views on the subject were unclear. He already had become so much a part of my life. Even though I didn't understand, I couldn't shut him out. Not now.

I heard the garage door open. I glanced at the clock—5:00 p.m. Steve was home from work. Henri scooted off the sofa and I did the same.

"How come there are no lights on in here?" Steve asked, bending over to pet Henri.

Folding the blanket, I looked at him. "I'm sorry—I..."

"You were sleeping. I can tell by your eyes."

"No, I was just resting."

"Must be nice," Steve stated sarcastically.

"Actually, it was. I decided to take a break from seeing Mom."

"Good, well you can help me get supper ready."

"Sure. What are we having?"

"You tell me."

"You usually bring something home," I said, standing at the kitchen counter.

"Well, I didn't—so you can get off your lazy ass and get something."

"That's fine—tell me what you want?" I asked. I didn't dare tell him I wasn't hungry. My stomach was upset.

"Forget it—I bought swordfish and clam cakes."

"Can I help?" I asked.

"No, I'll take care of it—you can set the table."

Steve was at the kitchen counter, and I was behind him reaching into the cabinet. We both turned at the same time and collided. I dropped the plates and they crashed to the floor, shattering into large shards.

"Oh my God," I said.

"Now look what the fuck you've done."

"Don't worry—I'll clean the mess," I said in tears.

I got out the broom and dustpan and swept up the scattered pieces. Then I grabbed two more plates and the silverware and set them on the table. Afterward, I went into the living room until dinner was ready.

"Aimee," Steve yelled from the kitchen, a half-hour later.

I walked in and took my seat at the table. Steve was looking at me. "What?" I asked.

"Can you get me something to drink?"

"Sure. What do you want?"

"I don't know."

I grabbed two cans of Pepsi from the refrigerator. When I put one in front of him, he asked, "Can you get a glass?"

I got up and went to the cabinet, grabbing only one; I drank from the can.

I felt him looking at me again. I looked back. "I'm sorry, honey, I didn't mean to yell at you."

"You yell at me all the time and it's really hard on me." I broke down, tears streaming. Steve came over and hugged me, kissing my forehead.

That night I was restless, tossing in bed. What had I learned about Rob confused me. I had only one person to talk to about this. Dr. Bentley. I hadn't even mentioned our relationship to him yet. But now I was anxious to ask him about Yoni and Tantra. I wanted to tell Vicky, but I was afraid she'd judge Rob—unfairly.

I woke up in a sweat, trembling. I lay awake the rest of the night. I knew I had to keep this to myself—to keep Rob from being torn down, ripped apart, but why I wanted to protect him, I had no idea.

Chapter 53

Dr. Bentley asked, "Would you like a cup of coffee or tea?"

"Tea, please." I watched him grab a mug from a drawer in his desk.

Handing it to me, he said, "The machine is right over there—just push the red button. It heats up quickly. The box of tea bags is on top."

"Thank you." I noticed it was decaffeinated.

"How are you feeling overall?"

"Worn out. The adrenaline flares alone are draining. Never mind the goings-on."

"Are you sleeping any better?" *All you have to do is look at me.*

"No, not really. I sleep a few minutes here and there—you know, like naps. It helps."

He stared at me. "Are you telling me everything? I had a client who left here and called me afterward and said she wished she had told me everything."

He knows.

"I'm trying."

"I'm not here to judge," he said.

I don't care what they say, they're judging even if they don't verbalize it.

I looked at him, debating. Should I—or shouldn't I? My heart was pounding. His response could kill me. Literally. Rob had been my secret. My love. My savior. Even if right then—for the first time—I felt like I didn't know him. They say if something seems too good to be true... *Angels only fly in heaven.*

"I have a friend—male friend," I finally spilled.

"Do you see him?"

"No, he lives on the West Coast."

"How do you know each other?"

"We met at a party here months ago." He nodded. "We talk every day. He's helped a lot."

I tried to hold back my emotions, but I could feel my cheeks getting wet. He handed me the box of tissues. I took a handful and wiped my tears and blew my nose.

"He's been so caring and thoughtful. And he lightens my days—my spirit. I don't know what I would've done without him..."

"Are you in love with him?"

"Yes, I believe so." *Even after what he revealed to me.*

I held my breath, waiting for him to tell me—this is wrong. These feelings can't be real. Rob is just temporary, a band-aid to cover the wound—that can only heal from within. But instead, he said, "Okay."

Since the doctor seemingly wasn't judging me, I felt better about sharing more. Other than Rob, nobody had ever listened. Paid me any attention. And if they had, it wasn't obvious.

"I keep a journal."

"Do you write in it—daily?"

"Yes, nearly my whole life."

"When did you start?"

"My mother gave me a diary when I was a kid. She told me my secrets would be safe in there."

"And were they?"

"So far. I still have that diary. I haven't opened it in decades." Mom threw out everything I loved—my stuffed animals, my dolls. Stuff that she thought took up too much space or had been around too long. Part of it was her OCD. I hid my diary, though. My secrets. She could take anything from me, but I wasn't going to let her take that away.

"Any reason you haven't looked back or read what's inside? Aren't you a little curious?"

"I think some things are best left alone. Forgotten." *But is anything really forgotten? Or forgiven?*

"But you must have kept that diary for a reason."

"Maybe. I don't know."

"How would you feel about me reading some of it?"

I squirmed in the chair. "Why?"

"There might be things in there that have contributed to your anxiety and sleeplessness, that you're not aware of. Something buried in your subconscious. That could help me to be able to help you better."

I said nothing for a while, looking down at the floor. Then I looked up, my eyes met his. "Okay."

"You sure?"

I nodded. "Yeah."

What the heck—he wasn't going to blab to anyone. He couldn't. Even if he did, who would care?

That night while Steve was watching TV, I ventured upstairs. Inside the bedroom closet, I moved aside extra blankets and pillows and grabbed the wooden chest with the small padlock on it. I never forgot the combination. How could I? 8-8-6-6. (August 8, 1966) I opened the chest and found the diary. The little key was still attached to the outside.

I was tempted to unlock its contents, but my hands were trembling fiercely. A nefarious fire-breathing dragon was in there. In the deepest darkest catacombs of the dark dungeon—waiting to incinerate me. A voice inside repeatedly said, *"Wait."* I grabbed the diary. *Wait for what?*

> *Sunday, August 13, 1966*
>
> *Dear Diary,*
>
> *Mom stuck me in the kitchen sink to wash me. The water was so hot, it burned my skin. She scrubbed me all over. She said Dad could take me away from her—for neglect.*
>
> *I am so happy Daddy came today. But I was so sad when he left. I think he is the best daddy in the whole world. I block my ears when Mom says bad things about him.*

> *Friday, September 8, 1966*
>
> *Mom says I can't go roller skating with my friends. She said I will fall and break my ankle. Or my arm. She doesn't let me do anything. I stayed in my room and studied phonics.*

> *Wednesday, September 20, 1966*
> *I wanted to go to Susan's birthday party after school, but Mom said I had to go to Catechism. I cried. I did not want to go with Father. He laughs at his own jokes. They are not funny at all. And he squeezed my hand too hard when he took me to his house. God wouldn't hurt me.*

I thought I heard Steve coming up the stairs, so I quickly closed the diary and stuffed it in my purse and put everything back the way it was.

"What are you doing?" he asked.

"Nothing. I was just resting."

"Resting? You rest all day."

"Do you have to be so sarcastic? I have a lot on my mind—and you know I don't sleep well."

He mumbled something under his breath. "Well, I'm going to bed now—I have to work in the morning."

"Okay. I'll grab my pajamas and read for a while on the sofa."

Chapter 54

After Steve left for work, I drove to the beach. Something about the sand and the ocean in the morning twilight with its violet hue and its serenity—it had a way of settling everything. Me. Waves were gently lapping the shore. Seagulls squawked above and others ran the shoreline hunting for crabs and small fish. I inhaled deeply a few times, breathing in the salty air. Exhaling slowly. The beach was void of people, and the night's high tide had washed away any sign of human or animal imprints. The sand was now smooth and untouched.

I laid down the woolen throw and sat, taking in all that surrounded me. I kept my mind blank and let my eyes focus on what was before me. The water. The fine, white sand. The sun was rising in the pink sky.

An hour later, I packed up my gear and walked back to the car. Instead of returning home, I stopped at Dunkin' Donuts.

Mom was on the edge of her bed, trying to figure out how to put her shoes on. "Can you help me?" she implored.

"Yes, of course," I said, putting the coffee and donuts on the top of the bureau and bending down.

"What's...," she asked, pointing to the bag.

"Donuts. Here," I said, handing it to her. "Open it."

She pulled out the honey-dipped, setting it on the nightstand.

"Can you take me to the bathroom?"

"Yes, Mom."

"Hurry. It's coming."

The bathroom was shared with another room. Someone was in there.

Mom wailed.

"It's okay, Mom—you have on a Depend."

"What?"

"A diaper—I will clean you up after."

She moaned.

I wondered where the aide was, hoping to get out of my

pledge. I had to commend those nurses' aides; it took a special kind of person to fill that role. Their work was demanding and exhausting.

While in the process of wiping Mom clean, Tanya, the young aide, came in. "I'll take care of her."

Tanya said she would give Mom a bath. Mom reeked of poop. I waited in her room, thinking how depressing this all seemed. Unable for one to think normally, care for oneself.

Then I heard my phone ping. I should hold off responding. I needed him.

Hi.

What are you up to?

I smiled. *About 5'7. Unless I shrunk.*

I've missed you.

It'd only been a couple of days, but it seemed like an eternity. I think he wanted to wait till I'd cooled. Tantra and Yoni were never discussed again. Like it was just a dream. And quickly forgotten when you wake. *And when did he have time for this practice—when he was always with me? Always with me.*

My heart beating faster, I took a deep breath. *I've missed you too.*

Can we talk?

Maybe later—I'm with Mom right now.

Okay.

I went back to concentrating on Mom. After she got cleaned up, we held hands and walked down to the solarium, where it was bright with sunlight. We sat at a small table and worked on a child's puzzle. She was having a hard time now, putting even those large pieces together. Afterward, we went to a wooden toy chest in the corner of the room. It was filled with stuffed animals. She picked out the cutest black and white bear and held it close to her chest.

It seemed strange watching her cuddling this animal; it reminded me of the panda she had bought me when I was three. She promised me that bear, which I had admired in the store, if I stopped sucking my thumb. I stopped immediately. But I knew bribing Mom with an animal or anything else wouldn't make her come back to who she once was. *Aimee, you have to face reality.*

We walked out of there into the dining room, also used as an activity room.

"Mom, are you getting hungry?" I asked, knowing she'd never had the donut or the coffee.

She shook her head. Food of any kind, even sweets, was becoming a challenge. I didn't push it anymore. It wasn't going to make a difference. The inevitable was nearing with each passing day. I looked around at the other residents, some accompanied by relatives or hospice workers. I studied each one, wondering what their life was like before. Who were they? What did they do for a living? Doctors. Accountants. Lawyers. Housewives. Waitresses. Janitors. Teachers. What did they look like when they were young? Do they want to be living like this now? I imagined them—talking. Walking. Dancing. Those people were able-bodied and had sound minds. Now they all seemed to converge—no one was better or different than the other. Human beings just existing. Waiting.

Why God? Why?

"Aimee," Mom said. I was shaken out of reverie. Hearing her still call my name and seeing that glow in her eyes made me understand why we want our loved ones around as long as possible.

After a couple of hours, I went home. Henri greeted me at the door. I picked her up in my arms and nuzzled my nose against her cheek. "Hey girl, I missed you too." I held her until she got antsy and wiggled out of my embrace. I made coffee and sat down at the kitchen table, enjoying the quiet.

Then I picked up the phone and texted Rob.

Hey, you still wanna talk?

My phone rang a minute later.

"Hi. I can't go without hearing your voice for long."

"I know—me too," I admitted.

"I wanna see you—in person again."

"How? You're like a world away."

"I don't know—we'll figure it out."

"Yes we will—we have to." Although, I think it was just a fantasy. Besides, how could I leave Mom, especially now?

"What would you like to do when we're together?"

"I just want to look at you," I said.

"And then what?"

"Kiss you. Hold you. Make love to you."

"No. Make love *with* you, not *to* you," he corrected me.

"You're making it hard for me to breathe."

"What we do to each other."

I couldn't stop feeling him. Desiring him. Constant craving. Obsession?

Chapter 55

I took the diary out of my purse and handed it to Dr. Bentley.

"Wow, this is in good shape," he said, looking at all sides.

"Mom taught me to take care of things," I said.

"I won't read any of it now, unless you want me to?"

I shook my head. "No, that's okay. I did open it last night though, and read a few entries."

"Is there any of it you'd like to talk about?"

"Remembering can be painful—right?" I asked him. *Painful times. Painful memories.*

"Sometimes yes. But also, it can be the first step to healing."

I nodded.

I watched him put the diary in his desk drawer. "I'll read some later. And don't worry, nothing will happen to it." He must have read my mind.

I hesitated. "Do you know anything about Tantra?"

"I'm familiar with it. But vaguely. From what I understand, it's an ancient healing that works with the chakras. I have referred couples to someone I know in that field and heard it has greatly helped their marriages. It's a spiritual path. Why do you ask?"

"My friend, you know the one I told you about on the West Coast—well, he's a Tantra *Yoni* practitioner."

"Have you researched it?"

"Not really." *I freaked out when I opened the site.*

"I can look it up right now," he said, turning to his desktop.

"No! Please don't!" I didn't mean to yell.

"Actually, I have a pamphlet here if you'd like one," he said, taking it from a holder on one of the bookshelves and handing it to me."

"Oh, thank you, Doctor."

"I haven't looked at it—a friend of mine had dropped off the flyers a few months ago." There was silence for a minute. "So how is it going with your friend—did you tell me his name?"

"No, I don't think I did. His name is Rob. And things are going as good as they can."

He nodded and stared at me. Waiting. Always waiting for more.

"He's married too."

No shock on the doctor's face. I'm sure he'd heard this before. He was careful with his words to me; he knew I was hanging on by a thread. *And this Rob guy seemingly makes her feel better.*

"Is there anything else you'd like to talk about?"

"I am finally accepting the reality that Mom will be leaving soon."

He looked at me. *He doesn't believe me.*

"I think I am, anyway. Truth is, I really can't think of death." Long time here—then gone. A permanent goodbye. Body to ashes. Just a memory.

Chapter 56

"It's almost Lent," I mentioned to Rob.

"Yes, it is. Do you give up something you enjoy?"

"Even though I don't go to church, I still do. It's usually chocolate."

"Chocolate?"

"Yes, I crave it sometimes. Maybe all the time. Especially when I'm stressed. It's so good, yet too much can be bad for you. Like anything, I guess."

"So, what are you going to give up this year? I hope it's not me."

"Well," I stuttered. "I just thought that maybe—you know, we should take a break. This would be the perfect time. Just to see..."

"See what—if it's real?"

"Yeah, I guess," I said quietly.

"I know it's real but if that's what you want, I'll respect your wishes."

"I just think giving each other some space might be good right now..."

"I understand. It's been really hard—for both of us."

"It's not going to change the way we feel. We have nothing to worry about." *Do we? Forty-six days!*

***

Sometimes, I felt like I was on a seesaw, one minute up high, the next plummeting to the ground, anticipating that rise again. I thought stopping communicating with Rob would bring some normalcy back into my life. Whatever that was. I knew it would be hard coming off an adrenaline explosion. But I needed to do this—for my sanity. I was sacrificing someone who meant so much to me, but I also needed to practice some self-discipline.

The six weeks of Lent seemed never-ending. The longest forty-six days of my life. Rob had gotten to be my addiction, and I was having withdrawals in his absence. Nothing was exciting. I was on autopilot, drifting through each day. Waiting for the next twenty-four hours to be over. I ate chocolate. Dark. White. Store-bought. Homemade. I devoured Milky Ways, Snickers, Hershey, and Heath bars. It served—temporarily. But certainly, didn't come close to taking his place.

My feelings hadn't changed for Rob. I wondered if his had. I was reassured when I awoke to the sound of his text.

I reached down the side of the bed into my purse and grabbed my phone.

I smiled as I read, *Hi, Happy Easter!*

Happy Easter.

Hey, think of me looking at you, when you take your first bite into that ham.

I laughed. *Okay.*

My phone vibrated again. He sent me a smiley face.

I shoved the phone in my purse, smiling.

I could hear Steve downstairs in the kitchen, preparing the food. The Easter tradition. Prepping the ham and simmering it in mustard and brown sugar. Cutting up the carrots, peeling the potatoes, and stuffing the celery with cream cheese and walnuts. I knew there would be roasted onions too.

Not to be in Steve's way, I lay in bed and waited for him to be done before cleaning up. I loved and hated the holidays. I liked the concept of how a family gathering should be during these times—loving and grateful—but I resented that they never were.

I donned my bathrobe and slippers and sauntered downstairs. "Morning. Smells good," I said, smiling.

"The water is boiling for your coffee."

"Thank you."

"What were you laughing about?"

I shook my head. "When?"

"A few minutes ago."

"Oh, nothing really. I must have been thinking about something. Can I help?"

"Nope—everything's done."

"What time will it be ready?"

"Around three."

"Would you mind if Vicky came for dinner? She'll be alone."

"Doesn't she have family?"

"No. I mean not here. Her kids live too far away—California."

I already knew Vicky had no plans—I would've asked her sooner, but I thought it was better to ask Steve at the last minute. Hoping he'd be in good spirits on the holiday.

"Tell her to bring something," he said.

"She never comes empty-handed."

"But she's looking for a handout."

I took a deep breath. "Whatever," I said, biting the inside of my cheek.

I opened a drawer of the dining room hutch and took out the pale green, linen cloth adorned in butterflies and flowers and spread it across the table. Then I set matching placemats for three: Vicky, Steve, and me. I took out Mom's white china dishes and the gold-lacquered silverware from its wooden case.

Every Easter I'd arrange a big basket, adding green grass, tossing in chocolate bunnies and jellybeans, and wrapping it with pink or blue cellophane. Eventually, I began envisioning grandchildren being here coloring eggs and hiding them. Their precious faces with big smiles and eyes full of sparkle, filling the house with laughter and joy. I had always loved kids since I was a kid myself and wanted some of my own. *Aimee, you need to face reality.*

Thanksgiving, Christmas, and Easter were all special to me when I was young. I think more because my father was always there, making them fun. Now I dreaded them. Mom and Steve had always sabotaged them by being volatile and mean, making the rest of us uncomfortable, squashing any cheeriness the holidays brought.

On Easter, 1988, my dad had arrived at Steve's and my new house still in his church clothes, looking as handsome as ever. He sat in the living room, minding his own business, when Mom walked in and started on him. "Still seeing that slut? You look old enough to be her father."

Dad never said an ill word against Mom, but she spewed hateful remarks until he finally got up and left.

The sight of him reiterated that memory from decades earlier; the one incident she couldn't forgive or forget. Mom was tactless, hurtful. She gave her opinion straight and unfiltered. She didn't care about hurting anyone; seemingly she wanted others to feel her suffering as she pointedly showcased her own pent-up anger and hurt around everyone.

"Mom, look what you've done. He's gone. Couldn't you be nice for just one day?"

"Nice? He walks around town with that slut. You condone this? That should bother you," she said glaring at me, wrath in her tone.

"Yes, it bothers me—but it's ***his*** *life. I still love him—no matter what he does."*

"I'm going home," she said. She grabbed her purse and out the door she went.

"Mom, please stay," I called after her.

Vicky arrived an hour before dinner. I handed her a woven Easter basket packed with a dishtowel, two potholders, two wine corks, jellybeans, and homemade chocolates.

"This is really nice," she said, staring at the purple wrapping and bow. "You didn't have to..."

"Shush, I wanted to."

We sat on the sofa, eating the candies and yakking about our childhood Easters. I could see Steve in the kitchen getting frustrated just by the way he was shoving things around on the stove and slamming drawers and cabinets. He never wanted me in the way when he was working in the kitchen, but he didn't like it when I wasn't there helping either. And he couldn't stand it if I was enjoying myself with anyone else.

"Steve, do you need any help?" I hollered from the living room.

"What do you think?"

I shook my head, got off the sofa, and walked to the kitchen.

"Get the bowls for the vegetables."

Steve carved the ham and placed it on a platter while I

scooped carrots and peas, the roasted potatoes, and onions into bowls and set them on the dining room table.

"Don't forget the applesauce and rolls."

"I won't," I said.

At the table, I knew Steve was waiting for our approval, his eyes shifting from me to Vicky.

"This is delicious," Vicky said after a mouthful.

"Yeah, it's really good, Steve," I added. "You always do a great job."

Steve looked satisfied.

After the meal, I scraped the dishes and washed them. And after dessert Vicky went home.

"I saw Vicky didn't raise a finger to help," Steve said.

"She's not into cleaning up—"

"That was obvious."

I ignored his comment; I wasn't going into detail about her life.

Chapter 57

The next morning, I got a text from Rob.

Hi. Can I call?

Yes.

My phone rang.

"You make me so happy inside, I could sing aloud," Rob chirped.

I smiled. "Please let me hear you."

Silence.

I listened to him breathe, light and composed.

"You there?" Rob asked.

"Yeah, I'm here."

"What are we going to do? This is hard, isn't it?"

"Yes, very hard."

"Aarrgghh!"

I knew he was feeling all that I was. We wanted to be together in person. Yet that seemed impossible.

"As much as I want to talk to you, I have so much to get done today. So please write and when I get home, I will look for your words," Rob said.

"Okay. Have a nice day."

After he hung up, I poured myself another cup of coffee and went to the computer to write. Henri purred at my ankles, looking to be held. I picked her up and cradled her in my arms, petting her. After a few minutes she had enough love and jumped off my lap. I tried to focus on the story, but I had too many questions for Rob reeling in my head. *Why do you like me? Why are we still in the same place? Why aren't we doing anything about this?*

Why? Why? Why?

I went to my email and typed a new message to Rob. The first: Why?

I know you like me, but I want you to tell me why.

I had to know since I'd had a bad reaction when he told me about his work with Yoni and Tantra. I needed to be more open-minded and educated on these practices. He continued being my friend and sharing loving energy. *Maybe if circumstances were different. Maybe if...*

I washed the dishes, threw in a load of laundry, and vacuumed the floors. Other than a little dust and cat fur, the house looked decent. Although the rooms were tasteful, handsome really, and cozy in a traditional style, they were short of joy. Happiness. Love. All the things that mattered—that made a house a home.

Were Rob and I in a friendship, a romantic friendship? Or were we just keeping each other company, steering us away from our loneliness?

After an hour of sitting on the sofa wondering and wallowing, I got up and went to the nursing home. Mom was in the Namaste room, sleeping soundly in a reclining sofa lounge. I had sunk in next to her in a tufted club chair, waiting for her to open her eyes. Smile and say my name. I knew someday soon they'd remain closed. Forever. Instantly, I was distracted from those sad thoughts as I dissolved into my surroundings—feeling the positive energy immediately. Taking a deep breath, I drew in the calming scent permeating the room. The soft lighting and beautiful nature scenes with relaxing music, on the TV above the fireplace, was very tranquil. Peaceful. I wanted to remain here. Fade away.

When the only other resident was gone, I quietly chatted with the pretty, olive-skinned young aide. I read her name tag.

"How is Mom doing, Claudia?"

"She has her good days—she sleeps more now."

I nodded.

When Mom didn't wake up after an hour, I left.

In the car, my phone pinged. I knew it was my email. I looked and it was from Rob. I hated reading emails on my phone; I don't know why but I preferred reading them on the computer. But I couldn't wait to see his response, so I opened it.

Dear Aimee,

The question you asked, why do I like you? Well, most people have the answers to that question right away, for instance, I like you because you are cool, or I like you because you are nice. We already know that and never have to say it; it just is. But really? Our relationship is much deeper than that! It holds hidden treasures and truths beyond the murmur of syllables and sounds. Beyond trying to uncover them with words. It is like the warm breeze at the ocean or the leaf that falls in autumn—never uttering a sound. It is like the sweet smell of lilacs or the butterfly passing by. We just take it in. It does not have to be dissected.

Just the question itself, why do I like you? Who can describe the universe—or even the flavor of vanilla or chocolate?

I smiled.

Chapter 58

"How was your Easter?" asked Dr. Bentley.

"My girlfriend came over and the three of us had a nice ham dinner."

"Sounds like you had a good time."

I nodded. "We did."

"How are you and Steve getting along?"

"Nothing really changes—he's not going to change. I wish sometimes he'd divorce me, but he never will. And I can't think about my future right now."

"And Rob—how's that going?"

"It's weird—when I think it can't get any better, it does. I feel fortunate to have him in my life. Not only am I crazy over him, but I also don't know what I would've done without him."

The doctor nodded. He doesn't say much, mostly listens. But I know what he's thinking—Rob is doing the trick right now. Helping her get through this hardship. Married men don't leave their wives. It's just a short fix.

"I have been reading your diary."

He probably thinks he knows me now.

"And?"

"You went through a lot as a young girl. And keeping those secrets bottled up all those years had to be difficult. I'm sure there were things you wished you could talk about with someone. Someone you trusted and maybe could help in some way."

"Yes—but I didn't feel like I could tell anyone. Anyone that would believe me." *I had to keep my promise.*

"You realize, as a child, none of that was your fault. The adults had the power."

"And I always obeyed." *I was the good Catholic girl. An angel, he called me.*

Chapter 59

It was a warm and sunny spring morning; the trees and shrubs were blossoming. I was in the kitchen with a cup of coffee in my hand, staring out the window at the season's promised delivery, when I heard Steve calling out my name. "Aimee, come outside."

Steve had gone out early and returned a few hours later with a yard of mulch and small pots of annuals and perennials for our little garden in the backyard.

I opened the window and yelled back, "I'm not dressed yet."

"It's okay. Just for a minute."

I tied the belt around my robe and walked outside.

"I bought some flowers for you to plant. They were on sale. Besides, by the time *you* get planting, summer will be over. And by the way, I got mulch and another bag of planting soil."

Then maybe you should plant them.

I looked at the variety of yellow and orange, which weren't my favorite colors. I had mentioned this to him several times; it never penetrated. I had no idea what kind of flowers these were. Not pretty like a dahlia or a clematis.

I had no interest in planting any flowers, regardless of my preference for color. Steve had already killed any joy that would emanate from this otherwise soul-healing project. Still, I went back in the house and darted upstairs and threw on a pair of old jeans and a T-shirt and whipped my hair into a bun. I went back downstairs and headed out to the garage. I grabbed the planting gloves, shovel, trowel and hand rake. Then I went to the shed and got the wheelbarrow. I began removing the dried brown leaves from fall, as well as the weeds and other debris that had accumulated in the flowerbed throughout the year.

When the bed was cleared for the planting of the flowers, I dug the first hole and took a perennial out of its pot to set in the ground, neatly packing fresh topsoil around it. A bumblebee whirred nearby. I waved it away.

I hadn't realized Steve was standing a few feet away, watching me. "You're not doing it right—you need to make the hole bigger."

"I think it's just fine."

"And you're putting in way too much potting soil," he said.

"Then why don't you do it?" I said, raising my hands.

"I'm just trying to help you, honey."

"Please leave me alone—let me do this." He walked away.

I felt the sun's heat on my head and back as I continued planting, thinking of Rob. Wishing he was here helping me. Tears filled my eyes, escaping down my cheek. I quickly brushed them away with my shirt sleeve. I imagined him and me working side by side, converting this fruitless patch into a lovely little garden. A sanctuary. Ours.

Later, while texting Rob, I mentioned the garden and what I had wished for.

I will make you a garden someday.

I'd love that. When? Where?

You're like a flower to me. A beautiful rose. I can just see you blossoming in the spring. What is this spell you have on me, Woman?

I guess it's the same one you have on me.

I need a dose of Vitamin A—A for Aimee. Like right now.

You got it.

Rob sent me a heart and hugging emoji. I closed my eyes and imagined his arms around me, warming not just my outside but reaching deep within.

Chapter 60

Steve and I were invited to a cookout, mutual acquaintances of our friends, Diane and Joe. Since Diane knew them better than I did, I called her and asked her what she thought I should bring. I wanted to make a good impression.

"Hey, isn't this the couple who said they liked Rob's music?" I remembered them getting up to dance to one song.

"Yeah, why?"

"Well, I thought it'd be nice to bring them the extra CD that Rob sent me."

"Are you *still* talking to him?"

Her authoritative tone took me by surprise. I don't know why she said it like that. "Yeah, occasionally. Hey, I have to go—Steve is calling me. See you there."

I mixed salad greens in a large bowl, then I cut up and added cucumbers, radishes, Greek olives, shaved carrots, and red peppers. Steve crafted a fancy fruit display out of a watermelon base, filled with green and red grapes, kiwi, cantaloupe, and melon.

After showering and blow drying my hair, I donned a yellow sleeveless, knee-length dress and threw on a light blue shrug. Even though it was nearly seventy with bright sunshine, there was still that cool ocean breeze. Then I added silver hoops and the bangle bracelet I'd bought in Provincetown. Lastly, I slipped my feet into brown leather sandals for the first time this year.

The old Cape house on 6A in Barnstable was surrounded with new birth: the lush lawn, the matured oak, maple and beech trees, and the rose and azalea bushes showing signs of blossoming. Nearby, a cluster of robins and sparrows hovered, chirping harmoniously.

Steve had long disappeared into the house.

Inside the sliding glass door of the summer room, Diane greeted me with folded arms, her forehead creasing. Her puffy lips twisting. I could see she had an attitude.

I smiled. "Hi. So good to see you." I hadn't seen her since our dinner party months earlier.

"When he was here," Diane rambled with a scowl, "his hands were all over me."

"What? Who?" I had no idea what she was talking about.

"Rob—who else?" Fire raging in her dilated pupils. She had waited till now to tell me this.

I stared at her in confusion. This wasn't the man I knew.

"He tried to get me into this cult he's a part of," she sneered.

"Cult?"

"Yeah. He's crazy."

I had never seen Diane this upset. Was she jealous of our friendship? I mean, as far as she knew, Rob and I were just that—friends. Newly acquainted. Was she trying to get me upset—make me dislike Rob? *Why does she think he's crazy?* I didn't ask her to elaborate—I clammed up.

The rest of the afternoon I tried to remain calm and keep my face void of what I was feeling. I was glad we were sitting at separate tables, and that I only had a side view of her. Once or twice, I glanced Diane's way. I noticed a bottle of wine on the table in front of her. *Please don't drink too much.* I didn't need her to make a scene. She really didn't know anything.

***

I couldn't wait to talk to Rob. When Steve and I got home late that afternoon, I told him I needed some exercise. "I'm going for a walk."

In the woods, I texted Rob and told him he needed to call me ASAP. He said he would sneak away. I waited anxiously.

"She said that your hands were all over her and that you were trying to get her into some cult."

"I've known Diane for years—she's very possessive. She doesn't like to share anyone. I think she's mad because you and I are friends."

"I don't understand—why would she be upset about that?"

"She's a funny woman—she's hard to figure out. When she's friends with someone, she thinks she owns them."

"Do you think she's in love with you?"

"No," he said flatly.

"Are you sure? I could see how women could fall for you."

"You have nothing to worry about, my sweet lady."

I took a deep breath. "Okay."

I believed him. I didn't know Diane well enough—she could be a meddler. There were signs of jealousy too.

Chapter 61

I got up before Steve; I was tired from watching every hour pass. When he left, I went back to bed till 8:00 a.m. Then I got dressed, did the morning dishes, and wrote out a grocery list.

While in the supermarket I heard my phone ping. I knew it was Rob.

I'm getting some groceries.

Get some olives.

?

Just get them, please.

Okay, since you asked so nicely.

When I got home, I put away the groceries. Except for the jar of olives. I figured Rob was going to give me a nice recipe that required this fruit.

I grabbed my phone from my purse and texted him. *I'm home. What do you want me to do with these olives?*

He called me.

"Open the jar and take one out," he said in his deep, luscious voice.

I unscrewed the top and took out one with my fingers.

"Got it."

"Put it in your mouth, close your eyes, and just keep it there."

"Hmm."

"Savor it slowly. Feel its texture. Swirl it around. Let your tongue caress all of it."

I do as he says. "Hmm."

"And?" Rob asked.

"Dense. Firm. Deliciously bitter," I whispered.

"God, you turn me on."

"Can I bite now?"

He was quiet and then I heard him moan with desire. "Yeah, gently."

I heard him breathing deeply. We both remained silent.

"Maybe I should go now," I said.

Rob texted me an hour later.
You drive me crazy. What are we going to do?
Find a way to see each other.
I went online searching for airline tickets.

Chapter 62

It was mid-September, the early morning clouds had scattered, and a veil of sunshine opened above me. Knowing I'd be sitting for a long time on the plane, I wanted to move my legs. In the large parking lot, I closed the car door and circled the harbor; boats were still in their slips. Then I continued my walk to the beach. It all seemed surreal to me that in a few short hours I'd be boarding a flight to Oregon.

I'd let Steve know at the dinner table before I bought the tickets that Rob's family had invited me to come and stay. Steve seemingly wasn't curious or bothered by my decision. He didn't appear upset. Or even question me. Ask me why I was going. Absolutely no dialogue between us. He kept his head buried in the newspaper. The whole thing was bizarre since Steve knew I hadn't met Rob before that night at Diane's house. Maybe he felt I needed to get away. Plus, I have always been faithful. Was he truly unaware of what was going on between Rob and me? *Are we that much out of touch with one another?* Or maybe he just didn't care. Either way, it was sad. Still, I was relieved and grateful there was no tension before I left because not only did I need to see Rob, I needed to get away. Period.

All fears I had of flying, especially alone, seemed to dissipate. This calm fell over me. Vicky had driven me to Logan. I felt composed on the ride there. I had never taken a trip or gotten on a plane alone. Just the thought of it had always made me anxious. The few flights I had taken with my husband were only a couple hours or so in the air. And that was a little nerve-wracking, especially when facing claustrophobia and panic attacks. Craziest thing—I wasn't feeling nervous or scared. I felt none of that.

I was looking forward to seeing the man who'd had such an impact on my life in the past year. And I had absolutely no expectations. I had to know what this gamut of emotions was all about. Maybe just a fantasy? Maybe I'd gone a little crazy, but I felt like I was going to go out of my mind if I didn't see this beautiful man I'd been falling in love with—soon! Though we were separated in person every day, we were together emotionally and spiritually. Even sensually.

To avoid paying more for extra luggage, I'd stuffed everything into two small suitcases, taking clothes in and out for days. I had already shipped Rob body lotions, makeup, mouthwash, and even my hiking boots. I figured it would be easier that way. Vicky and I shopped at Macy's weeks before the trip. I bought PJs, a couple of V-neck tops, and a pair of black jeans.

Rob told me not to bring anything fancy, that I needn't impress anybody. "This isn't Cape Cod. We're pretty laid back here," he'd said. I only partially listened. Even though we had only met once—briefly—first impressions are important, despite what he had implied. I wanted to look nice. That's all. I wanted him to have the same attraction he had for me when we first met. He made me feel sexy, attractive. Loved.

The airport was new to me. Vicky stayed until I made it through security. I turned and waved. I was walking what seemed like forever, especially carrying a suitcase and a tote I had overloaded, until I reached the terminal that I was supposed to be at. Alaska. When noticing where I was to wait before being called to board, I stopped at a variety store and bought a large bottle of water and a protein bar. While standing in a long line at the register, I kept juggling my luggage and purse. My new shirt opened, for the third time, revealing my bra, grateful that I wore one. Rebuttoning was obviously a waste of time.

When it was time to board, the flight attendant stopped me and told me I had too much baggage. *Don't we all.*

"What!" I panicked.

"You can try to put your purse in one of the carry-ons," said the flight attendant.

I thought, OMG, they are overstuffed now.

Anyway, I had to move aside and attempt this. *I'm not going to miss this flight, even if I need to throw away some of my clothes!*

Somehow, I did it! I crammed my purse into the duffel bag. I was screaming *Yes!* inside. Then I worried she'd weigh my bags and they'd be over what was allowed. When she nodded me on, I didn't look back.

I, at last, got on the plane and I had no idea where my seat was. I was trying to hold everything and glance at my ticket and the numbers above as I followed the people in front of me. *Why are the aisles so narrow?* My blouse came undone again and my white bra was flashing. *Maybe I should have worn a fancier one.*

I had never placed a bag in any compartment before. I could barely lift my medium-sized suitcase, never mind hoist it up that high. Muscle loss from weight loss. And hitting fifty soon didn't help. Somehow, I managed. I stuck the small tote under my seat, since my purse was inside. I finally dropped in my seat, sighing. I looked up and saw a dark-haired middle-aged attendant staring at me. "You're in the wrong seat. Your seat is over there," she said, pointing with a sour puss.

"Sorry," I muttered, and stood up.

Not everybody my age has flown before. Give me a break. She glanced at me weirdly. Like I was trying to steal someone else's seat. Ah, I finally landed where I belonged. Yay, I got a window seat! I could read my newest book, *The Longest Ride* by Nicholas Sparks. How coincidental. Or maybe I'd just stare into the blue sky and drift with the clouds.

A smartly dressed, heavyset woman, soaked in a fruity perfume, sat next to me, her slender husband beside her. And a friend of his beside him, on the other side of the aisle. My first thought: What if I need to go to the bathroom? *I won't drink much.* Soon after takeoff, dinner was served. I suddenly became hungry as I watched the woman next to me gobbling a salad with chicken, but I wanted to avoid any stomach issues. *Maybe Rob will take me out to eat.* I tried reading, but my eyes burned—I'd hardly slept the last two nights. Some guy was hacking away a few seats in front of me, exposing us to who knows what.

Five and half hours went faster than I'd imagined, we were descending into Portland. I thought my anxiety would reach its peak—but nothing. Not even a hint. I was about to meet this guy who knew me better in just eleven months than my husband did after twenty-two years of marriage, and I wasn't even nervous.

When I exited the plane, I saw a gentleman standing there who resembled Rob. After all, significant time had passed, and we had only met once. I thought it must be him, even if he looked older than I remembered.

I bravely approached the gentleman. "Rob?"

"No. I don't know you," he said.

"I'm sorry. I haven't seen him in a long time," I mumbled, embarrassed.

I walked away and sat down in one of the chairs. Waiting.

I watched the rest of the passengers hustling toward an escalator that would lead them upstairs to their luggage—at least that's what I assumed. I was the only one left, other than that same gentleman.

He came back over to me. "Are you waiting for someone?"

"Yes," I replied.

"Well, only passengers are allowed in this area. You have to go upstairs to luggage claim."

"Oh, okay. Thank you."

I proceeded to follow the last of the throng. When I stepped off the escalator, I looked around and still I didn't see him. *What if he never shows?* It was only a whim of a thought; I called him.

"Are you here?"

"Yes. I've been here for a while."

"Where?"

"In front of Starbucks."

"Okay. Look for me."

After walking aimlessly through the airport, dragging my luggage, I, at last, spotted him. Standing there waiting. I dropped everything in front of him and leaned my body into his. It seemed to fall naturally. He pulled out a picture of me from his shirt pocket, a recent pic I had sent him in an email of my husband and me in North Carolina a year earlier. He had sliced out my husband.

"Oh, you forgot what I looked like?"

He smiled. "Just want to be sure."

Rob grabbed my luggage and we walked to the parking garage. It was only eight o'clock there, but it was 11:00 p.m. for me. *Sleep is overrated.* Driving through Portland, I surveyed the streets the best I could in the dark. He pointed out landmarks: Hollywood Theatre, Voodoo Doughnut, The Old Church, Portland Old Town neon sign, Governor Tom McCall Waterfront Park, and Portland Center Stage at The Armory. He knew what I'd be interested in seeing.

"Are you hungry?" he asked.

"Yeah, very."

I felt his eyes upon me, but I just stared out the window and only met them when he spoke.

"How about the Outback?"

"Sounds great."

The cheerful hostess greeted us and steered us toward a booth. Rob sat next to me, instead of across from me, which made me feel more comfortable, less awkward. He had already eaten dinner so to be polite, he ordered a Caesar salad. I chose the house salad and filet mignon with sweet potato.

"How was your trip?" he asked.

"It was good."

"Smooth ride?"

I nodded. "No turbulence whatsoever." I looked at him. "I can't believe I'm really here!"

He smiled. "Me neither."

Two booths in front of us, there was a young couple and a toddler. The child kept turning around, trying to win our attention—flashing big smiles. He had the most beautiful chubby face with sparkly dark eyes and long eyelashes.

"Hi, sweetie, how are you?" I asked, giving him a wave.

His young parents turned and smiled.

"How old is he? What's his name?" I asked.

"He's eighteen months. His name is Logan."

"Hi, Logan. I just came from there—an airport named Logan," I said, when he batted those long eyelashes again.

It was like he understood, grinning wider. To think I was old enough to have a grandchild, but that was never going to happen. Still, I yearned for it—even just one. One I could love and spoil.

During our meal, our conversation was light. Rob was very much a gentleman, not sizing me up and down. I was at ease; it felt natural sitting next to him. Like I'd been with him a million times, even though it was a first date. And I felt no apprehension. We had nothing to pretend. We'd already told each other nearly everything, which made this meeting easy and comfortable. *And so right.*

After dinner, Rob took me to the Holiday Inn, a few miles from where he lived, where I'd be staying for the next couple of nights. Another first for me. I wondered how my psyche would handle this, but I was not concerned. As old as I was, sadly, I rarely ever left the nest, ventured anywhere alone. From my mother to my husband. *I was a prisoner. Theirs.* Rob had invited me to stay at their house. Yeah, right! I was to sleep in his granddaughters' bedroom when he was sleeping in a nearby room with his wife.

I registered at the desk and handed Rob the extra key.

When we entered the room, I collapsed on the king-size bed. Rob snapped on the big-screen TV and sat at the end of the bed watching *The Golden Girls*. He even laughed. His laugh made me laugh. There was no TV in his family home, so he appreciated this one. The two of us alone on this big bed, I was surprised when he didn't jump on me right away. Most guys would have pounced at the opportunity. Especially after our longings, our hunger for each other all these months. I eventually rose to wash up and slipped on my PJs—shorty shorts and a T-shirt. I could feel his eyes on me as I walked from the bathroom to the bed.

It all seemed surreal. Here I was, thousands of miles from home, alone with someone I had never been with, yet it felt like I had been with him… always.

He lay on the bed next to me. We hugged and then his lips met mine. And when our tongues braided, it was indescribable. Something I'd been waiting for a long, long time.

Our bodies, at last, together, and natural as the flow of a river. I could feel his erection through his pants, wanting me. "No, not now," I whispered. *You fool.* Oh, how I wanted him. But it needed to be more than instant gratification. He said not a word, respecting my wishes, making him more desirable than ever. After kissing me tenderly again, he walked over to the wash sink and threw water over his face as if he needed to wash away our kiss. His sin.

I hated seeing him go that night, but I knew in a matter of hours I'd be with him again. In fact, it seemed like I'd just shut my eyes and he was sending me a phone message. He, his older son, Calvin, and his grandchildren were on their way. Rob had said they couldn't wait to meet me; maybe he couldn't wait to introduce me.

When they arrived, I was fixing the bed, making it presentable. It was an awkward situation, them coming into the hotel room. What should I say? *Hi, I'm your dad's, your grandfather's friend.* A friend they'd never met. *Yes, I am the mysterious woman who will be spending a lot of time alone with him. And you have no trouble with this?*

Calvin said, "Hello," and held his hand out to shake mine. He was dark and handsome. And what a smile. Obviously, he'd inherited his father's features and skin tone.

"Nice to meet you," I said, taking his hand.

Then I was introduced to the two young girls. Shayna, the oldest at fifteen, and Kiley, eleven.

"Hi, girls."

"Hi," they both said shyly, looking away, as they surveyed the hotel room.

Rob had said Shayna read a lot. *The Longest Ride* by Sparks was on the bed. "I hear you like to read. Have you read this one?" I asked, picking it up and showing her.

Shayna looked down at it. "Yeah."

"Did you like it?"

She shrugged. "It was okay."

"Just okay?"

I looked at the younger girl, Kiley. "What grade are you in?"

"Sixth."

"Do you like school?"

She nodded.

The girls were a bit aloof, quiet, or maybe they were a little shy around a stranger. Or smarter than the adults; they weren't being fooled. I was their curiosity, I'm sure. After a few minutes Calvin said they had to get going; the girls had to be back at their mother's home at 10:00 a.m. Calvin and his wife had recently divorced. Rob had said that Calvin's wife had been physically abusive; she would throw things at him and kick him. "Once, she yanked his glasses off his face and stomped on them. Another time she came at him wielding a knife and screaming she was going to punish his children." Rob said she even began an affair with her dentist while they were still married. *Why did he take this abuse?*

Rob had driven his own car, so he stayed after they left. We were alone again. We hugged and kissed. When he French kissed me, his tongue in my mouth sent pulsating waves of erotic electricity all the way down to my toes.

"My wife wants to meet you."

My eyes popped wide open. "That's nice," I said.

This was odd to me. But everyone was acting like I had been a part of their family. Forever. So I pretended too. What did they think I was to Rob? A Facebook friend? An email friend? A phone friend? I wondered if they even asked Rob how we met or knew each other.

"I told her that you like to walk, and there's a spot where we go that has beautiful redwood trees and a river." *What else did you tell her about me?*

"Yeah, a walk sounds great—especially after that long plane ride."

He drove us to his small apartment that he and his wife, Carol, rented from Calvin. I still couldn't believe Rob had asked me to stay there. It had nothing to do with the place itself; it just didn't feel right.

A kitchen merged with a living room and a small bathroom veered to the left beneath a stairway. I followed Rob upstairs. He showed me the room where he had suggested I stay to save money. Where his grandkids bunked when they came for an overnight slumber. How could he ever think that I could sleep in the same house as him and his wife? Just knowing they'd be a few feet away in the same bed together bothered me. When I had no right to feel that way. After all, I was the other woman. Although he made me feel like I was his only woman, always calling me "his" lady.

He never brought me into their room. I was glad but still I wanted to see where he slept. What the room looked like—what was on the walls, in the closet, on top of his bureau?

Once the grand tour was over, his wife soon arrived home, full of chatter and laughter.

"Hi, how are you?" I said, not knowing what else to say.

Her long, gray hair lay softly down the back of her matronly figure. She had fine spun eyelashes over hazelnut-shaped grey-blue eyes. Was I supposed to hold out my hand to shake hers? Should I embrace her? Nothing seemed appropriate given the circumstances. Rob had said she and I were much alike. I wondered now in what respect. We certainly didn't look alike. Maybe he saw me with blinders on too.

That felt awkward. A quick introduction and she began filling her husband in on what went on that morning with her friends at some school event. *Yuck, that piercing laugh.* She rarely looked at me. As if I was transparent.

I am his emotional affair. And you are allowing me to be alone with your husband for days; this could lead to a physical affair too. Is this bravery—trusting of another—or absolute craziness? I wonder if you would still feel that way if you had heard our phone conversations—or saw all his writings to me. I needed to let this go; I was not there to try and figure her out. I was just grateful to her that she had given me this opportunity.

We soon got in the Hyundai Tucson; I sat in the back seat. Carol drove us into a residential neighborhood where she parallel parked. We got out of the car and headed toward a wooded trail lined with large redwoods. *Maybe this is where she is going to kill me... us... her husband and me.* We trekked single file. *Should I follow behind Rob, or should she?* Ended up, she led the way, and I hiked in her footsteps, Rob trailing behind me.

In our meandering stroll, we met a woman with a beautiful long-haired German shepherd. We stopped and talked with her for a moment. Finding out she was from the East Coast, I proceeded to tell her about the shepherd we had to lay to rest when I was a kid. Nice little conversation we had, but I could see Rob and Carol had lost interest and continued without me. Maybe they'd forgotten I was with them. I'd eventually catch up. I was walking with my lover's wife—it felt surreal.

We continued following the leader, without words, until we halted at a babbling brook.

"There is usually salmon swimming here," Carol said, staring into the clear water.

"That's cool. Too bad there aren't any now. We could've had salmon for dinner," I said.

"Wrong time of year," Rob said.

"Have you ever fished here?" I asked.

"A couple of times," he said.

The tour ended after we reached the river, and we walked back to the car. The combination of fresh air and moving my legs was invigorating, and I appreciated the walk among those amazing tall redwoods. Honestly, though, I didn't understand why Carol came along; there were no words exchanged between the two of us. I think I would interrogate the hell out of a woman my husband brought home. Maybe Rob had portrayed me as a saint. *God, do I give that impression?*

Chapter 63

Rob wanted to drive his own car on the trip, since he was most familiar with it. So I told his wife I'd pay for the rental car for her to drive while we were away. I supposed that was the least I could do. I still had a tough time believing she was letting us go away together. *Why am I dwelling on this?*

Calvin had even left his father a note, with cash, on the counter that morning before heading off to work.

"What did he say?" *It finally hit him that this wasn't right?*

"He said have a great time. And he left me a hundred dollars!"

"Oh wow. That was really nice." *He's approving of me. Approving of us going away together?*

Rob planned to take care of gas and meals, and I agreed to pay for the sleeping arrangements. Only fair. And he wasn't a rich man. We were packed and ready to go. Rob charted our itinerary, taking along a map from AAA since we had no GPS. And he made sure we had plenty of protein bars and bottles of water he'd bought at Trader Joe's. He knew what I liked and what I could eat; we had discussed it several times on the phone.

There was little he didn't know about me.

I watched him fasten his seatbelt; I followed. Rob was a conscientious driver, and right away I felt at ease. I was able to relax for once and enjoy the sights and surroundings. I inhaled deeply and rested against the seat.

Our first stop was the summit of Mt. Hood. Already sheathed in white, it was magnificent. Took my breath away. It had been a while since I'd seen mountains. I think the last time was in New Hampshire, the White Mountains. The ocean, the woods, the lakes, and the mountains were God's gifts for us to appreciate and cherish. Be thankful for.

The cultural center and museum had authentic Indian artifacts, and I was particularly drawn to the feather headdress that went to the floor. The deerskin costumes were beaded with dyed porcupine needles in intricate patterns. I even imagined slipping my feet into those soft moccasins. We soon ventured into the Timberline Lodge, built with the largest logs I had ever seen. When I first entered, in front of me was a beautiful stone fireplace; I could literally walk into it without bending my head.

Before leaving, we snapped a couple of pictures of each other standing in front of the entrance.

"Up close, the mountain isn't as pretty without a lot of snow," I mentioned, gazing.

"Some things are meant to be admired from a distance."

"I guess."

Then eyeing me from head to toe, "You're prettier up close."

I shook my head, smiling.

Leaving the base of the mountain, we stopped at Trillium Lake and sat on the dock, engaging in small talk with a trout fisherman, who had recovered his broken line and found it had a fish on it. An occasional dappled trout would leap from the smooth glassy lake, creating ripples. We sat quietly, gazing at the mountain, its reflection painted on the water. The sun was at its peak in a cloudless sky.

Two young Asian women came walking through the forest path toward us. "Would you mind taking our picture?" the smaller of the two asked, handing me her phone.

"No, I'd be happy to." They gathered. "Ready?" I asked. They nodded. "Smile."

They returned the favor by snapping one of us, the happy shot mirroring how Rob and I felt for each other. More than ever, I wished time could stand still. But I knew deep down nothing has permanence—not even love. I kept those thoughts at bay and lived in the moment because that's all we are really given.

Rob never rushed anything. I needed his calm disposition. He made everything enjoyable, even when we were doing nothing. For once, I had no thoughts or worries of what or who I had left back home. I didn't feel guilty leaving Steve, and he didn't even mention my departure. Mom seemingly didn't know who I was anymore, and she was sleeping most of the time now, so she wouldn't even know if I was there.

We strolled through a cleared, wooded stretch and eventually perched on a cast-iron bench. Two chipmunks were chasing one another. We were essentially alone. I was hoping he'd kiss me.

He didn't.

"Look," he said, pointing. "An eagle."

"Wow, it's beautiful. Must be an incredible feeling to be able to soar above everything."

We followed the eagle's flight until he eventually came to rest on a high limb, its majestic stature exemplifying confidence. "King of the land," I said.

"Do you know what it means when one sees an eagle?"

I smiled. "No, but I know you're going to tell me."

Whenever I spotted an animal or bird during my walks, Rob would let me know what it meant. If he didn't know, he would get out his spiritual animal book and read to me the predestined sign.

"It's the symbol of freedom, spiritual protection, bringing courage and wisdom—to do or become anything."

"Anything?"

"Yup." He smiled. "What if you were gripped by that eagle's talons and lifted and taken far away and dropped. What would you do?" Rob asked.

"I wouldn't look back. I would enjoy the flight. It would be the adventure of a lifetime. I could just imagine being dropped somewhere I've never been before. It would be exhilarating not to have a choice on whether I should go. Placed away from everything and everyone. All my fears and anxieties would disappear like they never existed. I would be free!"

Rob just looked at me.

I wanted him to talk more, yet I liked that he didn't. Talk can get messed up; words misunderstood. I could relate to him, read him, in a different, nonverbal way. A spiritual way.

I found Rob a "mysterious man." He was bad, yet so good. I liked both sides of him. Even his darker edge intrigued me. It was like he was in a constant battle with the two. There was always that diabolical side in life—all good can become boring. He had mentioned more than once that there was a dark side to him. "I mean, I didn't kill anyone," he had said. I wondered if there was more than I already knew. I was afraid to ask. Part of me wanted to. Without spoiling the mystery or ruining the good I saw in him.

I captured a few pics of Rob sprinting among the trees. One time, he posed like a respectable, thinking man, resembling the classic Rodin statue. Partially kneeled in a squatting position, knuckles resting beneath his chin, he stared into the distance, holding a thoughtful gaze. A prophet? I wondered who he wished to emulate. Who inspired him. We had never really discussed our faith, our beliefs. Only briefly about our Catholic upbringing.

"Do you want separate rooms?" Rob asked when we arrived at the hotel. "I'll pay—I want you to feel comfortable."

I shook my head. "No. We're both adults here."

That night, our first real night together in the hotel, we shared a king-size bed. He wore his jockeys and a T-shirt. I wore a long nightgown. It was awkward at first. Neither one of us had slept with anyone other than our spouses since we married. *At least I think he hasn't slept with anyone else.* We nestled beneath the cotton sheets, just holding each other. I felt the softness of the sheets on my toes, and my legs when the gown rose with movement. Sleeping with Rob was different and special. He was special. Matchless. I kept waiting for him to leap, satisfy his longings, but he didn't. No advances. And every limb of him was warm. Unmoving. Calm. Respectful.

Is this a test?

We got up around eight the following morning, dressed, packed up, and headed out. We stopped for breakfast, skipped lunch, and munched on protein bars till dinner. Surprisingly, being Oregon's rainy season, every day we had sunshine.

"The weather couldn't be more perfect," I said, feeling the warm rays on my skin.

"Mother nature is looking favorably on us. The powers that be knew you were coming."

I smiled.

Passing through Warm Springs Reservation, we noticed wild mustangs galloping in the desert fields. Their shining midnight, chestnut, and calico coats glistened as they sped like lighting.

"There are so many of them. Healthy looking and beautiful too," I said.

Running free.

"I think there are over seventeen herds in Oregon. They are the South Steen Mustang. They have been here for a long time—native to the land."

"Amazing," I said, staring, as Rob slowed so I could watch them.

Then he pulled off the road, so I could enjoy the lava formations at the Deschutes River. While taking pictures, a state policeman pulled in behind us. Rob got out of the car, and I followed; the two of us walked over to the trooper.

"You're not allowed to be parked on the Indian Reservation."

"We're sorry, Officer. We had no idea," I said.

"Where are you from?" the officer asked.

"Well, I'm from Massachusetts. Rob's from here. I'm just visiting."

"Can I see your license?" he asked Rob.

Then the officer looked at me. "Yours too, please."

I picked up on the policeman's accent. "Are you from Ireland?"

"As a matter of fact, I am."

"I have a little Irish in me—I hope to see Ireland soon. I hear it's incredibly beautiful. I have heard so many talks from friends about their wonderful visits there," I rambled on nervously.

"It *is* beautiful—and very green."

"What brought you here?"

"More opportunity in the U.S. Can't make any money there," the officer said.

"Yes, that's true. I mean, at least that's what I hear."

He stared at Rob. "Do you know you look like Robert Durst?"

"Is he a movie star?" I asked.

"No, he kidnapped and murdered his girlfriend."

"Yikes. No, Rob wouldn't hurt a fly." *How would I know that?* My mother always warned me about the quiet ones; she'd said stay away from them—they're sneaky. Untrustworthy—cunning like a fox.

"That's good. All right, you folks have a good day," the officer said, returning our licenses.

I smiled. "Thanks. You too, Officer."

When we got back in the car and put on our seatbelts, Rob looked at me. "Were you flirting with him?"

"Maybe a little—I didn't want you to get a ticket."

He grinned, shook his head, and started the car.

At Smith Rock, we saw brave climbers. From the bottom, staring up at them, they resembled ants. Slowly moving. Between the warm air and the steep hills, I struggled with the hike. It must have been obvious to Rob; he immediately took my purse to lessen some of the exertion. And he didn't seem to care what others thought. A real gentleman.

"So, what do you think?" he asked as we walked the curvy dirt pathways.

"This place is incredible," I said, looking at the wide river. Then turning back, staring up at the climbers: "I think it's insanity—but I can just imagine the adrenaline rush they get."

"Like the one you give me?"

"You mean like we give each other," I said.

"I like that."

I smiled, feeling my cheeks getting hot.

"Have you ever hiked or climbed?"

"No," I said. "But I always wanted to. Have you?"

"Yeah, when I was younger. Much younger. I hiked Mt. Washington."

"Oh, wow. That must have been some high."

He smiled. "Being with you is a high," he said, taking my hand in his.

Leaving there, we headed to Sisters, Oregon. We stopped for dinner at Bronco Billy's Ranch. It was noisy—I mean the place was rocking—and we had to yell back and forth, which made us laugh. The burgers and fries were good, and they filled our hollow bellies. It was getting dark, and we were tired. We needed to find a hotel before it got too late.

After we showered, Rob opened the bottle of red wine he'd brought along. Something we needed after that long hike.

"We don't have glasses," I mentioned.

"Sure we do." He got up and walked over to the big desk, in front of the bed. He grabbed the wrapped plastic cups next to the ice bucket. Before I finished the glass, I laid my head on his chest and wrapped my arm around his waist. I thought I would close my eyes for a second. Hadn't realized I dozed, until I heard something. Rob was talking in his sleep, more like weeping. Crying out for his daddy. Calling out for him in sadness. Dregs of a nightmare. Was he missing his dad or was he feeling guilty for not being able to save him? Or maybe Rob felt he was carrying on, cheating, like his dad did to his mother. I wanted to comfort him. Ask him what his dream was about, but I just lay there and listened, hoping he'd reveal more.

The following morning, we showered and gathered our things and put them into the car. Rob drove up to the front desk, and I got out and returned the key.

"Did you folks have a nice stay?"

"We did. Thank you."

When I came out of the office, I noticed alpacas grazing on a dewy field. "Hey look—alpacas. Or are they llamas?"

"Let's go see. I'll park the car closer."

"They're adorable," I said, moving my hand above the wired fence to rub the head of one that bravely approached us.

"They really are."

On a smaller parcel of grassy land rested an old covered wagon. A posted metal sign on the wagon read, "No touching or sitting inside." So we snapped pictures of each other standing next to it.

We stopped to have a late breakfast at Charlotte's Bakery and Café. A quaint little place that offered organic smoothies, juices, and a variety of gluten-free, homemade goodies. Rob had quiche and I tried the gluten-free pizza.

"Hey, how's the quiche?"

"Really good."

"How's the pizza?"

"Delicious."

We sat and ate in silence, enjoying the food.

"I think I'm going to get a slice of that pumpkin bread for later. Do you want something?" I asked.

"Yeah. Grab me a coffee, please."

Leaving the café's parking lot, Rob got a phone call. From a woman, I surmised. "No. No, this is not a good time. Okay. Bye." Short and sweet. I was hoping he'd tell me who it was, but he didn't. I wanted to grill him, but it would ruin our trip. Besides, who am I? I'm not even his wife. I didn't want him to think I was jealous—the jealous shrew. Truth be told—I was. *Did he touch her? Did he touch her there—give her an orgasm? Was she the one?* Even though I had forgiven, how could I forget?

The sun was still shining brightly in a cloudless cerulean sky when we stopped at the Black Butte Ranch. Several fenced-in horses trotted in a large open field. I thought of the apples we'd each grabbed from a fruit basket near the register at one of the restaurants.

"Hey, I'm going to the car to get an apple."

"Good idea—horses love them," Rob said.

Soon, an old black horse trotted over. He approached more slowly when he got closer to the fence, sniffed the fruit, but never went for it.

"I think this horse is blind," I said.

"What makes you think that?"

"Look at his eyes—it's like they're clouded."

"Maybe a cataract," Rob said.

"Could be."

"What would you do if I became blind?" Rob asked.

"Take care of you—be your eyes."

"Where'd you come from?"

I just smiled.

We walked hand in hand over to the pond, crammed with jumping fish and ducks gliding, while squawking geese flew above. We sat on the grass near the water's edge, enjoying the tranquil surroundings. It reminded me of the wall painting at

Bellview of the couple on the grass, looking so in love. And here I was—with Rob in a similar setting. It felt like I was dreaming.

Forty-five minutes later we were in the car headed toward the mountains. The road was long and curvy. Traffic suddenly stopped, for a half-hour or more, while tree men were working. Rob was patient. I rolled the window down, and I could smell the embers of destruction. The forest had had fires, ground scorched and hundreds of trees now devoid of life. It made me sad; the forest, like the ocean, was special. *Poor Mother Earth.*

I turned toward Rob, leaned over, and kissed him on the cheek. "I love the way you crunch your nose like a little rabbit."

"I'm not used to these glasses," he said, crunching it again. Smiling as he glanced at me.

***

It was a long drive to the ocean. We arrived at The Seafood Grill just as the sun was starting to set. It was romantic having him next to me while we ate our dinner. Afterward, at the car, Rob pulled his guitar out of the back seat, then took my hand. "Come with me."

Sitting on the sand, he began to play and sing another beautiful song he had written for me. It was romantic. I wanted this dreamy moment to last for all time. Mesmerized, I watched his lips move, his chest rise, and his fingers strumming those strings. When he finished, he put the guitar in the case and knelt behind me and started rubbing my neck. I closed my eyes and felt the wind blowing strands of my hair. He said, "Breathe in through your nose and out through your mouth. Slowly." He repeated it. And we did that breathing technique till I was calm and clear like I'd never been before. We stayed on the beach, laying under the stars.

Later that evening, when we got comfortable in our room, Rob asked, "Would you like a massage?"

"Yeah, that would be nice. Right here?" I asked, patting the bed.

"I need to use oil. It will stain these sheets. I'll get the table."

"Are you sure? I know you're tired too. You've done so much driving."

"I'm good."

Wow, he's going to oil my body; it will make it easier to glide his long, smooth fingers over me.

As I lay there waiting for him to return, I wondered how many other women he'd given massages to. Did he touch them the way he was going to touch me? When he got back to the room, I watched him set up the table and get the oils ready.

"I need you to take everything off." That statement awarded me a flashback—that Mongolian woman had asked him to do the same.

"Okay," I said, feeling nervous. But I trusted him.

He handed me one of the hotel towels. "Here, put this around you."

I obeyed. I lay on my stomach and waited. Then I felt his hands in my hair. As he massaged my head, any negative thoughts disappeared. Before he applied the sweet almond oil to his hands, he wrapped my hair in a bun. He started at the nape of my neck and moved to the blades of my shoulders, dissolving any tension. He continued slowly toward the middle of my torso, down along the back of my legs, until the landing of my feet. Then he bent over, showered my toes in soft kisses, and smeared them in oil.

"Do you want to turn over now?"

It sounded more like an instruction than a query. I slowly lifted myself, turned to one side, and lay flat on my back, giving myself to him. He gently took away the towel.

I closed my eyes in trust, letting my mind wander. I knew I should fight the devil's temptation; it was a harmful desire like a heroin addict craving the needle for elation. I lusted for his virility inside me. To reach that pinnacle, the ultimate high.

Rob's oiled hands maneuvered the front of my neck, toward my chest; my nipples erected. He gently shifted strands of my hair that had loosened from the bun off my shoulders. "Do you want me to examine your breasts?"

Examine my breasts? That's random—never heard about that being asked during a massage.

I opened my eyes. "No," I said quietly. Though my insides

were screaming, "**Yes**." I wanted him to but if he did, I was going to have an orgasm. I could barely hold back now. How could I be one of those women? Just another one that he satisfied with his smoothness. His trust. His understanding. No, no, no! I won't be just another. Damn him.

He worked my shoulders, moving down my arms. Then I felt his soft, long fingers gliding along my torso, to my inner thigh. I closed my eyes. My body quivering. I was trying to keep control. I wasn't sure how much more I could take. I didn't need to deprive myself of the long-deserved satisfaction. Fulfillment. I waited for him to touch me there, but he didn't. He was just torturing me. *I hate him—I love him.*

I would have to reciprocate. Oh, how I wanted to. First time ever I wanted to give all of myself to someone. As much as I loved him, that voice inside my head returned, reminding me that we were both married, but that voice was so minuscule I dismissed it. What rushed in more dominantly was of the woman he'd relieved. *"I only did it to one woman so far."* So far? I could envision him touching her, giving her that orgasm, and it made me sick inside. Or maybe I just wished I **was** that woman. But now I was just a number. Number two. *You should never have told me this. You ruined it for me—you ruined it for yourself.*

I wanted to be his number one.

But I could never be now.

Though he'd claimed he received nothing from that experience sexually, I was having a hard time believing him. I wanted to trust him in every way, but *they* had put their trust in him too. I knew I wasn't special, but he had made me feel like I was. I was sure he made them feel the same way. Did any of those other women go away with him? Stay with him—sleep with him? I was the lucky one. *Don't fool yourself*, said my inside voice.

He talked about how spiritual Tantric sex was and not focused on the climax but everything leading up to it. Okay, we'd led up to it. So now what? If he keeps touching me this way… maneuvering his fingertips slowly and lightly across my body… making tiny hairs on my skin rise… I wanted to feel someone in this way—all my life. But I couldn't allow it to happen. Not this time. *"I could just watch him walk by me and come in my underwear."* I could now relate to what Mom meant about her beloved Irving.

When Rob came from the bathroom in his briefs, I stared. His dark-toned body was unblemished and solid. He had a physique of a much younger man. My eyes crept to his flat, firm stomach and his manly part bulging in his underwear, which was more than adequate. I knew he could satisfy me. *Sex is a broken promise. Pain. Insecurity.*

We teased each other, turning one another on. I knew he was as horny as I was. Then I sat up and said, "No." He listened. HE LISTENED. I was happy he respected my wishes. Partly. There were no more advances. Why? Damn, I wanted him. More than I ever wanted anybody, but I, instead, with my entire being—resisted it. Him. Because I wanted it, us, to be right. And for him to never desire another. Never!

"I think it would be best—you sleep over there," I said, gesturing toward the other bed.

Am I insane?

"Okay."

Okay—that's it? Is he insane too? No other guy, at least the ones I had known, would ever put up with that. They might have even tried to rape me. Rob accepted my rejection. And exhibited zero signs of anger or disappointment. Why is he being so compliant? Submissive?

Control. Respect. Tantra.

In the morning, he slid under the covers next to me. I smiled and laid my head on his chest. I wrapped my arm around his stomach, letting my hand feel its smoothness. My fingers inched down toward his groin. I told myself no and stopped myself from reaching further beneath the sheets. *God, I want to feel him. Why am I fighting this?* I know we both wanted to make love—but he gave me intimacy, which was even better.

For now.

God, I love this man. And I hate that I love this man; he's not my man. He doesn't belong to me.

***

The country road headed to the coastal mountain range through Alsea was long and barren. Poverty stricken. There were small houses and business structures. These edifices were now rundown and abandoned. It appeared as if some had tried to make a go of it at one point, but the area never developed. The rundown shacks, in bold blue, red, and yellow, might have been fruitful trades at one time. A place where I would have felt welcomed.

Rob stayed in the car while I ran from one side of the road to the other taking pictures.

When I got back to the car, he said, "Hey, did I tell you, you have a great behind."

"You've been staring at my butt?"

He smiled. "How can I not—it's part of you."

I shook my head and smiled.

My phone rang. I checked the screen—it was Steve. I answered to see if everything was okay at home.

"Why haven't you called? You've been gone for days—not one word from you. What the hell," Steve yelled.

"Is Mom okay?"

"How the hell do I know?"

I saw Rob waving his hand, expressing to cut Steve off. "Tell him you can't hear him."

"We're in the mountains—the reception's poor here."

"What am I, chopped liver?"

"No, of course not. I gotta go—everybody is getting back in the car." I had told Steve I was touring with Rob's family. "I will call you later."

I didn't.

About an hour later we arrived in a small but charming fishing village. It reminded me of Provincetown with the beautiful artwork on some of the big, old wooden buildings. As we ventured near the water, I noticed seals sunbathing on the docks. "Oh my gosh, look," I said, pointing. "Seals."

"They aren't seals. They're sea lions."

"Sea lion? I've never seen one."

"Well come on," he said, grabbing my hand, bringing me closer.

"They're really cute—with their long whiskers. And there are so many of them."

"Too many can attract sharks."

"Really—that's not good."

"No, so you wouldn't want to swim here."

I shook my head.

After snapping pictures of each other, we strolled through the little village viewing the quaint and vibrant blue, red, yellow, and green shops; one with a line of people waiting to go inside.

"I wonder what's going on in here," I said, peering into the big glass window. "Oh, look, homemade chocolates. Want some?"

"No, I'm good."

"I would love to have some. Does your wife like chocolates?"

"Yes, she does."

"Great."

We stood in the long line for nearly a half-hour. When we got to the counter, I ordered a half pound for both Carol and me.

Afterward, we went to the car and headed north on Rte. 101, the coastal route, stopping at small towns on the way. We parked in front of a gift shop and walked across the street. There was a brick alleyway complete with a cluster of refined boutiques stocked in chic clothing. Shoes. Boots. Blown glassware. Pottery and more. A tourist trap. Still, we were tempted to enter but thought better of it. Besides, I had no more room in my suitcase.

As we walked onto the beach, I saw tsunami warnings posted everywhere. I had never seen anything like this before. I wondered if they just went up.

"Should we be scared? Are these warnings for now?"

"No, those signs are always up."

"Have you had one here—a tsunami?"

"Not as long as I have lived here."

"I suppose a disaster can happen anytime. Anywhere?"

"True. We can't worry."

I remember overhearing the gift shop's keeper and a customer talking about how the state of Oregon was in great danger of having a major earthquake. All I could think about was losing Rob to this disaster. Not from natural causes or an accident or even another woman, but to Mother Nature! An earthquake was a real possibility, but people chose to ignore it. And here too, no one was running for safety.

It was windy and chilly by the coast, but when Rob held my hand in his while walking along the shore, my whole inside warmed. The surf was roaring. Several others were strolling the beach, some dipping their feet in the cold Pacific, flirting with the waves. Rob pointed out a big boulder in the distance surrounded by terns and puffins.

"That's called the Haystack Rock."

"It's so big."

"Third tallest in the world."

"Really?"

"Yup. At lowest tide, you can walk to it. Usually, you'll see crabs and starfish and limpets clinging to the rock."

"What's a limpet?" I asked.

"Marine mollusk—like a snail.

"Oh."

A Newfoundland dog, running free from his owner, veered our way. Rob reached out to it. The hound scampered over and sniffed his hand. Rob bent over and petted him; in return the dog gave him a sweet lap of his tongue, then dashed back to his owner.

"He liked you," I said.

"Briefly—he didn't stay long."

"Maybe he was afraid to."

Rob looked at me. "Nothing to fear here."

I smiled. "I know."

Walking hand in hand along the beach, I felt light, and the happiest I'd been in a long time. *Togetherness—this is what a good marriage should be like.* After about half a mile, I stopped and released my hand from his. Then I bent down and wrote a message to him in the wet sand. "I Love You Roomy." He said nothing, smiled, and wrapped his arm around my waist, pulling me closer to him.

Our days together bolted like a speeding bullet. I was wishing something would delay my return. Maybe a storm, an accident, I got too sick to board. I wanted to stay longer. Or maybe forever. I could hear my mother's voice, "Aimee, you have to face reality." *Why? What good does it do?*

Noticing an Italian café, we went in. There were gluten-free options, and we decided to share a pizza. While waiting for our order, we used the restrooms. Since we were pressed for time to pick up his wife at the airport—to return the car she rented—we took the pizza to go. While Rob drove, I fed him. The traffic was heavy and came to a halt several times. I could tell he was nervous, knowing his wife was counting on us to retrieve her. It was the first time I'd seen Rob anxious during the entire trip, but it was understandable.

"We can't change the traffic," I said. *Why do good things come to an end?*

"I know. But she'll be waiting."

She could wait forever as far as I was concerned—they all could. For the first time, his body showed unease. Almost agitation. I could even see it in his eyes. Seemingly, wanting to return to her. Or maybe, not wanting to return at all.

Carol had been standing in the dingy rental car parking garage for quite a while before we got there. She had to be upset, but she said not a word. Her face was unreadable. I moved from the front, passenger's seat to the back. She avoided eye contact with me during the switch. Rob didn't apologize for being late, and she didn't scold him. She never asked either one of us how our trip went. Why would she?

"I have to stop at the bank before we go home," I heard her say to him.

He nodded, "Okay." He was so smooth, his wife in the front seat now, his lover in the back. *Or am I his friend—lovers make love.*

While she was inside the bank, Rob looked at me in his rearview mirror. "Did you have a good time?"

I nodded with a wan smile. "Yes."

"I'm glad."

Our trip was over, but our time together wasn't. Not entirely. We still had a day and a half to explore. Either more places or each other. I knew I would no longer be sleeping with him through the night—she would. Was it wrong—a sin—wanting to feel good with someone who made me happy? Someone who treated me with respect? Accepted me for who I am? *For the way I was?*

And Rob, like myself, was a romantic in every sense of the word. Everything he uttered was like poetry to my ears. And it wasn't about him opening the door for me, sending me greeting cards. Or even bringing me flowers. He was someone with patience. One I could communicate with, someone who liked the same things I did. Someone who deeply cared and seemingly understood me. Who had an abundance of empathy and love, not just for me, but for those around him.

He loved me—he loved her. Who will he choose?

The next day after picking me up at the hotel and taking me for breakfast, we drove to the Portland Women's Forum State Scenic Viewpoint. It was foggy, and soon it began to drizzle. Rob and I went back to the car and put on our rain jackets. I quickly snapped some photos. Then we both stood there, like the rest of the onlookers, staring out at the picturesque view before us. Rob draped his arm around my waist, pulling me closer to him. I leaned my head on his shoulder and let the rain drip on my face.

***

That night, I had dinner at Rob's house with the whole family, including the daughters-in-law and grandkids. I wondered what they were thinking. Not one of them asked about the trip, where we went. What we did. *Why would they?*

Everyone was pleasant and seemingly accepting of me, but something felt off. I didn't fit in. Belong. *The oddball.* Rob eluded any attention or affection toward me and his wife. He seemed void of emotions, detached from reality. I felt as though I was sitting amongst the Waltons in *The Twilight Zone*. Perfect family deception. I was invisible to them—seemingly they were looking right past me. I finished my dinner and immediately took my plate and everyone else's over to the sink and began washing. The least I could do for their hospitality. Besides, I felt awkward.

Then Calvin asked his father if he had taken me to the Rose Garden in Portland.

"No," Rob said, shaking his head.

"Oh, why not? Dad, you should have taken her there."

"I know. We didn't have time."

I was surprised Rob hadn't made the effort; he had talked so much about the roses in Portland Garden. I loved the way he always compared me to a rose or another beautiful flower. "Strong and sweet."

In the living room, I sat in a hard chair. Carol was across from me, a few feet away, in a love seat, in sweats. She just stared at me, shooting daggers. Like I had done something terrible. *You're the one who let your husband go away with me. If he was my husband, I'd tell him not to return.*

Rob's younger son, Tyler, brought out his guitar and began playing and singing—breaking the tension. He had his father's musical talent. His voice was nice, but there was no comparison to Rob's. Maybe I was just partial. His father's stage presence and charisma were missing. Tyler glanced my way a few times, maybe looking for my approval, reminding me of the night I first heard his father.

Carol went to bed early; she had to work the next day. Rob and I stayed in the living room and talked. He showed me the music albums he'd collected through the years, and a journal he'd kept where he had written over two hundred songs. As we sifted through them, I felt like I was a teenager again on a first date, with Rob's mom upstairs. How could Carol sleep?

Chapter 64

The next morning, Rob picked me up at the hotel for more sightseeing. Our last day. Another beautiful, sunny day with a gentle breeze. Multnomah Falls was mesmerizing with its willowy waterfalls, falling smoothly like glass, swooping into infinity pools. The water was so crystal clear, I wanted to bathe in it. Feel it cascading over me. Cleansing my body. My soul. We climbed the steps and got sprayed in one area near the top; the radiant sapphire descent was purely astounding to watch. We laughed and snapped pictures.

Afterward, we walked back across the road. Before we got back into the car, Rob took my hand and walked me beneath a rickety wooden bridge. There, he stopped and faced me, holding both of my hands in his. He stared into my eyes. "I've fallen in love with you." Then he kissed me tenderly. Lovingly. Other than the omitted kneeling on one knee and the giving of the ring, it felt like he had just proposed to me. My insides stirring, every cell of my being electrified.

"I love you too." We wrapped our arms around each other and kissed again, even longer. I wanted time to stop—right here, right now. He took hold of my hand and we walked to the car.

He had waited and his timing was perfect. He could have said how he loved me when we were in bed together, luring me in to change my mind about making love with him. Or any time during our trip, for that matter. But no, he said those words of adoration when he believed it was the right time for me to hear them.

But what did this mean—for the both of us? Was it taking us any further?

***

Knowing it was my last night there, I was restless. I couldn't sleep. I got up at 2:30 a.m., ran the bath, and soaked. I knew it wouldn't be long before Rob would be there to take me to the airport. I wasn't ready to leave.

As soon as I got out of the tub, Rob was at the door. He said he couldn't sleep either. It was my last chance to make love with him, but we would have been rushed, and I wanted to wait until we saw each other again. I wanted it to be right—in every way. We'd see each other again. I was sure of it.

In the airport, Rob tagged all my bags and stayed with me until I got through security. I turned around and mouthed, "I love you."

He put his hands together, forming a heart.

I sunk in a chair at the airport away from everyone and closed my eyes. I had an hour to wait before boarding the plane home. I was only there ten minutes when Rob texted me.

I'm still sitting here.

Where?

In my car.

Your car?

Yes. Crying.

Crying?

I just miss you already.

I took a deep breath and typed, *Me too.*

We'll see each other again—soon.

Tears forming in my own eyes. *Yes. Yes, we will.* We had to.

When I finally boarded the plane, I dropped into an aisle seat with a lavatory wall behind me, leaving it impossible to recline. Sitting up straight, I fell asleep. Suddenly, my head dropped to my neck, jolting me out of a peaceful rest. Luckily, no one occupied the other two seats, giving me room to spread out.

Inside Logan Airport, Steve was waiting for me with open arms. I strode into them. He hugged me tightly. Then he looked at me. "Honey, I missed you so much." I could see the love he had for me in his eyes. I was bothered that I wasn't feeling the same sentiment. Yet I had no remorse.

Chapter 65

Even though it had only been a few days since Rob and I had seen each other, it felt like we'd been apart for weeks. I missed him. Terribly. If anything, the feelings I had for him were stronger. He wasn't just a fantasy or a figment of my imagination. He was the man I'd been longing for all my life.

Visiting Mom wasn't the same; she had lapsed into another state of feebleness. Her body was growing smaller and weaker, hardly any flesh to protect her frail bones. She slept most of each day in a fetal position, moaning in pain. Even the morphine injections they were giving her seemed of little help. I'm not sure if she knew I was even there. Although when I talked to her, her face contorted, and her forehead wrinkled. I could see her eyes moving under the lids—like they were scolding me. I think she was angry with me—I wondered if it was because I hadn't been there. Or was it just my own guilt?

"Mom, I'm here," I said, gently touching the top of her head, lightly combing her hair with my fingers. "I can tell you are mad at me. I went to visit that man I'm in love with. I hope you understand. I didn't desert you—I would never do that.

I want to let you know—in case I haven't said so lately—I think you're a wonderful mother. And I love you very much," I said, lowering my head, kissing her cheek.

I thought I saw a faint smile, a tear falling from the corner of her eye.

Sometimes I just wanted it all to end. Be over with. Mom wasn't going to get better, and I hated seeing her suffer. Would I ever get Steve out of my life? And I was starting to believe that Rob and I would never be together. Insecurities and fear hampered the pathway to our happiness. I felt powerless. Immobilized, as if a boulder was crushing me—my heart. I just wished things could be different.

When I returned home later that day, I got a text from Rob that made me sadder.

The sun has gone away; the sun that warmed me.

The rain has returned in full force.

The winter will be long,

But that summer-like sun that we felt when you were here—I will remember—to bring joy to my heart.

You bring joy to my heart.

I missed him so much. Our love had only grown stronger after being together. Even with our ups and downs. There was confusion many times when our emotions went on overload. But we forgave each other—nothing could tear us apart. At least that's what I'd come to believe.

Another text.

When you were here, I wanted to put a ring on your finger.

Ohh?

That statement was wonderful, but I didn't know what he was saying except that I liked it, and I didn't question his reasoning. Of course it made no sense, since he was married, yet it made perfect sense to me.

While I was walking, I got another text from Rob.

I have loved only two women in my life. You and my wife. Tell me what to do, please.

I can't—you have to make that decision on your own.

Do you want me?

More than anything. You know that.

I have a lot to sort out. Give me some time, please.

Of course.

Thank you.

There hadn't been too much contact since our last text, but this time I wasn't worried. I knew he was working on making a big decision on who he wanted to be with. More. He had more to lose than I did. He had his sons nearby and his precious grandchildren, whom he adored. They had been so much a part of his life.

For my birthday, Rob sent me a gift. Unexpected. I opened the package and stared in awe. It was a pen and ink drawing. A forest gleaming with birds and daffodils. Two deer, a fox along a stream, and a couple of squirrels on a tree's trunk. He was not only thinking of his future, but he had also been spending a lot of his time making this for me.

There was exquisite depth to this human being, and that was just another part of him I loved.

"I don't know what to say—this is so beautiful. I love it! Thank you so much. It's one of the best presents I've ever received."

"It's my pleasure—my lady."

"I can't wait to frame this, so I can hang it."

"I wish I had done a drawing of you —when you were here."

"Me?"

"Yeah. I would've drawn you without any clothes on."

"Naked?"

"Sure, why not—your body is beautiful."

"I don't think I'd want a nude pic of myself—especially at this age. I'd only want you to have it—to think of me, remember me."

"I wouldn't need a picture to remember. I have you etched in my mind—all of you. I will never forget."

I took a deep breath. Nobody had ever appreciated me—all of me—the way he did.

Chapter 66

My phone rang at 2:30 a.m. Seeing it was the nursing home, I knew what had happened. The call I knew that would eventually come. Hospice had been with Mom for a while now. I let the phone ring, go to voicemail, and I just lay there numb the rest of the night.

The days following were a blur. I was floating through the steps of doing what was required when someone dies. Discussing various flower arrangements with florists, the funeral director—regarding the wake and visiting hours—and the town as to when the gravedigger was to come. I didn't have to worry about picking out a casket. Mom never had indicated what her wishes were because death was not a subject she would discuss. "I don't want to be buried in the ground having bugs crawl on me." This was the only thing I remembered her saying.

I searched my closet for something to wear. Black attire was no longer considered a tradition for mourners, since it was no longer focused on the bereavement of someone's passing; more of celebrating the deceased's life. How can one dress cheerfully in the presence of another's loss. Still, I found black attire to be the most appropriate. *Stunning and morbid. Respectful. Superior.* However, I discarded my black garments when I turned forty. They reminded me of him.

> *Wednesday, May 21, 1969*
>
> *Dear Diary,*
>
> *Week after week, Father forces me to swallow his "snake". It makes me sick! He doesn't care! When will this end? I hate this promise! Why God? Why?!*

What baffled me more was how people expected you to get on with your own life after a certain amount of time. They may as well put a date on when to stop feeling. Cold. Unsympathetic. Detached. *It's not your mother.*

Other than Aunt Sara, Jeff and Amanda, Cameron and Casey and my close friend, Vicky, only a few locals paid their respects at the funeral home. Afterward, Steve and I and a scant number of others attended the graveside memorial.

I carried the beautiful decorative urn, painted with butterflies and birds, from the funeral home to the graveyard and left it where she was to be buried. Mom would be wondering why I'd put this lovely vase into the ground. *I didn't want to put you there either.* The gravedigger was already waiting a few hundred yards away. *Routine.*

I read the back of Mom's obituary card; I'd picked this poem from a binder filled with choices they had handed me at the funeral home. They were beautifully sad poems. For some reason, I chose this one.

Do not stand at my grave and weep.
I am not there; I do not sleep.
I am a thousand winds that blow.
I am the diamond glints on snow.
I am the sunlight on ripened grain.
I am autumn's gentle rain.
When you awaken in the morning's hush,
I am the swift uplifting rush.
Of quiet birds in circled flight.
I am the soft stars that shine at night,
Do not stand at my grave and cry,
I am not there,
I did not die.

—Clare Harner

Afterward, I invited everyone back to the house including the pastor, Joseph Crowley, who had conducted the service. Steve and I had a mini buffet: appetizers, finger sandwiches, deli meats, and desserts. Pastor Crowley, a lifelong local man in our small town, regaled us with stories of my grandfather, whom I hadn't known. He rambled about my grandfather's chickens and cows and other livestock at the home Mom was born and raised in. I wondered if she'd met happier times in those earlier years. *Broken home. Probably not.* I remembered that old black and white photo I had found of her when she was a little girl, standing alone beside her house, looking sad. Despondent.

A couple of hours later, everyone was gone. I put the leftovers away and washed the dishes—like just any other day. Steve gave me a long sympathy hug and a kiss on the forehead.

He retired to bed.

***

I needed Rob there for me, more than ever, and he stayed away, which hurt deeply. No phone calls, no emails, no texts. Not even a stinking sympathy card.

"Where were you?" I cried when he finally called three days after the funeral.

"I wanted to leave you alone with your family during this difficult time for everyone."

"You know that I consider you family. The same way you considered me part of yours. I'm closer to you, more than anyone here! I needed you," I cried.

"I was always there for you—maybe silenced, but I prayed for you and your mom every day."

Fuck the silence. Fuck the prayers—fuck all that.

"You've been with me every moment of this difficult journey, every moment and then silence? I don't understand. Help me understand."

"I'll write you a letter to explain and mail it you."

"A letter? Are you kidding me? We're not going to talk about it?"

"I think it's the best thing for now."

"I thought my husband was the abusive one. Isn't abandonment a form of abuse?"

"Aimee, you're upset right now. We'll talk another time."

Another time! I wanted to go off on him; he was making me crazy. *Fuck you, Rob.* My insides were torn from the loss of my dear mother. I don't know what I would've done without him. And he'd been with me all along, supporting me, through her illness and now it was like he was abandoning me. How can someone who's been warm and caring turn stony and indifferent overnight?

***

A few days later, I received the letter in the mail, typewritten. Not even a personal salutation or signature. And the words, the letter's contents in between, were calculated. I wasn't sure who this person was anymore. There was nothing heartfelt here, just contradictory BS. A waste of ink and paper. A sympathy card would have been more personable.

Dear One,

Though you think your friend abandoned you in your time of need—this was not so. For months, caring and compassion were always there. When you seemed so alone without help, prayers were said every morning and evening for your strength and stamina.

When your mom was at her worst and you were worried, listening ears and a quiet mind paid attention.

When everyone else was busy and you were drowning in your loneliness—a tear far away was also being shed.

When you were with mom, and she looked like she was on her last breath—I was breathing from a distance for her.

When your emotions were high, and frustration was becoming a norm—a soft, caring voice attempted its best to soothe you.

And without you knowing—distant healing was sent in the night when the vales between worlds were thin, so the angels would hearken to the call for all to be better.

And when you were suffering—the person who abandoned you suffered too.

In the desire to be the only teddy bear to comfort you—selfish desires were put aside, so your family would hopefully unite and be one during your mom's journey from this world to the next. Right or wrong—the silence came from purity of the heart. This writer is hoping that the receiver of this letter would know in her heart that selfishness was never and would never be the writer's motive.

By stepping away, true love for you and your family's unity was, and will always be, my reason for your perceived abandonment.

My pen is lost for further words and its strength lost like the northern geese who are fading in distant skies—but never forgotten.

People at the funeral will weep and cry, tell stories about their love for your mom and how they will miss her—while I abandon you in my months of caring and in silent prayer for your mom—the lady I did not know but came to know only in my heart. And the love you so freely gave to her.

Me

This didn't sound like Rob. *Is it me?* Or was there something going on in his life that he hadn't shared. "Dear One." I have a name. Signed "Me." Seriously?

I took the letter and stuffed it in my purse. Then I grabbed my jacket from the hall closet and the car keys from the kitchen counter.

My car tires tore over the shell driveway, spitting shards in both directions and pinging the wheel rims. Tree twigs scraped the doors and brushed both sides of the windshield. Birds whizzed from tree branches. I was relieved when I saw Vicky's car in front of her house. I parked behind her car, grabbed my purse from the passenger's seat, and hustled to the door. I knocked. And knocked. I hadn't called ahead to let Vicky know I was stopping by.

She answered, still in her nightgown. *It's three o'clock in the afternoon.* I knew Vicky stayed up most of the night and usually slept in late. "Sorry to barge in on you like this."

"No problem. I've been sleeping alone lately. But maybe not for long," she said with a smile. "Would you like a cup of tea?"

I nodded.

I had heard that tea was quite the solution, a problem solver for the Irish. Maybe that's why my grandmother, on my dad's side, drank so much of it, along with her evening highballs. Right now, I could down a highball. Or two.

I broke down and told Vicky how Rob seemed to be acting differently since Mom passed. I needed to talk to someone other than my therapist.

"Maybe he just didn't want to be in the way while you grieved—wanted to give you space, time," Vicky said.

"Why couldn't he have just said that? Instead of making me think he just deserted me—when I needed him more than ever."

"You know he's different—you've said that yourself."

"I know, but it still hurts—badly. He's always been so compassionate and attentive. I don't get it. Granted it hasn't always been perfect between us—but under the circumstances how can it be?"

"You have to stop this wondering—it's not going to change anything."

"It's just that I know him so well—I feel like he's pulling away. And I don't know why—I don't know what happened. What I did."

"It doesn't mean you did anything—I mean, how long can this go on? Neither one of you is making a move."

"That's not entirely true. I started a letter to Steve, letting him know I intend to divorce him. Rob doesn't know yet. And Mom—she was my priority. But now that she's gone, I have the time to see what's ahead of me. Decide on what I really want to do. Was he not seeing that?"

"I'm sure he did—but maybe he was afraid of that. Maybe he thought about how the opportunity of being together could be a real possibility now. And he got scared. Didn't know what he wanted—or couldn't handle it. Who knows? And who knows what his wife is saying to him? She could be threatening him. You don't know how much power she has over him."

"I wonder if he thought I was depending on him too much. I was becoming needy. But this was a death for God's sake and not a stranger's death. I needed to be able to lean on him like he always wanted me to. And he knew my husband couldn't give me what he was able to. That's why I had turned to him in the beginning."

"Maybe you both just need time away from each other."

"Yeah, maybe."

But I knew if we parted, there would be no return. A perfect love is not real. Just doesn't exist.

Chapter 67

"How are you feeling?" Dr. Bentley asked.

"I'm okay," I said. Inches away, he stared at me in his chair. He was watching my body language—I tried to be conscientious of my hands and feet, and I sat up straighter. *Like I was in front of him—the priest.* He seemed particularly focused on my hands. I think that's where some people reveal a lot of their nervousness, either by chewing their fingernails or making a tight fist, till their knuckles paled.

"Honestly, I feel relieved. Is that wrong? I mean, I'm sorry Mom got ill and all, but it's been hard..."

"You know—it wasn't a healthy relationship."

I nodded. "I know," I said quietly. "I just didn't know how to stop—how to change things."

"Well, now you've been emancipated."

What? I am not a child who's divorced from her parent. Death separated us.

"It's weird—I do feel a sense of freedom. It feels good and scary at the same time."

"I'm sorry—I can't hear you," he said, moving closer to me.

"I don't know why I'm whispering, except I'm afraid my mother will hear. Maybe get angry or be hurt."

He flashed a weak smile. "I wouldn't worry—I'm sure she'll understand."

He stared at me.

"Have you heard from Rob?"

"Yeah," I said quietly.

"How's that going?"

I shrugged. "As good as it can be, I guess."

I glanced out the double window behind his desk. I saw a variety of birds: sparrows, robins, even a blue jay amid the trees. I watched squirrels scurry up and down the oak trunks, out to the limbs. Nothing to concern themselves with but food and chasing their mate. In the distance, I noticed two swans gliding across the pond. I wondered if they were an item.

"Look at the swans," I said, standing up and pointing. *Distraction.*

Dr. Bentley turned around and glanced out the picture window. "Yeah. I have seen two out there lately," he said.

"I wonder if they are a couple—they're so beautiful."

"Yes, they are, but they can get really nasty—I've seen them fighting out there."

"Like people do, I guess."

Dr. Bentley, relaxed in his chair, his hands folded in front of him—waiting for me to unburden.

"I love him—I'll always love him," I blurted, poking my tongue into my cheek. "But he's not strong enough to leave. He's afraid. Afraid of change—or afraid it won't work out. He established his roots long ago. As much as I believe he loves me, he can't leave. He has grandchildren he adores. He feels secure in his environment, and I think he feels he owes his wife something for saving him from destruction when he was young. He's just not stable enough. He still carries guilt, and had such a dysfunctional childhood—he feels calm and safe in his setting. Although, I know he's not truly happy—being there," I said, taking a second to catch my breath. "His marriage was probably the only thing that has been a success for him. The whole home life, having his own family, gave him a sense of steadiness and an unconditional love, something he didn't have as a kid."

"Did he tell you this—or is this how you're feeling?"

"No, he didn't directly say these things—but I got to know him so well..."

"I do feel, from what you've told me, that you two may have similar personalities."

"It's more than that—we're like twin flames. Do you know what a twin flame is?"

"No," he said.

"It's this intense attraction you find with someone—that comes immediately. The way it did with us. More than that—it's a deep spiritual connection. One soul—two bodies. That other person becomes the other half of you. Like you are mirrored. If it has never happened to you, it can't be explained." *The doctor has never felt it. That's why he's still single.*

"And your emotions go over the top. Your head goes into the clouds—you get more confused every day. Everything you feel—both good and bad—gets stronger. Even overwhelming. You can't sleep at night." *You can't sleep at night!*

"Your twin flame shows you what's holding you back, like your fears and insecurities, so you can grow and come out stronger. But it goes beyond, far beyond the butterflies and fireworks of just an infatuation. Twin flames share so much. It's crazy, yet real and beautiful. Google it when you have time."

I took another deep breath and remembered the email from Rob—after I'd sent him the readings on a twin flame:

I was so dazzled by the readings, but mostly about the deep feelings that emerged so quickly. It was like a tsunami of emotions. It came unexpectedly.

Family—children, many years and You. You!

Oh my, oh my!

Rob was the kind of person who would give up his own happiness to spare others' pain.

"He wanted me to help him choose—between his wife and me. I told him he had to make that decision. I knew I could convince him, but I didn't want him to have regrets..." I trailed off.

"You shouldn't have to convince him."

True, I thought. *But who will?*

Chapter 68

After Mom's passing, my relationship with Rob spiraled downward, and after a few months, it was over. This whole fable of "us" that we had built up, our hopes and dreams, our plans for the future. *There was never a future for us—because there was never an "us," only what I imagined. You imagined.*

We had hurt each other—but not intentionally.

Like one coming full circle in life. Our emotions had been in constant rotation, up and down and around like a roller coaster ride, full of fear and excitement. Then the joy we gave each other turned crazed with sadness and pain from separation. With him not taking any action on his marriage, our relationship ended the way it began—furious, manic, and quick. Although the love I still had for him, was never going to fade.

And the love he had given me, I would carry through eternity.

His last text to me:

It seems like I have hurt you enough. I must keep the life that has been given to me. Thank you for all you have done for me. I will always love you.

***

I took a seat in the waiting room. I watched Dr. Bentley through the window, between the two rooms, finishing up his lunch at his desk. Then I scanned the bookshelf, filled with magazines, along with the cutest stuffed bears and dogs and unicorns. Dr. Bentley didn't seem like the fuzzy type. I was sure they were donated for the children. But I thought the doctor only worked with adults. The younger adults' children perhaps? I grabbed a copy of *Psychology Today* and skimmed through. Always interesting articles. I stopped at a book advertisement. My eyes widened. And then I heard the door of his office open. I looked up. "Come on in."

"Can I tear something out of this magazine?" I asked.

"I prefer you didn't."

"Okay. I'll be right there," I said, rummaging through my purse for paper and a pen. I quickly jotted down the title of the book and the ISBN#, then I stuck the magazine back on the shelf.

I sat down in the chair and took a deep breath.

"Everything okay?" he asked.

"Yeah. Why?"

"You seem distracted." I think he was curious as to what I'd found in the magazine.

"No, I'm fine."

"How's everything going?"

"It hurts still. This affair I had might have been morally wrong, but it saved me in a way. I felt lost. Alone. God brings people to us at various times in our lives, sometimes for reasons we don't understand."

Dr. Bentley never discussed religion. He might have believed in God, but I got the impression he didn't partake in any religious formalities. "Yeah."

"But now I keep trying to find negative things about Rob, so I can hate him."

"You don't want to do that."

"I do. Then maybe I won't think about him so much—and this pain will go away." *Love is pain.*

"There's no way of telling if it would've worked out. It could be good for two or three years, and then it could change," he said.

Yeah, maybe once I indulged in all the sex he dreams about with me. All that my body craves with him. The years of pent-up sex I had forfeited to be an angel, his angel, the good Catholic girl.

"Yeah, like anything. I only wish I'd had the chance—to find out."

I never knew how much to tell Dr. Bentley—or what subject mattered most each visit. But I always spilled my emotions if they were still fresh, usually with tears. Today, though, all I could think about was getting home to my computer.

When I got home, I looked up the book on Amazon and ordered it.

Ten days later, I received it in the mail: *Tantric Sex.*

"What do you got there?" Steve asked, seeing the package.

"I ordered a book," I said nonchalantly. I knew he never read, so I wasn't worried about him having any interest.

"Aren't you going to open it?"

"Nah, I know what it looks like—I have another book to read first."

The next morning, after Steve left for work, I took the package from Amazon from my bureau drawer and opened it. My hands were trembling. I was feeling the same emotions I had when I was in my twenties, after ordering a book on orgasms. Guilty and ashamed.

But then as I began to read, I saw the author was educated and her words were written eloquently. No trashy content. And the writer, herself, had grown up with a strict religious background. That said to me—not everything taught is ideal. Dead right. I read every word, every paragraph to the end. Absorbing. I learned that Tantra is an ancient art of awareness, mindfulness, applied to the self and body in daily life. I realized Rob was exercising Tantra and was actively committed. In Tantra, sex was not practiced for a quick gratification, or just for the sake of performing the act, but as a means for going *beyond* sex, for improving one's health, balance, couple relationships, even self-control, and eventually reaching higher states of consciousness. *Far better than going for the quickie. Then your partner rolls off and leaves you feeling empty.*

Afterward, I had a better understanding of Tantra sex. The book assuaged my bad thoughts. It could be beautiful with the right partner. But why did Rob have so much passion for it if his wife wasn't interested? Maybe I was just being naïve—married or not, he'd been searching for a Tantra partner. And maybe he had been hoping I was the one. And if I had been more receptive, maybe he would've chosen me. Not her.

***

Dear Journal,

I am sitting on the sofa in silence, numb—there is no more hope, worry, or even wonder left. Mom is gone, God has taken over. "Aimee, I just want you to be happy," I hear Mom say.

Rob is gone too. He may not be dead, but he might as well be. Like he was there for a purpose and then he was no longer needed. Had Rob concluded this or had the universe decided? What gave them that right? Neither one had that right. No one asked me what I wanted.

The emptiness I feel right now is like the air outside—still and cold. No sunshine or rain, just gray skies—ominous and threatening. I suppose—like purgatory. A timeless limbo. Where there is no bad, yet nothing good either. No emotions stirred by love or excitement, or even sadness or loss.

I am just existing.

I decided not to type this and got out a subject notebook. And began writing on the lined white paper.

Dear Steve,

I hate to have to write this to you instead of talking in person, but I don't want to argue or fight about what I have to say. Things haven't been good between us for so long now. You know it as well as I do. I don't know exactly when or how or even why we started drifting apart. Whatever the reason or reasons—it happened. And neither one of us is to blame. Each day I am sad about how we, as a couple, go on with our day as if we lived separately, ignoring each other. And when we talk, it's rarely pleasant. Sometimes, I feel like I'm living with a stranger; there are no kisses, no hugs, no making love. We only touch each other's flesh at night by accident. Either in dreams or just restless limbs. We have said and done terrible things to one another. Hurtful things that cannot be erased or taken back. Our marriage has become loveless and holds resentment. I don't want to live like this anymore. I want us to find the happiness we both deserve. But, please, I beg you to try and understand. I don't want this to end badly—I am asking you for a divorce. I hope we can resolve this peacefully without harsh words or actions.

Aimee

I folded the letter carefully in four parts and stuck it in my underwear drawer. *I ought* to pack my things and find a place to stay before delivering it. I looked around the house; despite the unhappiness here, it was still my home. And I loved it—I loved

Steve once too. I believed that. It wasn't always like this.

I took a deep breath and called Cyrus.

"I'm sorry to hear," Cyrus said with sincerity.

"This might sound cliché, but it's been a long time coming."

"Does he know you want a divorce?" I imagined Cyrus sitting there at his desk taking notes, his dogs nearby, wearing the wrist compression for his carpal tunnel.

"No. I haven't mentioned it—I did write him a letter."

"A letter? And how did he respond?"

"Well, I haven't given it to him yet."

"Oh."

"I am planning to—today," I said, twirling locks of my hair around my index finger.

"I don't usually handle divorces. Will he contest it?"

"I hope not—it would be a lot easier. And all we have really is the house. No children."

"Any assets other than the house?"

"I have a little money saved, but not much."

"We will still need a financial statement from the both of you and a certified copy of your marriage certificate. You can obtain that from the town office.

"Okay," I said, taking a deep breath.

"In the meantime, I can start preparing the paperwork, get the separation agreement together. You'll both have to sign, and written in there will be how you're going to divide your property."

"Thank you very much, Cyrus."

"You're welcome. I'll be in touch."

Yeah, if Steve doesn't fight me on this.

I left the letter on his pillow. Then I picked it up and put it on the kitchen table where he sits. I couldn't be afraid, be a coward. I'd face him. Nervously, I picked up the letter again, and waited till he came home to give it to him. I paced back and forth, back and forth.

"Please come and sit," I said when Steve walked in, gesturing toward the kitchen table.

"What is it?"

I handed him the letter. "Just read it, please."

My anxiety was over the top, my insides were trembling, my hands sweaty and shaking, as I waited for him to read the letter. The end. Divorce, they say, is the next highest stressful thing to the death of a loved one. And I didn't think I could take anymore. But I wanted to get it all over with at once.

Be done. Find peace. *If that was possible.*

Steve's big shoulders suddenly drooped. Hunched over. His chin quivered and tears filled his eyes, spilling down his cheeks. I hadn't seen him this emotional since his father died, seven years earlier. I wanted to wipe his tears away. "Why? Why?" he asked. I wanted to recant everything I'd written, but only for a second. I knew he wasn't going to change. I knew I was doing the right thing, even though I felt terrible. Seeing him so upset, I started to walk over and put my arm around him, then stopped myself. I'd cry too.

Then he looked up at me with those puppy eyes of his, the ones I fell in love with, now red and sad. Making me feel worse. "I'm sorry—for everything," he said. "Is there anything I can do—to change your mind?"

I shook my head.

After a few minutes of silence, I said, "Cyrus is drawing up a separation agreement. We both have to sign it."

"Separation agreement?"

"I guess that comes first—before we go in front of the judge. And we'll have to divide our assets."

"No fucking way are you getting anything—I worked hard for this house."

"I'm not asking for alimony—or even half of what you worked hard for. But I do need to be able to survive."

"Have you lost your fucking mind?"

"Maybe I should leave now—I will get some things together." I had asked Vicky if I could spend a few days with her, not filling her in. I knew she was curious, but I'd wanted to make sure I'd follow through with my intentions. Fear wasn't going to intimidate me. Not this time.

I turned away. Then Steve surprised me.

"You don't have to—I'll sleep in the guest room," he said in a calmer voice.

I turned back. "You sure?"

"Yeah."

I hoped he didn't think I would change my mind. Even if he suddenly became sweeter. Nicer. It wouldn't last. I knew if I didn't stick to my guns and do it now—I might not. This wasn't the kind of life I wanted. Deserved.

Chapter 69

Even at two miles an hour, the car bounced over the narrow, bumpy, overgrown lanes. I was trying not to run over or collide with grave markers. In the three-hundred-year-old cemetery, older stones, ensconced in moss, had cracks or had broken in two and tumbled over. I'd come here with my mother when she visited her father, my grandfather, whom I never really knew when he was alive. She lost her father when I was two; I was too young to remember him. Mom would kneel before his grave, while silently praying. She would place a fresh wreath before leaving and wipe a tear from her eye.

No more tears, Mom; you're with your father now.

I stopped next to her stone, put the car in park, and shut off the engine. Opening the door, I grabbed the bouquet of flowers from the passenger's seat and pushed the door closed with my behind. I advanced a few feet and knelt on the partially frozen ground, laying the flowers. *Maybe I should have just brought a plant; I know these will shrivel soon or blow away.*

"Mom, I brought you flowers. A rose, an actual scented one, and carnations because I know they last longer. Not sure if you can see them, smell this rose, or even hear me. For that reason, I feel awkward talking—it's like I'm talking to myself, which I do often now. But I try not to in public. I guess I fear that someone will notice and wonder about me. But I'm in a graveyard—everyone talks to their loved ones in a graveyard. Right?

"Will you give me a sign, Mom, something, to convince me you are here? I often wonder because of the many ghost stories and sightings I have heard about in graveyards. I'm a bit of a skeptic; I like to witness things for myself. Christians have been saying since the Bible that you go to heaven or hell when you die, but I have doubts about whether those two places exist. At least, the way we visualize them to be. Either way, other than a common meeting ground for all you deceased, why would you be hanging around here? My theory is, which you now know better than me, that when we die, our souls are set free. *Yes. Free.* You know, to wander the universe. At least it makes more sense to me. We get to choose where we want to be. Even decide for another life—if we've had a crappy one here."

Suddenly, in the quiet, a blackbird appeared on a limb of a leafless tree nearby and began cawing, nonstop. The bird seemingly looked in my direction as if it were talking to me. There was not another creature around.

"Okay, is that you, Mom?" I asked meekly.

I kneeled on the cold, damp ground and placed the white carnations, with one red rose in the center, above where she lay.

"I've come to say goodbye, Mom. Not forever—I'm moving. Yeah, I know—it's hard to believe. But I need to get away. I need a fresh start. Steve and I are divorced. Though it had been a long time coming, it was easier than I anticipated. And it's been over with Rob and me for a while.

"It wasn't easy getting away from Steve, but I told him how I felt, and if he wanted to kill me—then kill me. I was done. I had to find myself. I know, how many have said that? But seriously, Mom, I don't want to depend on anybody anymore. I need to figure out who I am and where I belong."

Steve had cried and begged me not to leave him. I was like stone—I had no empathy. No tears. When he saw his tactics had no effect on me, he threatened me. "I'll hunt you down and kill you." *Do me a favor.*

"Go ahead, do what you have to do, if that will make you feel better," I'd said to him.

"Mom, there's nothing keeping me here anymore. I don't need some of the memories either. So I won't be visiting as much. I am hoping, in my belief, if our souls are really set free, that I can talk to you anytime. Anywhere." *Like I do with God.*

"I know the hurt, the loss you felt when it was over between you and Irving. But I also know now, how you felt when you were in love with him. You can't replicate that kind of attraction—it's a rare find. You can't enlighten another if they've never felt that way with anyone. I'm so glad we both got to experience that love in our lifetime. Even if it didn't work out the way we had hoped it would.

"I love you."

Chapter 70

I drove slowly down the long driveway to Vicky's, taking in all that lined its path: tangled thorny vines, soft hollows, and beautiful mature chestnuts and oaks. The trees' enormous trunks were swathed in a rich two-tone ivy, emerald and jade. Bushy-tailed squirrels with muk-muk warnings, racing here and there—appearing confused. *What is right. Safe.* Cardinals and sparrows chatting as they soared. Eventually settling on branches. I knew I'd miss this. And I'd miss Vicky even more. Greatly. My anxieties seemingly vanished or never existed whenever I was here, and in her presence.

Vicky opened the front door the moment she saw me pull up. "You fit it all in the car?" she asked.

I looked back at my new Honda Pilot. "Yup. I packed two suitcases of clothes and left everything else." I smiled. "Except for two adult coloring books."

"I'd be happy to go with you and help you find a place—get settled in?"

"I would love you to, but I have to do this on my own."

"I get ya, girl," she said, handing me a cup of tea. "Brave move. The right one."

All my fingers clutched the cup, providing warmth to my cold palms. Then I steeped the mint bag inside. In and out. In and out. Finally, I looked up at Vicky. "I'm not going to lie, Vicky, I'm scared. I AM SO SCARED. But it's now or never."

"You're stronger than you know."

"How did you do it?"

"It's never easy—but I knew if I stayed with my husband, I might have hung him—by his balls," she said, winking. I laughed. "Whether you realize it or not, things couldn't stay the way they were. You haven't been happy—for a long time."

I nodded. Change was hard, since I hadn't known any. Never wanted any. Until now.

"Who the hell am I going to show my potential prospects to?" she said, pouring us both another cup of tea. Then she scooted into the kitchen and brought out a plate of gluten-free Oreos.

"God, I'm going to miss you," I said, watching her place them on the table. My eyes were watering up.

"We will talk every day. I'll be there more than you'll want me—you're not going that far away."

"True. But to me—it's a world away."

"That's because it's all new. Hold your head up. High. And keep it there."

I nodded. "I will." I took a deep breath and stood up. "I better get going, before I really get messy on you."

"Wait," she said. "I made you something."

"You didn't have to... What is it?"

"Just open it," she said, handing me a little white box.

It was a beautiful sodalite pendant. I learned from her that this stone was great for relieving anxiety and dispelling fears.

"It's lovely and the blue is amazing," I said, taking it out of the box. "Help me put it on. I lifted my hair, and she clasped it behind my neck. "This will help keep me focused, calm, for sure. Thank you."

We embraced tightly, and tears filled both our eyes, escaping down our cheeks.

"Get out of here, before there's a puddle on my floor."

I wiped away tears with my palm. "I'm leaving. See ya."

When I got in the car, I turned and waved.

Chapter 71

Maine—One Year Later

I went to Jack's Cafe to grab a sandwich and came to a halt. I was thinking, it can't be —looks like Rob. Nah, no way, I thought. His head was down, but I knew that stature, his mannerism. He looked exhausted. His windswept hair was cut short and had gone silver and his face had more creases, but he still had charm and was slim and fit.

Still, it was never his looks.

I lingered in front of his table. "Excuse me." He looked up. "Rob?" We just stared at each other.

"Sit," he motioned. "Please."

But instead of sitting next to him, like we did in Oregon, I sat across from him.

"What are you doing here?" What did it matter what he was doing there? The fact is—he just was. "I mean, you're so far away from home." I wondered if he and Carol were on vacation. I knew they both loved New England, and had been to Vermont a couple of times. "How long are you guys here for?"

"It's just me."

"Oh." I wondered why he'd come this far alone. Of all the places in the country—why here?

I saw him look down at my hand, staring at my ring finger.

I shook my head. "No, I'm no longer married. It had been long over even before we..." I trailed off.

I noticed he wasn't wearing his band, but that didn't necessarily mean anything. I recalled that he wasn't wearing a ring when I was with him for the week.

"You?" I asked, looking down at his left hand.

"She's gone." His eyes watered up. "Cancer. She was sick for a long time."

"I'm so sorry. I truly am." I believed he loved her, his way. He'd had a lifetime with her.

"I know. Thank you," he said quietly.

We sat a while without words.

He broke the silence. "Are you getting something to eat?"

"Yeah," I said and stood up. "Can I get you something?"

"No, I'm fine. I had some chili."

"The chili is amazing here."

"I have to agree," he said.

I stood and turned, hand signaling to the owner. "The usual, Jack," I yelled. I always ordered a turkey sandwich with spinach and cranberry sauce, and a small cup of chili. "Hold off on the chili, please." I had become a regular there.

Jack gave me the thumbs-up. "You got it, Aimee."

When I sat back down, Rob smiled at me. "So, how you've been?"

"Good, really good."

"I can see that."

I stretched my legs and accidentally touched his beneath the table. Old feelings began to emerge, my insides stirring like they'd never stopped.

His dark eyes penetrated mine, the way I remembered.

"You look amazing."

I took a deep breath and smiled. "Thanks."

"My friend, Jay, told me about this place. He used to live here."

"Really."

"Yeah. Long time ago."

"Probably hasn't changed much."

"The real reason I came, I heard you were now living here."

There was silence between us. Then I asked, "How long you here for?"

"Few more days. I'm staying in a motel nearby."

"Oh," I said, taking the last bite of my sandwich.

We were both quiet again.

"I thought about you a lot—wondered how you were doing. Prayed you were okay," he said.

"I thought about you too." *Every day, waiting for you to call, text, email—telling me you missed me.*

I balled my sandwich wrapping and stood up. "Well, I've really got to get going. It was great seeing you."

I disposed of the brown paper in the waste barrel, placed the tray on the counter, and headed toward the door.

"Wait," he said.

I turned.

"What's your address? Can I stop by? I will call first—I'm sure you have a new phone number."

I hesitated, then grabbed a paper napkin and jotted it all down for him. "I still have the same phone number, but I wrote it down anyway."

"Thanks. Good seeing you."

"Yeah. You too."

***

The rest of the day, I walked around in a daze; I thought I'd moved on. Gotten over him. I'd vowed I'd never be subjected to that craziness again. But I never thought I'd get another chance either. We were both alone now. There was nothing stopping us—but ourselves. And it could be different.

Still, I wasn't sure if it was a good idea, giving him my address, my phone number. I had mixed feelings about seeing him again. But I wanted to. We never did get closure—or at least I didn't. I needed that from him.

Chapter 72

Rob didn't wait long to call—I heard from him that night. "Are you busy tomorrow?" he asked.

"I have a class in the morning, but after that I'm free."

"How about after lunch—say around 2:00 p.m.?" he asked.

"Sure. That's fine."

"Great. See ya then."

The idea of being alone with him delivered this numbness. We were meeting again, and I didn't know how I felt. He was such an enigmatic man. But that was a part of him that captivated me. Maybe everything we once felt was gone. Or maybe there was never really anything at all, just the pretense of sin that made it so compelling—exciting.

When I heard his car pull up, I met him outside.

"This is your place?" Rob asked, looking around.

I nodded. "Yeah, just mine. After the divorce, we sold the house. Everything was divided. I had enough to buy this," I said with open arms, looking at the cabin and the land. "It's not much—plenty for me though."

I watched him take in the surroundings, as if he was evaluating it. He laced his long fingers behind his head as his eyes fixed on the mountains. I wished I could see into his mind, his soul.

"It's really wonderful."

"It truly is. Sort of like Mt. Hood, I suppose," I said.

"Except there isn't just one mountain out there—look at them. They go on for miles," he said, staring.

"And more than the beauty and serenity, the people here are so nice—always willing to help one another. The way it was when we were growing up."

"Do you miss home—the Cape?"

"Maybe at first. But it didn't take me long to feel welcomed."

"So, what do you do for fun around here?"

"I'm learning how to ski—on the beginner's mountain. And I'm taking creative writing at the college in town."

"I always knew you were a good writer."

I smiled.

We sat for hours talking, the way we used to on the phone. But this time in person. His voice, distinctive and unique, still emitted a powerful effect on me. One I tried to ignore.

"You getting hungry?" I asked.

"A little."

"I bought some hamburgers. Thought we'd cook them on the grill."

"Sounds wonderful. Let me give you a hand," he said, following me into the house.

"Yeah sure," I said. We worked side by side on the butcher block table. Something Steve and I never did.

"I can make a mean patty," he said with a smile.

"I bet you can."

"I bought corn on the cob a couple days ago at the farmers' market. Do you like corn?"

"Sure do. We can wrap them in foil and toss 'em on the grill too."

"I've always husked and thrown them in a pot of water."

"Well, it tastes really good—not waterlogged," he said.

"Oh, okay. Let's do it."

While Rob was wrapping the corn, I threw together two salads of romaine lettuce, cukes, radishes, tomato, and red onion.

"Grab yourself a drink from the fridge," I said to him, after he placed the cobs on the grill.

While grabbing the plates and silverware, I saw him looking inside the refrigerator. "Oh, sorry, there's not much in there," I said. "Other than Kombucha and almond milk."

"No problem. Tap water is fine."

"I have some lemons."

"Perfect."

We slipped on our lined jackets and woolen hats. Then we carried the food upstairs, through the loft, to the upper deck. Sitting at the pub table in high back chairs, we watched the sun fade behind the mountains, and talked about everything from the surroundings to things that had happened since we parted. I learned that Carol had been diagnosed with cancer while Mom was dying. No wonder it was difficult for him to be there for me too. I felt terrible. I was so consumed in my own grief, I'd jumped to conclusions. Wrong ones.

"That's why your family was so accepting of me," I said softly.

"Yeah. They didn't want me to be alone after she passed."

We were both silent for a moment.

"I just remembered—I have a bottle of Merlot that I never got around to opening. A housewarming gift from one of the neighbors. Red okay?"

"Red is good."

I hustled downstairs and grabbed the wine from under the sink and a corkscrew from the silverware drawer. Then I seized two long-stemmed wine glasses from the cabinet and hurried back and put them on the table.

"Well, what are we waiting for? Let's pop the cork, girl." I watched as he inserted the corkscrew, opening the bottle. He poured the wine into my glass first, then his.

He smiled and lifted his glass. "Cheers. To a new place. A new time. A new beginning."

"Yeah, cheers." I raised mine to meet his and clinked.

"I missed you," he said, looking into my eyes.

"I missed you too. What happened?" I probably shouldn't have asked, but I needed to know.

"Aimee, I couldn't be the man you wanted me to be."

"I never asked you to be anything but you. I loved you just the way you were."

"Crazy and weird."

I laughed. "Yeah, that too." I think that's the part I liked most," I said. "You were different. You always had this peculiar way of saying things."

"I felt I wasn't enough for you—I couldn't give you all the wonderful things you already had and deserved."

"That never mattered."

He looked into my eyes. "I know you said that, but it mattered to me."

"Things can never be the same. Can they?"

"No. But they can be better," he said, giving a reassuring smile. "You didn't want to be my friend. That hurt."

"How could I be?" He looked at me. "I couldn't be just a friend—to someone I had fallen in love with."

"I understand."

"Do you? Do you really?" I asked, looking into his eyes. My inner voice kept repea*ting: Just accept the now. Let the past lay dormant.*

"I'm really sorry—that was so wrong of me. I just didn't know what to do."

We said no more and watched the sun begin to set, the rolling mountains pretty and still. Two birds in a nearby birch were chatting to one another, seemingly narrating a story. Maybe ours. Then a myriad of purples and pinks spread across the evening sky. Casting a blush of radiance. On a perfect setting.

We finished the last of the Merlot. The alcohol warmed us, relaxed us, and our inhibitions perished, enabling us to reopen to one another.

"I have something to show you," I said, inviting him back into the loft, my bedroom.

"I kept this—hoping someday..." I said, opening the storage drawer beneath the bed, holding up a cotton and lace vintage nightgown. The sale tag hanging from a sleeve. "I found it in a high-end thrift shop and saved it—for when we were together again."

He took the gown from me, perusing it. After a few moments he said, "That someday is here. Please, let me see you in it."

It was the way he had melded things that always made me soften. I slowly unbuttoned my cardigan, taking it off, revealing a blue cami beneath. I lifted it over my head and unzipped my jeans, dragging them down to my ankles. I sat on the bed and Rob removed them. I stood in my bra and panties. Rob stared, his eyes longing. I turned and he unfastened my bra. Then I slipped off my underwear. Standing there naked, I shivered. But not from the cold.

"No," he said, when he saw me covering my privates, wrapping my arms over my breasts, and then interlocking my hands like a leaf to armor my vagina. "Let me look at you—all of you." Reluctantly, I dropped my arms to my sides. No one had ever observed, stared at my naked body. It was as though he was studying it. Admiring. Appreciating. I watched his eyes wander over me, my insides quivering. Then he stood in front of me, shielding my body with his. Taking my hand, he gently secured it against his chest, so I could measure every beat of his heart. Then he took his right hand and placed it on my heart.

"Close your eyes and just breathe. Slowly. Deep breaths."

I did and soon my insides calmed. Somewhat.

Then he picked up the nightgown from the bed and handed it to me. "Here, go," he gestured toward the bathroom.

When I came out, he said nothing at first. He just stared.

"There should be wings attached to the back of that gown. God, you look beautiful. So angelic."

"Thank you," I whispered.

"I thank you. I thank God for you, my lady."

I saw him unbuttoning his shirt. "Let me," I said.

I slowly undid one button after another, until I could fully see his olive-colored chest. His skin, seemingly, emitted a warm glow. After taking his shirt off, I stared down at his jeans. When I looked up at him, his eyes were giving me permission. I stood in front of him, my fingers fumbling. After unzipping the jeans, I pulled them below his buttocks. He sat on the embroidered armchair, so I could take them off his legs. His white Jockeys looked new. While wondering if I should remove them, he was already taking them off. Noticing his erection, my insides began to quiver.

"The last time we were together, I held back because you said Tantra isn't about the orgasm. Of course, I never really believed that. I'd bought a book on Tantra sex."

He looked surprised and then smiled, as if his dream, at last, had become real. "Wow."

"Yeah, and after reading it, I feel differently."

"You do?"

"Yeah, I mean it could be amazing with your partner—the

person you love." *But not doing it with other women if you are married! Let it go. Let it go.*

Never taking our eyes from one another, he wrapped his arms around my waist. I reached up, tilting my head back as I wrapped mine around his neck. Our lips joined in harmony like angel kisses from heaven. As if they were being introduced for the first time. Then our bodies fell in sync like never before. The sexual energy was divine. We dropped the illusion of our identities to become one. One body. One mind. One heart.

Dear God, how long has it been since any man has had me—or I him? I don't want to end up like my mother. I will surrender myself completely.

Rob laid me down on the bed. He gently removed the thin straps of the gown from my shoulders and my top collapsed, exposing my breasts. I watched his eyes follow his hand, his fingertips slowly tracing the contour of my body from my face to the subtle dimple of my hip, as if he was sketching me for one of his beautifully detailed pen and ink pieces. His hands were soft and silky on my skin, moving slowly over me like the artist he was—with all the right strokes, in all the right places. My firm nipples were signaling my groin, my breathing escalating. His feathery touches sending me into a euphoric haze as my hips arched. I wanted to drown in Rob's flood of passion, obliterating my misguided perception of love. I, at last, awarded him and myself.

In his arms I lay, nuzzled, snuggling into his chest like a cub against his mom. Tears were stinging my eyes and rolling down my face. Rob was gently wiping them away with his fingers. "I know these tears are of joy," he said.

I nodded.

"That was beautiful. You are beautiful, my lady."

"I love you. I always have—I always will," I whispered, looking into his eyes.

"I love you—you make me so happy. I have waited a lifetime for you," he said.

Then he held me, and we fell asleep in each other's arms.

The next morning, before breakfast, we made love again. The second time was even more satisfying, as we practiced taking our time. Learning where to touch one another, reaching ultimate pleasure. Words needn't be spoken.

After scrambling eggs, together we made pancakes with cranberries and chocolate chips. We ate on the deck and then Rob helped me with the dishes. I had to get ready for my writing class.

He kissed me lovingly on the lips, wrapping his arms around my waist, and I wanted to make love with him again. But Tantra wasn't about rushing.

Before heading out the door to go back to the motel, he turned.

"You don't happen to need a roommate, do you?"

I smiled.

Then his phone rang. He looked at his caller ID and pressed the ignore button.

His phone rang again. He answered.

"No, it's not a good time." I recalled that same response when I was with him in Oregon on our trip. "What? Yes, I will call you back—soon."

"Who was that—a woman?" I asked, fearlessly this time. "A client? Someone from one of your healing sessions?"

I looked him straight in the eye. Saw the guilt. *You still playing with vaginas? Tell me. Tell me right now!* I kept screaming in my mind.

He shook his head. "I have to go, Aimee. See you later."

He turned and left.

Chapter 73

The full moon was basking in the starlit sky. A ghost-gray mist, voiceless and heartless, draped the mountains. It had snowed for days; temperatures had fallen below freezing. I had been sleepless; my nights haunted, wondering if I was his only one. Or just another victim… I kept my feelings inside; I didn't want to lose him a second time. *God, why do I have to be this way?*

On the bed Rob and I fell, our lips still locked. I positioned myself on top, straddling Rob. I yanked his T-shirt up, pulling it over his head. I let my fingertips feel his abs. I bent over, looking into his eyes, and kissed each side of his cheeks before letting my mouth rest on his. I slowly moved my lips down his neck to his chest and over to his nipples, teasing them with my tongue, lightly sucking them. Then I let my tongue slide to his navel. Touching and caressing every inch of him. I slipped my fingers to his jeans, unsnapping them. I heard a slight whimper as he lifted his hips for me to remove them. I pulled them off his legs. His white Jockeys bright against the darkness—a bulge clearly visible. I laid my hands on both sides of his hips, yanking down his underwear—his fully erect penis so beautiful, so perfect. I wanted it. I wanted it inside me.

I cupped my hands around his balls and lowered my face to the tip of his erection and gently kissed, letting my lips linger there. "You're torturing me," he said. *Huh, the way you tortured me.* Then I glided my tongue slowly up and down his penis before fully grasping it in my mouth. Hearing him moaning, his breathing escalating, I pulled away. I didn't want him to come. Not yet.

I could feel myself losing who I was and wondering who I was becoming. But I liked being in charge—in control.

I got off him and stood up.

He opened his eyes and looked at me, puzzled.

"Give me a moment," I said, gesturing toward the bathroom.

Rob lay there naked in the middle of the bed, waiting for me. I went to the bathroom to undress and upon returning, in the dim light, I saw a shadowy figure. The hooded phantom swiftly, but quietly, approached the bed. Then I saw the gloved hands—gripping a long, pointed, gleaming instrument that resembled a knife. Blood dripping like an icicle from the eaves of a house on a sunny day. I was mesmerized as I watched the glow of the shiny object rise and fall. Rise and fall. Rob's legs and hands flailing as he cried out my name, "Aimee. Aimee, please…" My heart was beating rapidly. I opened my mouth to scream but was silenced by fear. I was holding my breath—I could barely breathe. Suffocating. I was sweating profusely. My fingers were tense, curled tightly in a fist. I finally yelled, "Stop. Stop. Please!" Then the phantom turned and gaped at me. I became paralyzed. *No, no!* To my astonishment—the face I saw, gazing back at me, *was My Own.*

I felt like I'd been floating above, watching a horror show and there should be a standing ovation for the performance.

The intruder seemed to suddenly disappear.

Am I having an out-of-body experience?

His blood oozing, I rushed to cover Rob's wounds with my hands. His eyes wide, he lay lifeless. He was cold and clammy. I cried out his name. "Rob, Rob." Willing him to return to me. Nothing. He was gone—really gone this time. After hours of sobbing, I fell asleep. I heard his soothing voice, and I felt myself slowly drifting deeply into the warmth of him, his arms holding me. Comforting me. Like that of a beautiful memory.

Chapter 74

I wanted to see Dr. Bentley—I needed to see him. But I knew I couldn't. Even if he liked me, had sympathy for me, and felt my act was justifiable, still, he would be obligated. He'd be sworn to the code of ethics, to do the right thing. Even if Vicky had proved to be my confidante, there were no guarantees. There wasn't a soul I could tell, a soul I could trust—but Him, God.

The slamming of the massive ornate door, and its echoing, made me jump. That familiar smell wafted through my nostrils, and that eerie quietness made me shiver. It was as if no time had passed. I was seven years old again, wobbling down the aisle. I could still see my classmates staring at me.

Other than attending a wedding or a funeral, it had been years, maybe decades, since I'd been in church for mass, even been considered a parishioner. I hadn't been to confession since I was a kid. As I sat in the pew waiting, my hands began to tremble. There was one older gentleman in a suit and tie, waiting to go in. Then a lady, I guessed to be around my age, sauntered out of the booth, appearing completely absolved. She looked my way, my eyes peered downward. I feared she knew me. Or maybe it was my appearance that drew the attention. I wore a black satin dress with a big gold cross.

The gentleman signaled to me with an open palm to go before him. I shook my head and said, "No, thank you." I wondered what sins he would have to confess. I couldn't imagine this sweet-looking gentleman with even one sin. But I learned—looks can be deceiving. When he came out, he nodded with a wan smile. I waited till he left, waited for the familiar slamming echo before entering the booth.

My legs near collapse, I kneeled and made the Sign of the Cross. I could tell from his profile that the priest was in his early to mid-thirties. *How does this young man abstain from sex?* I wondered.

"Bless me, Father, for I have sinned. It's been about thirty-five years since my last confession."

"Why so long, child?" I'm far from a child—but he's representing God—and I'll always be God's child.

"I have had no sins, Father." I was stunned. I just lied to a priest! In confession! *Or did I?* I felt I needn't tell him about the affair, since I felt I hadn't actually committed adultery. My therapist had said it was an emotional affair, even if he did see me naked. And adultery seems venial compared to what I've done.

"Go ahead, my dear child."

"Are you still sworn to secrecy, Father. I mean, what I tell you… you can't, you won't, tell anyone?"

"No, it stays with me. What have you done, child?" His voice so soothing and calm, non-judgmental. *Like Rob's.*

I felt a blockage in my throat. I coughed, to try and clear it. It felt like I was straining to get even a single word out. "I hurt someone," I finally spilled.

"We all hurt others—I'm sure it wasn't intentional."

"You don't understand… Father, I killed someone," I said so low, I'm not sure he heard me. Rob's cry was echoing inside my head.

"How?" Did he just ask me how? I wasn't sure how I killed him, but I told him anyway.

"An icicle. The kind that hang from roofs—after a big snowstorm." *Or maybe it was an ice pick?* "I stabbed it into his stomach like a knife. It had to be six inches long. I kept stabbing and stabbing until he…," I revealed, trying to catch my breath.

"That was clever," I thought I heard him say, followed by a stifled laugh.

Clever?

There was silence. "Is that all, child?" *I think that's enough.*

"Yes," I cried. Then I waited for my penance.

"Recite three Hail Marys and three Our Fathers." *That's it?*

I began the Act of Contrition, the sacrament of reconciliation. "Oh my God, I am heartily sorry." Then I had no recollection of the rest, though I had known it by heart. "Father, I forget. Could you please help me?"

"Repeat after me."

"Okay."

"O my God, I am heartily sorry for having offended Thee, and I detest all my sins because I dread the loss of heaven and the pain of hell, but most of all because I have offended Thee, my God, who are all good and deserving of all my love."

I repeated after him.

When I finished, I waited to receive the priest's prayer of absolution, bestowing forgiveness.

Forgiveness I didn't deserve.

The priest said nothing, but I didn't hear his window close. So I waited. Still nothing. My hands trembling, I slowly raised my head and glanced into the mesh screen. I yelped; I was frozen. Holding my breath, I squeezed my eyes shut. When I dared open them again, I saw… I saw not the priest, not the man of God, staring back at me. But the devil—the devil himself!

I exhaled and sighed deeply. *I surrender.*

I knew he had come to take my soul.

Blackness!

Chapter 75

"Miss Aimee, you have a visitor," said the tall, muscular orderly, named Rio, who looked like a gangster but had a gentle soul. He reminded me of the actor Robert LaSardo, his bare arms heavily tattooed with skulls and crosses, and other letters and symbols.

I sat straight up in bed. "Where am I?"

"You're in the Augusta Mental Health Institute. I'll get your visitor now."

I waited. Watching the door. My head was spinning.

Steve strolled in with a big smirk on his face. "Hi," he said.

"Hi," I said back. I was feeling a little groggy; must have been whatever they had me on. Steve looked good—refreshed. Looked as though he'd lost weight, and he was clean-shaven. His haircut was military style. And he was wearing new jeans and a black leather jacket.

"What are you doing here?"

"I came to take you home."

"Home? We're divorced."

"I want you back, Aimee. I can take care of you," he said, his callused hand touching my bare arm. *"I told you I'd never let you go—I'd hunt you down."*

I winced. "I'm fine. I don't need anyone to take care of me."

"You have to—they won't release you otherwise."

I shook my head. "I don't think it's a good idea."

"Why not—your boyfriend is gone. No one else is going to want you."

"He did—he loved me."

"He just wanted your body."

Maybe I wanted his.

"It's your choice—come with me or stay in this hellhole."

"I don't belong anywhere else." *I'd rather stay here. I'm paying my dues.*

Then he bent over and whispered in my ear. "Rest easy, honey—you couldn't hurt a fly."

"What are you saying?"

He flashed an evil grin.

"Okay," I said.

"Okay what?"

"I'll go home with you." *They say after one mortal sin, one kill, it gets easier.*

"Good. You made the right decision. I'll be back to get you in a couple of days, when the paperwork and formalities for your release are complete."

***

At 11:00 a.m., Rio escorted me out of my room, down the hall to my therapy session.

Dr. Richardson was the chief psychiatrist in the hospital. A Yale graduate. I guess I got one of the best. *Can even the best perform miracles? Mend the broken? Fix the unfixable?*

He studied his notes, then looked up at me. "Hi Aimee," he said, with a kind smile.

"How did I get here?" I asked.

"You passed out at the church two days ago and were taken to Maine General. When you woke up, you were hysterical. They had to sedate you, and then you were transferred here. How are you feeling now?"

They have me on so much medication, how can I tell? "Pretty good."

"You sleep well?" he asked.

"I did."

"I'm glad to see you've gotten some much needed rest. I know you've been under a lot of stress, and you've been anxious about sleep—for a long time. I've been in touch with Dr. Bentley."

I nodded.

"Well, after conferring with my colleagues, we concluded you had what is called a hypnagogic hallucination."

"A what?"

"A hypnagogic hallucination," Dr. Richardson repeated. "It can include seeing a shadowy figure, much like what you described, and is often perceived as an intruder—and it can seem real and very frightening."

"I was hallucinating?" I asked, shaking my head. "But it was me in that room—I know it was me."

"Yes. See, when the body becomes paralyzed during REM, the parietal lobe can become confused and create a projection of our 'self' elsewhere in the room."

"You mean I didn't hurt…?" *Kill Rob? Rob's not dead?*

He shook his head. "No. The authorities have found no evidence to back that. No knife, no body, no blood. Nothing." *I saw the blood—lots of blood.* "These hallucinations can create strong, intricate images in the mind that can be distorted in an unrealistic way. And the likelihood of anyone being killed by someone with an icicle inside a warm room is implausible. An icicle would melt in the hands before any fatal damage could occur."

Maybe it was an ice pick.

"Then where is he?"

"I can't answer that."

Chapter 76

When I got back to my room, I called Steve to let him know I wasn't going home with him. I couldn't go back there; nothing could revive that relationship.

I had no idea where Rob was, but it didn't matter now. Yet it did matter. Steve might have ignored me, verbally abused me, but one thing Steve never did was cheat on me. Rob paid attention to me, never said anything hurtful or unkind. And doled out a ton of compliments. But I knew Rob could love more than one. At the same time. Even if I could satisfy him, Rob could get tired of me. Of us. Still, I have never loved anyone more. *Take a chance. Live for once.* I checked my phone but there were no messages from him.

I texted him. *I haven't heard from you—is everything okay? I hope you're not angry with me—I don't recall what happened. Please call me if you get this.*

My phone rang immediately…

"You were upset—you thought I was talking to another woman. It was my granddaughter. She was having relationship issues."

"You went back home to talk to her?"

"Yes. Yes, I did, Aimee. She was very emotional—she is pregnant. When she told Cabot, the guy she'd been seeing—he told her he was married."

"Oh, wow."

"Yeah, she's having a hard time."

"I'm so sorry, Rob. There's so much I haven't told you. I've been going for therapy. And I've learned that a lot of our problems are because of the abuse I buried from my childhood. For years, I spent hours each week with a priest while my mother worked, and he exploited my innocence. When you told me about your Yoni practice, it just triggered bad memories of my past. I hated that part of you—and felt like I was going crazy because I loved you, and at the same time I saw in you—him. And I couldn't forgive you."

"Thank you so much for sharing, Aimee—I know that had to be tough. I'm not making love to anyone else—if that's what you were thinking. It's only you I want to be with. It's always been only you. I hope you can believe that." I nodded, but he couldn't see me. "Aimee, I'm coming back to you now. We will talk about this in depth when I get there. It won't be soon enough. I love you. I gotta go—my ride to the airport is here."

"I love you too."

Epilogue

I still can't believe we're back on the Cape. Driving down 6A again, I'd realized how much I truly missed this place. Home. When I left, it had sparked positive, even cumulative change. I chose to focus on my life and rely on myself rather than Mom or Steve or Vicky or Rob. Running away is never the answer. Maybe a temporary solution.

I heard a tap on the bedroom door; I looked up. "You ready?"

"Almost," I said with a smile, putting on my second earring. Rob was taking me to our favorite Italian restaurant, to celebrate our second anniversary together. We chose not to get married. Talking it over, we'd decided a legal document wasn't a confirmation of our love for one another.

I had allowed my life to torture me. But ultimately, we make our own choices. Right or wrong. Dr. Bentley is a good therapist, better than good. Therapy is tough work—not just for him. Me too. While living in Maine, we'd had our sessions on the phone. I still see the doctor, but now only a couple times a month. More if I feel I need it.

Dear Journal,

On Saturday, I waited till close to five o'clock before driving down that road. At the stop sign, I sat and stared at the priest standing outside the church's door. Parishioners soon exited and formed a line to greet him. Someone beeped behind me. Startled, I drove into the church's parking lot, giving me a better view. I hesitated for a moment—hearing Dr. Bentley's voice in my head. "Face your fears—your demons, Aimee. Don't let them intimidate you. You hold the power." "Yeah," I said out loud. I quickly turned off the engine and got out of the car, joining the long queue of worshipers. While waiting, there were no goose-bumps. My hands didn't shake or sweat. And there were no palpitations. Then I was in front of him. My hand accepting his. It was warm. Surprisingly, almost comforting. "Thank you for coming.

Have a wonderful day." I was there for a purpose. I looked at him and smiled genuinely. "You too, Father."

***

Monday

Dear Journal,

Today was even better than I'd imagined. I never thought I'd be a victim advocate; it's given rich meaning to my life. Helping someone is such a rewarding feeling. It has also helped me realize that I'm not alone. And I've never really been alone. Even all those times I felt like I was.

I read over her file again and took a deep breath. Poised and calm, I walked the corridor to the last door on the right and opened it. There was a young lady seated at a table, hunched over, with her hands wedged between her thighs.

"Hi Erica, I'm Aimee," I said, extending my hand. "I am your victim advocate." She slowly reached out her sweaty hand. "It's so nice to meet you," I said. When her sad eyes looked into mine, I immediately felt her pain. "I'm here to help. Nothing you say to me goes beyond this room."

There was a brief silence.

"I should never have worn that stupid skirt—it was too short. I just get tired of guys staring at my boobs. And they never look at my face," Erica cried. "I told him over and over again, 'No!' Maybe I didn't yell loud enough. It's my own fault."

"No," I said, shaking my head. I bent down and put my arms around her trembling shoulders. "It's not your fault—don't ever, ever blame yourself. Here…" I handed her the box of tissues.

Together—we went to her first legal hearing.

Justice!

Acknowledgments

... And then there was, at last, a story. A novel!

Writing is hard. If it looks easy, it's because the author did a good job. Several times through the years, I thought of giving up—even burning those drafts! The thing is, I never give up. Still, I couldn't have done it without the help and encouragement of these magnificent people in my life. No particular order—not one of you is more or less important than the other.

First, a huge thank you to two of my dearest friends, Sheila Mesner Smith and Jacquelyn Nesbitt for all the days, those grueling hours, we spent together going over and over the manuscript—not always in agreement but we worked it out. Thank you for putting up with me. I'll be forever indebted to you ladies.

I am enormously grateful for these friends and beta readers too, especially Debbie Hagen, author Liz Martinson, and Laura Trulli for taking time out of their busy lives for reading the story and giving their thoughts and suggestions. Sometimes I listened and sometimes I didn't. But more than not I did—listen, that is.

Jeralyn Bolinder Sebek, I admire your talent in doll making and so appreciated your tips.

A special thank you to Anne Speyer who was there in the beginning helping with the editing during a very heartrending time in her life—after losing the love of her life, her husband.

I feel fortunate to have found Angela Werner, my wonderful proofreader. When I was at my wit's end, you invited me to your house, and we sat and talked for hours. Or maybe I talked, and you listened. Your fresh eye was a godsend. Thank you so much.

David Aretha, author and editor, along with your expertise in finding things that needed to be addressed, I appreciate your kindness. And I'm so glad you enjoyed the story. It meant a lot.

Jacquelyn Mitchard, author and editor, thank you for steering me in a helpful direction in the beginning.

I am incredibly thankful for some of my besties—Pam, Kathi, Barbara, Penny, Kathy, Lynn, and Skip for just always being there for me along with their continuous support in my writing. If I have forgotten anyone, forgive me, it wasn't intentional—I'm older now.

And, of course, I acknowledge *You*, my readers, for investing your time and money in my book. Thank You!

Made in the USA
Middletown, DE
29 August 2024

59646780R00176